Three beautiful
sought-after ladies…

DIAMONDS
are for *Lovers*

Three powerful, sensational novels from
Jan Colley, Paula Roe and Yvonne Lindsay

Diamonds are a Girl's Best Friend!

January 2013

February 2013

March 2013

April 2013

May 2013

June 2013

DIAMONDS
are for *Lovers*

Jan
COLLEY

Paula
ROE

Yvonne
LINDSAY

Mills & Boon, an imprint of Harlequin (UK) Limited, Eton House, 18-24 Paradise Road, Richmond, Surrey TW9 1SR

DIAMONDS ARE FOR LOVERS

Satin & a Scandalous Affair © Janet Colley 2008
Boardrooms & a Billionaire Heir © Paula Roe 2008
Jealousy & a Jewelled Proposition © Dolce Vita Trust 2008

ISBN: 978 0 263 90286 0

025-0313

Harlequin (UK) policy is to use papers that are natural, renewable and recyclable products and made from wood grown in sustainable forests. The logging and manufacturing processes conform to the legal environmental regulations of the country of origin.

Printed and bound in Spain
by Blackprint CPI, Barcelona

SATIN & A SCANDALOUS AFFAIR

JAN COLLEY

Jan Colley lives in Christchurch, New Zealand, with Les and a couple of cats. She has travelled extensively, is jack of all trades and master of none and still doesn't know what she wants to be when she grows up—as long as it's a writer. She loves rugby, family and friends, writing, sunshine, talking about writing, and cats, although not necessarily in that order. E-mail her at vagabond232@yahoo.com or check out her website at www.jancolley.com.

Thanks to Richard Baird of Rohan Jewellery in Christchurch, New Zealand, who spent hours sharing his knowledge and passion for diamonds and let me peek over his craftsmen's shoulders, and to Max Rooney of Argosy Jewellery for the introduction.

To our intrepid editor, Melissa Jeglinski, who must have experienced a few conniptions with this project. And special thanks to a great bunch of girls: Bronwyn Jameson, Tessa Radley, Maxine Sullivan, Paula Roe and Yvonne Lindsay. Long live Desire Downunder!

One

"Danielle Hammond? I have a proposition for you."

Dani blinked, jolted out of a pleasant daydream, the Northern Queensland sun that had been warming her face at the outdoor café now hidden behind a wall of a man.

"May I join you?" The softly spoken deep brogue sounded more continental than Australian. She blinked again. It took a few seconds for her to understand that the subject of her daydream, the man she'd seen walk into her shop just minutes ago, had now crossed the road to the café and stood towering above her.

It took another few seconds to realise that she'd seen him before, and to swallow her jolt of dismay. It was him—what's his name—Quinn Everard!

The name exploded in her head as he tossed a

business card on the table and pulled out the flimsy white chair opposite her.

Dani eased her sunglasses down her nose and need-lessly read the card. "Quinn Everard. Broker." Simple, classy, on a satiny-silver card. They'd never met person-ally, but she'd seen his face in many jewellery publica-tions over the years.

His head turned toward the café door and immedi-ately a waitress materialised. He ordered coffee while Dani's curiosity ran riot. What could the great Aus-tralian gem expert want with her? He'd made it very plain, very publicly, that she wasn't good enough to wipe his shoes on.

"Did you see anything you liked?" she asked, sipping on the straw of her thick shake.

Chocolate brown eyes under thick brows scanned her face.

"In the shop," she qualified, easing one hot foot out of her shoe under the table.

"I was looking for you. Your assistant pointed you out."

"You were checking out my window. I saw you."

He rested his elbow on the table and subjected her to a leisurely inspection. Just another nail in his coffin, as far as she was concerned. Dani stared boldly back, seeing in her mind's eye his tall broad form as he'd scrutinised her display window. How she'd admired what looked like an Armani suit—a rarity in the tropics—and his smooth, rolling gait as he'd straightened and disappeared inside. He moved like a fighter, and who's to say he wasn't? There was a definite break in his nose, the telltale bump high on the bridge, and a scar, smooth and pale, traced the corner of his mouth.

His inspection completed, he sat back in his seat. "I've been hearing your name around lately."

Thanks to Howard Blackstone, Dani's benefactor, who'd nominated her as his featured designer for the annual launch last February. "The Blackstone Jewellery launch, probably." Blackstone Jewellery was one retail division of Blackstone Diamonds, Howard's mining and manufacturing company. Dani pursed her lips sardonically. "Oh, I forgot. You weren't invited."

A flicker of amusement deepened the creases on both sides of his mouth, showing up an unexpected dimple. "I've never said I don't find your work interesting, Ms. Hammond. Which is why I'm here. As I said, I have a proposition for you."

She relished the sharp stab of triumph. This man had never made a pretence of liking her stuff, yet here he was. What on earth could he want to proposition her about?

Dani could think of some things…and they were all tied up with sizing him up as a hunk a few moments ago, before she'd realised who he was.

Hopeful that the lick of attraction she felt wasn't written all over her face, she cleared her throat. "A proposition for *me?* April Fools was a couple of days ago."

"I want you to design a setting for a large and very special diamond."

This was very satisfying. The great Quinn Everard wanted her, Dani Hammond, to make him a diamond necklace.

Oh, but there was that one small problem. They hated each other.

She raised her head. "No."

His eyes narrowed.

"Diamonds aren't really my specialty." His words, aimed at her four years ago at the prestigious Young Designer of the Year Award competition, the one everyone tipped her to win, came back to her. He'd said something along the lines of "A jewellery designer should stick to what she knows and is comfortable with. Ms. Hammond may have cut her teeth on diamonds, but she has little flair and understanding of the essence of the stones."

That wasn't the only public dressing-down Dani had received from Quinn Everard. She'd assumed it was because of the spat between he and Howard years ago.

"Remember?" she asked sweetly, and received a coolly assessing gaze in response. How could he sit there in his gazillion-thread suit and not melt?

"I am offering a generous commission."

Now, that was interesting… "How generous?" A little extra cash and she could make the final payment on her loan from Howard. Of course, she'd repay his estate, since he'd died earlier in the year. Generous enough to include some new display cabinets, maybe? A face-lift for the tired signage?

Quinn took out what looked to be a solid-gold pen, wrote something on the business card and turned it around so she could see.

A surprised cough escaped and she jerked her head up at the numbers on the business card. "You want to pay me that to make you a piece of jewellery?"

He nodded.

The amount was obscene. Damn the spruce-up. This could be the deposit for the bigger, more modern and vacant premises two doors down.

"That's way over the odds. You know that."

"Yes or no?"

She shook her head, positive she was the butt of someone's joke. "The answer's no."

Quinn leaned back, not attempting to cover his displeasure. "You and your family have endured quite a bit of unwelcome publicity lately, haven't you? Howard's death three months ago. Not to mention his companion on the plane."

Tell her something she didn't know. No one survived when the flight Howard Blackstone had chartered to take him to Auckland one night in January, plunged into the sea. When it turned out Marise Hammond was on board, the media were beside themselves. Marise was married to Howard's arch enemy, Matt Hammond, head of House of Hammond, an antique and fine jewellery company in New Zealand. Matt was also Dani's cousin, although they'd never met because of the feud between Howard and the Hammonds that spanned three decades.

The reading of Howard's will a month later rocked the family to its core. Marise was named as a substantial beneficiary and a trust fund was set up for her son, Blake, giving rise to the assumption that Marise and Howard were having an affair. Who was Blake's true father, everyone wanted to know, Howard Blackstone or Matt Hammond? All the old family history and hostility had been bandied around for months.

Despite a growing anxiety, Dani feigned nonchalance. "So?"

"And poor Ric and Kimberley," he continued. "They must have been bummed when the TV cameras crashed their wedding."

That was an understatement. Dani grew up in Howard Blackstone's mansion, along with her mother and cousins, Kimberley and Ryan. Kim had recently re-married her ex-husband, Ric Perrini. Their lavish wedding on a yacht in Sydney Harbour was nearly ruined when the media sent in helicopters.

What did Quinn Everard know about that?

"I haven't officially met Ryan," Quinn resumed, "but I do know Jessica slightly. I think she'll make a lovely bride, don't you?"

She opened her mouth to agree, then snapped it closed. Ryan and Jessica had recently announced their engagement, but the wedding details were a closely guarded family secret.

"I have no idea what you're talking about," she said warily.

Ryan was the most private of people. That's why he'd asked Dani to help arrange a secret ceremony up here, away from the Sydney gossip-mongers. Port Douglas was an excellent choice. Chances were, the family members wouldn't be recognised, and there were any number of world-class venues and caterers to choose from. With Dani's help, arrangements for the perfect intimate wedding in three weeks' time were well under way.

"Really?" Quinn mused. "There are some lovely beaches up here, aren't there? I hear Oak Hill is nice."

Dani's heart sank. He couldn't possibly have found out. Almost everything had been confirmed and all participants sworn to secrecy. "Your information is out of date, Mr. Everard," she lied. "There won't be a wedding in Port Douglas, after all. That was just a ploy to get everyone off the scent."

"A ploy? My source seems adamant that on the twentieth of April, the van Berhopt Resort is staging a very special event. It looks fantastic on the Web site, just the place for an intimate, discreet family wedding."

She heard the sound of her own teeth grinding. "How the hell did you know that?"

He tapped his nose. "The diamond world is surprisingly small."

Dani knew when her back was against the wall. "That's blackmail," she muttered.

He shrugged, all traces of amusement gone. "It's business, Ms. Hammond. Are you so successful you can afford to turn down a commission of this size?"

Intimidation really got her back up. "Do your worst." She pushed her glass away and picked up her purse. This was precisely why she had chosen to live up here, away from the city gossip. "The Blackstones and I are used to media attention." Howard's womanising and close-to-the-edge business dealings guaranteed that.

Quinn stroked his chin. "Poor Ryan and Jessica, their beautiful day ruined. And the rest of your family—especially your mother—will they be so blasé? All that distasteful speculation, old family wounds reopened, over and over…"

"Leave my mother out of this," Dani snapped. That

was the worst of it. The Blackstone-Hammond feud had ripped her mother's blood brother away from her thirty years ago, leaving a massive heartache. With Howard's death, Sonya Hammond's dearest wish was to bring the family factions together again.

"I can empathise, being a private person myself." His tone was sympathetic—reasonable, even.

Dani jutted her chin out defiantly, despite a sinking feeling that he was right. Did she have the right to expose those closest to her to more scandal and shame?

"You could spare them all that unwelcome attention. Ryan and Jessica will have the day of their dreams. And you, Danielle, will make a lot of money."

She glared at him. Only her family called her Danielle. Up here in Port, as it was affectionately known, she went by Dani Hammond, the brand name for her jewellery. Most of the locals had no idea she was connected to one of Australia's richest and most notorious families. Those who did, didn't care.

Quinn shifted impatiently. "Yes or no?"

Could she bear her anonymity here to be shattered by all the old gossip and innuendo she had lived with all her life? And worse, how could she let him ruin Ryan and Jessica's day and put that hunted look back in her mother's eyes? "Bring your damn diamond to the shop, then." Grasping her change purse in a white-knuckled grip, she stood abruptly and scowled down at him.

Quinn Everard tilted his head, peering up under his brows again. Then he rose, gesturing to the cars parked across the street. "My car is right over there. Take a ride with me."

Her internal alarm sounded. It wasn't that she thought a man with his reputation would try anything dangerous. It was her reaction—her attraction—that worried her. And how could she refuse a man who held such sway in her profession, especially one offering dream money?

"I don't carry this diamond around in my pocket." Quinn frowned at her hesitation. "I've rented a house in Four Mile Beach."

Four Mile was an outlying district in the shire of Port Douglas, and where her apartment was. "I'm working."

"Exactly. Time is money, Danielle."

She eyed him moodily, weighing her options. "Whereabouts in Four Mile?"

He impatiently motioned her to start crossing the road.

"You may be famous," Dani said tightly, "but you're a stranger to me. I'm going nowhere without telling my assistant."

He inclined his head. "Number 2 Beach Road." He stopped beside a sleek black BMW. "I'll wait."

Taut with indignation, she poked her head into the shop and told Steve, her assistant, and told him where she was going. Then she got into Quinn's car. They spoke little on the short drive, but her eyes widened in surprise when they pulled up outside his house. She'd walked past here nearly every day on her way to work. Never a morning person, she needed the fifty-minute walk along beautiful Four Mile Beach to improve her mood.

The house was right on the sand dunes, surrounded by high walls. A discreet plaque on the wall by the entrance said Luxury Executive Accommodation. Dani had always wondered what it was like inside.

She followed Quinn through the gate and entrance into a large multilevelled living and dining area. The house was a blend of Asian and Australian designs, the furnishings rattan, leather and teak. Striking floral arrangements with birds-of-paradise and heliconias seasoned the air with tropical scents, stirred by lazily rotating ceiling fans. This place was even better than she'd imagined.

"Shall we?"

Quinn stood at the door leading to the stairs. Dani hesitated for a second. She didn't trust Mr. Quinn Everard one inch, but it wasn't a threat of physical violence that made her pause. More his attitude, the impression that he got what he wanted so effortlessly. He smelled good, looked good, obviously lived well. She'd need her wits about her with a man prepared to resort to blackmail to get his own way.

He opened the first door and intense light flooded what was obviously a dream workroom. In one corner, under the perfect lighting, sat an easel. A workbench ran fully down one side, two stools at the end and tool organisers that held an array of implements, everything from tweezers to gauges to loupes. There was a waxing station, engraving blocks, micro torch, rollers and grinders—everything she had in her shop, except the equipment was new and top-of-the-range and must have cost a fortune.

It slowly dawned on her that he expected her to work on his diamond here. A laptop sat open on a desk, no doubt with the best CAD software available. The desk and bench were lit with magnified true-light lamps. He must have had all this brought in, she thought dimly, lights included.

Dani ran her hand over the workbench. "You were that sure I'd agree?"

"I've questioned your motivation in the past, Ms. Hammond, not your intelligence."

She glanced over to where he leaned casually against the doorjamb, arms folded. "Why?"

"The diamond does not leave the premises."

"So I come around here when I feel like it? When I have a spare minute?" She shook her head. "That would take months."

Quinn turned to the door and stretched his arm out, indicating she precede him. His steady gaze challenged her to refuse.

Cautiously Dani edged past him, down the hall away from the stairs. She paused at the next door. He leaned past her, pushing it open, and she took a couple of hesitant steps forward.

Long white curtains stirred at the open window, and she heard the sea lapping the sand beyond the trees. A huge bed, covered with shiny satin in bold red-and-gold stripes, took up most of one wall. Purple-shaded lamps on the bedside tables matched plump purple cushions scattered on the window seat. Dani felt the smile start; it was a dream of a bedroom, and to think she could hear the sea. She was still smiling when she turned around to see Quinn in a long-legged lean against the doorjamb, arms folded, a pose that was fast becoming disturbingly familiar.

Her smile faded as his intentions finally sank in. He expected her to stay here—alone—with him. "No," she said firmly, even though he hadn't asked the question yet.

His dark head tilted. "Those are my conditions. You stay here and work on the diamond in the room provided until the job is done."

Frowning, she shook her head slowly.

"It's not negotiable."

Dani thought he sounded bored. "I'm not staying here alone with you."

His eyes were scathing. "Don't be puerile, Ms. Hammond. Just what do you think is going to happen?"

If his intention was to make her feel gauche and stupid, it worked. "Wh-what possible reason…?" she stammered, her cheeks burning.

"Security and expediency. It is an extremely valuable diamond and I am a busy man. I don't have time to sit around up here in Nowhere-ville for a minute longer than necessary."

Dani shook her head again. "No deal. Bring the stone to the shop. I'll work on it between customers."

Quinn's brows raised. "I don't think so," he said softly, and, turning, left the room. But the certainty of his voice, his potent male presence remained.

Dani waited a couple of seconds, worried. There was sympathy in his face as he'd turned away. Her refusal had not even registered. A vision of being locked in, of pushing against him, pounding against his broad chest to get out, made her head swim.

She was being ridiculous. Quinn Everard was an internationally regarded man in the gem and fine arts world. He was not going to kidnap her. She started off after him. "Look, if you're worried about theft, don't be. There hasn't been a robbery in town for years."

"You don't understand, Ms. Hammond." He turned so sharply to face her that she almost bumped into his impressive chest. "This is a very special diamond."

"It will be perfectly safe in the shop, and, anyway, I'm insured."

His eyes bored into her, making her heart thump. She stepped back hurriedly, excruciatingly aware that he hadn't given an inch.

"Have you heard of the Distinction Diamond, Danielle?"

"The Dist…?" Air punched out from her lungs and her heart thudded. Either that or her chin hit the floor. The Distinction Diamond was nearly forty carats of fancy intense yellow, originating from the Kimberley mines in South Africa. No one had heard of it for years. "You've got the Distinction Diamond?" Her swallow was audible. "Here?"

Quinn Everard could do scathing very well. Was it the curve of his lips or the dangerous glint that lit up his eyes? "No, Ms. Hammond." He turned his back and continued on to the door next to "her" room. "I have her big sister."

TWO

Quinn turned his back and walked into his bedroom, smiling when he felt her creeping presence at the door. Opening the panel in the wall that concealed the safe, he began keying the code into a digital keypad. The whole house was burglar and smoke alarmed, including this room and the workroom. The safe was dual combination and key, complete with trembler sensor. His company had the best security money could buy. After all, it was vital in his business.

He glanced to where she fidgeted at the door, chewing on her bottom lip. Quinn miskeyed and the thing beeped at him. He swore softly, ordering himself to stop thinking about whiskey eyes and plump bottom lips. She was on the hook. It was time to reel her in.

He went through the elaborate security measures

with exaggerated care, then took out a heavy steel box from which he lifted a hand-stitched leather case after a barrage of additional code numbers. A hydraulic mechanism raised a small velvet-covered platform on which the diamond sat. Reaching out, he flicked the desk lamp on. Then he faced her and tilted his head, giving her permission to come near.

She moved slowly into the room, her eyes on his face. The light from the lamp washed over her skin, and he thought again, as he had earlier on meeting her, that her face was all wrong, a contradiction. Wide-set, wild-honey eyes, a straight no-nonsense nose, and then rosebud lips, suggesting innocence and insecurity.

And just like earlier when he'd first looked at her, the impact jolted him. She'd attempted to tame her wildfire hair with a scarf, but still, dark red curls sprang up in interesting dimensions. Her colour sense was outrageous, combining a red-and-pink-striped top with a captivatingly short floral skirt. She was exotic, unconventional, bubbling over with life and energy. He knew more beautiful women, but none so colourful, so vibrantly original.

She looked down at the diamond on display for her, her eyes glowing. When she finally looked back at Quinn, the gratitude in her eyes stunned him. She would know well how few people had ever been given the opportunity to look upon this treasure.

Enjoy it, he thought grimly. If it were down to him, he wouldn't have Danielle Hammond within one hundred metres of this baby, no matter how interesting her face.

She put out her hand. It hovered over the glow and she hesitated. "May I?"

Half of him wondered what the diamond would look like against her skin, her hair. The other half protested, *Get the hell away from this diamond!* But he had his orders. He nodded tersely.

Her slim hand dipped and the middle finger stroked lightly, reverently over the crown of the perfect octahedron. Then she took her hands away, crossed them in front of her body and just looked down at the stone, as if giving thanks to a god. Her lashes made shadows on her cheek.

"Do we have a deal, Ms. Hammond?" he asked quietly, reluctant to interrupt what was obviously an awe-inspiring moment for her. As it had been for him when he had procured this very special diamond for his client six years ago.

"I have a choice?" she murmured.

He knew she didn't. No jeweller in her right mind would say no to this opportunity.

She continued, "Since you're blackmailing me…"

Quinn smiled at her nice recovery. "Of course I am." He knew that she would crawl over broken glass to get her hands on this stone, blackmail or not. Money or not.

He perched on the edge of the desk. "The conditions are these—you stay here in the house for the duration of the work. You work on it day and night if possible. You tell no one about this stone."

She sucked in a breath. "I have a life, you know."

"No, you don't." He shook his head decisively. "Not for the next few weeks."

"And my shop?"

Quinn had initiated a decent conversation with the

young hippie called Steve in her little shop this morning. "Your assistant needs more hours. His partner is pregnant. They're struggling financially."

Dani frowned. "You found all that out in a couple of minutes?"

"I did not draw your name out of a hat, Ms. Hammond," he said sharply. While he couldn't blame her for being surprised, his reputation alone should have swayed her. Put that together with one of the most incredible stones the world had ever seen and it was unfathomable that he was still trying to persuade her.

"What sort of setting?"

Quinn shrugged. "You're the designer."

"I mean," she sighed, "pendant? Brooch? What type of piece? I didn't see any cutting gear."

He drew himself up to full height. "You will not touch this stone with anything but your fingers, do you hear?"

Danielle Hammond rolled her eyes at him. "Of course not, but I may use other gems." She eyed him speculatively. "You are supplying findings? Platinum, diamonds, the whole deal?"

"As long as you keep the stone whole, you have carte blanche to design whatever you like. I will need to approve a model and a list of your requirements."

"This could take weeks…."

"You have three, less is preferable. The accommodation is acceptable?"

She nodded.

"I will feed you. Everything you need for the job is there. All you need to do is tap into your talent and work."

"Who's it for?"

Quinn opened his mouth, staring at her face. "A friend," he said shortly. "A special friend."

Dani nodded, and he could almost hear her mind ticking over. That was his brief; she was not to know who commissioned the piece. No harm letting her think there was a special lady friend. "Do we have a deal?"

She exhaled noisily and stared down at the diamond as if for reassurance.

Just to play with her longing, he closed the lid— slowly.

"I want half the money up front," she said, "and throw in Steve's wages."

He scowled. "How very Blackstone of you." Her family connections were his main objection to the deal. Quinn had no time for anyone bearing the Blackstone stamp and was sorely tempted to delegate this job to one of his staff. But it was a sensitive matter, one which he'd reluctantly agreed to handle personally.

He picked the box up off the desk, noting with pleasure the regret and loss in her eyes as she watched him put it away.

"This is going to be a barrel of laughs," Dani muttered from behind his back.

"The sooner you get on with it, the quicker we can go our separate ways." He banged the safe door closed. "I'll take you home to pack and make arrangements."

When he turned back to her, she was rubbing the side of her long pale neck, eyes closed, her head rolled back. Quinn teetered on the edge of a rogue wave of desire so intense that it stopped him dead in his tracks. Behind her, not two feet away, his king-size bed sprawled, inspiring all sorts of suggestive images.

Her eyes snapped open, finding his gaze immediately. "No need. My place is only a minute or two from here."

He gestured to the door. "I'll drive you," he said firmly, intent on getting her out of his bedroom.

Quinn prowled her living room while she packed and made arrangements to cover her absence from her shop. He was fond of his comforts, and the climate up here in Northern Queensland was not to his liking. Luckily, unlike Dani's tiny apartment in a dated resort complex, the beach house was equipped with an excellent air-conditioning system. He wiped the back of his neck while she scurried about packing with the phone plastered to her ear. The prospect of baby-sitting a spoiled girl with an artistic temperament and inflated opinion of her own talent, whilst sweltering in the suffocating humidity, was not a good one.

His internal temperature soared even higher when later that afternoon, after settling in at his rental, his house guest took a swim. Quinn's office window offered an unobstructed view of the pool. His work forgotten, he stood at the window, watching the long-legged, flame-haired beauty. She wore long shorts and an oversize T-shirt; perfectly respectable attire—until it got wet. Quinn turned the air-conditioning dial down a couple of notches and undid the top two buttons of his shirt.

For the first time in many years, he wanted, with a savage unrelenting intensity. He was certainly not celibate, but preferred older, cultured and financially independent women. Women with similar interests and social mores as he. Danielle Hammond looked to be mid-to-late twenties and certainly had the wealth of the Blackstones behind her, but they were light-years apart.

It was totally undignified to stand at a window, salivating over the sights of wet fabric clinging lovingly to a fine pair of breasts, and of water streaming down well-toned, lightly tanned legs. He was much too discriminating to crave the slide of her wet, spiralling curls on his burning skin. Wasn't he?

He returned to his desk, pushing aside the unwelcome intrusion. This wasn't supposed to be a holiday, he chided himself. The next Famous Paintings auction was only days away. It was frustrating to be stuck here for such an important date on his professional calendar, but at least he had a contact to inspect a very special lot number for one of his most important clients.

Clearing his head one final time, he refocussed his attention where it belonged. On his work. He remained at his desk until Danielle interrupted him, after the dinner hour. Apparently she was ready to work and wanted the diamond to be brought to the workroom.

Quinn set it up on the workbench and watched her circle the desk, her small digital camera clicking and whirring as she took snapshot after snapshot.

He was totally absorbed by her concentration, not to mention her lithe form bending and stretching, and the interesting strain of fabric across her rump and thighs as she crouched and circled. So when she suddenly straightened and looked at him, he was a few seconds behind the eight ball.

Her finely arched brows seemed to mock him. "What's she like?"

"I beg your pardon?"

"Your lady friend. The one you're giving the diamond to."

"Like?"

She looked at the ceiling briefly. "Her height and build. I don't want to design something dainty for a big strapping girl. Or vice versa."

Quinn hesitated. It wasn't an unreasonable request.

Tonight she wore flowing baggy summer pants of an indeterminate colour that fell between pewter and light brown. A purple lacy top accentuated her shape, which was, he conceded, a work of art. A strip of matching fabric tied bandanna-style kept her forehead free of springy curls, and lime-green beads circled her throat. "Five nine, five ten." He shrugged. "Slender but strong-looking."

Dani held the camera up, checking the images. Quinn noted with surprise that her nails were short and some of them jagged, as if she chewed them.

"Pale or tan?" she asked distractedly.

"Lightly tanned," he told her. "Freckles."

Click, click. "Okay. Hair?" When he didn't answer immediately, she lowered the camera and frowned at him. "What colour is her hair?"

Several superlative responses came to mind, but while he was deciding which best described her vibrant curls, her frown gave way to sarcasm. "You're a little unobservant, Mr. Everard. Do you have a photo, perhaps?"

His mouth quirked. "Red. Dark red." He pursed his lips, wondering when she would twig. "Curly."

Her brows arched up to kiss the edge of the bandanna.

"Rather multifaceted in style," Quinn went on, warming to his task. "Unconventional, definitely. Some would say bohemian, but that's not it... She's like no one else." And that was the truth. Her use of colour, breaking all the fashion rules, should have offended a conservative like himself, yet somehow, it charmed the hell out of him. Living with Danielle Hammond, he knew, would never be boring.

Dani pursed her lips sternly. "You have good taste in women, Mr. Everard," she told him smartly, and put the camera down with a sharp thud. "Contemporary bling, then, for the lady."

"Knock yourself out." Quinn pushed himself away from the doorjamb, trying not to be horrified about her terminology in reference to this diamond. He'd spent hours trying to talk his client out of this, citing Danielle's age and inexperience.

Surprisingly though, he smiled all the way down the hall, pleased with himself, and with her. Maybe the next few weeks wouldn't be so bad, after all. Dani Hammond had a bite to her. She seemed smart—almost street-smart—and Quinn knew all about that.

But how did she, with her luxurious upbringing?

Sightings of Dani were scarce the next couple of days as she immersed herself in her design. She worked late and rose late. Mid-morning she would request he bring the diamond to the workroom. He restored it to the safe on his way to bed. He kept the refrigerator stocked and was thankfully spared the ignominy of standing by the window like a Peeping Tom, because she didn't use the pool again. Most of the food he prepared went to waste as she said she was too busy to be hungry. Despite himself, and without seeing any tangible results yet, he was impressed by her dedication.

The third night, she joined him for dinner, an impressive meal catered by one of Port Douglas's surprisingly fine restaurants.

"Why me?" she asked over coffee. "You must know twenty world-class designers who would gnaw off their right hand to ingratiate themselves with you."

He tapped his teaspoon lightly on the cup, giving a brief smile. "But not you."

"Aren't you afraid I'll mess up your precious diamond out of spite since you're blackmailing me?"

"Then I would have to mess up your reputation."

"Haven't you already?" She raised and crooked her two index fingers in a parody of speech marks. "'Ms. Hammond has passable talent but chooses to use it working for chain stores....'"

Quinn rubbed his ear, amused. That was one of his missives in the *DiamondWorld Monthly* about a year ago. She'd had the cheek to respond in the next issue. He'd retaliated by saying she was "one step up from a Sunday-market vendor in a one-horse town, pandering to the tourist buses."

"A mere dent, which doesn't seem to have harmed

you at all. Although, why you would shut yourself away up here in the middle of nowhere is anyone's guess."

"Another snobby Sydney-sider," she sighed, giving him the impression this wasn't the first time she'd had this conversation. "I like the tropics."

"What's to like? A beach you can't swim in because of the stingers…"

"Only for a few months…"

"Insufferably hot and sticky weather…"

"I like it probably for all the reasons you don't. Especially now in cyclone season."

So the lady was into sultry, steamy nights. He sniffed and rubbed his jaw, clamping down on where that thought would take him. "Bugs and snakes…"

"You get those in Sydney," she countered.

"Not in *my* neighbourhood, you don't."

"They wouldn't dare," she muttered under her breath.

He ignored that. "No shopping to speak of. Is there actually any nightlife in town or does it shut down at five-thirty?"

"Remind me to take you cane toad racing while you're here," she said, then smiled wryly and leaned her elbows on the table edge. "Laid-back it might be, but there's an interesting dynamic of village charm and sophistication here. Port is famous for its restaurants and you never know which Hollywood stars or ex-American president you'll bump into around town or checking out the reef in their big chartered yachts."

His fingers tapped the tabletop, drawing her glance. "We know you like to play with the rich and famous, but you're limiting your opportunities here, Danielle. Why is that?"

"I do all right, and don't call me Danielle."

He inclined his head. "And 'all right' is enough?"

"For now." She sipped her coffee. "Tell me about you and Howard."

"You don't know?" he asked, surprised.

Dani shook her head. "I was at uni around that time. All I know is, he bristled every time your name came up."

That didn't surprise him. Back then, Howard Blackstone had thrown his whole vindictive weight against the young broker from the wrong side of the tracks. "I was just starting out," he began. Laura, his wife, was sick. His whole world was going to hell.

"Howard wanted to be nominated as the Australian representative to the new World Association of Diamonds. Everyone had finally woken up to the fact that our industry, the diamond trade, was subsidising wars in Africa."

"Conflict diamonds." Dani nodded. "What good could some worldwide association do against the one or two massive conglomerates who control the mines?"

Sharp, he thought, but then she had grown up in Australia's foremost mining family. "The association has definitely raised awareness. Even America, the largest bastion of consumerism, reports that a high percentage of people in the market ask for certification that their diamond is conflict-free."

"A certificate's only as good as the person who completes it," she stated, again rousing grudging admiration for her appraisal of a very grey area.

"So, the feud?" Dani prompted.

Quinn pushed his empty plate aside and leaned back. "Blackstone wined and dined me. He wanted my vote. I suppose he could have got the impression I was a solid bet, but in the end, a fellow broker asked and my vote went his way. To be honest, I expected Howard to romp in, with or without me."

"But he didn't." Dani nodded. "He likes—liked—getting his own way."

Quinn wondered about the relationship between her and Australia's King of Diamonds. "He lost the nomination by one vote, and took it a lot more personally than it warranted."

"Let me guess. You were off the Christmas card list."

Well and truly, Quinn thought grimly. Howard's wrath nearly sent him to the wall with his financiers. "He banned me from accessing the Blackstone mines. I had to borrow heavily to source the stones I needed offshore."

If it hadn't been for one or two friends in high places—notably Sir John Knowles, owner of the diamond upstairs—Quinn's fledgling business wouldn't have survived.

Dani whistled. "That must have hurt. The broker with no diamonds."

"It put me in a very bad situation," he agreed.

She glanced around the room, her eyes resting on a magenta orchid in the corner. "It doesn't seem to have had any long-term consequences."

"No thanks to the Blackstones."

"Have you approached Ric or Ryan? They may be willing to ease the ban now."

Now that Howard was dead, Quinn thought scathingly. His dislike of the former head of Blackstone Diamonds wasn't just business. Howard had made it personal. How ironic that he was sitting across an elegant table with his nemesis's protégée. "I can manage without the precious Blackstone mines, thanks."

Dani's gaze sharpened a little. "Forgive and forget, hey? The man's dead."

He couldn't forget. The slights in the papers. Door after door closing in his face. The old-boys banking networks, determined to pull him down. "It's hard enough starting out without the most influential man in the business doing a number on you."

And all while he was barely keeping his head above water to cope with his wife's terminal illness.

And that's where Howard's vindictiveness really came into its own. Quinn could overlook the loss of business, the tearing down of his reputation, the condescending snubs by former backers. He would never forgive the look in Laura's eyes when he couldn't give her the one thing she wanted above all else.

It never failed to surprise him how much it grated after all these years. "Howard Blackstone was a manipulative, vindictive bastard."

Dani blanched, and just for a moment, he felt a needle of sympathy. Was it possible that someone in this world mourned the man so many hated?

"You know all about being vindictive, don't you?" she asked tightly. "Wasn't that what marking me down at the awards was about? Or the slagging off you gave me in various industry papers?" She drained her cup and banged it down on the saucer. "Maybe you and Howard aren't so different after all."

"Maybe you just aren't that good," he suggested, eying her evenly.

"If that's so," she snapped, "why am I here?"

"I don't know, *Danielle*." He stressed the syllables of her name. "Haven't you got work to do?"

She glared, and in the candlelight, her hair and eyes crackled like embers. "Luckily, it's a big house, Mr. Everard. Why don't we keep our distance?"

She shoved herself to her feet and stalked from the room.

Three

"Fine by me!"

Dani slammed the door on his retort and stomped up the stairs, muttering to herself.

Granted, Howard Blackstone had been no angel. His abrasive nature combined with immense wealth was the perfect enemy magnet, but that aside, he had provided a good life for her and her mother. Sonya and Dani Hammond were two of the very few people in this world who truly mourned him.

She opened the workroom door and banged that, too. Bloody man!

Sonya had moved in with Howard and her sister, Ursula, when she was twelve years old. After their first-born was abducted, Ursula became depressed and took her own life. Howard was inconsolable so Sonya stayed on to look after her niece Kimberley and nephew Ryan. When she became pregnant, Howard persuaded her to remain and bring up her child with all the advantages his own children enjoyed. He paid for Dani's education, and over the years, they'd forged quite an affectionate bond. Sometimes she thought he liked her better than he did his own children.

Her mother had refuted that. "He loves Kim and Ryan fiercely. He enjoys your company because he has hopes for you rather than expectations of you."

People didn't know the real Howard, Dani thought belligerently, tearing off her latest mishmash of a sketch. His faults were legion, but she and Sonya saw a side of him he didn't show to many. They would always be grateful.

By unspoken mutual consent, Dani and Quinn avoided each other the next day. She needed to pinpoint a design, but every time she looked at the diamond, her ideas changed. She held it up to the light, admiring the purity, depth and distribution of colour throughout. There was a cynical old saying popular in her trade: a polished diamond is only rough ruined. How she wished to have seen this beauty before it was cut.

Dozens of pages littered the floor under the sketch pad as she pared back the initial outpouring of inspiration into a few shapes vaguely resembling a setting she might be able to work with. About the only thing she knew for sure was that the setting would be platinum because it complemented a diamond's finest qualities so perfectly, especially fancy pinks and yellows. Dani intended the stone to be the star, not the setting.

As the hours passed, ideas rushed through her mind, most disappearing a few seconds after their arrival. She played around on the software Quinn had provided, but the solution eluded her and the beautiful diamond taunted her on its velvet pillow. Finally she took it from the display box and slid down to the floor with it in her hand, loving the milky coolness of it in her palm.

Quinn walked into the room with a plate in one hand and utensils and a wineglass in the other. He stared at her incredulously for a moment, then turned to set his load on the desk. Dani pressed back against the leg of the workbench, suddenly wondering what her hair looked like. Had she showered today or not…?

She gazed at him, thinking how seriously appealing he was. He wore pleated charcoal chinos and a light polo shirt that accentuated the breadth of his shoulders and had her peeking at his strongly muscled arms. Boat shoes, no socks. His platinum Rolex flashed as he leaned forward to switch a lamp on.

"What are you doing?" he asked, staring down at her sternly.

"Thinking. What's it look like?"

After a pause, he nodded at the food he'd brought. "Eat."

"What time is it?" She raised her head to peer out the window. It was dark. Where had the day gone?

"Eight." He frowned at the sight of the uneaten sub he had brought up at lunch, the cold cup of coffee beside it.

Still holding the diamond, she uncrossed her legs and rose, drawn by the smell of the food. A twinge in her stomach reminded her she'd had little to eat today, if anything. She replaced the diamond in its box and reached for the wineglass first.

"How's it going?"

The wine was smooth. She swallowed and opened her mouth to answer but was hijacked by a huge yawn. "'Kay."

It wasn't okay yet, it was driving her nuts. Inspiration never came easy. She could spend hours or even days on an idea and toss it because of a niggling suspicion she had seen it somewhere. Originality was paramount.

His large shoe ventured out to drag a ball of screwed-up paper toward him. "What time did you work till last night?"

She shrugged, still smouldering a little from their altercation the night before. It would be better if he'd just leave her alone with her thoughts and her food.

"Eating and sleeping will be tolerated on an occasional basis."

Had he made a joke? Emboldened, she moved closer to the food he'd brought, suddenly ravenous. "Thanks." The wine had cleansed her palate and spiced her appetite, and she sniffed appreciatively.

"Is there a problem with your setting?" He bent to pick up the ball of paper by his shoe.

"No." Dani picked up the fork and stabbed at a floret of bright green broccoli. "I haven't nailed it yet, but don't worry. I will."

Quinn tossed the ball of paper into the trash bin. Then he moved to the easel and tilted his head at the latest sketch, one she hadn't torn off yet. "Have the graphics I supplied been any help?"

Dani shook her head and cut into tender lamb drizzled with a sauce that tasted of paprika. Software was great for learning on, but most designers she knew preferred to work freestyle.

He moved to the desk where she sat and laid his hand on her portfolio. "May I?"

Dani stilled mid-chew. His past comments about her work still rankled. Yet here she was, staying in luxury accommodations, being catered for to her heart's desire. Awaiting the payment of a colossal sum of money, and all for the privilege of working on an incredible diamond.

She shrugged. Whatever he thought of her stuff, he'd paid her an enormous compliment by commissioning her. Quinn Everard, the great Australian gem expert, wanted *her* to design for him. Not Cartier. Not JAR. Dani Hammond.

Quinn flicked the desk lamp on and stood, one hand in his pocket, the other leisurely turning the pages of the big black binder. He studied each page intently, unmoving except for his lashes dipping and rising as his eyes moved over the page. She watched under the guise of chewing and swallowing.

His shirt clung to the contours of his chest and hinted at an impressive-looking abdominal ridge or two. Fine dark hair sprinkled his forearms. The harsh light of the lamp picked out definite traces of silver in his side-burns. Mid-thirties, she guessed, with plenty of exercise to keep him toned and strong.

She tore her eyes away before he caught her, suddenly feeling way too warm. Quinn was too big for this room, too enticing and wickedly attractive.

His deep brown eyes were suddenly on her face. "These are good."

She hadn't realised she was holding her breath, but now it suddenly left her in a rush. "Oh. Thanks."

"You have improved, matured."

Improved? Matured? *Don't go overboard with the compliments, mate.* "Thanks," she sniffed, and turned back to her nearly empty plate.

"Maybe," he continued, "you chose the wrong piece for the awards."

"You were the only one who thought so."

That was a lie. She had thought that, worried about it. Her entry for the Young Designer Awards was a wide gold bangle featuring pink and white Blackstone diamonds. It was supposed to capture the sweep of the outback ranges and show the riches within. Although it was a stunning piece and created comment from whoever saw it, Dani had never felt peaceful about it, never felt that she actually got it.

Quinn Everard, the judge, was the only one who had seen past the "wow" factor and found it wanting.

"Now, this…"

He flipped the pages back to where his thumb had marked the spot. She stood up and moved beside him, inhaling a warm masculinity so clean and refreshing that the air in the room was revitalised. Dani nearly swayed with the pleasure of being close to him, her fatigue from the long day washing away.

She looked down at the book. "The Keishi!" This was one of her first pieces, and still a favourite. Nineteen millimetre champagne Keishi pearls strung on white gold interspersed with gold roses, each centre a small round blue sapphire.

"This would have won you the award, just for colour and lustre alone."

She thrummed with pleasure. "I wanted to enter it. People said it wasn't high value enough."

Quinn looked into her eyes and her heartbeat stuttered.

Heat bloomed inside and filled her. She couldn't look away for the life of her. This close she picked out the fine lines at the corner of his eyes; the scar by his mouth she wanted to trace with her finger to see if it was as smooth as it looked. His eyes were dark and a little perplexed, and then he looked down at her mouth.

"Trust your instincts," he said softly.

Oh, boy, if he only knew what her instincts were telling her now. He was so close, his breath wafted over her face. She felt her body tighten, sway slightly in his direction. The man was a magnet, her own personalised magnet. The back of her neck prickled and dampened under the rumpled hank of hair she had twisted and last looked at ten hours ago.

Ten hours ago? She stepped back hurriedly, thinking how dishevelled she must look. There was probably broccoli in her teeth, and she remembered now that she had not showered today....

Dani had her pride. She didn't even know if she liked this man, but if succumbing to an intense attraction was an option, she would at least be clean and fragrant.

"I—I think it's time for bed." She groaned inwardly, thinking, *You smooth talker, you.* Her embarrassment was heightened by how strangely husky her voice sounded.

"It's only eight."

She ran her tongue over her teeth. "It's been a long day."

Quinn nodded, and in the process, his eyes swept over her chest and lingered long enough to tell her what she already knew, that her nipples were tight and hard, visibly so.

She didn't dare look down. "You can take the diamond to bed," she said weakly, then wanted to clap her hands to her head. Verbal clumsiness didn't sneak up on her often, but she'd made the world team tonight.

Quinn's mouth twitched.

Her cheeks stung with heat. No doubt his "lady friend" would be so much more sophisticated, never a hair out of place or a word out of turn.

"You look hot, Dani," Quinn said smoothly, and there was no mistaking his amusement.

She cleared her throat. "You could check the air-con in here. These lights really raise the temperature."

"They do, don't they?"

She'd made enough of a fool of herself. "Good night." She escaped without waiting for his response.

Quinn let his head roll back and stared at the bright lights on the ceiling. "Control yourself," he muttered, his weakness taunting him. Had she noticed his arousal? He'd sure noticed hers! The sexual charge he got just from being in the same room was beyond a joke, and he was toast once he clapped eyes on her chest.

So despite her snippiness, the lady was interested.

That added a new dimension to the proceedings. He'd not so much as touched her, but he knew instinctively that they were sexually compatible, or more aptly, explosively combustible!

Interesting… He looked down at her empty plate, remembering why he'd come up here in the first place. Quinn was tired of his own company, bored eating alone—which was weird since he was used to it. Preferred it, in fact. His life was a never-ending roundabout of fancy dinners in up-market restaurants, with the added non-bonus of countless airline meals.

But his apartment in Sydney was ordered and peaceful. To his mind, a cheese sandwich in front of the wall-to-ceiling windows that showcased the most beautiful city in the world was far more enjoyable than any two-hundred-dollar meal he had ever eaten.

A throwback, he supposed, to the chaotic mealtimes at home when he was a kid.

Quinn grew up with loving but eccentric parents who filled their huge old Sydney home to overflowing with troubled foster kids. He shared everything as a boy: his parents' love and time, his room, toys, even his wife, who moved in while they were at university. She was studying to be a social worker and loved helping out with the kids. Quinn shared her right up to the day she died of a brain tumour, aged twenty-six.

These days, he didn't share so much anymore, but still loved his parents dearly. Although he wished they didn't keep asking him when he was going to get around to giving them grandkids. Quinn's response hadn't changed since he was twenty: "I learned growing up that there are too many unwanted kids in the world."

He picked up the boxed diamond and took it to his room to lock away. Then he collected her empty plate and the food he'd brought at lunch. His phone rang as he descended the stairs. Matt Hammond calling from New Zealand.

He'd met Matt before since they were both shareholders of several different companies, including Blackstone Diamonds.

"Can we meet up in the next week?" Matt asked. "Among other things, I'd like to thank you properly for bringing the pink diamonds home."

Last month, Quinn had authenticated four pink diamonds for Matt's former sister-in-law, Melbourne supermodel, Briana Davenport. Briana found them in her apartment safe after her sister Marise was killed in the plane crash. Quinn was astonished to find they were from the Blackstone Rose necklace, stolen from Howard nearly three decades ago. He told Briana they must be returned to their rightful owner. At her request, he'd delivered the stones to Howard Blackstone's estate lawyers.

It was well publicised that Howard's will had been altered shortly before the crash to bestow his jewellery collection to Marise. Quinn was less clear on whether the stolen necklace would be included in the jewellery collection, since it was not specifically named and still listed as stolen. He had to be sure he was not acting illegally. It would pan out better for Briana, his client, that way.

After deliberation, the lawyers declared that the Blackstone Rose necklace *was* included in the jewellery collection. Since Marise hadn't changed her will before the accident, the pink diamonds now belonged to her spouse, Matt Hammond.

"I'm holidaying in Port Douglas for the next couple of weeks," Quinn told Matt now.

"You're kidding! I'm coming up there myself in the next couple of days. We can catch up then, if you're agreeable."

Quinn wondered if Matt was coming to Port Douglas to see Dani. They were cousins, but from what he'd heard, the rift between the Blackstones and the Hammonds included both Dani and her mother, Sonya.

"In the meantime," Matt continued, "I'd like you to put the word out. I'm willing to ask no questions and pay top dollar for the fifth Blackstone Rose diamond, the big one."

The centrepiece of the old necklace was a pear-shaped 9.7 carat diamond. The original Heart of the Outback stone was just over one hundred carats in the rough. Stones lost a lot of weight in the cutting, especially if the cutter wanted several diamonds from the one stone. Some cutters went for weight, which did not necessarily correlate to value; fire and brilliance came from the shape the cutter chose.

In this case, the cutter had done a masterful job, realising a creditable thirty-eight carats in total. This, along with the name and the legend, accorded the stones a massive price tag. The last big intense pink Quinn could recall coming up for auction several years ago—an unnamed twenty carat, pear-shaped beauty—fetched six million dollars. The Blackstone Rose diamonds could sell for as much as half a million dollars per carat, more if they were sold together.

Although laser identification wasn't around when the stones were cut, the Blackstone Rose's thief must have sold the big stone on the black market for it to have disappeared without a trace. Quinn had extensive connections, and there was always someone who could be persuaded to sell information about less-reputable art and gem collectors. A pink of this size would cause comment wherever it turned up.

Quinn hung up, thinking that his whole existence lately—professional and personal—seemed to be tied up with the Blackstone and Hammond families. First Matt and the pink diamonds, now his enforced cohabitation with Danielle Hammond. His very *personal* existence stirred again when he recalled the desire in her eyes a few minutes ago, heard the huskiness of her voice. He knew that he was destined to spend another night alone in his bed, dreaming about her intriguing face and lithe body.

He would have Dani Hammond, he decided. It would help while away the hours in this sauna until he could return to civilisation.

He grinned as he stripped and slid between the sheets, allowing himself the uncharitable thought that tupping Howard Blackstone's little girl would be like thumbing his nose at the old man, dead or not. That would be twice in a month he'd shafted the old goat. Howard must have turned in his freshly dug grave when the Blackstone Rose diamonds came full circle to a Hammond again.

Four

Soon after 6:00 a.m., an ungodly time for her, Dani crept out of the house to watch the sun rise over the beach. The tide was high and the temperature around twenty. Yawning widely, she stumbled through the ten-metre stretch of trees that fringed the beach, then slipped off her sandals and carried them down to test the water.

The physical response she'd had to Quinn in the workroom had played on her mind all night. Her fumbling efforts to gloss over it, knowing he'd noticed her tongue practically hanging out, made it ten times worse.

This man was not her friend. More than that, he already had a woman, a special woman, judging by the value of the gift he was having made for her. But why did he have to be so gorgeous? How was she to exist under the same roof for the next two to three weeks without succumbing to his charms?

She knew how. Remember Nick…remember the humiliation.

The water licked around her toes, a cool surprise, reminding her that winter was on its way. She remembered a cool winter's day two years ago. On cue, her cheeks burned for no one but her and the breeze as she walked on deserted Four Mile Beach. Nick had nearly finished her.

Dani should have known better, even back then. Twenty-five was hardly wet behind the ears. Nick had wined and dined her, swept her off her feet in an indecently short time. Promised love and marriage and forever. And even though she'd lived all her life in a fishbowl being targeted by the Sydney tabloids, she trusted him.

Until the day she'd left the house to go to a wedding dress fitting and found ten journalists camped outside the gate in the rain. To this day, Dani loathed large black umbrellas. They reminded her of vultures waiting for someone to die.

The journalists gleefully filled her in on the details. While she'd been sitting at home happily planning her wedding, Nick had been entertaining a well-known soap actress in an alleyway beside a nightclub. The photographs were pornographic. When confronted, the louse drunkenly accused Dani of misrepresenting her position in the Blackstone family. It had finally sunk in, despite her repeated insistence, that far from being an heiress, his fiancée was penniless and illegitimate.

Howard came to her rescue, just as he had for her mother years before. Dani wanted nothing more than to disappear. A few months backpacking around Asia eased her pain a little but caused her mother tremendous worry. Tired of the constant media scrutiny, she refused to return to Sydney, and Howard agreed to bankroll her business here in Port, where no one knew or cared that she was Danielle Hammond of Blackstone fame.

The sunrise was beautiful, reminding her of why she loved this place. She filled her lungs with sea air, knowing she had to resist Quinn, because if she didn't, there would be far worse heartache than Nick had inflicted. And that would spoil this beautiful place for her forever.

She turned around at the halfway point, feeling stronger and determined to finish this job quickly and eliminate the temptation. But her heart fluttered as a figure in blue shorts and a black sleeveless T-shirt jogged leisurely toward her. She had forgotten he liked to run in the early morning before the heat and humidity gained purchase.

Quinn slowed as she approached. "Too hot to sleep?"

Whether it was there or not, Dani imagined a sardonic twist to his mouth, and her hope that he would ignore her stammering reaction to him last night faded. He knew. And he wanted her to know he knew.

"Have a good run," she said as politely as she could muster, still walking steadily toward the turnoff through the trees.

But Quinn began jogging backward, facing her. "Did you know Matt Hammond is coming to town?"

That was unexpected. She slowed. "No, I didn't."

Dani had never met Matt in person. He'd attended Howard's funeral in February but kept an icy distance from the family. She'd wanted to introduce herself but decided, under the circumstances, to present a united front with the family of the man who had raised her.

She'd met Matt's brother Jarrod a couple of times and liked him immensely. But Matt was understandably bitter about Marise's presence on the ill-fated plane and her inclusion in the diamond magnate's will. Especially when a lot of the bad press zeroed in on the paternity of little Blake, Matt and Marise's son.

"How did you know that?" Dani asked.

"He called last night."

"Called you?" She frowned.

Quinn stopped jogging and propped his foot on a half-buried log to retie his laces. "We're both in the gem trade. That's not so odd, is it?"

Dani hovered nearby, curious.

"When I told him where I was, he said he was on his way here himself. I assumed, since you're his cousin, it was to see you."

She shook her head. "He wouldn't come here to see me."

Quinn utilised the log to stretch his calf muscles. Dani couldn't help but notice the dark hair salting his long strong legs.

She wrenched her mind back to Matt. Why would he seek her out? And what was his business with Quinn? A mutual dislike of Howard Blackstone was their only connection as far as she could see. "What exactly is your business with Matt?"

Quinn stilled, his hands on his thighs. "Is that anything to do with you?"

"Is it to do with the Blackstone Rose diamonds?"

"What do you know of the Blackstone Rose diamonds?"

Dani exhaled. "How they mysteriously turned up at Howard's lawyers a month ago and they had no choice but to send them to Hammonds." Suddenly it all fell into place. "*You* found them. *You* sent them back."

"I didn't find them. I was given them. A simple authentication job."

"Who from?"

"You'll have to ask Matt for the details, but they're his property, fair and square."

"I told you, I don't know him." She sighed. "He came to the funeral but wouldn't have anything to do with us."

"You should be more picky whom you fraternise with," Quinn said lightly. "Is there anyone in the world Howard Blackstone hasn't rubbed up the wrong way?"

"The feud wasn't all Howard's doing, you know."

"Tell me about it."

"Everyone knows. You must know."

"I know what the papers say." Quinn sat down on the log and patted the space beside him. "I want to hear it from an insider."

She sat tautly, aware of his big hot body just inches away, warming her side. A trickle of sweat crawled down his temple and she bet his back would be slick, too. Why didn't that turn her right off, instead of accelerating her pulse to alarming levels?

She bent and picked up a handful of white sand, letting it run slowly through her fingers. Since Howard's death, the Blackstone-Hammond feud origins had been printed and reprinted. Dani was sorry if her rendition was reminiscent of a bored teenage boy recounting his summer holiday to his class, but frankly, she was tired of the whole thing.

"Jeb, my granddad, and Howard were friends and partners after Howard married my auntie Ursula. Uncle Oliver, Mum and Ursula's brother, was left behind in New Zealand to run the family business. Anyway, when Granddad Jeb got sick, he signed over all his mining claims to Howard. Naturally, this didn't go down too well with Oliver."

That was an understatement. According to her cousin Jarrod, even after a stroke five years ago, the old man still got apoplectic at the mere mention of Howard Blackstone.

"He was particularly upset when Jeb gifted the Heart of the Outback stone, his most famous find, to Auntie Ursula." The massive pink diamond was part of Australian folklore, but as with many other exceptional diamonds, it brought its own share of bad luck with it.

"Howard had it cut and set into a fabulous necklace he called the Blackstone Rose."

"Rubbing salt into Hammond's wound," Quinn murmured.

She nodded. Oliver was incensed that the name Hammond was now completely usurped of its rightful place in the history of the famous Heart of the Outback.

"But after James, Howard's firstborn, was abducted,

Auntie Ursula became depressed. To cheer her up, Howard threw a huge thirtieth birthday party. Everyone was there, even the prime minister." Dani smiled, remembering her mother's awestruck tone as she'd described the finery, the dresses, the beautiful decorations. "But it all ended in tears."

"The night the necklace was stolen," Quinn murmured.

Everyone had their theories. Some thought it was a failed ransom attempt. No doubt Quinn thought Howard had hidden the necklace to collect the insurance money. "Howard accused Oliver and things got pretty heated," Dani continued. "Oliver denounced his sisters and said they were dead to him…." She turned to him, lowering the depth of her voice and adding some volume, "'So long as you have anything to do with a Blackstone!'" She wagged her index finger at him.

He smiled at her. Really smiled, and her insides melted.

"You missed a bit," Quinn admonished.

"What? Oh well, you obviously know about poor old Auntie Ursula toppling into the pool…."

"After drinking too much."

She put her finger to her lips. "We don't talk about it," she whispered dramatically. "In the melee, Howard accused Oliver of engineering the kidnapping of wee James, as well." That fact was probably not as well known as the rest.

Unfortunately, that accusation was the one thing Oliver could never forgive. He and his wife, Katherine, could not have children of their own. Jarrod and Matt were adopted.

"Nice bloke," Quinn said, an edge to his voice.

"You have to remember that he'd lost a son," Dani countered. "And whatever rumours you've heard about his womanising, Mum says he really loved Auntie Ursula. It can't have been much fun watching her struggle with depression."

Quinn didn't look impressed or moved. Whatever had gone down with him and Howard must have been spectacular. She sighed. "I don't get it, Quinn. Matt has a legitimate right to be angry, especially after the past few months. But your little spat was years ago. I wonder, why do you hate his guts still, even after his death?"

"Curiosity killed the cat." His tone was cool.

It had to be more than just the diamond-association vote, Dani reasoned. Quinn was a very successful broker, one of the most prominent in the world. She refused to believe that he still held a grudge because Howard had made life a little difficult for him years ago. "You know, your dislike of Howard borders on obsession."

He cocked a cynical brow. "That so?"

"It's too personal. What did he do? Take a woman from you?"

His bark of laughter rang out, startling her.

"Professional jealousy?" she guessed.

Or maybe she was needling, trying to pick a fight. Trying to find some external conflict to justify the internal conflict of wanting him. "He beat you to the deal of a lifetime?"

Quinn's brows knitted together. "Howard Blackstone never beat me at anything."

"Or maybe you've heard the stories and decided that you are the missing Blackstone heir." She was joking, of course, even knowing it was a terrible thing to joke about.

Howard alone always had faith that his firstborn, James, would walk through the door one day. He'd never closed the investigation and must have had a strong lead just before he died, because he changed his will. The new will effectively cut Kimberley out, favouring instead his oldest son, James should he be found within six months of Howard's death.

Naturally the press enjoyed this extra twist to the ever-changing, always-enthralling saga of the Blackstone family. Several candidates had been discussed and discarded over the past months, including Jarrod Hammond, Matt's brother. You had to hand it to Howard, she thought with a spark of admiration. He sure knew how to keep the paparazzi guessing.

Just like Quinn kept her guessing, mostly about how long it would be before she gave in to an unusually severe case of the hots… Reining in her errant thoughts, she returned to the topic of the missing heir. "Let's see, you'd be about the right age, mid-thirties. And I heard somewhere that you'd grown up in a foster home."

He spread out his fingers on his thigh, snagging her gaze for a moment. Tension curled his fingertips around his muscled leg, tension that radiated toward her in a hot cloud. Dani tore her eyes away and braved a look at his face, hearing the waves just a few metres away as if they were sloshing against her ribs.

Quinn gave no sign that he agreed or disagreed, but a rising sense of incomprehensible excitement pushed the next words from her mouth. "What, did you go to him with your theory and he laughed you out of the room?"

He stilled for a long moment, then slapped one hand on the log right beside her leg and heaved to his feet, turning to loom over her. The smell of him, sweat and soap and desire, swamped her. Then his other hand slammed down on the log on her other side.

She was trapped.

His face descended quickly to within an inch of hers, so close she could almost feel the scrape of his morning beard.

"You've got it very wrong, Danielle," he said, his soft voice at odds with the dangerous blaze of warning and desire in the espresso depths of his eyes.

Her stupid joke had pushed him too far.

"I'm not the missing Blackstone brother," he murmured, his chin dipping as he inched closer. His pupils were enlarged, the centres pinpoints of fire that hypnotised and immobilised.

"Because if I was," he continued in a low murmur that made the hairs on the back of her neck leap to attention, "I wouldn't do what I'm about to do."

Dani knew what he was about to do. She saw it coming like a train wreck—and she was chained to the tracks. It was inevitable that her head tilted back and her fingernails dug in to the rough surface of the log, bracing her. The cords on her neck stretched, rigid and tight. She watched, wide-eyed, as his face and mouth crossed the last millimetre, the point of no return.

If she'd been standing, her knees would have buckled at the first taste. They stared at each other until his salty mouth with its silky tongue started teasing hers, then she felt her eyelids flutter and close. He kissed firmly, not touching her except for his mouth, yet involving her senses totally. Every kiss she'd ever experienced was just window dressing; she'd been waiting for this, the real thing. Every man she had ever kissed before was a boy, and Quinn was here to show her how a man kissed.

Where were her cautionary affirmations? Where was her regard for that unknown woman, waiting somewhere for her diamond? That woman, at least, would understand, would realise that to be kissed like this was impossible to resist.

Dani wouldn't have stopped it; he taught her that in just a few seconds. How beautiful and right it was that she sat on a log in her favourite place in the world at sunrise, and the door to perdition was open and inviting. With his tongue stroking hers, his lips commanding hers to give him more, desire pushed her to where the sunrise would claim her, consume her with pleasure.

Then he raised his head abruptly and she sagged back onto her log, gasping for breath. The young sun disappeared behind him as he straightened, and all she could think was "I've done it now."

Quinn looked down at her, his eyes a swirling brown storm of intent. "Did that feel like a cousin's kiss, Danielle?"

While she was still trying to collect coherence and dignity—and maybe some form of protest—he turned and jogged away, his strong legs pumping, his back bristling with tension.

She registered a sharp pain in the tip of her middle

finger and raised her hand to her mouth to nibble at the splinter.

She was so out of her depth.

Five

Thankfully Quinn left her alone for the rest of the day and she completed the first of several wax models she would make in these initial stages. Dani worked late, said her good-nights from his office door and went to bed, trying to dampen down the memory of the kiss. But even though she'd had little sleep the night before, it still eluded her tonight.

She tossed and turned, listening to the waves through the open window. She considered a walk along the beach, something she did sometimes when troubled or unable to sleep. But she discarded that idea, knowing all she'd see was his face, all she'd feel was his mouth on hers.

Finally at about 1:00 a.m. she rose and threw on her robe, hoping that chocolate milk might help.

Downstairs, Quinn's office light was on, the door ajar.

She halted for a minute that seemed to stretch on forever, her heart thudding in her ears. All was quiet so she crept closer and pressed her ear carefully to the wooden door. Then his voice sounded and Dani nearly leapt into the air. She only let her breath out when she realised he was on the phone.

Who could he be talking to at one in the morning? A nasty combination of guilt and jealousy clawed at her as she wondered about the special woman in his life. Perhaps it was a long-distance love affair and that's why he was calling so late. *Hi, honey, I kissed someone today....*

But it was soon apparent this was a business call—exciting business. From what she could make out, he was in the middle of a live auction, bidding by phone. When she heard him murmur "Five million," her decorum abandoned her and she straightened and inched forward, snaking her head around the door.

Quinn sat at his desk, the phone to his ear. She felt the leap of interest as his eyes swivelled toward her, a palpable, inescapable sense of awareness, zeroing in on her. He'd rolled his shirtsleeves up to his elbows and undone his top buttons. One hand rested on a file in front of him, under a half-full glass of some amber liquid. The desk lamp was on, but otherwise the room was in darkness.

Dani lingered in the shadows, although he gave no sign that he was either displeased or happy with her presence. But he did not release her from his gaze. She leaned against the door, her heart thudding along in the silences that punctuated his infrequent responses.

After a couple of minutes, Quinn sipped his drink and then laid the receiver down and turned the speaker phone on, all without taking his eyes off her face. She took that as something of an invitation. Here was an opportunity to have a glimpse into his world, see the negotiator at work.

She moved a few steps farther into the room and rested her hands on the edge of a chair to keep that barrier between them.

The voice on the speaker was unmistakably English. She heard the name of a well-known auction house and the words *lot seven*. Presumably the auction was being conducted in London. Dani wondered if the man on the phone was a bid clerk from the auction house or an employee of Quinn's.

The item being bid for was a famous painting by a contemporary Irish artist who'd died in the sixties. She only knew that because Howard had one of his paintings. She wasn't sure how many bidders there were for this particular item. The bids were relayed to Quinn as they happened, although Dani heard nothing of the activity in the auction house, only the man's voice. The pauses in between bids seemed interminable. They probably weren't, but she guessed there was a lot of tension on the other side of the world. Lord knows there was enough in this office.

Would he smile if he won the bid? Celebrate with a drink? She held his gaze, and no doubt her face was alive with questions. His, however, was framed in intense concentration that held her captive.

The price was now up to eight million pounds. Dani

inched a little closer to the desk, marvelling at his calm. It probably wasn't his money he was spending, but if it'd been her, she would have buckled under the pressure. The next million took only two or three minutes to be disposed of. Still Quinn looked at her face.

"Ten million pounds, sir?"

He didn't flinch, but she did. While she'd been thinking about him, about his face and concentration and possible means of celebration, she had waylaid a couple of million.

Quinn quietly affirmed.

Ten million! That was *how* much in Australian dollars? For a painting?

The next pause was a long one. Dani was halfway across the room now, just a few more steps to the chair in front of his desk.

"The other party has just bid eleven, Mr. Everard."

"You may proceed," Quinn said quietly, and flexed the fingers of his right hand.

Dani covered her mouth with her hand and moved to the desk. The tension was killing her, but how cool he was. No sign of emotion crossed his features. He might have been reading the paper.

The minutes crawled by. Twelve million came and went. Her throat felt like sandpaper and she swallowed. Quinn lifted the glass and moistened his lips, then held it out to her.

Cognac. She would never smell it again without remembering this night. It slid down her throat and washed her lungs with heat. Slowly she rolled the glass over her forehead before setting it down on the desk. She had to lean well forward to get it within his reach, so she edged one hip onto the desk, twisting around to face him.

His eyes were inscrutable. A trickle of sweat began its journey down her spine, surprising her. She arched a little as the fabric of her silky robe slid over and cooled the moisture. A tiny flicker of that mahogany gaze told her he'd noticed, but not one muscle in his face twitched.

"Mr. Everard," the bid clerk's nasal voice intoned. "The other party has entered into a consultation with his client. Are you happy to hold?"

"Yes."

Dani's breath gushed out and she stretched her tense limbs and rubbed the back of her neck, thankful for the intermission.

"By the way, Quinn..." The man on the line lowered and warmed his voice. "That commodity you were interested in? A blank wall so far, I'm afraid. However..."

Quinn shifted but made no response to her raised brows. "Go on."

"A gentleman of my acquaintance has recently returned from visiting the big house on the other side of town. He owes me certain favours."

Quinn chuckled. "You run with the most appalling crowd, Maurice."

"I will let you know directly if I can be of any further assistance." There was a muffled crackle and muted voices. "I think we are ready to resume, sir."

"Thank you," Quinn murmured, his eyes back on Dani's face.

She lost the ability to judge time in the airless room. The performance may have lasted ten minutes or an hour. The last two million pounds advanced and Dani took another sip of liquor, her nipples prickling with the knowledge that he watched her every move. Rather than push the glass across the desk, she walked around to his side, placed it in front of him and leaned against the desk beside him. Quinn swivelled in his chair to face her, still holding her prisoner with his eyes.

Fourteen million pounds.

Dani swallowed.

Fourteen-point-two million. The other bidder had opted to chop the bid. Quinn offered no objection, neither did the auctioneer, apparently. Dani cleared her dry throat and helped herself to another sip of cognac while he watched.

Fourteen-point-five million. The room spun a little, which could have been the cognac. It was like a vacuum in here. Quinn Everard stared at her calmly, steadily, and the bid rose another massive increment. The tension was unbearable.

The skin of her throat and face tickled and she swiped at it, somehow agitated and afraid for him. She could not even contemplate him losing now, not after this. Not when she felt so sensitised, so aware of his gaze gripping her, holding her up.

Fourteen-point-seven million pounds for lot seven, going once. She chewed on her thumbnail, praying. Her chest rose and fell as each breath tortured her lungs.

Fourteen-point-seven million pounds for lot seven, going twice. Dani sucked in a massive breath, held it. This was it!

It was over! Quinn had won the bid.

Air gushed out from her lungs and she slumped momentarily, but then elation poured through her like the most illicit rush. She leapt in the air, her arms high above her head, her hands fisted in victory. For the first time in many minutes, maybe even an hour, Quinn was not looking at her. He stared at the file on the desk. His shoulders were rigid.

"Congratulations, Mr. Everard, and thank you for participating."

He exhaled slowly. "Thank you, Maurice." He paused, as if about to add something, but then looked up into Dani's face. "Thank you," he repeated, and she saw that his teeth were clenched. His hand shot out and hit the switch of the phone. Then he was standing in front of her, gripping her waist hard. He dragged her forward into him, his body like stone against her soft, yielding form.

She wrapped her arms around his neck and sagged against him, burying her face in his shoulder. Quinn moved so that her head tilted up, her throat exposed.

Bite me, she thought, her blood screaming in her ears. She was leaping out of her skin. Never had she reached this peak of excitement in her life, and she couldn't begin to think of consequences, other women, her heart, his hatred for Howard.

As if he'd heard her plea, Quinn lowered his head and nuzzled the hollow at the base of her throat briefly, then took her mouth hard. The taste of leather and almonds from aged cognac filled her mouth. His need for her came from farther down where his groin pushed into the silk-clad vee of her thighs. With a strangled gasp, she pushed back, feeling the distended ridge of his fly, every link of his zipper.

His tongue lashed hers, teeth knocked and scraped. She gasped breathlessly when his hand cupped and squeezed her buttock, forcing her forward. Then his hand ran down the short robe and to the sensitive back of her thigh, lifting it high and hard against him, so that her leg came up and wrapped around his hip. Her mind splintered with a desperate need of carnal contact.

She got it in spades, and the more she jerked against him, the higher she went. Grinding and straining, she became something—someone—she had no control over. She was on a collision course with a cyclone, building higher with every lash of his tongue deep in her mouth and every hard, fast thrust against her hot centre. And then he gripped the soft inside of her leg from behind and moved up, his seeking fingers sending a bolt of fiery energy searing through her. She lost the battle to be aware of her actions or his. All she knew was a wave of scalding pleasure that fisted and ebbed and fisted again and again, driving everything out of her mind.

She sagged against him, trying without success to halt the slide of her leg down his. Boneless, still swimming in pleasure, she trusted him to hold her up because her only tenuous grip was one hand around his neck. The other arm was behind her, palm pressed into the desk and trembling.

Quinn dragged her thong down her legs and made short work of the knot of her robe. While she still lagged, he plunged his hand into her hair and lifted her face to his.

His eyes snapped at her, fierce and hot. "Again."

"Yes." She sucked air into her lungs and pushed up off the desk and the madness started again.

Hands tore at clothing, mouths scraped over heated flesh, breath gushed from screaming lungs. When she got her hands inside his shirt, they slid on his slicked flesh. Cool, calm Quinn Everard was sweating, her mind crowed. She had reduced him to this, a wild animal desperate to copulate, so far removed from the suave, sophisticated businessman he was.

Where had she come from, this wanton, panting woman using her teeth and nails, taking his tongue into her mouth as if it was a drug she was addicted to? She was a nice girl about sex, only did it with someone she really cared about. One didn't do nasty sex when one had lived in a fishbowl all one's life, just like one didn't do drugs or drunken rampages, either.

"Do it!" the nice girl panted, desperate to have all of him now.

His hands tangled in her hair. "You think I have any control over this?" he gasped, holding her face up and scowling down into her eyes. "That went when you walked into the room."

The only answer she was capable of giving was to pull his torso against her and swipe her breasts back and forth, again and again. His crisp chest hair scraped and burned her nipples, spurring her into intensifying her efforts with his pants fastening. She finally got his pants down and at last he was naked, in all his pure, proud, masculine glory, roped with muscle, rough with hair, fierce with need.

There was a brief halt when he clapped a hand to his head. "Wallet?" Feverishly, he picked up his pants, slapping the pockets, then his face cleared and he reached behind her to the drawer and drew his wallet out.

Grateful for his foresight—protection hadn't even occurred to her—she took the pack from him and made it memorable, smoothing the condom over his hot, hard flesh with a dedication that had both of them holding their breaths for long seconds. He was built. Even her wildest daydreams hadn't done him justice. Then he groaned and grabbed her hands in a viselike grip. This agitated man before her, streaked with sweat and with rumpled hair, was a side of him she could come to like. But right now, her body was screaming for him, she needed more than *like*.

Then his palms were covering her breasts and his mouth was stealing her breath and the eye of the storm moved on, throwing them into a sexual frenzy again.

Quinn kept one arm firmly around her back for support while the other swept clear the surface of his desk. Then down she went, clutching at his shoulders and arms, dragging him down, too. Limbs tangled, teeth gnashed, her heart threatened to explode out of her chest. The storm overtook her, both of them. The air was filled with grunts and bumps and harshly drawn breaths. He dug his fingers into her hips and dragged her forward. She felt heat meeting heat and then the delicious, brimming slide of his total invasion. For a second, the absolute shock and pleasure of him deep inside immobilised her. Then she strained up, locked her legs around him and held on for the ride of her life. He kept one arm under her to shield her from the unforgiving desk. The other he plunged into her hair, pulling her head back to give him access to her mouth. Bodies and mouths locked together, she threw herself heart and soul into a coupling so intense, as full of the fire and brilliance of the diamond upstairs, that she wondered if they'd survive or just combust.

Her second orgasm slammed into her, making her falter and lose her rhythm. Her legs relaxed suddenly from around him, splaying wide as coils of sensation pumped and flowed to every extremity. She sobbed with delight and Quinn straightened a little, lifted her higher, changing the angle to drive new pleasure into her. She was assailed by so much sensation, she couldn't contain it and was swept away in another inferno of red-hot pleasure that never cooled, only soared higher. Somehow she held on, lifting her legs around his waist again, rising to meet him, until she felt the change in his grip intensify, his arms becoming so rigid, her hands lost purchase. But he gathered her whole body to him, right off the desk, threw his head back and in a groaning rush of breath that went on and on, he pumped, again and again, and then collapsed on top of her.

Minutes later sometime in the next millennium, Dani stirred and tried lifting her head. She was trapped with Quinn's face buried in her hair on one side. It was an interesting predicament, unable to move, the harsh light of the desk lamp only inches away, burning her face and revealing all her flaws, no doubt. Quinn's heartbeat, right on top of hers, rattled away at an impossible rate. She swivelled her eyes to the side, saw the devastation on the floor, clothes mixed with papers and with cognac.

Her hair scratched and whispered on the white blotter pad. She blew softly into his ear, repeating the gesture when there was no response. His lashes flickered and he turned his head and licked his lips. Slowly his eyes focussed on her.

"You okay?" he asked weakly.

Dani's dry lips stretched in a strained smile. Oh, man, was she ever!

He blinked apologetically, lifting his torso a couple of inches. "Sorry. I'm squashing you."

Quinn Everard was embarrassed, she thought. Like her, he probably didn't do nasty sex.

That made her smile wider. "I never took you for a desk man."

He blinked, looking appalled. "I'm not. I'm…sorry. Did I hurt you?"

She bit back a full-on smile. "Only if you call pleasure pain."

They shifted jerkily, which brought about an interesting sensation since he was still inside her. He lifted a little higher and ran his eyes down her body, making her squirm. Distracted by her belly button jewellery, he tugged lightly on the barbell she wore; a triangular knot of sterling silver, studded with deep red Swarovski Austrian crystals. "Did you make this? It's very pretty."

Dani made belly button jewellery only for herself. The precious stones she preferred working with were too expensive, since they were destined, for the most part, to be hidden under clothing.

His big hand, spread wide, covered her belly, then moved slowly up to pass lightly over the tips of her breasts. She squeezed around him, as tight as she could, pleasuring them both. Smiling, he bent his head and tongued a rapidly hardening nipple, even as she felt him harden inside her.

"I think I can dredge up some finesse, if you'd consider giving me a second chance."

"While I have nothing at all against the desk man—" she smiled and put her arms around his neck, arching up into him "—I wouldn't be averse to some finesse in the very near future."

Six

Quinn declared the next day a holiday to celebrate the results of the auction. He'd made all the arrangements by the time she'd showered, and within the hour, they were at Port Douglas Marina boarding a bareboat charter catamaran named *Seawind,* a ten-metre flared-hull beauty with mainsail.

They sailed out to the Low Isles and snorkelled around the breathtaking underwater garden of the Great Barrier Reef. But by late morning, the area was overrun by hordes of tourists on day trips, so they set sail for a small inlet to put into and enjoy the hamper the charter company provided.

The weather was perfect, calm and clear. Quinn was happy to find that on the water the humidity didn't bother him at all. Either that or he was becoming acclimatised.

"This is the life." Dani appeared from below deck with her lime-green sundress on again; he liked the bikini better but she'd burn easily with her skin. And at least he now knew exactly what was under that dress. It would give him something to do later, peeling it off her....

He offered her a plate and glass from the hamper and she stretched her legs out along the seat, sighing with pleasure.

"Ever sailed before?" he asked.

"No. Howard was never interested in boats."

Quinn popped a cheese-topped cracker in his mouth. "Did you get on?"

"With Howard?" She considered. "Most of the time. He wasn't averse to sharing his opinion on clothes, friends, music and so on, but I suppose that was his right since he paid the bills."

She unscrewed the cap of the chilled sauvignon blanc wine and held it up to him.

Quinn had his mouth full but shook his head, holding up a bottle of water instead.

Dani leaned back on the seat with her wine and a plate of nibbles. "He was kinder to me than to the others. I was never going to run his company, so I guess he went easier on me."

"He bought the shop for you, didn't he?"

"It was a loan, one I've nearly paid off."

"Why do you think they never married?" Quinn really wanted to know why the bastard never publicly acknowledged Dani as his daughter.

"Who?" She looked blank.

"Your mother and Howard."

She took a sip of wine, her brow wrinkling. "Why would they marry? He was her brother-in-law."

"They obviously liked each other well enough to stay together all those years," he mused aloud.

"They were a bit like an old married couple, I suppose, when he wasn't out putting it around…" She grinned.

"But she still stayed?" Don't tell him Sonya wasn't in for all she could get. Quinn had never met Sonya Hammond, but the Sydney press had long speculated on the relationship between the womanising Howard Blackstone and his sister-in-law. No matter how often the Blackstone publicity machine denied it, Dani's paternity was subject to debate on a regular basis. Most— Quinn included—assumed she was Howard's love child.

"I know everyone thought Mum was his mistress," Dani said moodily. "I've lived with the scandalised looks and whispers all my life. But my mum has more class in her little finger than all of them."

"But there was you." If Howard didn't want to acknowledge his love child, why did he flaunt them, keep them in his house?

Her gaze was unwavering, if a little cool. "Howard's not my father," she said tiredly. "Look, I know you hate him and I know he has—had—his faults. But he looked after us." She looked down, picking at the hem of her dress. "Which is a lot more than can be said for my real father."

"Who is…?"

"Who cares?" she shot back. "Not him, that's for sure."

Quinn held up his hands, remembering the cliché about redheads and temper. "Sorry. Touchy subject, huh?"

He sympathised but was still reeling a little to find she wasn't Blackstone's daughter. That was a turn up for the books.

"Not touchy, boring." Her voice dropped. "He didn't want us. End of story." She stared moodily out at nothing but sea, and the sun glinted off her copper curls. "I wouldn't have minded very much if Howard was my father. At least he was there."

Quinn supposed he should feel guilty. Sleeping with Dani wasn't a victory over the old man, after all. Regardless, it still felt damn good.

And then she smiled brilliantly, unfolded those glorious legs and came to stand close and rummage through the hamper. "Who taught you to sail?"

"My father." Quinn spent many a Saturday morning on the water as a kid until his parents decided the boat was a luxury and the money would be better spent elsewhere.

"Was it very rough, growing up in a foster home?"

"Rough?" He smiled. "Sometimes. Bloody noisy. It was more or less open house. I doubt even Mum and Dad knew how many kids were under the roof at any one time."

"You called them Mum and Dad?"

"They are my mum and dad," Quinn said, bemused.

"Well, yes, but how long were you with them?" She looked confused.

Quinn scratched his head. "All my life. I think you've got the wrong end of the stick. I wasn't a foster kid. All the other kids were."

Dani's face cleared. "Oh, I see. So you and your parents ran a foster home?"

"Something like that," Quinn agreed. "They have a big old villa in Newtown, off King Street. Lots of rooms, all in various states of disrepair, and a kitchen that's the size of a hotel dining room."

"Not at all what I imagined for you."

She moved back to her seat, but her enticing floral scent lingered and he sniffed carefully, keeping it for himself. "What did you imagine?"

Dani grinned. "A grand old mansion with a butler. Everybody dressed for dinner and speaking very *na-i-cely*." She gave an apologetic shrug. "Sorry but you're just so damned refined."

Quinn chuckled. "My parents would love that. They are the most unpretentious people I know. Old hippies, very socially aware. They don't care about money or nice things, only sharing what they have with the less fortunate." He paused. "I'm sure I embarrass them, successful capitalist that I am. Not that they don't hit me up every couple of months with some harebrained fund-raising scheme or other."

She crossed one shapely leg over the other, snagging his attention, holding it for seconds. What was this hold she had over him? She was younger than him by seven years, but that wasn't the allure. He'd found her his equal in maturity and intelligence.

"You must have seen some sad things, though."

"Kids are selfish." He opened his bottle of water. "I was too busy marking my territory."

"Is that how you broke your nose?"

Quinn gave her a resigned smile. "Yep. That was Jake Vance, actually."

"Jake?" She sat up.

"You know him?" Something in him bristled. He'd be surprised if she didn't know of Jake; he was one of the most talked-about entrepreneurs in Australia. But as he was his best friend and also quite the ladies' man, Quinn wasn't sure if he liked the idea of Jake and Dani being friendly.

"Not very well. I met him a couple of times. He was at Kim and Ric's wedding, with Briana Davenport, actually, pre-Jarrod."

Quinn nodded, relaxing. "I'd heard that."

"Tell me about the broken nose," Dani prompted.

"We didn't see eye to eye when he first came to stay." Quinn absently rubbed the bridge of his nose, recalling the mother of all his teenage fights.

"Jake Vance was a foster child?" She sounded disbelieving.

He supposed it was difficult to think of Jake like that when the whole country associated him with immense wealth.

"Not exactly. He had a mother, but there were some problems, mostly to do with his stepfather. He ran away from home, looking for work in the city and things didn't pan out the way he'd hoped. Ma and Pa got to talking to him on the streets one day so he turned up at home."

Quinn as a teenager was well used to sharing but liked to be asked nicely. Jake didn't ask nicely. Quinn wasn't about to lose his standing as top dog in his own house. The battle was epic, and at the end of it, neither boy could stand. And that was the start of a long and valued friendship.

"He's my closest friend now. He and Lucy my foster sister. She was abused from the start. Came to us when she was eight and just stayed." He caught her horrified look. "She and Jake had a thing a few years back, but now she lives in London. Corporate banker," he finished proudly.

"How awful." Dani shuddered. "What makes people such monsters?"

"I don't suppose people start out that way," Quinn said thoughtfully. "But it's not that hard to be careful if you don't want a baby."

Dani nodded sadly, and he realised that was probably close to the bone for her. "Not these days, anyway," he qualified, not meaning to suggest her mother and the mystery lover had been careless.

"So have the things you've seen and heard put you off having kids?" Her voice trailed off when a shadow passed over his face. "Oh, I'm sorry, Quinn." Dani looked very uncomfortable suddenly.

"That's okay. I was married, yes."

"I remembered as soon as I'd asked. Laura Hartley, wasn't it? I only know because she was at PLC around the same time as Kim. I was a couple of years after."

"Ah." He nodded. "I didn't know that." PLC— Pymble Ladies College, a private college on the North Shore—had an excellent academic reputation, but it was strictly for rich kids.

"I'm sorry," Dani repeated quietly. "I remember now hearing that she'd died."

Quinn stared out over the waves. "We married when we were still at university. Laura wanted to be a social worker, whereas her parents…" his voice hardened as he continued, "They had other ideas. Sure, they sent her to a nice school and tolerated her going to uni, but they didn't intend their daughter to get her hands dirty. She was only marking time till the right rich husband came along." He smiled bitterly. "When she moved in with me on the cheap side of town, her family disowned her."

"What was the family business again?" Dani's brow wrinkled. "I remember they had stores all over the country. I think they were friends with Howard."

"Soft furnishings." Quinn swallowed, but it didn't erase the familiar burn of anger that flared up at the mention of Howard's name. He may not have caused Laura's death, but he sure influenced how she felt in those last days.

"How old was she when she died?"

"Twenty-six. It was sudden, only a few months from the first symptoms till the end."

"I'm so sorry," she said again, her golden eyes pools of sympathy.

"Don't be. I wouldn't swap those few years for anything, not a bit of it." He leaned forward and poured a little wine into a glass, mindful that he was skippering the boat. "She loved our life, my parents. She loved that we took in the unwanted and the street kids." Some of the good times flooded in, making him smile. "Every time I turned around, she was sitting in a corner, talking to some snot-nosed kid. They confided in her, told her everything.

More than Mum and Dad, even." He looked down at the wine in his glass, swirled it around before tossing it down in one gulp. "That was the hell of it. She would have gone places, helped so many. Why she had to die is beyond me."

It was his one taste of true failure. He couldn't understand how it could happen, how she could be taken.

How could he not have saved her?

He rubbed his chin. Part of him would always love Laura, or more accurately, love that time of his life, when he was young and silly enough to believe in forever, believe he and Laura were invincible.

But Howard Blackstone had tainted the memories. He'd never forgive him for that.

And as he tried and failed to swallow the hard knot of bitterness, he found himself wanting to justify it to Dani. He called himself a swine for doing it, for doing what Howard had done to him. Tainting the memories.

But he wanted her to know. "You want to know why I hate Howard so much?"

Dani blinked at his harsh tone.

"The bastard ruined the last weeks of Laura's life."

She visibly paled. "I didn't know he knew her."

"He didn't. But you're right about him being friends with the Hartleys. After the World Association of Diamonds vote went against him, he did all he could to blacken my name. That was fine, I could take care of myself. Laura always had faith her folks would come around and accept our marriage. But with Blackstone whispering in their ears, filling them full of hate, they turned their backs, even knowing she was terminal."

Dani's mouth dropped open in dismay, and she looked away as if she couldn't bear to look at his face. Yes, it hurts, doesn't it, he thought bitterly. She'd thought Howard was some kind of saint. Well, now she knew differently.

"When everything went to hell and the tumour came back, I went to them, begged them to come. Not that we ever gave up hope..." Laura would not permit anyone to think for a minute she wouldn't beat the cancer. "But they tossed me out. They said Howard had told them all about me. How I couldn't be trusted, how I was after her money, how she was my meal ticket out of the slums." His head rolled back and he breathed deeply of the warm air. "They couldn't even give her peace at the end," he said with disgust.

"I—I didn't know."

How could she?

Now that the anger was out, as always, it quickly faded. Time did that. Blackstone had a black heart and that wasn't Dani's fault. It seemed even being six feet under was no barrier to hurting people.

"They didn't deserve her, Quinn," she said quietly. "You did."

He sighed, thinking that Dani had her own problems. At least he had great family support. He suspected she'd never felt part of a real family. He'd glimpsed a vulnerability in her, an insecurity. He remembered it from long ago, when he used to notice such things. Loneliness, a need to belong.

Somewhere along the way, he'd just plain stopped looking.

The hell with it. Today was a rare day, one that didn't come along very often. She was sexy, fun, talented. Available. Why was he wallowing in the bitter past? And in some ways, telling Dani was kind of cathartic. She knew the man, knew his faults. She gave him a slightly different perspective.

Quinn would never forgive or forget, but he could let go a little more. That's what time did. And the fact that she wasn't Howard's daughter had to be a good thing, right?

He set his glass down, sorry that he'd made her sad. He wanted the warmth of her brilliant smile back, and perhaps he wanted to warm her a little also. When he held out his hand to her, she smiled up at him and he saw understanding and empathy. When he bent to kiss the soft, fragrant flesh just under her earlobe, her skin steamed up quickly and her pulse quickened under his mouth.

This was about sex, he reminded himself. Unbelievable and uncomplicated sex. If it made them feel good and if no one expected anything more, where was the harm?

He lifted his head to see her mouth turned up in sultry understanding. Quinn resolved to give her as good as she gave.

He pulled her to her feet and downstairs to the cabin, peeling her clothing off on the way. The salt from her skin tingled on his tongue as he revealed and then tasted every delicious inch of her. He made her stand still, legs braced, and made love to her with his mouth. She rocked on her heels with the sway of the vessel under them, clutching his head. His bitterness and her insecurities melted away as he tipped her onto the bed, slid deep into her body and looked into her eyes, and they became one with the motion of the sea.

"How's it going?"

Dani looked up from her workbench, where, days later, she was once again engrossed. "Today I start on the chain."

She was working with platinum, always a challenge but one she enjoyed. Many jewellers found the metal too soft and dense to work with, but with practice, it got easier and the rewards were worth it.

"You chose diamond cut and not snake," he noted approvingly.

Dani nodded. "It's classic and doesn't kink so much." She picked up her torch again and resumed her work. Quinn pulled up a stool. It was becoming a habit of his to come in here and watch her work. He seemed fascinated by the whole process.

"It must be exciting to create something from start to finish and know it will outlive you." He was flicking through her portfolio again, he did that a lot. On every page, he found something that interested him and would ask her how she decided on that particular combination of texture or colour. She broke all the rules, he told her, and yet her jewellery worked beautifully.

Dani was buoyed by his interest. He really seemed to get her, to share her vision of the relationship between gemstones and precious metals. Being a designer was a solitary occupation. Most people were only interested in the end product, not the journey of creation. It was nice to have someone to share ideas with for once.

Several days had passed since the boat trip, each one slightly cooler and calmer as the fitful cyclone season waned and autumn woke up. Dani barely noticed the weather since she only left the workroom to finalise a few last-minute wedding arrangements for Ryan and Jessica or to make love with Quinn.

She glanced over to where he sat at the desk, flicking through her portfolio. So far she'd shied away from badgering him on the intended recipient of the yellow diamond. He was an honourable man, despite the coercion he'd used at the start. She had to believe that. A loyal man who wouldn't make promises and trifle with her feelings.

It wasn't her normal way of doing things, but she had to be grown-up about it. One disastrous relationship had only added to her lifelong feeling of not being good enough, firmly entrenched in second best. But that wasn't Quinn's problem. They were from different worlds. This wasn't a "relationship" so much as a "situation"—and as far as situations went, it wasn't a bad one to be in.

So long as she didn't try to make it into something else.

Her phone rang and she put her torch down. It was Steve from the shop to say Matt Hammond was there to see her. She gave him the beach house address and prepared to meet her cousin for the first time, face-to-face. Several minutes later, understandably nervous, she let Quinn answer the door while she hovered a few steps back.

"Danielle?" Matt Hammond looked from one to the other, a confused look on his handsome face. "I didn't realise you knew each other," he said, taking Quinn's proffered hand.

Quinn stepped back and motioned her forward with a reassuring smile. "Dani's doing a little designing job for me."

She looked up into Matt's face. He was nearly as tall as Quinn, leaner, with thick sandy hair and sharp grey eyes that reminded her of her mother's.

"Come in and sit down." Quinn led the way to the living area, offered refreshments and then discreetly withdrew.

Dani twisted her hands together, unsure of the reason for his visit, hoping it was a genuine overture to get to know the Australian side of his family. Her first tentative questions concerned Blake. It was a tricky subject after the months of speculation about his late wife's infidelity and his son's paternity. But when she asked if he had a photo, like any proud father, he produced several from his wallet.

The snapshots showed a dark, rather serious-looking little boy. "Three and a half," Matt responded to Dani's query about his age. She dredged up the courage to ask if she could have one to send to her mother and Matt readily handed over a couple.

"Are you here on holiday?"

"I thought it was time we met," he said simply. "I also wanted to talk to Quinn, but had no idea I'd find you together."

Dani felt her cheeks glow. "As he said," she quickly inserted, "I'm helping him with a designing project."

"Good for you." Matt smiled. "A recommendation

from Quinn Everard is a valuable thing in this business. I saw the catalogue for the February launch, by the way. Your pieces were impressive."

Dani beamed. She'd had a lot of work as a direct result of the Blackstone launch, proving that Howard, who'd talked her into being the featured designer, had known his stuff.

But best not to mention that name in this company, she thought.

"And that is another reason I'm here," Matt continued. "You've heard, I suppose, that four of the Heart of the Outback diamonds have been returned to me?"

Dani nodded cautiously, noting his use of the Heart of the Outback—the Hammond diamond—as opposed to the Blackstone Rose diamonds.

"I have an idea and I'd like you to be part of it."

Her response was measured. Was this a ploy to upset the Blackstones? "In what way?"

"I want to make an heirloom necklace from the Heart of the Outback diamonds, to be kept in the Hammond family and worn by future Hammond brides."

Dani's mouth dropped open. "Matt, that's a wonderful idea!"

"Hopefully my father will think so, too."

She nodded. Bringing the Heart of the Outback stones—Jeb's legacy—together again for the next generation of Hammonds would surely ease the old man's bitterness in his last years. "Matt, my mother would so love to restore some sort of relationship with Oliver and your mother, and you and Blake, too. Do you think there is any hope of that?"

Matt's silvery gaze was steady and open. "I have no problem with Sonya, Danielle. But there is a lot of water under that bridge and I can't speak for Dad." Then his voice softened. "Small steps? Starting with you designing the Bridal Rose necklace?"

The Bridal Rose. Emotion almost overwhelmed her. "It would be an honour," she mumbled, staring fixedly at Blake's photos to hide a sheen of tears.

Although she was close to her cousins Kim and Ryan, and had never doubted her mother's love, finding a place she felt she belonged had always eluded her. To have found a new family and have a part in reuniting its members was a privilege. She and Matt seemed to click, just as she and Jarrod had.

Then a more selfish elation sneaked up on her. First, the beautiful yellow diamond upstairs in the safe, and now the pink Blackstone Rose diamonds. What were the chances of being offered two commissions with stones of this calibre? And at only twenty-seven years old! "What a pity the fifth diamond hasn't come to light."

"I'm working on that," Matt said mysteriously. "In the meantime, I'd like you to design the necklace as if there *were* a fifth diamond—the centrepiece. Can you do that?"

"Of course. Can you give me a couple more weeks to finish what I'm doing here?"

He acquiesced. "I hadn't thought further ahead than getting an answer from you."

"Well, you have it." She smiled happily. "I would love to do it. And I'm rapt you thought of me."

Matt's smile was slow to start but it lit up his face.

"You are a very talented designer and a Hammond. The perfect choice."

They talked for an hour about the jewellery trade and little Blake, and ended on his brother Jarrod's recent engagement to Briana. Dani thought it must be strange for Matt to see his brother marry his late wife's sister, but Matt confided he'd always been fond of Briana. More relaxed now, she mentioned the rumours doing the rounds a few weeks ago, suggesting Jarrod Hammond was really the missing Blackstone heir. To her relief, Matt did not seem offended at hearing the Blackstone name.

"Jarrod's birth mother may have something to say about that," he retorted.

Dani was surprised. There had been no mention of Jarrod's birth mother in the newspaper stories.

Matt's mouth tightened. "I've met her. She taps Jarrod up for money every so often, then disappears under whatever rock she crawled out from."

Her heart went out to Jarrod. Impossibly handsome, a successful lawyer, a beautiful new fiancée, and yet that suave exterior hid its own personal pain.

But at least he knew who his mother was....

As if her cousin had recognised her momentary sadness, he turned it on its head by agreeing to talk to his brother about a family get-together soon. "Briana has dragged him along on one of her modelling assignments overseas. Poor beggar." He pulled an amused face. "But maybe when they get back, we can have a bit of a get-together."

It was tentative but, still, it was an overture. "And Blake?" she asked. "And my mother, too?"

"Why not?"

The three of them had a wonderful dinner at a famous outdoor restaurant in the middle of a copse of huge tropical palms. Quinn toasted her when he heard about the Bridal Rose commission, saying it would really put her on the map in the designing world.

He turned to Matt. "I thought I had a lead on the fifth diamond, but the trail has gone cold, I'm afraid. I'll keep you posted."

Matt was clearly disappointed but still raised his glass to both of them. "I appreciate it, Quinn. Someone must know something. And Danielle, I am looking forward to working with you on the necklace, hopefully with all five stones."

It was truly one of the best days she'd ever had. Her mother would be over the moon that Matt had made contact, and to have the opportunity to rewrite the history of the Heart of the Outback Diamond was such a buzz. To think Quinn might have a hand in locating the fifth stone… It was the perfect end to the perfect day.

Until she walked in on them talking business some time later on her way back from the bathroom. She wasn't eavesdropping, but one palm tree looked much like another and she came in from a different direction to find Matt had moved into her seat and they had their heads together. Something made her pause behind the nearest trunk when she heard the name Blackstone.

"I have already spoken to three of the minor shareholders," Matt said. "If you were to get behind us…"

She heard Quinn's voice. "If you're serious about

this, you need Jake Vance on board, not me. I only have a handful of shares."

"I'm meeting with Jake next week, but listen, they're on shaky ground. The Blackstone empire is crumbling with Howard gone. Perrini and Ryan snap and snarl at each other and Kim spends all her time calming them down. I just want to keep the pressure on."

Dani's rosy wine-glow faded fast, leaving a nasty feeling that her cousin wasn't playing fair.

She waited to hear how her lover responded.

"I'm not interested in a dogfight, Matt. My few shares are performing adequately."

Dani relaxed a little and peeked around the tree trunk.

Matt had leaned back and put his hands behind his head. "I thought you'd jump at the chance to shaft a Blackstone, given your history."

Quinn frowned. "My beef was with Howard, not Blackstone Diamonds."

"Or," Matt continued nonchalantly, "maybe you're mixing business with pleasure."

She saw Quinn's eyes glint dangerously and couldn't expel her next breath.

His voice was low and cool and she had to strain to hear him. "Dani is private business, all right?"

Though her heart was beating loud and fast, mostly for fear of discovery, she heard Matt apologise. "But if I can get Vance on side, you'll go with us?"

"If Jake says sell, I'll sell."

She stayed behind the tree for a few more seconds, trying to make sense of all the emotions. She felt strangely buoyant that Quinn hadn't denied there was something between them. Keenly disappointed that Matt Hammond clearly wasn't ready to embrace the reconciliation of the two family factions just yet. Would he ever be?

And somehow uneasy that she was consorting with the enemy. Perhaps two of them.

Seven

"Quinn, have you heard a rumour about a corporate takeover of Blackstone Diamonds?"

His eyes snapped open. That was out of left field.

Quinn had been lying in bed, idly thinking that his sporadic sexual encounters rarely involved morning sex, especially dreamy morning sex with the same woman. He was always rushing off to a meeting or a flight. Maybe he'd been missing out all these years.

Now he abandoned his reverie to answer Dani. "You stopped screaming your delight one minute ago and suddenly you want to talk business?"

She lay with her head on his chest, her hair a riot of curls against his skin.

Quinn turned his head to look at the clock. Seven-thirty. Time he was up. "Yes, I have heard something. You want coffee or are you staying in bed?"

But she was persistent. "Do you think Matt is involved?"

Had she heard something last night?

Matt's request to sell his shares or support a takeover bid had not surprised him; Quinn had heard he was polling all the Blackstone shareholders for support. He was getting it, too.

But not from him, at least not yet. His fingers rasped over his chin. "What is this inquisition before I've had my coffee?"

She kept her face down on his chest, a fact he found strangely worrying.

"I heard you," she said in a small voice. "Last night at the restaurant. Talking about selling your shares in Blackstone."

Quinn's eyes narrowed in the dim room. Scratch all those nice thoughts about waking up with the same woman. He didn't know whether to laugh or be offended. Who the hell did she think she was? "Eavesdropping, Danielle? If you heard us, you'd know I turned him down."

She lifted her head and looked him right in the face. And it hit him: she was serious.

The urge to laugh disappeared. "A company takeover," he said, twisting his finger around a springy red curl, "is very complicated. It needs the support of the board and the requisite number of shares. I'm Little League in Blackstones, Dani."

That was the truth. He had very few shares himself. But he knew Matt was in for more than the Blackstones knew about—and climbing. And Quinn knew who else had a substantial portfolio.

"But if Jake Vance asks you to sell…?"

Quinn stilled. She had heard everything. And she was right out of line. He was not in the habit of justifying himself to anyone, let alone a woman he'd known for a week or so, even if the sex was amazing.

He injected plenty of cool in his reply. "Yes, if he gave me a good enough reason, then I'd sell."

Disappointment darkened her eyes, and just the fact that he recognised that pissed him off. There was no room for emotion in business. That was the dictum that Jake Vance, corporate raider, believed in, and Quinn agreed wholeheartedly, damn it!

"Quinn, what hurts the Blackstones hurts me, you *do* get that, don't you?"

Time to remind both of them this was just a fling. "Just because we're sleeping together, Danielle," he said coldly, "doesn't give you the right to ask about my business dealings."

She flinched. He knew that because he felt it in his chest and stomach, which lay under her torso, in between his legs where she'd squeezed her thigh, over his shoulder where she'd draped one of her arms.

But he held her gaze. He wouldn't negotiate on overstepping boundaries. After a long moment, he nudged her, indicating he wanted to get up. She moved over to her side of the bed. When the hell did they get into his-and-her sides of the bed anyway?

His refection stared balefully back in the bathroom mirror while he wondered what had suddenly happened, what had changed. One minute, he was savouring the delights of a very sexy body. The next, he was wallowing in guilt, thinking about someone else, considering someone else's feelings. Just how deep was he getting here?

Somewhere out on that boat, she'd stirred up some long-buried need to protect. His parents, his childhood home had always been a port in a storm, a harbour for lost and needy souls. Quinn had forgotten what it felt like, until now. Was that what Danielle saw in him? Was she searching for such a port?

He ran the tap and splashed his face, making sure it was good and cold.

This was supposed to be a brief fling, a bit of fun to while away the heat of the day while he was stuck up here in the middle of nowhere. Wanting her every minute of the day in the limited time they had together was acceptable. Thinking about waking up to her every morning was probably teetering on the edge and would have to be addressed—and soon. It had been years since he'd considered relationships and he was perfectly happy with his life just as it was.

But justifying himself to her was definitely off limits.

Steve called at breakfast to ask if Dani could mind the shop for a few hours; he and his partner had an ultrasound to attend. Quinn went into town with her. She was quiet but not snippy, and he had some ideas for marketing he'd been thinking about. He pushed aside the feeling that giving her some decent advice may assuage his guilt somewhat.

"What are you doing here, Dani?" he asked, after a customer walked out with a very nice pair of pearl earrings that she'd gotten for a bargain, he noticed.

Dani looked up from locking the cabinet. "Making a living. Just."

Quinn paced out the tiny interior. The display was funky without being crafty; the quality of her jewellery was too high for that. But the premises were second-rate, security was inadequate and the whole place needed a complete overhaul. "Is it success or failure you're afraid of?"

Dani ran her eye slowly around the shop. "It could use some attention, I know."

"How did you end up here, anyway? Why Port?"

She scratched her neck and shrugged. "It's where I stopped." She picked up a cloth and bottle of glass cleaner and walked out from behind the counter. Today she was almost conservative in below-the-knee tights, high-heeled sandals, a mushroom-coloured tunic with voluminous sleeves and a huge orange silk rose pinned to her lapel.

Why he always noticed her attire was beyond him. He questioned her again. "What were you running from?"

Dani walked to the display cabinet on the other side of the shop and turned her back on him. He heard the hiss of the spray cleaner, saw the sleeves of her creamy shirt rippling as she rubbed and polished. "I was engaged."

As soon as she said it, he remembered a couple of sketchy details. Actually, what he remembered was watching it on a TV news programme and wondering how it qualified as news.

"I was engaged to someone who was convinced, even though I denied it repeatedly, that I was Howard's daughter and, therefore, a Blackstone heiress."

She moved around the cabinet, rubbing intently, but didn't look at him.

"I remember," Quinn murmured, noticing two distinct spots of colour on her cheeks.

"You remember the scandal."

She did look at him then and he saw that it wasn't so much pain setting her mouth into a thin line and colouring her cheeks. It was embarrassment.

"The media had a field day." She gave a tight laugh. "There were some really funny headlines. I would have laughed myself if…" Her eyes slid away and she moved to another glass-topped cabinet. "Do you know, he even demanded his ring back, until Ryan paid him a visit on Howard's orders."

Quinn exhaled. "I'd say you had a lucky escape."

She rolled her eyes and the smile she had forced disappeared. "I just got tired of it. I'm either the illegitimate love child, the scheming gold digger or the poor stupid fool whose fiancé got caught with his pants down. Just one more brush to tar me with."

She fell silent and continued to rub vigorously at some imaginary mark.

"Why here?"

She raised her shoulders. "I love the beach and the climate. It's far enough from Sydney that most people don't even know I'm related to the Blackstones." She glanced at him briefly and grinned. "And I'll admit to a bit of poetic license. The population is pretty transient here. I can be whoever and whatever I want."

Images of a wan face, tamed hair and indeterminate clothing flitted through his mind. He'd seen her featured several times in newspaper spreads or television reports. But he'd never noticed her beauty, her animated smile and sparkle, until he'd met her up here. Now he found himself consciously holding his breath when he heard her come downstairs in the mornings, wondering what jaw-dropping mishmash of colours and textures she would amaze him with today.

Quinn put his hand out. "Come here."

He led her outside and then turned her and gestured to the faded lettering above the door. "What does that say?"

"Dani Hammond. Fine Jeweller of Port Douglas."

"Fine Jeweller," he repeated. "We both know how much study and work experience it takes to be able to put those two words after your name."

He put his hands on her shoulders and turned her to face him. "Is this what you envisaged while you were putting in the work?"

Her head dropped a little. "Not really."

"What did you see?"

"What does anyone see just starting out? I wanted to be the best."

"Didn't you want important people to come to you, celebrities and royalty and private collectors?" he asked.

She pursed her lips. "I suppose…"

"Would Howard Blackstone have put his money up if he thought this was as far as you'd go?"

"Ouch!" Her eyes flashed and Quinn wondered if there might be a little residual anger from this morning.

"This," he said as he turned his palm up to indicate the shop front, "isn't good enough. Not the shop or the location."

He showed her back inside. "You have the connections, Dani. If the Blackstones won't help, invest in a marketing company. Maybe my people can point you in the right direction."

Dani frowned, not convinced. "Listen, I have so many orders from the February launch, I can barely keep up."

But Quinn was pacing again. "You need to move. Sydney…" He caught the negative set of her mouth. "Melbourne, then. Hell, why limit yourself? You're good, Dani, great, even. Why not New York or Europe?"

She put up a hand. "I was thinking of a couple of doors down, actually."

Quinn stopped and looked at her, put off his stride.

"The vacant shop two doors down," she repeated patiently. "It's nearly on the corner of the mall, so there's lots of foot traffic. It's twice the size and very modern."

His head went back and he stared down his nose at her. *Why* wasn't she getting this? "You want to be the best? The best in Port Douglas?"

"Yes, I do remember the one-horse-town comment," she said testily, her cheeks firing up.

"Hey, it's your career. But no one will ever know you if you don't give your profile a kick up the backside."

She stepped up to him, head thrown back, fingers curled into her palms, those golden eyes positively steaming. And Quinn realised, too late, that yes, she really was still sore about this morning.

"I can't be too bad," she said hotly, "since you practically *begged* me to design the necklace for you."

"Hey, it wasn't my idea," he retaliated. "In fact, I argued against you being allowed within ten feet of that diamond."

* * *

It was like a blow to her gut.

This morning he'd inflicted a neat cut, chosen his words carefully to put her in her place. She wasn't to question him, wasn't to expect anything from him.

This was punchier, without preamble or foresight. She realised from the stunned look on his face that he hadn't intended to tell her.

A deathly hush descended. So Quinn Everard wasn't here on the pretext that she was the best designer around. Crushed, she felt the blood drain from her face.

What did she expect? He had only just finished belabouring the point. The best—hah! Who was she kidding? He'd been right, again and again. This wasn't what she'd imagined for herself. Her shop was pathetic, and Howard had given her the loan but never stopped harping on her about moving back to Sydney and getting serious about her career.

Quinn inhaled and opened his mouth to speak, but she had to get in first, before she crumpled. "Who is your client?" she asked quickly.

"Dani, for what it's worth, I now have complete confidence in you."

Fine jeweller, indeed. Somehow she managed to keep her chin steady. "Am I not to know who hired me?"

He shook his head. "I'm sorry."

She should have learned by now never to get ideas above her station. She was second best. Always had been. The stigma of illegitimacy. Nick. Hell, even

Quinn Everard with his designer awards and chain-store quips.

She now felt justified to ask about the woman she was supposedly making the necklace for, a subject she had conveniently put to one side once he started blowing her mind in bed. "The diamond isn't for your girl-friend?"

Quinn looked away. "That was your assumption, one I chose not to correct."

She'd been feeling guilty for an imaginary girl-friend—not that the thought of wrecking someone's life had stopped her, or him. She was just some floozy to while away the hours with up here in the middle of nowhere. He was bored, he was hot. She was available.

Her mother always told her it was okay to make a mistake as long as you learned from it. Obviously Nick's betrayal was no deterrent for making huge lapses of judgement where men were concerned. She had known Quinn a bit over a week, a record time for her to sleep with someone. And that would reflect badly on her, she suspected.

But was she strong enough to keep away from his bed?

The next few days dragged by. The necklace pro-gressed well, even without Quinn's encouraging presence. It was as if all her frustrations poured out into the design. Without consulting him, she altered the model she'd supplied for his approval—that is, his client's approval—and worked fifteen-hour days. Ryan and Jessica's wedding arrangements were well in hand.

Quinn kept to himself and a kind of polite peace enveloped the house.

But by night, it was a different story. Dani was her own worst enemy, reliving their lovemaking over and over. He was a drug she was addicted to. To stop herself from marching into his bedroom, she began justifying his actions. After all, she was being paid an enormous amount of money and an enormous compliment to design a necklace for the most beautiful and valuable stone she was ever likely to see. What did it matter that it was for a client and not him?

And it wasn't like he had tricked her into bed, either. She'd practically ambushed him while he sat at his desk, conducting his business. She couldn't blame him for that.

Had she really expected that something more could come of this "situation" she had rushed headlong into? She was out of his league, not even in the same stratosphere.

One night he told her that Jake Vance's mother had passed away. "The funeral is Friday. Come to Sydney with me and catch up with your family."

She considered it dubiously. "It will put me back on the necklace. I wanted to finish it before the wedding on the twentieth."

"Relax. I'll put it in a bank vault here. I'll charter a flight for Thursday afternoon and we'll return Saturday."

It was the excuse she needed to keep away from him. She went all out for the next few days and made good progress, barely sleeping at all.

And that's probably why she fell asleep on the private plane.

She awoke slowly, fuzzily, dreaming of Quinn, so it was no surprise at all when she saw his face mere inches away. And when he leaned even closer and brushed her mouth with his, she closed her eyes again, didn't even *think* of resisting. After all, that was how the dream was supposed to go. Reliving their lovemaking was how she'd spent every night since the fight.

She stretched toward him, allowed the dream to part her lips, to feel the tip of his tongue seek and find hers. She combed her fingers through his thick hair and her heartbeat quickened and banged loudly in her ears. But she wouldn't open her eyes just yet. She didn't want this to stop, didn't want him to disappear.

His hand moved on her thigh, skimming her silk underskirt over her heated skin. Each stroke lengthened, higher and higher until she shifted restlessly, craving more. Another hand caressed her neck and face as they kissed. The seat belt dug into her hips, making her wriggle against it. Every part of her strained toward him, this faceless lover, this man with his tongue in her mouth, one hand moving down over her blouse to cup and stroke her breast, the other moving ever higher, scorching her thigh. Her arms were trapped against his chest, unable to move far with his weight leaning into her, but she moved toward him, trying to touch him, to inflict some of the same torture on him.

Breathing heavily, he grasped her wrists and stilled her.

"Open your eyes, damn it!"

She did and almost quailed at the tortured desire in his. Desire and regret.

Regret for wanting her or for hurting her?

Wide awake now, she gave a shuddering breath, laid her head on the rest and just looked at his face. The heat of passion still smouldered sullenly in the pulse beat on her wrist where he gripped her, and in the aching tips of her breasts and deep inside her centre. But her breathing slowed and she searched his scowling, troubled face, trying to read what he was thinking and feeling.

His breathing had calmed. Gradually the grip on her wrists eased and became more of a caress. He, too, leaned back in his seat facing her, watching her.

Finally his eyes softened and he spoke. "You'll stay with me tonight."

It wasn't a question, or a demand. And—God help her—her heart leapt in her chest with welcome. She'd intended to take a cab to the Blackstone mansion in Vaucluse and surprise her mother. But Dani would take what she could get from Quinn.

Time with him was short and she knew there'd be less of her when their fling ended. The fight had torn them apart physically, and because it was unexpected, the end was hard to accept. Now she had the opportunity to say goodbye properly, make it special. Dani was going to make the most of the day or days she had left with him, and damn the consequences.

They spent the rest of the flight looking at each other. Not kissing now but touching, sweet touches to their hands, cheeks, throat, hair. His eyes burned for her, and that and his touch kept her at a simmer for the remainder of the flight to Sydney, the seemingly endless taxi ride to his building and equally interminable elevator ride to his penthouse apartment.

Giddy with desire, they barely made it inside before he was ripping her clothes off, pushing her up against the wall opposite a massive picture window that showcased beautiful Darling Harbour, Sky Tower, the harbour bridge and the opera house. He took her there and Dani welcomed him into her body and came again and again as the lights of the city swirled behind her eyes like a kaleidoscope on drugs.

Eight

Dani survived the fierce hug and pulled back to survey her mother. "You look…different. Did you get highlights?"

Her mother patted her hair self-consciously while Marcie, the Blackstone housekeeper, bustled around the table.

Sonya Hammond usually wore her brown hair in a neat bun, but today she'd allowed several long spiralling tendrils to escape, giving her a completely different look. Was it her makeup or the unusually colourful teal blouse she'd teamed with smart-looking slacks? Her mother was the epitome of conservative elegance, but today, Dani thought she looked younger somehow, mature-chic. "Have you had a facial or something?"

Sonya ignored her question and instead tsked at

Dani's earrings. "Must your earrings always arrive before you do?"

"I thought these were quite demure." She touched one gold bar with a plaque of smoky quartz on the end. Since she had reinvented herself up in Port Douglas, some of her more bohemian creations stunned her mother, though Sonya was too nice and too fond of Dani's strong sense of individualism to criticise without humour.

"Sit. How is it you're here when we're seeing you in a few days?"

"I told you I was doing a little job for Quinn Everard." Dani leaned forward and sniffed appreciatively at the urn in the middle of the table. "Mmm. Pumpkin soup."

"Yes, I couldn't believe the cheek of the man, after all he's put you through."

The whole family had witnessed the deterioration of Dani's professional reputation at Quinn's hands. Dani tried to ignore the little pang of hurt at her mother's words. "Anyway, he has a funeral to attend today so I came down with him. I need some shoes for the wedding."

"What colour is the dress?" Sonya asked quickly. "No, don't tell me, I'll try to keep an open mind."

Marcie appeared with a soup bowl and a platter of warm Turkish bread and set them down. Her mother looked pointedly at the urn. "Eat up, I have an appointment. Ryan's picking me up any minute."

Dani ladled some soup into her bowl. "I thought you'd want to supervise," she said dryly, "but we can do dinner later and maybe I'll treat you to the movies or something."

Sonya looked uncomfortable. "I can't, dear. I have an engagement. The theatre, actually."

"Oh?" That was unusual. Sonya hardly ever went out in the evenings. She swallowed her soup, watching her mother. New clothes, new hairdo, appointments and engagements… "Who with?"

"Garth, actually."

"How is old Garth?" Dani was relieved. Garth Buick was the Blackstone company secretary and had been ever since Dani could remember. He was probably Howard's closest friend, a nice man, she recalled. A widower for a few years.

"He's not old," her mother said with an edge to her voice. "He's very young and fit."

Dani's spoon stopped halfway to her mouth and the two women locked gazes for a long moment.

Sonya reddened and looked away first. "Close your mouth, Danielle. It's just friendship. He's been teaching me to sail."

"Right," Dani said weakly. "That's great, really."

And it was, she told herself as she slathered butter onto the warm flatbread. Her mother had given her life over to raising her daughter and Howard's kids and then running his household and being his hostess. Whatever Dani's father had done to her, she'd completely withdrawn from relationships outside of the family.

Either that or she'd been walloped with a massive dose of unrequited love. Dani wondered what it would be like to love someone so completely that you never wanted to risk it again.

Was Quinn still in love with his wife? It must be six or seven years since Laura died. Did he still miss her, measure every other woman he met against her? Was Dani about to discover what her mother had all those years ago, that you couldn't compete with a dead woman?

Sonya's smile was resigned. "I can just see your mind ticking over, my girl. Poor old Mum, the dried-up old prune, wasting away for the love of Howard."

Dani shook her head admiringly. How did the woman do it?

"But no," her mother continued. "He was so devastated when Ursula died. I knew then that he would never risk giving his heart completely again. And I didn't intend to be one in a long line of his discarded women."

Clever woman, because that was exactly the way things had turned out. Howard was notorious for his womanising and had never committed to any of them.

Her mother sighed. "I may as well get it over with. My appointment this afternoon is with a real estate agent. I'm looking at a house over in Double Bay."

"But…" Dani was stunned. Her mother leave Miramare? "You have a permanent right to reside in this house." Howard's will stated that.

They both cast their eyes around the room and out to the vista beyond. The first-floor suite Dani had grown up in was much more informal than the rest of the house but still boasted spectacular views of Sydney Harbour and the Pacific Ocean. Sonya combined a love of antiques with a warm, comfortable style of her own. Miramare was a show home, she liked to say, but her suite of rooms was just a home.

Dani could not imagine her mother anywhere else.

"I rattle around here by myself now," Sonya said broodingly. "And what if James Blackstone comes forward? Howard was convinced he was alive or he wouldn't have left the mansion to him in the will."

"This is your home. You are legally entitled. James, if he exists, will just have to accept that." She pushed her plate away, suddenly not hungry. "Besides, what about Marcie?"

"There will always be a place for Marcie. She knows that."

"You've talked about it?" Dani frowned, a little indignant that her mother hadn't shared this with her first.

"I'm just looking, dear," her mother said airily. "When Garth suggested this place was up for sale, I decided to have a peek, that's all."

"Garth suggested... Wait a minute, doesn't Garth live in Double Bay?" Dani didn't know whether to be affronted or delighted, but in the end, delight won out. She couldn't help grinning as her mother fidgeted. It was about time Sonya thought of herself after a lifetime of looking after everyone else.

Sonya cleared her throat. "I'm not moving in with Garth, okay? I'm just looking at a smaller house that happens to be a few blocks from his."

Marcie passed by the table. "I've made up your bed, lovey."

"Oh, I'm not staying."

It was her turn to fidget as two sets of eyes swivelled toward her. "I'm twenty-seven, for crying out loud!"

Marcie scuttled out, grinning.

"Is he as nice-looking as his photo?" Sonya asked.

Dani shrugged. They'd be here all day if she was to outline the myriad ways Quinn Everard appealed to her.

"Do you like him, Danielle?" her mother insisted.

"Would I spend the night with him otherwise?"

Her mother's piercing gaze made her feel about ten years old, as usual. She reconsidered her defensive attitude. It had rarely worked in the past. "I suppose. But he's out of my league."

Sonya raised her aristocratic nose. "Must be hard to walk with that huge chip on your shoulder."

"You haven't met him. He's smooth." *And sometimes rough…* "He owns himself, very self-assured. Supremely comfortable with himself, his place, his ability. And he manages to convey all this without making the minions around him feel inferior." She rolled her eyes ruefully. "Even though it's painfully obvious that's exactly what they are."

Her mother rested her chin on her hand, a faraway look in her eyes. "You do like him," she said softly, and a silence descended as Dani tried and failed to think of a suitable rejoinder.

"Why don't you both come to dinner and the theatre with Garth and me tonight?" her mother asked.

Dani shook her head, somewhat relieved. "He won't be back until late."

"Oh." Sonya looked disappointed. "You, then."

"I'm not playing gooseberry." She was pleased her mother was stepping out but one tiny part of her wanted to think about this for a while. Dani had few enough absolutes in her life already. To think that she may never visit her mother at Miramare again was a sobering thought. "I have heaps to do on this flying visit, honestly," she lied, and decided to change the subject. "You'll never guess who came to visit last week. Matt Hammond."

Sonya's eyes lit up, just as she'd known they would. Dani rummaged through her bag for the photos of Blake that Matt had supplied. Her mother fell on them.

"What's more," Dani added, "he wants me to make him an heirloom necklace from the Blackstone Rose diamonds, though I'm not sure if that's for public consumption just yet."

"I can't believe it! What's he like? Tell me everything!"

"Nice." At least, she had thought so, thought they clicked, but that was now coloured by the conversation she'd overheard. "Really nice."

"You don't sound convinced," her mother said dubiously.

"Oh, I am, it's just that Quinn was there and they were talking business."

The doorbell rang downstairs and Sonya's face fell. "Not now." She grimaced at Dani, obviously wanting to hear more about her nephew. "That'll be Ryan."

"Don't tell him about Matt," Dani whispered.

Ryan looked pleased to see her and they spent a couple of minutes discussing the wedding plans. She was thrilled to see how utterly happy he looked. He and Jessica were expecting twins in a few months. Jessica was blooming, Ryan told her, but worried she'd already outgrown her wedding dress.

"What brings you to Sydney?" Ryan asked.

"I needed special shoes for my dress," she explained.

He rolled his eyes at Sonya. "God help us…."

Dani's fashion sense for these big occasions was legendary. "Don't be mean," she grumbled. "I've gone to a lot of trouble for this wedding. Keeping it quiet has been the hardest thing I've ever done." *Moving into Quinn's house, his bedroom, exploring his body, welcoming his touch…and all just to keep their wedding under wraps.*

Dani smiled, suddenly feeling quite kindly disposed to Ryan Blackstone. "Quinn was coming down for a funeral so I tagged along."

Ryan's brows rose. "Sonya told me you're doing a job for him. I was surprised, given your history."

She shrugged away a pang of hurt. "Client's request."

"Jessica knows Quinn slightly, likes him, I think." His face lapsed into a smile she had never seen on him before. "Still, she likes everyone these days."

Dani's eyes nearly misted over as she witnessed Ryan's happiness. He'd always been a troubled soul. His brother's abduction and mother's suicide were enough of a burden. Add to that the offhand way Howard treated both him and Kimberley, consistently choosing Ric Perrini over Ryan when it came to Blackstone Diamonds. She crossed her fingers under the table and silently wished Ryan all the happiness in the world.

"Who died?" Ryan selected an olive and a slice of cheese from the table. "Quinn's funeral?"

"Jake Vance's mother."

"I'd heard Everard and Vance were chummy. Has

Quinn said anything about Matt Hammond sniffing around?"

Dani shook her head, not looking at Sonya.

"Apparently Hammond was in town last week seeing Vance. The rumour doing the rounds is that Hammond and Vance are out to set up a corporate takeover of Blackstone. Seems Matt's been polling all the shareholders for support."

Sonya opened her mouth. Dani shot her foot out and connected with her mother's ankle. What good would it do for him to know Matt had been in Port talking business with Quinn, too? He'd turned him down.

Sonya prudently said nothing, and she and Ryan dropped Dani at the bus stop for the central city and headed off to their real estate appointment. But even the prospect of shoe shopping did little to quell a growing disquiet. Should she warn the Blackstones about the Jake-Matt-Quinn connection? Was she being disloyal to the family who had provided for her all her life?

She let herself in to Quinn's apartment using the key he had given her. Her feet ached and all she could think about was his large Japanese bath, so it was an unwelcome surprise when the sound of loud voices greeted her.

Four people stood around the island in Quinn's kitchen. A pretty woman with long, tied-back greying hair, looked up first. A tall, lean man stood beside her with one arm draped loosely around her shoulders. Quinn, too, had his arm around someone's shoulders. Someone beautiful, in a lilac suit, with a chic blond bob and striking eyes.

Dani couldn't really take in much more than that.

But then Quinn's eyes beat a path to her face and she felt the energy as if he'd shone an intense spotlight onto her.

"I—I'm sorry," she stammered. "I didn't mean to intrude." God, what must they think? She had his key. "I thought you'd still be out."

Then Quinn dropped his arm from the blonde's shoulders and walked toward her. His eyes shone as he drew her into the circle. There was no mistaking the warmth in his voice as he said, "*This* is Dani," as if he'd been waiting for her to come, dying to introduce her.

As it turned out, this was much better than her anticipated bath. She shook hands with his parents, Gwen and Joseph, and with Lucy, his foster sister, who had the most beautiful, sad violet eyes.

They were ribald and rowdy, and so close, they finished one another's sentences. It was incredible to see Quinn in this light. Outside of the bedroom, his reserve set him apart from everyone; he seemed untouchable. His parents were nothing like that, and when he was with them, neither was he. There was so much warmth, humour and concern for one another in this kitchen. She loved her mother dearly but she'd never stood around a kitchen counter with her family members, drinking, joking and sharing memories.

Yes, it was a sad day for the Everards, but as often happens with funerals, the relief of getting through it sometimes manifests itself in a need to drink. "Especially when you're Irish!" Joseph intoned, holding out his glass for a top-up, while Quinn shook his head at her, mouthing, "He's not Irish."

Dani thought back to the tensions that had accompanied Howard's funeral; the reserve, the constant media crush, everyone watching one another to make sure they didn't fall apart, or wondering who knew what about Howard's eventful life.

That all seemed a million miles away. Corporate takeovers, too, seemed a million miles away. She swapped blueberry muffin recipes with Gwen, had an eye-popping dance with Joseph to a Leonard Cohen song, and Lucy confided she had discovered Dani's knickers under the couch.

"Must be his other girlfriend," Dani told her. "I never wear them."

"I don't think so." Lucy laughed. "Quinn *never* invites a woman to stay over here."

Everyone left a couple of hours later and Quinn ordered in pasta, which they ate in his tub. She lay across from him as he struggled to keep his eyes open, and cautioned herself to guard her heart. Her expectations of people were too high. A throwaway remark by Lucy, the warmth in his eyes when she crashed their party…there was danger in allowing herself to hope she could ever be admitted to the circle of love she had just glimpsed.

Her fingers swirled the water in front of her, making a whirlpool, and Dani recognised she was in an uncontrolled spiral. She was falling in love, and not only with Quinn, but with the idea of his family, too.

Quinn came into his living room to see Dani standing in front of the window looking out at Sydney's skyline, her bag by her feet.

Yes, he thought. He'd wanted her here, to see what she looked like, see if she'd fit. And if that hadn't prompted him to take a swan dive off the balcony, then he was going to try her out on his parents. Only they had preempted that by inviting themselves over last night.

And hadn't that gone well?

The polite tension of the past few days in Port Douglas had made him miserable. Being relegated from lover to boss shouldn't have bothered a man who, since Laura's death, hadn't considered forever. At thirty-four years old, Quinn had never wondered till now whether he was missing out on anything.

He hadn't expected to enjoy her so much.

Dani turned and smiled at him and he gave himself a mental shake. "All packed?"

What the next step was, he couldn't be sure, but Quinn knew one thing. Where Dani Hammond was concerned, he was at least prepared to admit that there would be a next step.

She nodded and reached for her bag, just as Quinn's phone rang. It was Sir John Knowles, former prime minister, outgoing governor-general, and close friend and mentor of Quinn's. A call he had to take.

He walked into his office and after very little preamble, Sir John got to the point of his call. Incredulous, Quinn listened to the man's earth-shattering admission, and in seconds the feeling of peace Quinn had woken with was ground to dust.

"Taxi's here." Dani stood at the doorway to his office, holding her bag.

Quinn covered the mouthpiece of his phone. "I have to take this. You go on and I'll meet you at the airstrip."

She left and he returned to his phone call. Based on Sir John's admission, Quinn had no alternative.

"I want out, John."

The older man's quiet voice begged him. How could he turn him down?

"I've become personally involved. I won't lie about something like this."

"Please, Quinn, just another few days. I wouldn't ask this of you if it wasn't the last chance I have."

"Allow *me* to tell her, then."

"I can't risk her refusal, don't you see? And I haven't told Clare yet. Not about the prognosis or the other."

The old man sounded sick and alone. His last chance. Quinn had heard that before, had lived with his failure for seven years.

But still, it was a lousy thing to do. "You don't know what you're asking."

"I do, believe me. And I wouldn't ask it of anyone but you, because I know you won't let me down."

"Quinn, will you come to the wedding with me?"

He sat back in his chair and displayed the same careful expression he'd had since they got back from Sydney three days ago.

Dani was worried. The rumours Ryan spoke of in Sydney had now been aired on television. The shareholders of Blackstone Diamonds were restless, despite an assurance from Kimberley in the paper this morning that all was well.

Perhaps if he knew the Blackstones, was personally involved, he wouldn't be so hasty to offer his support to Matt.

Quinn set his pen down. "That's not a good idea," he said slowly.

"Why not?"

"It's a family occasion. With the events of the past few months, everyone will be feeling a little nostalgic." He looked at her steadily. "My history with Howard is bound to raise comment. I don't want to rub everyone's nose in it."

"I don't think anyone will—"

"I'll let you know if I change my mind, okay?" He picked up his pen again, his eyes unreadable. "How's the necklace coming along?"

"Okay." The client had imposed a deadline for completion—the twenty-fifth. She was on track, Dani thought, assuming she kept her mind on the job instead of wondering what Quinn Everard was up to.

Nine

"Look who I found on the doorstep." Dani was on her way out to collect various members of the Blackstone clan from the airport when Jake Vance's face appeared before her. She left the guest with Quinn, gave her apologies and rushed out to her task.

Quinn's smile faded at his friend's grim expression. What was up? Jake kept a brutal schedule. He didn't just show up on a whim.

Quinn waved Jake into a seat. "Coffee?"

"You have something stronger?"

Quinn narrowed his gaze but held up a bottle of cognac.

"My old mate Hennessey." Jake nodded gratefully.

Quinn poured two generous snifters.

"No wonder you're AWOL." Jake's head gestured to the door where Dani had just left. "Well, more AWOL than usual."

Quinn stayed silent and sipped his drink, waiting for Jake to come to the point.

The silence stretched, then Jake leaned forward and placed his glass on Quinn's desk. "Sounds important."

"I didn't say a word," Quinn retorted, exasperated.

"Exactly," Jake said smugly. "Not often you have a girl stay over at your apartment."

"How did you…?"

"Lucy."

"You and Lucy are talking?" Quinn leaned forward, arms folded on the desk.

"Don't get excited. She called the day after the funeral, before she headed off back to England. Just a friendly take-care-of-yourself call."

"She was worried you wouldn't want her at the funeral," Quinn mused. Jake was ripped to shreds when Lucy left him after several years together. Quinn tried not to take sides and loved both of them, but he never wanted to see that hurt inflicted on either of them again.

Jake shrugged. "I appreciated it."

"What brings you up here? Bottom fallen out of the market?" Quinn hoped it was nothing to do with Matt Hammond and his Blackstone Diamond shares. He didn't need any more secrets upsetting the applecart with Dani.

Jake took a healthy gulp of liquor, screwing up his face. "In a roundabout way, it concerns the little lady who just rushed out of here with her tail on fire." He fixed Quinn a stern look. "Drink up. This is going to come as a shock."

Quinn listened in disbelief as his closest friend related how his mother, shortly before she died, told him he was not her birth child. She'd found him as a two-year-old at the site of a fatal car accident. The car had been washed into a river and the two other occupants were dead.

Jake rubbed his eyes wearily. "I thought she was delirious. And when she insisted that I was Howard Blackstone's son, I was sure she was delirious."

Quinn's eyes felt like saucers. He raised his hand. "Back up. This was before she died?"

"I didn't mention it at the funeral because…well, I just didn't believe it. But I've been going through the house." He opened the briefcase he'd laid on the other chair and took out a large scrapbook. "It's all in there, Quinn." He patted the book. "God Almighty, I've never been so scared in my life."

Quinn rose with the bottle and walked around the desk to top up Jake's glass. He perched on the edge of the desk and put out his hand for the scrapbook.

Jake kept talking as Quinn flipped the pages.

"How I was kidnapped as a toddler by the housekeeper and her boyfriend. How they sent a ransom note and Howard did all he could to get me back, but on the way to pick up the money, the car crashed."

Quinn glanced at him periodically while reading the newspaper clippings. He tried to imagine the dark-haired little boy in the photos as a grown man, even as his rational mind rejected the notion. He glanced up at Jake's dark green eyes, coal-black hair and at the fully formed widow's peak—as opposed to just a hint of one in the baby photos.

"My mother happened on the accident and it all went a bit haywire. She'd lost a baby the year before to SIDS and was on the run from her deadbeat boyfriend. She was going somewhere where no one knew her. Anyway, she was probably a little crazy at the time—hormones, grief, whatever—so she picked me up and passed me off as her own."

Quinn got to the last page and snapped the book shut. The dates could work, though it would make Jake a year older. It must be true, or else a very elaborate hoax, but why would April, Jake's mother, lie at the end when she had nothing to lose?

"My God," he breathed. "You're a Blackstone."

"I'm *not* a Blackstone!" Jake countered, then he put his face in his hands. "What the hell am I going to do now?"

They talked and drank all afternoon. Quinn suggested a DNA test to eliminate April as his birth mother.

"Already done it," Jake said. "The results should be through in a few days."

They agreed he should talk to his lawyers and accountants. It was common knowledge that Howard Blackstone's amended will instructed a six-month delay of disbursements pertaining to James while his whereabouts were investigated. Jake thought April's ex-husband, Bill Kellerman, must have got wind of the investigation and threatened her, so she decided to forewarn him.

The living Blackstones were not likely to welcome him with open arms. Matt Hammond's intention to stir things up in the Blackstone boardroom was another complication. "You'll need Matt onside in case they turn on you," Quinn warned. "And watch your back. Ryan and Ric Perrini are chips off the old block. Don't trust anyone. The Blackstones have a leak somewhere in their organisation." That much he knew. Someone close to the Blackstones was providing little snippets of information to those in the industry. That was how Quinn had stumbled onto Ryan and Jessica's wedding plans.

When Dani arrived home a while later, she popped her head in the office to ask if they wanted coffee. Though they both probably needed coffee by this point, judging by the depleted brandy bottle, they declined.

"Don't worry," Quinn reassured his friend when he saw him staring after Dani. "I'll keep it quiet."

Jake turned his head to look at him. "You serious about her?"

The million-dollar question, Quinn thought, leaning back and folding his arms. "Define *serious*."

"I couldn't define squat at the moment."

Quinn had given considerable thought to the question but was little closer to an answer. At his mother's funeral, Jake had spoken of the importance of family, which made Quinn think of the relationships that were vital to him. He was as proud of Lucy, who'd dragged herself up from nothing, as if she were his real sister. Watching Jake grow into the confident, successful business baron he was had been one of Quinn's greatest pleasures in life, and he had no qualms that however upsetting the situation with the Blackstones became, Jake would face it squarely and prevail. Even his parents were constantly motivated to change things for the better. They were now busy fund-raising for a caravan to take to the inner-city streets as a drop-in centre for the street kids of Newtown.

Quinn loved them all and was proud to share in their successes, but sharing was nothing new for him. He'd grown up sharing everything until Laura died—and then he had nothing left. He'd closed himself off, kept his motor idling, but somehow had stalled here in Port Douglas.

He was passionate about his work, hugely successful, but he did have to question whether or not he was growing. Because from where he sat, he was doing the same things he was five years ago, while everyone else had moved on.

Quinn stared at a point somewhere above his friend's shoulder. "I've always felt it was unfair to ask a woman to sit around waiting while I'm off travelling the globe."

"Liar!" scoffed Jake. "You've never even *considered* asking a woman to sit around waiting for you."

Quinn grinned and picked up his glass. He made a thoughtful study of his friend through the amber liquid. "There's this woman I know in Milan. I see her every three or four months for one or two nights. I like her, but we both know that's all it is, a one-night stand every so often. I remember her birthday, I buy her nice things, take her out somewhere nice…." He emptied his glass in one swallow, grimacing at the burn. "But that's all there is. I was happy with that, damn it!"

"About time." Jake stood and approached the desk, tipping the bottle up to empty the last drops into Quinn's glass.

"You can talk!" he retorted. His grin faded. "She's like no one else. Every minute with her is a keeper. Suddenly, my life, which I've always thoroughly enjoyed—"

"Stinks!" Jake nodded sympathetically.

"No!" Quinn drained his glass and his eyes watered. "It just seems a bit lame, that's all."

After he poured Jake into a cab and sent him off to the airport, Quinn went to find Dani, nursing a moderate headache from the effects of the brandy. She lay mostly submerged in a bath full of fragrant bubbles, chewing her nails. He tapped her hand away, admonishing her. "You going out, I suppose?"

She nodded. "I didn't think you would want to come."

Quinn sat on the edge of the bath, the steam and the brandy fuzzing his brain. He most certainly didn't want to spend the evening with the Blackstones.

Then again, maybe it would help Jake to know something of the family dynamics. Who was top dog, who was most likely to oppose his appearance, and who—if anyone—might offer the hand of friendship.

An idea was forming....

"Quinn, have you told anyone about the wedding?"

He squinted at her. Her hair was mostly piled up on top of her head, a long coiled strand clinging to her damp shoulder. "Nope." He reached out and tugged the curl gently, straightening it. It bounced back when he let it go.

"It's just, I know Port Douglas, and there's something going on. I can smell a press photographer a mile off."

He blinked as her words sunk into his brain. "You think *I* tipped off the press?"

She reached out and touched his knee, leaving a wet

patch, but Quinn's indignation faded fast when her movement stirred up the bubbles and a very pink and pert nipple peeped out of the froth.

"No," she answered. "I just think there's something going on, something not quite right."

He bit back the words before they tumbled from his mouth. *"With us, you mean?"* Where the hell had that thought come from? Whatever he did, he could not get into a deep and meaningful conversation after half a bottle of cognac. He dipped his hand into the steaming water and rubbed his face. "I probably deserve suspicion." After all, he had blackmailed her about the wedding in the first place.

When you thought about it, he deserved to be hung, drawn and quartered for all the lies he'd told, all the secrets he withheld. Layer upon layer of secrets. Just when he'd decided he might take a chance on her, look ahead a little—*kapow!* And then *kapow* again. First Sir John, and now Jake. What next? And however could he justify it to her?

She looked up at him thoughtfully. "I didn't think you would contact the media. I just…" She sighed and reached to the side for a sponge, her knee bending up out of the water. "I just so want this day to be perfect for Ryan and Jessica."

Perfect? Quinn knew what was perfect. A smooth pink knee foaming with bubbles. He felt hard as a rock suddenly and licked his dry lips. "Jake," he croaked. "The press will be after Jake."

She looked up at him, a relieved smile forming on her delectable mouth. "You think?"

"He attracts attention wherever he goes. You planning on finishing that?" He nodded at the sponge resting on her knee. The thought of it was attracting all sorts of attention in all sorts of places.

"What was he doing here, anyway?"

Quinn reached out and took the sponge from her hand, his fingers digging into its soft porous depths. "Business. Lift your leg."

"My leg?" Dani hesitated, probably expecting a more expansive reply to her question about Jake's unexpected visit.

Quinn's eyes shifted to hers, challenging her. He had business in mind, all right. Funny business.

And he didn't want any more questions—or any more guilt.

Holding her gaze, he moved his hand into the water and soaked the sponge. Sultry understanding glowed in her eyes. Forget Jake. A trickle of steamy sweat slid down his temple. Forget Blackstone and the press and the shares. Forget life-altering secrets. The swish of streaming water filled his ears as her shapely, heat-flushed thigh rose up from the foam, and then her calf and foot flexed prettily. Quinn caught hold of her foot, washing it while she squirmed.

He cleared his throat. "I've been thinking, may I change my mind and come to the wedding, after all?"

The little smile that curved her lips warmed him. "I'd like that," she said slowly, watching as he dipped the sponge and stretched her leg out. "I'll set it up tonight," she promised.

Quinn stroked the back of her calf and thigh with the

sponge. Water dripped down his forearms and onto his thighs and he thought he must be one sick unit because the warmth and wetness of it only fuelled his desire more.

"Exactly how long do I have to get you clean before you go out?"

Ten

The day of the wedding had finally arrived.

Quinn knocked on her door to say the car was here. Dani was on edge, swimming in questions. Would he like her dress? Would her family like him, and vice versa? What was Jake doing up here? Why were the media swarming all over town, sipping coffee in the cafés, propping up the bars everywhere she turned?

And Quinn's sudden turnaround about accompanying her to the wedding. What was that about?

She made a final adjustment to the chiffon scarf she had cleverly twisted into her long French knot, picked up her purse and joined Quinn downstairs, loving the light in his eyes as he watched her descend.

And would he leave for good once she finished the necklace? Dani worried about that most of all.

They were driven to a helicopter port and, minutes later, were lifted up and over the rain forest to a beach just a few miles south. Dani had inspected the premises previously but was unprepared for the beauty of the place from the air.

The entire van Berhopt Resort hovered above an unsurpassed vista of rain forest and sea. Built on a raised knoll, the lodge appeared to be suspended over the secluded beach below, like a bird about to launch into the air. With a body of glass and steel, somehow it merged with the surroundings, complementing the bird's-eye view. For one breathless moment, Dani thought they were going to land on the massive curved roof that arced above the building, its eaves on all sides overhanging and imposing.

"Spectacular!" Quinn breathed in her ear as the helicopter thankfully set down a couple of hundred metres away from the lodge.

Dani could imagine the reaction of the wedding guests as they were flown in pairs to this incredible secluded paradise. Golf carts took them up to the house. The reception was to start at four-thirty with cocktails and nibbles, then the marriage ceremony. Afterward, there was a sumptuous buffet, featuring the best the tropical north could offer. Only the bride and groom would stay the night here, with the guests being ferried back to their hotels in Port by limousines. It was a small gathering of only twenty family and friends.

In his platinum tux and mahogany-and-silver-striped tie, Quinn Everard was the perfect escort for a tropical, late-afternoon wedding, sophisticated and breathtak-

ingly handsome. His cool against her flamboyance.
Dani proudly took his arm and walked through the
lobby out to the pool area where the guests were already
gathered. Ryan and Jessica had arrived first to settle into
their suite. Several other couples lounged around the
pool, being served by white-jacketed waiters with silver
trays that glinted off the blue water. Dani waved at
Sonya and Garth on the other side of the pool and
prepared to present Quinn to Ryan Blackstone.

"Well, well," said Ryan as they approached. "Quinn
Everard, I presume." He held out his hand. "Welcome
to the lion's den."

Quinn smiled and took the proffered hand. "Congratulations, Ryan. It's a pleasure to be here."

Jessica offered Quinn her cheek. "How lovely to see
you, Quinn."

"Jessica, you look stunning."

And she did. The bride glowed in a jewel-encrusted
champagne gown, a stunning clasp of rose-gold and
pink diamonds in between her breasts. "A gift from
Ryan," she whispered to Dani, who was so taken with
the brooch, she instinctively reached out and touched
her fingertips to it. The lovely gown flattered her
rounded belly and no amount of sparkle could eclipse
the proud smile on Jessica's face or the warmth in her
beautiful brown eyes.

While Quinn and Ryan chose drinks from a tray,
Jessica turned to Dani and hugged her. "I can't thank
you enough for all you've done. This place just takes
my breath away."

"I thought you'd like it."

"Everything is just perfect, Danielle. The setting, the weather, the menu you chose and, oh my God, the suite! I don't intend moving out of there for a week!"

The bride took Dani's arm and walked a few steps away. "You look positively beautiful. That colour has no right looking so sensational with your hair…"

Dani expected a few raised brows about her dress, especially from her mother. Strapless and backless, the fabric was hummer orange but the chiffon overskirt was made up of thousands of tiny overlapping patches of deep pink blush and vivid orange. When she moved, the patches rippled with the richness of the sunset.

"You and Quinn look cosy together."

Dani smiled. "I appreciate his invitation at such short notice."

Jessica nodded and sipped her orange juice. "I've met him socially a few times at launches and jewellery expos. He's charming and knows his stuff. And more handsome than any man has a right to be."

Dani helped herself to a delicious morsel from a platter offered her by a server, thinking she wasn't going to argue with Jessica's assessment.

Her soon-to-be cousin-in-law eyed her speculatively. "Is this part of the job description or likely to grow into a more permanent position?"

"I think I'll keep our positions to myself for the moment, Bridezilla." She stopped, her smile fading, and stared across the pool. "Would you look at that?"

Her mother and Garth were putting on a display for Kim and another couple she didn't know. Dani realised it was quite a well-rehearsed tango.

"Did Sonya tell you they were taking lessons together?"

"No. She mentioned sailing." Dani sipped her champagne. "They look good together."

"They *are* good together," Jessica murmured.

Dani felt a twinge of regret that she wasn't in the loop when it looked like this relationship was already quite advanced. But she shook it off. Her mother had never looked better and Dani was thrilled for her. It would just take a bit of getting used to. "Only last week she fobbed me off with the 'just friends' bulldust."

Dani moved to Quinn's side and slid her arm through his. "Let's go say hi to my mother before she dances into the pool and is swept out to sea."

Quinn and Sonya hit it off immediately, and Garth, the Blackstone company secretary and long-time friend and confidant of Howard's, showed no sign of any residual prejudice toward Quinn. Kimberley also greeted him warmly and Dani learned that they had met before in the diamond houses of Europe.

She sensed a slightly cooler dynamic from Ric Perrini toward her escort throughout the evening. She couldn't put her finger on it so decided not to worry about it, wanting nothing to spoil the beautiful wedding she'd helped arrange.

Ryan and Jessica became man and wife as the sun slid beneath the rain forest behind them, setting the sea in front ablaze with light. As if on cue, cockatoo and fruit bats set up their dusk chorus. It was a beautiful ceremony with a stunning backdrop, and there was barely a dry female eye in the place.

Afterward, everyone filled their plates from an amazing buffet of mud crab, ostrich, the local barramundi fish, and many other delicacies popular in this part of the country. The long table accommodated everyone and sat above the pool and the terraced grounds leading to the white sand beach. Jessica announced that the guests should sit next to someone different with each course. Dani knew everyone except a couple of school friends of the bride and her parents. Jessica's father was in a wheelchair but he didn't let it slow him down at all, and his wife and daughter were very attentive.

Sonya whispered that she was seriously considering making an offer on the house she and Ryan had viewed. Her mother living elsewhere than Miramare meant the end of an era was under way. Dani may not have known her father, but at least she'd had a family home, of sorts.

But there was a freshness and vitality to Sonya that Dani couldn't remember seeing before. Her life had been mapped out so young with a child of her own and the responsibility of Kim and Ryan. It gladdened Dani to think her mother was finally going to live a little.

At the next switch, she chatted to Jarrod Hammond and his beautiful fiancée, Briana. The handsome lawyer seemed very much at ease given the bad blood between the two families. Over dessert, she told him how pleased she was to see Matt in Port Douglas a couple of weeks ago. "He hinted that we might all get together soon, Blake, too."

"Great news." Jarrod sounded enthusiastic and

turned to Briana. "We'd be happy to host some sort of gathering in Melbourne, if that suits everyone."

Briana nodded enthusiastically and then responded to the bride's summons at the other end of the table.

Dani looked to where Sonya was deep in conversation with Garth. "Mum can't wait to meet him."

"Meet who?" Ric Perrini, resplendent in white, sat down in Briana's seat.

Dani liked Ric immensely. No one was more thrilled than she when he and Kimberley remarried last month. Despite their long separation, and the fact that relations were not always warm between Ric and Ryan, he was as much a part of the family as she was, in her mind. He'd stuck up for her over moving up here after the humiliation of her broken engagement. She was especially grateful for the support he'd been to Sonya in the past difficult months, and for bringing Kimberley home where she belonged.

"Matt Hammond," she answered. "He came to see me last week."

Ric's eyes shot to her face. "Here?"

She nodded, suddenly unwilling to mention her latest commission. Matt hadn't asked her to keep the Bridal Rose necklace a secret, but the Blackstones could not be expected to applaud the stripping of Howard's legacy and name from the famous pink diamonds. Dani wanted nothing to spoil this night.

"And what," Ric asked, glancing at Jarrod, "would Matt want to see you about, little one?"

Dani often felt like Ric's little sister. "Business of course, old man."

Ric's blue eyes sparkled. "You being such a hot businesswoman, Danielle," he quipped, "Hammond better watch out he doesn't lose his shirt."

Dani was distracted by a slight tension to Jarrod's jaw. Would this stupid feud ever disappear? Sure, it was decades in the making, but why did the younger generation continue to suffer? She turned back to Ric. "Not me, silly. Quinn."

"You called?"

Quinn's sleeve brushed her bare shoulder as he leaned over her to set his dessert plate down.

"Ryan wants a word," he said quietly. His breath trickled into her ear, reminding her of how she loved his voice and how much she had missed hearing it for the past hour. Closing her eyes, she leaned slightly back into him and inhaled, familiarising herself with his warmth and bulk and the unique scent of him that made her feel most like a woman. His woman.

Reluctantly she looked up the table to where the bridegroom stood talking to the manager of the lodge. Ryan's grim expression told her something was wrong. "Problem?" she whispered to Quinn, rising.

"Could be." Quinn put his hand on the small of her back and they walked up the length of the table.

"There's a reporter at the reception desk wanting confirmation of our wedding," Ryan said tightly. "I really don't want this to become a circus." He glanced to where his bride sat with her parents and Kimberley, looking for all the world like she didn't have a care.

"I'll go and talk to him," Dani began.

"I'll go," Quinn said quickly. "If he's from Sydney,

he'll know your face and that you're connected to the Blackstones. The vultures won't think for a minute I would be invited to a Blackstone wedding."

Ryan and Dani nodded, seeing the sense in that. "What will you say?"

"That I'm entertaining important clients from overseas. We're staying the night and will be leaving first thing in the morning. That way, hopefully your honeymoon will go undetected."

"Do you trust him, Danielle?" Ryan asked as they watched him follow the manager out to the reception desk.

She nodded, but unbidden, his threat to reveal the wedding plans to the media on the day they met pressed down on her like a grey cloud. "Don't worry." She squeezed Ryan's arm, swallowing her concerns. "Quinn is the soul of discretion. Nothing is going to spoil the night."

Two hours later, it seemed she was right. The champagne flowed and the party had become quite lively. Finally the bride and groom announced they were retiring to get started on their wedding night. One by one, white stretch limos pulled up to the lobby and the guests piled in and were treated to more champagne they didn't need on the way back to Port Douglas.

Dani and Quinn joined Ric and Kimberley in the back of the last car. Ric, still smarting from the media scrum at his Sydney harbour wedding six weeks before, thanked Quinn for getting rid of the press. "How the hell did they find out? I swear, when I discover who is keeping tabs on our family…"

"I'm starting to think it's someone in the office,"

Kimberley said thoughtfully. "There have been too many coincidences lately."

Dani felt pleasantly tired and snuggled into Quinn's side. "Quinn thinks the press are in town because Jake was here yesterday."

"Jake Vance?" Ric lifted his head. "What was he doing here?"

"He came to see Quinn," she replied. "They're friends."

The atmosphere in the limo chilled. In the dim interior, she saw Ric's nostrils flare and Kim's forehead crease with consternation.

Ric exchanged glances with his wife. "You've had a busy week, Quinn. First Matt Hammond, now Jake Vance." His fingers rasped over his chin. "Somebody is buying up a whole lot of Blackstone shares. You know anything about that?"

There was a long silence while Dani kicked herself for making the inadvertent comment.

"I might," Quinn said eventually. "What of it?"

"I knew it!" Ric said through gritted teeth. "I knew Matt Hammond was involved."

Kimberley put a hand on his arm, but Ric leaned forward and fixed Quinn with a piercing stare. "Hammond's called on both you and Vance in the past week or so. Do you expect me to believe you didn't discuss your Blackstone shareholding?"

"You can believe what you like. You know we're all shareholders. And for the moment, I'm happy with the status quo." Then Quinn, too, leaned forward, bringing his face close to Ric's. "And that's all I'm going to say about that."

His tone was dangerously low and loaded with warning. The two men eyeballed each other while Dani and Kim exchanged worried glances.

"I don't trust you, Everard," Ric said softly.

"Why should you?"

"Are you using Danielle to get an in with the family?"

"Ric!" Dani and Kimberley protested together.

"Watch your mouth," Quinn murmured.

The hairs on the back of Dani's neck rose. Danger throbbed in the air between the two men. Quinn pressed forward and slightly into her side, as if to shield her.

"Can you honestly tell me that you three are not plotting a takeover of Blackstone Diamonds?" Ric's voice was equally low, equally full of threat. "It's a reasonable request, Quinn."

"It's an unreasonable request," Quinn said evenly. "And I'm not privy to Matt's business dealings. But I'm happy with my minor shareholding." His chin rose. "At the moment."

Ric's eyes narrowed but he sat fractionally back, a little of the tension leaving his face. "And Vance?"

"What of him?"

"What's he been meeting with Matt about in Sydney?"

"Jake's business is his own…but I think he has other things on his mind right now."

"Jake's mother just passed away," Dani supplied in a small voice.

"But if he asked for your support?" Ric wasn't letting it go just yet.

Quinn paused while Dani held her breath.

"If he asked," Quinn said heavily, "I would support him."

Ric inhaled, glaring, but Kim beat him to it. She dipped her dark head between them and fixed both men with a formidable look. "That's enough! It's a happy day, damn it!"

Eleven

The car dropped Kim and Ric off at their hotel in town and set off for Four Mile. The tension remained, waves of it, and Dani and Quinn barely spoke. At least the actual wedding had gone off without a hitch, but the argument in the car had raised a barrage of questions that only Quinn could answer. Maybe because of the way they met, she would always have these reservations about him. That was a sobering thought.

They got out of the car and she stopped him from going inside. "We need to talk. Let's go out on the beach."

"You'll ruin your dress."

She shrugged and walked to the end of the road and the copse of trees that led out onto the sand. "I think better out here." She looked back at him. "And you have to tell the truth on my beach. It's my special place."

She was glad he didn't argue. The cover of darkness and the sound of the waves eased her nerves, which would help her ask the questions she needed to. Right now, she was more afraid than she had ever been in her life.

They walked slowly, aimlessly, onto the soft, thick sand. Dani slipped her sandals off, picked them up and turned to face him, her heart in her mouth. "Quinn, I want to know that you're not plotting to bring down Blackstone Diamonds."

He stood very still, looking at her for such a long time that she thought he wasn't going to answer. Would he cut her down again, tell her she had no right to question him? In the darkness, his eyes were unreadable.

Finally he spoke. "To tell you would be to betray a confidence."

She licked her dry lips. "I won't betray your confidence, but I need to know I mean more to you than a few shares."

Quinn inhaled deeply, his chest rising, his eyes boring into her. The silence stretched between them, and again she almost lost hope that he would speak.

She began to turn away, burning with humiliation.

Quinn reached out and caught her hand. "It's Jake. It's about Jake."

Her heart sank further. So Jake Vance *was* planning a corporate takeover, and Quinn had decided to be involved. Ric's words in the car—*Are you using Danielle to get an in with the family?*—returned to taunt her.

When was someone ever going to want her for her?

A full moon broke through the heavy cloud above, bathing everything in an eerie bluish-grey light.

"He..." Quinn's head rolled back and he sighed heavily. "There's no easy way to say this. Jake has reason to believe he is James Hammond Blackstone."

Dani jerked, staring at him stupidly. "Sorry?"

Quinn repeated himself.

Her reservations fled. That was the last thing she'd expected. "Doesn't he know who he is?"

"He thought he did."

"I don't believe it."

"He doesn't, either. That's why he's getting a DNA test done to prove that April—his mother—is his birth mother."

Her hand slid out of his. "He told you this yesterday? That's why he came?"

"It was the first I'd heard of it." Quinn nodded. He proceeded to give her the rundown on Jake's version of events.

"Jake didn't believe her. She was on morphine at that stage, and he thought her mind was going. But when he was packing up the house, he found a scrapbook and it's all there, Dani. Dozens of news clippings about the kidnapping and the housekeeper and her partner who took him. Toys and a blanket from the car that matched what was taken from James Blackstone's bedroom."

Dani's shoulder rose and fell in a helpless movement. "You're telling me this woman, this April, goes to the store one day and comes home with a baby and no one thinks anything of it?" She laughed disbelievingly. "That was big news back then, Quinn, all over Australia. She'd never have gotten away with it."

"He's still looking into it, but it appears that April had a baby who died the year before. At the time she found

Jake—James—she was running away from an abusive boyfriend. She moved around a lot and ended up in South Australia, where no one knew her." He exhaled and looked down, moving his shoe over a sandy mound of crab balls. "I knew April. She had her faults, mostly due to the men she hooked up with, but she was a decent woman. And she loved Jake. There was never any doubt about that."

Dani clasped her hands in front of her and rocked on her heels, sinking into the cool sand. "Oh Lord, this is really going to… So he's not trying to destroy Blackstone Diamonds, after all?" She gave another short sharp laugh. "In fact, that would be counter-productive since he is now the heir."

"Maybe," he warned. "Not confirmed yet."

In a tiny way, although this was earth-shattering news, Dani was a bit relieved. At least he wasn't plotting to bring about the downfall of her cousins. "So why did you suddenly change your mind about coming to the wedding?"

"I wanted to see everyone together, how they all get on, and who Jake's greatest opponent might be when—if—it all comes out." He exhaled. "I think we've established that."

She realised he meant Ric. "If Jake really is family, Ric'll accept it. If he does anything to hurt the company, that's a different matter. It's Kimberley and Ryan—especially Ryan—I'm worried about." Dani turned, rubbing her arms. Quinn slipped off his jacket and placed it around her shoulders and they began to walk slowly back the way they'd come. "I have to tell them."

Quinn inhaled sharply. "No!"

"Quinn, this is too—"

He grasped her arm firmly, turning her. "He won't get the results of April's DNA till next week. If that confirms that April is not his birth mother, then he is going to have to persuade Kim or Ryan, or both, to take a DNA test to prove Howard and your aunt were his parents."

Good luck with that, she thought, imagining Ryan's response to that request. "Quinn, I can't keep something like this from them. It's not fair."

Quinn smiled tightly. "Who said life is fair? Dani, there is a leak in the Blackstone offices. Kimberley said as much tonight. Do you realise the media frenzy something like this will generate? You have to keep it quiet until it's proved that April is not his birth mother." His eyes were grim. "Don't even tell your mother. Garth could be the leak, for all we know."

"Garth? He wouldn't!"

"Probably not. But there is no sense upsetting everyone till we know for sure."

Dani pulled the sides of his jacket closer, chilled by the realisation that on top of all this upset, there would be publicity. Lots of publicity. "God, I hate secrets. I can't even imagine what this is going to do to the family, after the year we've had."

"If it turns out that he really is part of the family, then that's a good thing for everyone, right?"

"Possibly." Possibly not. "Families aren't my strong point. Perhaps I have a jaundiced view." She raised her hand, nibbling on a fingernail. "How would you feel if it was your long-lost brother?"

Quinn considered. "Family's family to me," he said thoughtfully, pulling her hand away from her mouth. "But I suppose if a complete stranger suddenly appeared and wanted to take over the reins of all I'd worked for…" He held his palm up when she began to speak. "And just remember, it was Howard who changed his will to include James, it wasn't Jake's idea."

"Poor old Howard," Dani murmured with genuine sympathy for the man who had never given up hope. "He died before seeing his dream come true."

Quinn nodded. "It must be tough to lose a child."

Dani had her own views on that. "Not for everybody." Her own father had never looked back. She put a hand on his shoulder and raised a foot to slide her sandal back on.

Quinn took the remaining shoe from her hand and bent to put it on her foot. He remained squatting, peering up at her. His face was in shadow, the moon behind him. "Aren't you the least bit curious about your own father? Don't you want to know who and why?"

She looked at him sharply, wondering how the heck he'd known what was going through her mind. "Why should I? He's never been curious about me."

Even as the words left her mouth, she knew she was lying. She'd begged and cajoled, but her mother wouldn't be moved on that subject. *"Forget him, Danielle. He didn't want us and we're better off without him."* She wouldn't even confirm or deny if he was actually still alive.

Quinn slowly rose to his feet. "What if you found out that it wasn't his fault, wasn't his idea to stay away?"

"Then he is a lame excuse for a man," she declared.

What kind of a man made no phone calls, sent no birthday cards—not even once. Even if her mother hated him, it was no excuse to ignore his child. "He never gave a damn, end of story."

She cringed at the tight, self-pitying tone of her voice and turned and walked toward the house.

"You know, there is something my parents and Laura did with some of the kids at home," Quinn said from behind her, and she slowed to let him catch up. "Many of them hadn't seen or spoken to their parents in years. Many had been abused or beaten or just ignored. They used to say, 'If you had the chance, if your mother or father was standing here right now, what would you say to them?'"

Dani hesitated. "I wouldn't say anything. He means nothing to me."

Quinn caught her hand and turned her to face him. "If he was here, right now, Dani, and prepared to listen…?"

With a moody sigh, Dani looked past him, down to the waves lapping the sand. What would she say, indeed? She stared into nothing and tried to imagine what he looked like, this make-believe father. Would he be tall, have red hair like hers? A kindly face?

She could stare into nothing all she liked. There were no answers there. She'd already looked, many, many times.

"I'd say 'you're late.'" She looked into Quinn's face. "I'd say 'you're too bloody late!'"

The next day, they met Sonya for brunch at her hotel before the Blackstones took off for Sydney in the company jet. Her mother knew nothing of the argument in the car the night before with Ric, and Dani did not intend to enlighten her. Besides, the bombshell about Jake was the overriding topic in her mind.

During the meal, a reporter stopped by the table to ask for confirmation of Ryan's wedding. They did not confirm or deny; Ryan and Jessica deserved privacy on their honeymoon. After he'd gone, Quinn suggested that the exaggerated media presence in town was due to the imminent arrival of the governor-general, who'd been invited to officiate at the annual ANZAC Day festivities. Dani peered at the article in the morning newspaper detailing the commemoration of Australian and New Zealand military action in WW1. "Every year they drag some poor old dignitary out at five in the morning." She grinned. "Not that I'm complaining since it's a public holiday."

"You don't admire Sir John?" Quinn asked.

Dani shrugged. "I don't particularly admire any politician."

"He's not a politician," Quinn pointed out. "He is the governor-general, the Queen's representative in this colony of ours."

"But he was prime minister once." Dani rolled her eyes. "What a lot of fuss. The mayor is putting on a posh reception at the Sea Temple. VIPs only. Three TV stations, local and national celebrities—and all for some boring old—"

Sonya sighed heavily and put her hand on her purse. Dani looked up from her paper.

"I'm going back to the hotel," her mother said,

pushing her chair out from the table. "I think I have one of my headaches coming on."

"I thought you wanted to see the shop." Dani had been looking forward to showing off her new spring pieces. She also had a surprise for her mother and for Quinn. Yesterday, she'd secured a lease for the bigger shop a few doors down from hers. Whatever Quinn thought about the location, Dani Hammond was on the way up.

But Sonya got to her feet, looking pale. "I'd rather see if we could leave a little earlier and get the flight over with as quickly as possible," she said apologetically.

"You were perfectly fine a minute ago," Dani pouted in the flurry of activity as everyone rose from the table. "We'll see you upstairs."

"No, it's fine. Take care, darling." She hugged her daughter tightly, whispering "I *do* like him" into Dani's ear. When she pulled back, Sonya's eyes were suspiciously brilliant. "But I love you," she whispered, touching her cheek, then was gone.

What was that about? Dani wondered, feeling a little uneasy. Her mother wasn't given to emotional goodbyes. Perhaps she was sick. That wasn't the first time she'd had a migraine when they'd been out.

Maybe she and Garth had had an argument....

"Perhaps she just had a little too much champagne last night," Quinn commented, practicing that weird way he had of seeming to see inside her head.

"Probably. I'll call her later."

They drove back to the beach house and Dani's mind

turned to other matters. "Now that the wedding is over, I'd better get busy on the necklace."

"Yes. And if you finish it on time," Quinn murmured, "I have a surprise for you. How would you like to strut the red carpet wearing something fabulous, be the envy of all your friends?"

Her eyes shone as he told her he had an invite to the governor-general's reception—"The one to honour some boring old—"

"True?" VIPs liked jewellery. What a showcase! "How did you get an invite?"

"He's a friend."

"Sir John is a friend?" Dani unfolded the paper on her lap and peered at the photo of an old guy in an old suit that boasted a row of medals.

Somehow she couldn't see him and Quinn out on the golf course together. "He's too old and too frail to be your friend."

"Not at all," Quinn demurred. "He's an avid collector. I trust his recommendations and judgement above any man I know. I've dealt with him for years."

This was a chance to meet someone close to Quinn.

A chance to show off some of her pieces.

She sat back in her seat, already thinking that her lilac organza dress would be perfect for the occasion.

"*If* you get the necklace finished on time," Quinn warned.

The next two days, she closeted herself in her workroom, forbidding him to disturb her until she'd finished. Platinum was a fascinating metal, though it required a great deal of attention. As it was extremely pliable when heated, just one gram could be drawn to produce a fine wire more than two kilometres long. Luckily she didn't require quite that much. The cage she was making to encase the diamond was very delicate, but the density of platinum ensured its durability.

Finally it was done. Dani emerged, bleary-eyed, from the workroom to find Quinn sitting at breakfast, reading the paper. She glanced at the date on the paper, the twenty-fourth of April. The deadline was safe.

Quinn rose and picked up a cup from the tray on the table, concern in his eyes.

Dani stopped him as he picked up the coffeepot. "No, I'm going to bed."

"How's it coming?"

She hesitated, feeling almost nauseated with all the emotions raging inside. She was exhausted, relieved, cautiously optimistic that he'd like it. But mostly she wondered if this would be the end for them. "It's finished."

A small, slow smile appeared on his face. "Show me."

Dani backed away. "No, I'm too tired. And too nervous. You go look at it and formulate your hopefully complimentary comments later."

Quinn eased back into his chair. "All right. Get some sleep. I'll take you out somewhere nice tonight, just the two of us, to celebrate."

Dani nodded and climbed the stairs to bed.

Quinn walked into the workroom and immediately noticed that she'd tidied up. The workbench was swept clean, the tools stacked in their place. He thought how tired she'd looked and wondered if she had slept at all.

The necklace was up on its bust on the desk. Quinn switched the desk lamp on, pulled the chair well back and sat.

He was still there an hour later.

He looked first for impact, and got it in spades. A diamond inside a diamond. Mere filaments of platinum, like the gossamer wings of a dragonfly, held the huge trilliant-cut stone suspended inside a web cage. Platinum was the perfect setting for the intense yellow stone. It contained no alloys to tinge a diamond's brilliance and its reflective qualities enhanced the colour without distracting from it.

Quinn moved the bust from side to side to see every angle and put his judge's cap on. Innovative design, effective use of the gem, quality of workmanship, wearability. Ten out of ten in all categories. It was beautifully finished, totally professional, fresh and original.

And more conservative than he had originally feared, given her propensity for large, striking jewellery. The essence and personality of the diamond shone through, as a stone of this beauty and importance deserved.

Had she chosen this design, he wondered, as symbolic of herself, hiding in a cage of her own making? Was she brave enough to step into the limelight and let herself shine?

Quinn really was going to have to talk to her about moving to Sydney and marketing herself properly. His broker's brain started ticking. If this piece went to auction it would cause a stir. Just off the top of his head, he could think of three collectors who would pay a king's ransom for it.

But then he remembered. It wasn't going to auction. The owner of this necklace had quite a different purpose in mind.

That night, on their way out for dinner, Quinn placed the necklace around her neck and showed her what it looked like.

"Quinn, I can't," she protested, but her eyes were bright with excitement. "I'd be too nervous. What if someone sees?"

"Everyone should see, just for tonight." He tugged gently at her dangly angel earrings. "I think these are superfluous, don't you?"

She smiled at him in the mirror, her hand already reaching to dispatch the earrings. "You really like it?"

Quinn had spent the past couple of hours in bed with her showing her how much he liked it, but she deserved every indulgence. He nuzzled her bare shoulder, keeping his eyes on her reflection. "It is truly outstanding. *You* are truly outstanding."

He meant every word. It had come to him earlier in the workroom that he wanted to be the key to unlocking Dani's self-imposed cage. Throughout the day, waiting for her to wake up, he'd nurtured the idea, considered it, like the necklace, from every angle. More than that, he allowed himself to expand on practicalities, like geography, career, family. All the things he'd thought about in his apartment in Sydney.

Guilt had forced him to step back since then, but

Quinn was tired of denying it. He wanted to share in her life and wanted her to share in his. But there were still so many secrets and lies between them. Breaking Jake's confidence the other night had been about reassuring her, giving her something, because he knew he was about to inflict the most monstrous betrayal of all.

Over dinner, looking across the table at a masterpiece of design and the work of art wearing it, Quinn sought to be the perfect dinner companion, attentive and charming, as he knew she expected. But the food and wine were ashes in his mouth. He prayed her generous nature would forgive him.

Later he took her to his room and commanded her to strip until she wore only her high-heeled sandals and the necklace. He took the clip from her hair, letting it flow like a river of fire. Standing behind her as she peered into a mirror, he watched her face and saw that she, too, was struck by the beauty of her creation, and by the way her own beauty enhanced it.

He'd known she would look like this, but he drank the image in, in case it was all he'd have in the years to come. Her eyes mirrored the fire and sparkle of the intense yellow diamond, her irises ringed with gold. She moved her shoulders, a tiny repetitive sway from side to side, watching the diamond leap to life between her breasts. The perfect setting.

Quinn's large dark hands moved over her lush body, down the length of her torso, over the soft feminine curves of her bejewelled belly. He'd pulled the bed stool over in front of the mirror and now eased them down, bringing her slowly down onto him. Her legs parted and her eyes locked on his while he moved his hands over her, cupping her breasts, teasing her inside thighs, stroking her intimately. He made love to her tenderly, watching her hair ripple like firelight. The stone between her breasts changed the colour of her eyes to sheer, shimmering pleasure. When she shuddered and smiled her love and satisfaction back at him, he closed his eyes and allowed his release to engulf him in a wash of colourful ecstasy. And he knew he'd done the unthinkable. He had fallen in love with Dani Hammond.

Twelve

Sir John Knowles was tall and thin with drawn cheeks and a pallor of fatigue. She'd read somewhere he was in his early sixties, but from where she stood, Australia's most beloved statesman looked a lot older. To his right stood a birdlike woman, elegantly attired, her hands clasped tightly in front of her.

"Is that his wife?" Dani whispered to Quinn.

"Clare." Quinn volunteered nothing else.

Dani rolled her eyes and hoped he would loosen up a little once the formalities were out of the way. He'd barely spoken all day, except to reiterate how talented she was. She only hoped his client, whoever he or she was, thought so, too.

Quinn's approbation thrilled her except for an inexplicable feeling she could not define. It was nothing more noteworthy than his eyes sliding off hers just a fraction too soon, a watchfulness throughout the day, a hint of regret, even.

But then she remembered their lovemaking last night. Dani had never associated tenderness with this man, but last night she'd drowned in it, had truly felt special and cherished. Oh, there were logistical problems—the fact that he lived in Sydney, that he travelled constantly. But how could he make love to her so tenderly if he intended to leave her?

She rubbed her arms, pleased with her decision not to go with the summery organza dress. Her belted floral tunic, master-and-commander jacket and ankle boots might be a touch unconventional for a stuffy reception of this kind, but this was about exposure. The keishi-pearl-and-sapphire necklace was far too feminine to be trumped by lilac. It needed to rise above the bold, and triumph.

She fingered the necklace absently, looking down at the red carpet they inched forward on. As she did, she recalled the light in Quinn's eyes as she'd emerged from her bedroom earlier tonight.

"You always keep me guessing and you never disappoint," he'd said, giving her a little twirl.

Now Quinn's grip on her arm tightened and she realised they were at the front of the queue at last. He placed his hand over hers, staring resolutely ahead. The dignitary seemed to lose a little of his stoop when he saw them.

"Quinn," Sir John said simply, reaching out with both hands and clasping his.

"May I introduce—" she heard Quinn say as he tugged her forward "—Danielle Hammond."

Sir John took Dani's proffered hand and enclosed it with both of his. He stared down into her face for such a long time that she felt her smile stretch and become stale.

Quinn shook hands with Sir John's wife, then reached into his inside pocket and took out a long rectangular box. Ignoring Dani's wide-eyed comprehension, he offered it to the governor-general. With one last bony squeeze of her hand, Sir John released her and took the box from Quinn. Without opening it, he passed it to his wife.

Dani's smile froze. So the necklace—her necklace— was for Sir John, or at least his wife. The woman who smiled tentatively at her now.

Loss hit hard, followed by dread. It wasn't unusual to feel emotional when she sold a favourite piece, but right now she was just plain worried. Quinn had inferred she should make the necklace as if she were going to wear it. Somehow she couldn't imagine that necklace, that bold diamond, around this woman's neck.

Sir John turned back to her, and if he noticed her stricken expression, his calm smile didn't waver. "Thank you, my dear." He tilted his head at the jewellery box his wife held.

It's too young for you, Dani thought.

"Would you do me the honour," Sir John said, "of joining my wife and me for a drink in our suite in a little while?"

Quinn answered for both of them. "Of course, Sir John."

Dani could barely contain herself until they were out of earshot. "I don't believe it! He's your client?"

Quinn nodded, directing her over to a waiter with a tray of drinks.

"Oh, Quinn," she whispered loudly. "You encouraged me to make something contemporary. Something I would wear myself." She shook her head, very worried. "It's too young for her."

He handed her a glass of wine. "Dani, the necklace is perfect."

"But…" If only he'd told her, given her a picture of the woman or something. "She'd prefer brilliants all over it, possibly other gems, or pearls… Damn it, I should have gone for pearls."

Quinn took a long sip of wine, then tipped her chin up with his finger. "Sir John knows jewellery. He will see exactly what I see. You're world class, Dani Hammond, in every way."

Her nerves calmed somewhat. She trusted him. Quinn had too much integrity to let her fall flat on her face. His own professional reputation was at stake, too.

It was still a tense hour and a half until the mayor appeared and requested they follow him. And she still crossed her fingers on the way.

The mayor waved them into a luxurious suite and then left. Sir John and his wife sat on one of two settees. Behind them, French doors opened out onto a large balcony. Dani caught a glimpse of twinkling blue water from the lighted pool below.

On a coffee table between the settees sat the open blue velvet box.

Sir John rose and came to greet them, his smile born of real warmth rather than the restrained politeness of the reception. He seemed a little younger than before, more sprightly, and hugged Quinn, who warmly reciprocated. Then he led Dani to the settee.

She felt too nervous to accept a drink. Mrs. Knowles sat staring at the necklace while the two men made a little small talk. Then they sat, too.

An awkward silence descended. Everyone's eyes seemed to gravitate toward the open jewellery box. Quinn sat beside her, his shoulders back, as tense as Dani had ever seen him. He didn't look at her once.

Her eyes moved restlessly from one to the other, wishing someone would speak. After at least a minute of this, she began to pray for the floor to open up and swallow her. Finally she couldn't take the tension a moment longer. "Is something wrong with the necklace?" she blurted out.

Quinn grasped her hand, still without looking at her. She heard Mrs. Knowles clear her throat and murmur something that sounded ominously like "Poor child."

Sir John lifted his head wearily, fixed his wife and then Quinn with a stern look and said quietly, "Would you leave us?"

Mrs. Knowles rose quickly, looking at Quinn. With a last squeeze of her hand, Quinn rose. Bemused, Dani, too, started to rise.

But Quinn laid a heavy hand on her shoulder, pushing her gently back down. "Stay," he murmured, giving her shoulder a firm squeeze.

She subsided, completely confused now. Quinn and Mrs. Knowles left the room together and closed the door quietly.

What the hell is going on?

An ominous foreboding swamped her. If he didn't like the necklace, why couldn't he just say? She could change it, fix it; he was paying enough. She'd be happy to consult with his wife on the design.

Dani looked longingly at the closed door, wishing she was on the other side. With Quinn.

"He's a good man," Sir John said quietly, following her gaze.

She settled back in the seat, calling on all her composure. "Is your wife unhappy with the necklace?"

Kindly hazel eyes searched her face. He was very tall, as tall as Quinn, but his clothes and his skin looked like he'd lost weight in a hurry. "Clare thinks, as I do, that you're very gifted. But—" he cleared his throat and leaned forward "—the necklace is not for Clare." He picked up the open box and held it out to her. "It's for you."

She must have misheard. "Sorry?"

The box shook quite markedly in the old man's hands so she sat forward and put her hands on it to steady it.

"Quinn found the diamond for me six years ago, you know." His voice became a little less thready, a little warmer. "I always intended you to have it."

They sat there both holding the box in midair until he pushed it gently into her hands and she had no choice but to take it.

"You're starting to scare me, Sir John."

The man took a deep breath, looking earnestly into her face. "This is my apology and my legacy to you, Danielle, for I am your father."

I am your father.

Dani lowered the box slowly to her lap, her lips moving soundlessly. *Her father.* The two words chased each other around her head. Of all the things she might have expected at this glittering occasion, this was not one of them. And why didn't Quinn tell her? Did he know?

A piercing pain in her chest confirmed his betrayal. Of course he knew. He'd set her up.

Her father. She searched his face, thinking there must be some kind of connection, some kind of familiarity, surely. A proud nose, pockmarked with age and infirmity. A still-strong chin but sunken cheeks that whispered of pain. His bow tie seemed too tight around his scrawny neck, wormed with loose flesh. A plain white shirt covered what looked to be a wasted chest.

Dani stopped searching. There was nothing of her in this old man. She'd walk past him on the street and not feel the slightest hint of recognition. She wouldn't look at him twice.

A lump of anger slowly formed, not just toward him but Quinn as well. And her mother. She must have known this was coming. Dani let it burn just under the surface, wondering if he could see it on her staring face.

Sir John must have realised he wasn't going to get any help from her. He picked up his glass and sipped.

"I was the leader of the opposition. Your mother, Sonya," he said, his voice caressing the word, causing Dani to suck in air, "was helping out in the campaign office."

She swallowed heavily but managed to keep quiet.

"I was recently married to Clare, whom I'd known all my life. I noticed Sonya, I own to it. We were friends but nothing would have happened, for we were not bad people. I took my marriage vows seriously, and your mother was not the type of woman to wreck a marriage."

Don't tell me what my mother is, she wanted to snarl. *Don't even speak her name.* But she held her tongue.

"But then your aunt Ursula died. Your mother was inconsolable. I'd tried so hard to keep away from her. We'd both tried. The consequences were much more serious than my marriage, my career. I would have risked that happily for Sonya. But it was the party, the one that was going to take the country into the new decade...."

Dani had a sudden and savage insight into why she hated politicians, the way they tried to justify everything.

Sir John closed his eyes. "I intended only to offer comfort, but one thing led to another. She fell pregnant almost immediately."

In the dead silence that followed, a million questions and accusations swamped her. She knew she had to consider those different times, her mother's unenviable situation, the lure of a powerful, charismatic man. Heck, she was no angel herself. But her anger seemed to suck up her compassion for now. She'd get to it later, away from here.

"I loved her very much," the old man said plaintively. "Please never doubt that."

Her heartbeat sounded in her ears, loud, slow,

ominous. "Sure you did," she said softly, feeling the hot breath of her anger like fire in her throat. "That's why you kept in such close contact."

He closed his eyes briefly, his thin lips drawn in a slash of anguish. "I don't expect you to understand, but I am more sorry than you will ever know."

Dani clenched her teeth and looked down at the necklace. So sorry he was buying her off. Didn't he know she came cheap? A cup of coffee would have done, a bunch of flowers on her birthday or graduation. A simple phone call.

"I've thought about you every day." His voice was high and thin.

But not enough to get in touch. Her hand seemed to jerk up of its own accord, jabbing toward the balcony. "How fortuitous the ANZAC Day commemoration was up here this year. After twenty-seven years, you could kill two birds with one stone."

Sir John took a long time answering. "I'm so sorry, my dear. I wanted very much to be part of your life, but it wasn't possible. You see, Howard blackmailed me to keep away."

No. He wouldn't. A huge fist closed around her chest. Please say it's not true.... "Wh-why, what possible reason...?"

"The miners had been on strike for two years. The government was making a bad fist of it." His pallor became even more washed out and he inhaled deeply. "Industry was being crippled. My party promised to crush the strikers. Howard—all industry leaders—could not afford for us to fail."

And an affair outside marriage, a teenage pregnancy in those days would have been the death knell for the party.

How could Howard do it? She wanted to moan and scream with rage and betrayal. What right did he have? She wrapped her arms around her middle, still holding the jewellery box.

"I'm so sorry," the old man—her father—whispered, and she tried, she really did, to dredge up some compassion. But the rage was hot and hard and impossible to swallow.

"I'm dying, Danielle. Lung cancer."

The words hung in the air between them while she clutched herself, rocking. His eyes beseeched her.

Her brain was going into overload. He was dying. He wasn't here because he wanted to meet her, to get to know the bastard daughter. He was here to assuage his guilt before the end.

She couldn't breathe. The keishi necklace dug into her throat and the anger coursing through her wasn't hot and hard anymore. It was stone-cold fury.

Dani stood abruptly, holding the jewellery box. "How dare you!" And without any rational thought at all, just a need to rage, she threw the box at the wall behind him. It hit with a dull *thwack*, bounced off the cabinet and fell to the floor. The platinum cage holding the diamond glittered, the chain spilled out onto the white tiles.

"You selfish old…" Some kind of insane respect stopped her from saying the word *bastard*. He was after all, the governor-general of Australia.

Sir John remained seated, his head bowed, his sunken cheeks even more pronounced and impossibly pale. But she didn't care. She jerked into action, heard the quick, sharp click of her heels, and then she wrenched the door open and ran smack into Quinn's chest.

How dare he as well?

Dani reeled away, putting her hands up in front of her like a shield.

He spoke her name, took her wrists gently, and it required a superhuman effort not to slap him away, or slap his face.

Clare Knowles slipped past them and into the suite, looking very upset.

"How could you?" Dani demanded in a strangled moan. "How could you do this to me?"

"Dani, I'm so sorry."

"Let me go."

He tugged her toward a chair. "I had to. He's dying."

She resisted his efforts to sit her down. "How long have you known?"

Quinn swallowed and looked away. "Since the day we left Sydney."

Dani bit down on the inside of her mouth. She remembered the phone call, his polite excuse "I have to take this…" She had gone on to the airstrip without him.

She tasted blood. "You bastard," she said quietly.

He jerked his head toward the suite where presumably Sir John was being comforted by his wife. "Howard Blackstone was blackmailing him to keep away."

"Don't!" Her voice cracked. "Don't even speak his name. Howard was twice the man you will ever be."

He rolled his head back and sighed. "Dani, he's dying. He's my friend and he begged me and he's dying." He kneaded her hands between his.

"I told you the other night my father meant nothing to me. God, Quinn, we *talked* about it. You had a golden opportunity to tell me."

"Would you have come if I'd told you?"

She shook her head, trying to pull out of his grasp. "You set me up. I don't know how you could do that, take me in there and leave me." The tears started in earnest now and she was ashamed. Ashamed of crying, of upsetting an old man.

Of believing in Quinn Everard.

"I thought I loved you, but I couldn't love someone who could do that," she sobbed, her hands still imprisoned in his grasp. "I hate you."

"Quinn?" Clare Knowles stood in the doorway.

Dani turned her head away, not wanting to see or be seen by the woman, even as she registered the worry in her voice. But it was the slide of Quinn's stricken eyes from her face to the other woman's that gave her the will, the strength to push away from him.

Once again, she was second in line, never number one. Not good enough to be a daughter. Not good enough to be a Blackstone. Not good enough to be a fiancée.

Not good enough to be his...

Thirteen

Late on a public holiday Friday, the streets thronged with inebriated activity. Shortly after storming out on Quinn and her father, Dani stood outside her shop, looking in, drowning in self-pity and hating herself for it. How could Quinn do it to her, allow her to walk into the most important moment of her life unprepared?

And her mother—she had a lot to answer for. With a flash of anger, Dani pulled her phone from her purse and dialed. Sonya cried, saying she had dreaded this moment since learning of the official visit a few weeks ago.

"John called me a couple of weeks after Howard's funeral, wanting to contact you. I said no, you were happy, I begged him." She knew nothing of Howard's blackmail, but admitted that it was Howard who told her the leader of the opposition wanted nothing to do with her or her baby. "He gave me a choice: the stigma and scandal of bringing down the next government, or security. He said he would always take care of us. I had to do the right thing for you."

"Did you love him?" Dani asked tremulously. "My father?"

"I thought I did." Her mother sighed. "You have to understand, I was just nineteen. Overnight my life changed from being a carefree teen to suddenly being responsible for two kids, because Howard was so devastated by Ursula's death, he wasn't coping. John was kind, attractive, important."

Her mother begged to come up first thing in the morning, but Dani knew she was far too low to resist the coddling and entreaties to bring her home to Sydney. She asked for a few days' grace and hung up.

A group of people came out of a bar, weaving across the road, then scattering to let a screaming ambulance pass. Her reflection in the window fractured, just like her heart, and she knew she needed the sanctuary of the beach. At this time of night, it would be deserted.

She walked aimlessly onto the dunes toward Four Mile. There was no hurry; self-pity was a leisurely activity. The events of her day, her life, flashed through her mind, keeping her company.

An unworthy man had asked her at the ripe old age of twenty-five to marry him, and she'd accepted because he'd asked. All she wanted was to be the apple of someone's eye, the centrepiece. That episode had dented her heart, and now it had happened again. And what she'd felt for Nick was pathetic compared to her love for Quinn Everard. It was the difference between being strapped into a wheelchair in the rain or walking on the beach on a sunny day.

It was a bad night for the men in her life, she thought bitterly. A long-lost father who'd never acknowledged or contacted her had finally appeared, only to tell her he was dying. Her cherished benefactor had cruelly betrayed her and her memories of him would be tarnished forever. And the man she'd fallen heart and soul in love with had not uttered a single truth since the day they'd met.

The waves soothed her, as always. The beach was her friend. She knew every palm, every half-buried log, every crevice in the iron-grey sand.

Pushing Quinn from her thoughts, she cajoled her brain to accept and get used to two words. My father. My father, the governor-general. My father who is dying. The man whose nonexistence had shaped the way she felt about herself.

Which was, for the most part, not good enough.

But her feelings of inadequacy weren't his fault. Had she not had every advantage in life? She hadn't grown up on the streets like the kids that Quinn and his parents took in. She'd enjoyed a luxurious home, the best schools. Hell, she hadn't even had to raise the money to start her own business. Howard had handed it to her on a plate.

A pretty stone winked up at her in the moonlight. With her booted foot, she kicked it and watched as it skittered away in a satisfying arc. Okay, she had reason to be angry and hurt that everyone had lied. Her mother.

Howard. Her father. Quinn. But she could snack on self-pity till the cows came home. It was still a meager meal.

Her father's sad face swam in front of her eyes. How could she not even have given him a chance to explain? How long did he have left? Twenty-seven years and it all came down to this, compressed into a bitter pill of recrimination.

Oh God, what if the upset tonight had triggered a turn for the worse? Dani quickened her step, suddenly not aimless anymore. She couldn't turn her back on him, not when she didn't know him. Not when he was the one person she had missed all her life.

She was at the halfway point between town and Four Mile, another twenty minutes to either, if she ran. What if she was too late? Her breath came in gasps as she broke into a jog. She was so immersed in her prayers and panic, she didn't even hear the motorbike until it was nearly on top of her.

"Dani! Get on!"

What on earth? Quinn, tux and all on a filthy, mud-streaked dirt bike.

"Stop, damn you!"

Dani stopped, her chest heaving with exertion and amazement. He ripped off his helmet and thrust it out to her, his mouth a grim line.

She hadn't even begun thinking about Quinn, where he fit in her life now.

"Get on," he repeated urgently. "He's been rushed to Cairns Base Hospital."

With a cry of dismay, she shoved the helmet over her

curls and clambered awkwardly onto the back of the bike. She wrapped her arms around him as they gathered speed, squeezed her eyes shut and prayed for all she was worth.

Less than an hour later, they screeched to a halt at the entrance to the hospital.

"Go. I'll meet you in there."

Chilled to the bone by cold and worry, she rushed to find her father.

To her intense relief, Sir John had suffered a mild respiratory attack due to excess fluid on his lungs, a common symptom of advanced lung cancer, she learned. He was awake and fairly comfortable and would be kept overnight for observation, but would be discharged in the morning.

Dani spent the next hour sitting beside him, her hand covering his. He gazed at her, unable to speak because of the oxygen mask, but he turned his hand up and squeezed hers and even smiled once. His wife sat opposite and told them both that he must take the next few days away from official duties to spend some time with his daughter.

It was after 3:00 a.m. when Dani left the emergency unit. She was exhausted, rumpled and grimy and had no idea where she was going to spend the night. She certainly didn't expect Quinn to be sitting in the waiting room.

Despite everything, her heart warmed at the sight of him, his tuxedo crumpled, black hair standing on end. A far cry from the sophisticate who'd escorted her up the red carpet earlier in the evening.

That seemed a lifetime ago, so much had happened. So much had changed.

"How is he?" His eyes were rimmed with weariness and worry.

"Resting. They're keeping him in overnight, but he can go back to the hotel tomorrow."

"To the hotel?" He looked surprised. "Not home?"

"They've decided to stick around Port for a few days." She sat down, leaving a couple of seats between them.

"I see." He looked glad for her. "Is that good?" His head lowered and tilted, his eyes turned up under his brows.

Dani gave a tired smile and nodded. "That's good."

She took a deep breath and repeated the words in her mind. It was good. She had a lot of lost time to make up for. So did her father, and she was going to make sure he did.

"Can you explain how you came to be riding a motorbike on Four Mile Beach in the middle of the night?"

Quinn scrubbed at the dark shadow chasing his jaw line. "I initially thought you'd be at the shop, but then I remembered the beach."

He'd remembered. Her special place. "And the bike?"

His hand moved to his hair as he tried to repair the damage an hour of speeding on a motorbike in cool, damp air had inflicted. "An interesting sequence of events involving four boys messing about on the beach, my Rolex, a few bucks and a few choice threats." His mouth quirked. "Not to mention the possibility of being arrested at any minute."

Dani laughed shakily. "My hero."

My hero, the liar. Her smile faded.

So did his. "I thought you'd never forgive yourself if…" He nodded toward the emergency unit.

"That's why I started running," she murmured. "On the beach." She paused. "Thank you." It sounded wholly inadequate, but Dani didn't know what else to say.

There was an awkward silence. She rubbed her arms briskly, grateful again for her jacket and boots. Imagine the bike ride in her organza dress.

"Dani," he said softly, his eyes tormented. "I'm so sorry I hurt you like that."

She looked away. Did she want to hear it? Could she trust him, after all the lies he'd told? His were pretty big lies, after all. Not "You look lovely" or "Of course I didn't forget your birthday…" His lies involved blackmail, enticement, shady business goings-on, concealing a father.

But after all the crying and all the emotions of the evening, her anger had drained away.

Her sadness had not. "I know why you did it," she began. "You couldn't give your wife her dying wish. This was another chance."

"A chance to even the score," he mused. "You might be right. I figured I had the time to make it up to you. Your father is nearly out of time."

To make it up to her? He was asking a lot. "We've established that you're a loyal friend, then. Maybe not such a loyal lover."

Pain darkened his eyes even more. "I think I can be. It's not love for Laura that has stopped me falling in love these past few years. I didn't need it and I didn't miss it. I lived well, travelled incessantly, made a lot of money." He shifted forward in his seat, exhaling noisily. "I thought I was happy. Being alone, pleasing myself. I thought I had it all together. But you…"

"I what?" Her pulse skipped, but then, being in the same country as Quinn Everard made her pulse skip. Was he saying he wanted her, that it wasn't over?

"I won't lose you," he said fiercely, grasping her hands, "not when you've turned my life upside down."

She gently pried her hands loose and twisted them in her lap. A great wave of emotion and exhaustion blocked her ability to make sense of anything. Lord, it had been a long day, but she needed to focus. Did he mean he wanted to change his life for her? That he was interested in a relationship?

There was movement in the corner of her eye. Quinn Everard sat two feet away, fidgeting. The great negotiator who had calmly tossed away fifteen million English pounds on a painting, without so much as a muscle twitch, was fidgeting.

"You said you loved me," he muttered through clenched teeth.

"Did I?" Yes, she remembered, at the reception before storming out. "I also said I hated you."

"I wasn't looking for this, but then I found you." He turned to face her and grasped her wrists again before she could snatch them away. "You found me. I love you, Dani. I didn't want to, I tried not to, but I do."

Her head jerked up, but somehow she kept her hands calmly, quietly in his. "You—you love me?" She searched his face for guilt or pity.

Quinn sighed gustily. "Dani, you're smart, funny, vibrant. You're bloody frustrating and incredibly talented. I think about you every second, and when I'm not with you, I miss you, your smile and your colour." He spoke quickly, urgently. "You're the only person in more years than I care to think about who's made me feel this way." He lifted and shook her hands gently. "The only person who's *ever* made me feel this way."

"Oh." Her tongue seemed to be stuck to the roof of her mouth. Light-headed with surprise and excitement and love, she swayed drunkenly, hoping she wasn't about to pass out. The light in his eyes made her dizzy with hope but still afraid to believe what she saw in them. Afraid to trust in the love that shone out.

Quinn leaned forward and brushed her cheek with his thumb, and she realised she was crying. "Can you forgive me, sweetheart? I'll gladly spend the rest of my life making it up to you."

She dug her nails into his palms as joy swelled inside. Could it be true that everything she'd ever wanted was within her grasp?

And he was everything she'd ever wanted. Sexy as hell and well-respected everywhere. Loyal and warm toward those he loved. Encouraging and motivated about her work. She'd loved him, probably since the moment she set eyes on him, but definitely since Sydney. "I fell in love with you in Sydney," she blurted, finishing on a big sniff.

"I wanted you to come to my place, meet my people and see where we went from there. But I don't think I actually accepted it as love until the other night when I broke a promise to Jake. And then, when I saw the necklace…"

He shifted over to the seat between them and enfolded her in his arms. "You're dead on your feet."

Dani sniffed again, rubbing her wet face on his lapel. "How are we going to do this?" she whimpered. "You live down there. You travel all the time…."

His mouth moved on her hair and he tightened his grip. "I have a plan. Half the year up here—the cooler half, if you don't mind—and the other in Sydney. Steve runs the shop and when we're up here in Port, you design." He pulled back and tipped her face up, looking down at her sternly. "Then we go all out to promote you in Sydney, Dani. The whole works, launches, publicity, celebrity photo shoots. It's time to stop running, to show everyone what you're made of."

"Okay," she said cautiously. "But what about your business?"

Quinn shrugged. "That's what staff are for. I'll cut back on the travel, except for those trips where you can come, too, and tout your stuff in the big centres."

She closed her eyes, leaning into his warmth, so tired yet awash with exhilaration.

With Quinn beside her, she would never be afraid of success or failure again. She would reach for the stars, stamp number one on everything she touched. He would continually push her to be the best, and that's what she wanted, more than anything else.

Dani's heart burst with joy, even as she felt her eyes drifting closed. She came first for him; she was his precious jewel. Her father wanted her around for the limited time he had left. Her cousins would hopefully forge new bonds through the younger generation. Love and family, and all in such a short time.

She belonged.

* * * * *

BOARDROOMS & A BILLIONAIRE HEIR

PAULA ROE

Despite wanting to be a vet, choreographer, hairdresser, card shark and an interior designer (though not all at once!), **Paula Roe** ended up as a personal assistant, office manager, aerobics instructor and software trainer for thirteen years (which also funded her extensive travel through the US and Europe). Today she still retains a deep love of filing systems, stationery and travelling, although the latter is only in her dreams these days. Paula lives near western Sydney's glorious Blue Mountains with her family, an ancient black cat and a garden full of rainbow lorikeets, magpies and willy wagtails. You can visit her at www.paularoe.com.

A big hug and smoochy kiss to the Down Under
Desireables for your support, hand-holding and
encouragement: Bron, Tessa, Maxine, Yvonne and
Jan. To Linley, my personal GMC wizard and
finder-of-weak-spots. To MJ, who gave me such
insightful suggestions and made my writing that
much better. And my deep thanks to Andrew
Burden of Canberra's Aviation Search and Rescue
Centre who let me pick his brains about plane
crashes and rescues in order to get everything
just right.

One

Wealth and power hung in the expansive boardroom, permeating every cherrywood panel, every thread of the tightly woven carpet underfoot.

The huge panoramic windows played right into that powerful aura, offering an unobstructed view of Sydney's CBD to the right, the curved dome of the historical Queen Victoria Building to the left. Subtle track lights highlighted the boardroom table where one woman and three men were rising to their feet. Jake Vance recognised each in turn: Kimberley Perrini; her husband, Ric, and current CEO of Blackstone Diamonds; Ryan Blackstone, Chief Financial Officer; and Garth Buick, the company secretary.

Jake had stood in the same spot days ago.

At that time, the room had been tense with stunned denial after his little bombshell. Despite that, it was too good a coincidence for Kimberley to pass up; he'd seen the burning curiosity in her shaken expression. Now, judging by the shell-shocked looks, they obviously had their proof.

Finding out your previously dead brother was very much alive was a life-changing event, even if that bit of gossip had been press fodder for months. But when that brother stood to gain a substantial chunk of the Blackstone fortune...

He swallowed bitterly. This wasn't in his ten-year plan. Making his first million, breaking into the U.S. market, giving back to his mother's favourite causes, yes. Even, eventually, a wife and kids. But not this. Not becoming Australia's walking, talking answer to the freakin' Lindbergh baby.

"James...Jake?" Kimberley Perrini said tentatively, obviously confused about how to proceed. He gave a curt nod and remained silent as she settled for sitting at the table. He noticed her crisp business suit, the efficient pulled-back hair, the air of sophistication and privilege radiating out as if she'd been born into it.

He shoved the uncharacteristic bitterness away and instead focused on his game plan—detecting weakness.

It was awkward, this first face-to-face meeting with his sister. *His sister, for God's sake.* He ignored the deeper implication and completed his study. The similarities between Kimberley and Ryan were obvious: dark hair with that widow's peak, green eyes. But where hers held optimistic caution, Ryan Blackstone's were full of outright hostility. It was in every smell that infused the ostentatious room, every movement and gesture the man made in his thousand-dollar suit.

Jake glanced over the table to where Garth Buick sat. The

two younger men, Ric and Ryan, were on their feet behind him, as if standing gave them a psychological advantage.

Jake had used that tactic many times before.

"We had April Kellerman's documents analysed, as well as those DNA tests," Ric Perrini said now, indicating Jake should take a seat.

"And?" Jake sat and Ric and Ryan followed suit.

"It appears that you are James Hammond Blackstone."

As one, they released a collective breath and the expectant hush in the room fanned out, spreading like a blanketing drift of snow. The air was just as chilly, with most of the freeze coming from the two men who had battled for the CEO's position after Howard's death.

Jake steeled his features to betray nothing. Emotion meant vulnerability, which meant your enemies had a weakness they could exploit. Show nothing, reveal nothing.

"So Howard was right all along," Kimberley finally said.

Ric shrugged. "Looks like it."

She frowned and opened her mouth to say something, but Ryan interrupted.

"We asked you here to discuss a few things. One, your plans for Blackstone's." Ryan's even tone belied the storm in his eyes. "And we'd like to make an offer for your shares."

Jake stifled his surprise. Interesting. Business first. "I'm not selling."

"You haven't heard our bid."

"I don't need to."

"Listen, Vance. If this is about payback or revenge—"

"Why would it?" Jake raised one eyebrow.

The men glanced at each other, regrouping. Finally Kimberley said slowly, "See it from our side. You and Quinn

Everard are close. There's been a long history of animosity between him and Howard—"

Jake smiled, an action he knew would throw them off balance. "Not my problem. I'm sure you've had me researched. So you know I never let personal feelings stand in the way of a business decision."

"What about Jaxon Financial?" Ric asked.

Jake paused, letting the barb sink in without showing it'd hit a sore spot. "That was over eight years ago. And it wasn't my company."

"But you were accused of insider trading," Ryan probed, his astute eyes unwavering.

Jake eased back in the leather chair and stretched his legs out, a calculated show of nonchalance. "Accused. Not charged."

"You lost millions. The CEO fired you."

"And I returned the favour eighteen months later when I bought them out. Look, we can go over my chequered history for hours, but it doesn't change the facts. The way I see it, you have two choices. Fight me for the claim, which would tie us up in court for years, and see the shares plummet. Or work with me on this. Blackstone's has a problem. Besides the press leak you've failed to plug, the company has been floundering since Howard's death. Share prices are dropping. The power struggle between you—" he nodded at Ric "—and you," then Ryan, "is unsettling the board, not to mention your shareholders. They're getting antsy."

"How do you know that?" demanded Ryan.

"I make it my business to know." Before Ryan could interject, Jake held up a hand. "I plan to fix that."

"Why?" Ryan asked, his eyes narrowed.

"Because I can."

"I meant—"

"I know what you meant. Like it or not, Howard made me a beneficiary. You're worried about Blackstone's collapsing? I can fix it. It isn't personal. It's business."

"So this is all just business to you?" Kimberley asked softly.

"Well, it's certainly not about family bonding."

He didn't miss her brief flash of dismay as her eyes met Ric's briefly.

"So what's your plan?" Ric said smoothly.

Jake sized him up. Ric Perrini looked hard, with a reputation to match. He'd been Howard's surrogate son, the only one deemed worthy to take over Blackstone's. The man probably felt threatened. Hell, they all did.

Hardly surprising. Jake traded on his unpredictable reputation; it sent fear and respect into the hearts of his adversaries and made them careless.

That's how he won.

He looked back to Kimberley, who'd been staring at him in silence. When he met her sharp green eyes, she refused to look away.

"You're the spitting image of Howard," she said now.

Thrown by such a personal comment, Jake frowned. He wasn't sure she meant that in a good way, either. Should he thank her? Ignore it? He opted for the simplest approach.

"Blackstone genes."

Kim hesitated. "You know we all thought Howard was out of his tree about you," she finally said. "I just can't believe you're actually alive."

He lifted his eyebrows and gave her a small, wry smile. "In the flesh."

Kim paused, a moment too long.

"You have something to say," Jake said calmly. "Just go ahead and say it."

"Don't you have questions about the family?" she asked curiously. "About Howard? Sonya? Vince?"

"Not particularly. I have a very efficient research department."

"So where have you been for the last thirty years?" Ryan asked tightly.

"Queensland first. Then when I was about ten, South Australia."

"And?" Kim prompted. Jake let them dangle for a few seconds before conceding, "I was kidnapped by Howard's housekeeper and her boyfriend. Two months after the ransom note, around midnight, their car crashed into the Lindon River, five kilometres north of—"

"Newcastle, yes, we've read the police report," Ryan interrupted. "Everyone assumed you'd drowned in the crash and floated out to sea."

"April Kellerman was driving by when the car crashed. She pulled me free."

"And kept you."

The scorn in Ryan's voice sent a fierce surge of protectiveness straight to Jake's chest. "Don't judge what you don't know," he warned softly, piercing the younger man with a steely look.

Silence abruptly fell.

"We need to know more if we're to prepare a press release," Kim finally said, then paused as a shadow passed over his features. "You don't trust us."

"I don't trust anyone."

"That's a nice attitude to have," Ryan muttered.

Jake raised one eyebrow. "I'm not the one with the press leak."

Ryan tensed as Perrini said, "You know the press will fill in the blanks with whatever they can find, true or not."

"I know."

Despite a thorough going over, Jake was determined not to give anything away under everyone's searching eyes. Kim's small sigh a few seconds later was the only indication he'd won. *Won what?* The victory came with a surprisingly bitter taste.

"Your birthdate is wrong," Kim said finally.

"Excuse me?"

"James was born on the fourth of August, 1974, which makes you thirty-four this year. Your official bio—as Jake Vance—had you celebrating your thirty-fifth birthday on the first of September."

He knew that they were just numbers on a bit of paper. That it didn't mean squat. Despite his cold logic, a small lick of helplessness bloomed in the pit of his belly. In a nanosecond, cold anger flooded in to douse it.

Anger that was unjustified. Anger that actually shamed him. Blaming a dead woman would solve nothing.

Outwardly he shrugged. "So I'm a Leo instead of a Virgo."

Ryan's snort of dark amusement echoed in the quiet room, one that twitched Jake's mouth in all-too-brief humour.

Then Garth rose and withdrew a piece of paper from a folder. "As Howard's first born, you are now the recipient of a considerable amount of wealth." The man handed the paper to Jake. "You know about the third of Howard's shares— fifty-one percent divided equally between you, Ric and Ryan. You also own Howard's Vaucluse mansion, Miramare, although Sonya Hammond was given the right to reside there for the rest of her life. The remainder of Howard's assets—personal investments, artworks, cash—are now divided between yourself and Ryan."

Jake studied the details in silence, pausing only to chance a glance at Kimberley. Even Howard's rumored lover, Marise Davenport-Hammond, had come away with a seven-figure sum, yet for his eldest daughter, the wife of his surrogate son Ric Perrini, nothing. Worse, he'd publicly and privately humiliated her with the gifting of his Bondi beach house to Ryan, a house where her mother had drowned.

He had to hand it to Kimberley—she met his scrutiny head on, the cool green gaze a study in calm.

Garth continued. "There's also an article that stipulates three Blackstones must sit on the board—at the moment it's Kimberley, Ryan and Vincent Blackstone, Howard's brother."

"I'm not after a board position."

"We're not giving you one. Yet," Ric said, matching his cool reply. "But Vince has his own life and is making noises about retiring." He studied Jake's face. "And it all depends on what you decide."

"It's too early to make a decision."

"So just how are you planning to help the company?" Ryan asked tightly.

Jake gave him the once-over, only mildly surprised when the younger man, just like his sister, refused to break eye contact.

These Blackstones were tough.

"First, I need to get up to speed with all aspects of Blackstone Diamonds, starting with the financials and corporate structure. Then, I'll hold a meeting with the board and shareholders to reassure them of my commitment."

"Are you planning to commit?" Ric asked, leaning back in

his chair and crossing his arms. "Or are you going to break up the company after the shares stabilise?"

"How can I? I don't have a controlling interest."

"That's never stopped you before."

Jake studied Ric Perrini with renewed respect. If it came down to a vote, Matt Hammond held ten percent of the shares and had already pledged his support in Jake's favour. But that was purely because the man hated the Blackstones.

Jake didn't know these people. But he'd been in similar situations, ones that involved family, tradition and high emotion. You had to tread lightly. Be diplomatic. Get them onside with a small truth, at least.

"For now, I'm committed."

"That's not good enough," Garth snapped. "Howard built Blackstone's up from nothing. He wasn't a saint but he loved this company. He put his life into it, making it a successful, international brand name. His wish was to see that continue— with his family at the helm." The older man thumped the table with a clenched fist for emphasis. "After all these years, he never stopped believing you were alive somewhere. Even refused to put up a gravestone in your name. That's how damned stubborn and committed he was. And look—he was right. Don't you think you owe his memory—your family— more than a 'for now'?"

The impassioned speech made as much impact on Jake's composure as a feather on steel. He'd heard it all before, seen enough pleading, threatening and bargaining to not let it matter.

He held Buick in a cool stare until the older man let out a disgusted snort and settled back in his chair.

"A DNA test doesn't make a bunch of strangers suddenly family," Jake said calmly, ignoring the way Kim's face paled.

"I don't like this any more than you do. Make no mistake—this isn't about some newly discovered paternal ties to Howard Blackstone. I don't want or need the complication."

"So why are you doing it?" Ryan asked.

Jake smiled thinly. "To make money."

"You're a billionaire. How much more do you need?" Kim asked, her eyes astute.

Way too personal. Jake crossed his arms and met her gaze head-on. "Take my offer or not. You're quite welcome to maintain the status quo and let that press leak go unfound, watch the stock plummet, the shareholders pull out…"

"Or take our chances with you," Ric finished.

"Yep."

He rose to give them their thinking time and strode over to the cabinet to pour a glass of water. Unmindful of the hushed discussion at the other end of the room, he sipped slowly as he gazed upon the magnificent view of Sydney stretched in front of him, fixing on the familiar blue neon of his AdVance Corp across the bay, a physical manifestation of eight years' hard work.

He'd expected softer edges after Ryan's recent marriage, but the man's glare indicated a strong will. And, if the reports were true, an even stronger desire to prove himself in the face of Howard Blackstone's obvious preference for Ric Perrini. Just the sort of family infighting that jeopardised smart business decisions—which would, ironically, make his decision to keep them at arm's length that much easier.

For a week he'd immersed himself in this family—their history, their investments, even the salaciously unreliable gossip. He might be related to them on paper, but loyalty had to be earned. There were only four people in the world he trusted: His secretary. His chief of security. Quinn, who had voiced multiple warnings to watch his back. And his mother.

He didn't miss the irony. For someone with deep trust issues, he'd placed it with a woman who'd been living a lie.

"OK," Ric said at length. "Under one condition."

Jake turned his back to the window, placing his glass on the cabinet. "Which is?"

"No official announcements until we're good and ready."

Jake quirked an eyebrow. "And your reasoning is…?"

"You. The speculation alone will be enough to drop stock prices."

He smiled humourlessly. "And it conveniently stops anything from leaking out…unless one of you is the source."

Ryan visibly bristled, but Kim put a hand on his arm. "Your identity stays with us until we all agree on where and when to announce it," she said smoothly. "Not even the assistant we've assigned to you knows."

Great. A company mouthpiece to spout the latest platitudes about Blackstone's.

"Have you informed your solicitors and the private investigator?" Jake asked.

"We've called the P.I. off," Ric said.

Jake nodded. "So let's see what I can dig up on this leak before we start making anything official. A week, maybe two, should do it."

"Once people start seeing you here, it'll be hard to avoid speculation," Kimberley said.

"Which is why we've given you an office on the executive floor. Limited access. High security," Ric added.

"I don't need an office. But I will need complete access to your records."

"It's already done." Bitterness tinged Ryan's words. How much had it cost him to agree to that? For a brief second, Jake almost felt sorry for him. It disappeared when Ryan fixed him with a cold glare. He saw the enmity written in every muscle on the man's face.

"The only people who know the truth are family," Kimberley added.

Family. Jake's gut tightened at the word, but outwardly he just nodded.

"Vince will want to meet you," Kim said. "He's—"

"Howard's brother. Runs an opal mine in Coober Pedy. Lives in Adelaide and owns a ten-percent share. He's currently in the States on business."

"He's your uncle," Kim added calmly. "Then there's Sonya."

Jake heard the warmth in her voice, saw the emotion that briefly softened Kim's expression before she blinked it away.

An unfamiliar burst of injustice slammed into him, rendering him momentarily speechless. Sonya Hammond was a mother figure to these people. She was important.

He took a breath, quickly recovering with, "It's not necessary."

By the look on Kim's face he knew his response fell far short of acceptable. Well, hell. This wasn't exactly his dream situation, either.

Perrini said, "You'll have access to the internal filing and e-mail systems, plus a master key card to the building." He punched a number into the phone. "You understand that no files can leave the building, nor are there to be any unauthorised copies made."

"Naturally," Jake said smoothly.

Ric continued. "The elevator on the far right is executive

use only. It takes you to the basement, so there'll be no chance meetings with other staff. Your assistant, Holly McLeod, is outside."

I guess this means the meeting's over. "I'll need the current financials."

"I'll send them up," Ryan said curtly. He was the first to rise, striding over to the door and yanking it open. "Welcome to Blackstone's."

Holly McLeod waited as everyone exited the boardroom. Ryan, Ric and Garth were deep in discussion as they strode to the elevator. Nothing new there. They lived and breathed Blackstone Diamonds.

Then Jake Vance emerged and the seriousness of her predicament flipped her stomach.

It's nervousness. That's all.

He spotted her and gave a brief, humourless smile. "Miss McLeod."

Her softly murmured name tripped a breath of warm anticipation over her skin, one she quickly covered up by straightening the file in her arms. "Mr Vance—" she held out her hand "—I'm Holly McLeod. I'm to be your assistant for the duration of your stay."

When his long fingers wrapped around hers, her skin heated with the contact. It wasn't power he so clearly exuded. It was something much more seductive. Confidence? Control?

Intimacy.

The way his sharp green gaze swept her from head to toe, taking in her hair, her face, her business suit. The way those eyes probed hers until they finally came to rest on the small diamond solitaire at her throat.

She swallowed, withdrew and offered a key card, carefully avoiding his hand. "This will give you access to all the floors, plus the basement car park. You've been allocated a parking space for as long as you're with Blackstone's. I'll show you to your office now, if you like."

"No."

Holly blinked. "Sir?"

"It's Jake. I'm not staying." He stuck his hand in his suit jacket, pulled out a mobile phone and flipped it open. Without a second glance, he pocketed it. "You can give me a rundown of the company history in the car. Get the financials from Ryan Blackstone and I'll meet you in the basement."

She hesitated as he made short work of the corridor with his long, devouring strides. So he didn't want to view his domain, cast an all-encompassing powerful eye over the magnificent Sydney view. Of course. He had the mirror image from his North Sydney complex. Still, she'd anticipated questions, pulled all the relevant files and promotional material and put them on his desk. She'd made tentative meetings with department heads.

"Keep up, Miss McLeod," Jake said curtly as he pressed the elevator button.

Holly quickly regrouped and moved forward, apprehension giving way to irritation in the face of his cool perusal. "You're not authorised to remove files from the building, Mr Vance," she said shortly, refusing to flinch as his sharp eyes met hers. "But I'll go and personally make sure they're delivered up to your temporary office."

He scrutinised her with all the skill of a pro, but she returned his look steadily. *Oh, I know how you work, Mr Midas Touch.* The stare-down was part of his strategy, along with an emotionless, lay-out-the-facts style that most men grudgingly admired, despite his ruthless reputation. Men wanted to be him; women just wanted him. Period.

She pushed the elevator button repeatedly, tightening her grip on her file so it crushed up against her breasts like protective armour. "I think now's a good time to discuss how you'd like to work while you're here."

He frowned. "I don't expect you to be performing any personal assistant duties. I already have one."

"Holly is a wealth of information about Blackstone's. We're fortunate to have her," Kimberley said, from behind them. Holly ducked her gaze guiltily at the unexpected praise as Kim continued. "Make use of her expertise and gather as much knowledge as you can before deciding to invest with us."

Holly felt a confusing frisson of adversarial tension crackle between these two, like an argument was in the cards in the next two seconds. She'd never seen Kimberley be anything except utterly polite and professional, even to people she disliked.

Jake Vance, on the other hand, chose to do as he pleased, courtesy be damned.

"I need to speak to you later, Jake," Kimberley said pointedly.

"I can fit you in tomorrow."

"I'm flat out with Fashion Week but I can find time. I'll let Holly know." She gave up on the elevator and reached for the fire stairs door.

Jake turned to Holly when the door clicked shut, his face a study in controlled irritation. "It looks like I have myself an assistant, Miss McLeod." She blinked as he added, "As to how I work, it's quickly. I ask questions. You answer them. Simple."

She straightened her spine. "Do you have an agenda? A deadline or time frame that—"

"I plan on this taking no more than a week, ten days at the most. Every morning I'll decide on our timetable and we'll take it from there. I expect you to start work at eight and stay until everything that needs to get done is done. You need to work around my schedule and be available at my North Sydney office. Do you have other work commitments?"

She shook her head. "You're my first priority."

Holly watched in fascination as his sensuous mouth thinned, almost as if he were holding something back. His eyes, on the other hand, glittered for one second before he glanced away. "Let's start with the building layout and other assets." As if on cue, the doors pinged open and he swept his hand forward, indicating she go first.

"Our ground level is secured with high-end technology and a security desk, as you've seen," Holly began as they descended. "No employee gets in without their ID and a walk though the scanners. Visitors must be signed in and accompanied by an employee."

"What about the Blackstones themselves?"

"All executives are located on the forty-third floor with the rest of the board, and use this private elevator. Finance is on the thirty-fifth floor, PR on the twentieth. We also have an employee-only gym and health club, child-care center and cafeteria. We own the whole building, including the grand ballroom, shop fronts, bar and three restaurants that cover the ground, first and second floors facing George Street. Our employees get generous discounts at these and we have a standing table for executive use at each restaurant. We occasionally rent out our ballroom to other companies. Last year it was the B&S and Make a Wish Charity Ball."

She held out a glossy brochure that she'd helped design,

one that detailed the building's facilities. He just glanced at it, then back at her.

"No company propaganda. I prefer facts."

Right. Feeling as if she'd failed some kind of test, she tucked the offending material back into her folder. *Take a breath, Holly. Work out your strategy and stick with it.*

"The rest of the floors are taken up by HR, the press room and our other divisions."

"Which are?"

"Blackstone Jewellery, International Sales, Mining, Crafting and Design, Legal. I have a fact sheet of the departmental hierarchy and breakdown."

"I'll need that e-mailed."

She nodded and fixed her eyes on the descending numbers.

Jake crossed his arms and studied her profile before ending at the low, elegant sweep of dark hair that brushed past her ears and up into a stylish ponytail.

An unexpected stab of lust hit him low and hard, but with practised ease he stuffed it back. Still, it didn't stop his gaze from tripping back over her in leisurely study, taking in the navy suit that cinched in her waist, the V-neck shirt revealing a creamy throat adorned with one simple diamond on a gold chain. Down farther, her legs were encased in navy pants, ending in a pair of absurdly high sandals.

He found himself staring at those feet, the nails painted a subtle peach with the second toe sporting a diamond stud toe ring.

When she shifted the file in her arms and glanced over at him, he suddenly realised he'd been staring at the woman's feet.

He snapped his eyes up to meet hers and it hit him again. It wasn't the curve of her lips, nor the way her blue eyes tilted up at the corners. It was the tiny birthmark on the left side of her mouth, like some artist had painted it on to tease and tempt. To focus a man's attention.

A prime kissing target.

When she glanced away, her profile oozed cool professionalism. So why did that calm facade annoy him?

Jake was used to all the tricks when it came to business, but this was definitely a twist. They could've given him any old assistant, yet this gorgeous brunette's presence meant they'd obviously read the reports about Mia.

She was here not only to spy but to distract.

He scowled as his phone rang again. Expert, was she, held in high regard by Blackstone's? That was enough to give him pause.

He'd learned from his mistakes. If they thought a pair of cat's eyes and a kissy-mole would divert him from his purpose, they had another think coming. The press called him Mr Midas Touch, the bad boy of business, and if the Blackstones wanted an unfair fight, they would find out how bad he could be.

Two

So that was the great Jake Vance, Mr Midas Touch. Owner of the billion dollar AdVance Corp, corporate shark and Australia's third richest single man under forty.

Holly quickly dumped the financials on the desk of her temporary office, whirled out the glass doors and back to the elevators.

She'd been prepared for the arrogance, the intolerance of anyone he considered beneath him. He was unconventional, a risk taker. He made business decisions that wiser people labelled career suicide. But somehow he always managed to come out on top. Maybe because he gave the impression he had nothing to lose. Those who had nothing risked nothing.

But the Sunday feature article hadn't warned of the zing of attraction that had nearly floored her, the aura of power and control that stuck her tongue to the roof of her mouth and turned the words to dust in her throat.

Working at Blackstone's put her directly in the path of many powerful men. But Jake Vance…It was something in his face, the way his eyes had swept over her even as he tried to keep his perusal impersonal. Call her crazy, but she'd felt the air practically crackle with a weird sort of expectation.

The elevator doors swung open and she pressed the basement button impatiently.

Their gazes had locked just long enough for her to recognise the moment—predatory interest, an almost promissory flame in those deep green eyes. His mouth, a frankly sensual sculpture in warm flesh, had tweaked for a brief second, not enough to be called a smile.

Then he'd shut it down.

The only man in all her twenty-six years who'd forcibly smothered his interest.

No wonder he was at the top of his game. With that much control over his emotions, he was dark, brooding danger in an Italian designer suit. Heaven help a woman if the man ever genuinely smiled.

She curled her lip at the thought. Men in power—those who played God with people's lives—turned her blood cold.

Like Max Carlton, her soon-to-be ex-boss.

She'd been surprised when he'd approved her temporary transfer to PR eighteen months ago, but she'd had no time to worry if that approval came with strings, not when Blackstone's ten-year anniversary had been her top priority. Months later she'd been on the team organising Blackstone's Australian Fashion Week presence. It'd been a chance to show Kimberley Perrini her Blackstone's-funded studies were paying off, a chance she'd desperately wanted since graduating over a year ago. Then, last week, she'd been pulled from the glamorous event that was the ultimate dream of every Sydney designer to babysit Jake Vance.

She sighed, automatically brushing her hair back from her forehead. If only it were simply a babysitting job.

She finally arrived at the basement and found Jake standing beside a shiny silver Commodore, talking into his mobile phone.

She paused, taking in the perfect snapshot that oozed wealth and class, forcing her heart to slow down, to settle the stupid hitch in her breath. He looked up as she approached and, without pause, opened the back door for her.

Holly blinked. No limo? No uniformed driver? She slid into the creamy leather interior, a niggle of confusion creasing her brow.

Jake got in beside her, his phone call now finished. "Back to the office, Steve."

The car started with a gentle purr and the driver slid it into first gear, easing out the basement and into the traffic flow. And suddenly Holly realised Jake's attention was now focused solely on her.

Disturbingly focused attention in an even smaller space than the elevator.

She clicked on her seat belt, ignoring the way his green eyes grazed over her in concentrated study. When she'd first faced him it'd been a stretch to retain her composure. The natural command, the sheer sexuality he exuded had rocketed her pulse. Now in close, almost intimate, quarters, she felt the heated warmth curling up from her toes intensifying.

Here was a man used to getting his own way. He expected acquiescence, demanded it. He crushed anyone in his way.

"Besides the financials, what do you need?" She spoke calmly, that last thought aiding her steely resolve.

"How about you start with the Blackstone history?"

Holly gave him a curious look. "Anything specific?"

"Not particularly. Don't worry." His lips curved. "I'll stop you if it gets boring."

She blinked at his innocent expression. How could he make that neutral statement sound like such a sinful suggestion?

She concentrated on flicking through her documents to stop herself from flushing. Boring and Jake Vance were planets apart. Of that she was certain.

As Holly talked, Jake listened, carefully analysing not only her words, but her nonverbal cues. As they drove onto Sydney Harbour Bridge he noticed the way her eyes lit up when she recounted the intriguing history of the Blackstones. He knew all this, thanks to his research team. But it was more interesting hearing it from her lips than reading a dry hundred-page report. He asked questions and she expanded on the details, providing answers without hesitation. She knew her stuff.

Yeah, she's smart and attractive. But she works for Blackstone's.

He'd been blindsided twice before. Lucy had ripped out his heart when he'd needed her support the most. Seven years later, Mia had used her position as his assistant to violate his trust. He'd quickly learned a harsh lesson: To ensure his utmost privacy, no one was permitted to breach his tight security measures. His company had the strictest security checks, his private life had triple that. It just wasn't worth everything he'd worked his whole life for.

"Unlike other jewellers, Blackstone's issues only two glossies every year."

Focus. One second was all he needed to clear his mind, one second to shove his memories back into the past and concentrate on the here and now.

"Two catalogues," he repeated.

Holly nodded. "October and January."

"No Christmas issue?"

"No. Valentine's Day is our busiest time. We found our clients started shopping for Christmas as early as October. A Blackstone diamond is an investment. It signals superior quality and workmanship, something that women aspire to have, combined with the Australian mystique of the outback. Our branding says it all: the simple use of the word 'heart.' Some of our previous campaigns were 'heart felt,' 'heart's desire' and 'from the heart.' This is our most recent issue." She flipped open her folder. Jake gave it a cursory glance and focused on another magazine on the seat.

"What's that?"

Holly glanced down. "Our first issue. A collector's item, actually. There are only twenty existing copies in the world. That's Howard and Ursula. She's wearing the Blackstone Rose."

Unable to help himself, Jake slowly reached for the copy and stared at the cover. Looking every inch its 1976 date, the slim glossy brochure showed a candid but spectacular shot of a young couple in formal evening dress on the steps of the Sydney Opera House. Howard Blackstone in a tux, his wolfish smile triumphant. On his arm, Ursula was dressed in a strapless floor-length creation, her hair piled up into a then-fashionable beehive. The necklace around her neck was large and ostentatious, everything spectacular and showy that he'd come to expect from Howard Blackstone. There were five diamonds—four round stones with a teardrop shaped one dangling in the center. It sat high and heavy on Ursula's neck like a collar, a symbol of ownership.

The look in Ursula's face confirmed his impression. She was deeply unhappy. Sure, she smiled, but there was no joy behind it, the emotion in her eyes dull and resigned.

She had wealth, beauty and fame. Surely these things should have made her ecstatic, not miserable.

"When was this taken?"

"December 1976."

Two months after he'd been stolen. No wonder she looked miserable. And Howard, being the self-absorbed bastard he was, had probably convinced her to dress up and show off the diamonds anyway.

Despite himself, his chest tightened. Dammit. He dropped the magazine with a scowl, cursing himself for allowing that small weakness to take up space in his head. Emotion and business did not mix.

Holly's low, husky voice suddenly broke through and with the effort it took to flip a switch, he refocused. He turned back to face her, his face expressionless, as she continued.

"The Blackstone Rose came from a diamond called the Heart of the Outback. Jeb Hammond—that's Ryan and Kimberley's grandfather and Howard's father-in-law—gifted the stone to his daughter Ursula to celebrate the birth of James Blackstone, his first grandchild, in 1974. Howard then had it made into the Blackstone Rose necklace the following year." She paused. "Do you know much about diamonds?"

"Aren't they a girl's best friend?"

She gave him a smile that struck him as slightly patronizing. "Not this one."

"I thought every woman liked diamonds."

"I'm more of a sapphire girl," she admitted coolly. She shifted and straightened her back against the leather seat. "Diamonds are commonly judged by the 'four Cs'—cut, clarity, color and carat. The cut—"

"Determines its brilliance. Most gemmologists consider cut the most important diamond characteristic."

"Yes. There's no single measurement to define it…" Holly stopped. "But you're best mates with Quinn Everard. You probably know this already."

He nodded. "Some. Go on."

"Am I being graded on this?" She frowned. "Because if you're not happy with the information I'm giving you—"

"I am, Holly," he said curtly. "Please continue." After the briefest of pauses, she turned the page and showed him a studio shot of the Blackstone Rose sitting elegantly on black velvet. The camera flash had captured the reflection against one of the stone's polished surfaces, creating a starry burst of light.

He'd never understood the female obsession with jewellery but these were… "Impressive. The Blackstone Rose necklace was stolen on Ursula's thirtieth birthday, right?"

"It went missing around that time," she corrected him.

Jake eased his long legs forward, crossing them at the ankles. "A moot point now they've been found. For whatever reason, Howard bequeathed the stones to Marise, and now that she's dead, they're Matt Hammond's."

Holly paused at the mention of Matt. She'd read about the long-standing Blackstone-Hammond feud like everyone else, had pored over the numerous articles about their complicated history with a mixture of sadness and amazement. Matt's father and Kimberley's mother were brother and sister, yet because of greed, power and jealousy, the branches of the family tree had grown acres apart.

With a frown, Holly recalled the last few months that had been publicly played out in the media. Whatever the families' grievances, Matt didn't deserve to have his dead wife linked with notorious womaniser Howard Blackstone, to have her die in Howard's plane crash off the Pacific coast. His son Blake didn't deserve to have the memory of his mother tainted by salacious gossip.

Jake waited for her to comment, to echo what the press had feverishly dubbed the "Howard-and-Marise affair", but she remained silent. "And…?" he finally prompted.

"And what?" she replied calmly. "Look, Mr Vance, I'm not entirely sure what you want to know—"

"Dynamics."

"Sorry?"

"I'm interested in family dynamics. The mark of a successful family company depends on that family working together in a harmonious environment."

"The Blackstones have grown and thrived for over thirty years. You can't get more successful than that."

"It's not about monetary success. It's about respect, both for each other and their employees."

"What makes you think they don't have respect?"

"Howard Blackstone was a dictator. That much I do know. He was petty, vengeful and treated his employees and family like crap. He also relied on cronyism to stay on top of the heap." He suddenly leaned forward and Holly instinctively pulled back. "What I want to know is why people continued to work with him if he was such a bastard?"

Her eyes flashed, the first real display of anger escaping

her cool businesslike facade. "I don't know. Why do people still work for you?"

The air stilled.

Holly's breath hitched as her stomach plummeted. She'd done it now, offended the great Jake Vance to the soles of his imported leather shoes. With a pounding heart, she braced herself for the icy reprimand, a potent display of authority designed to put her right back into her place. Instead...

He smiled.

And what a smile it was.

Amusement creased his eyes, softening his jawline and bringing forth a dimple to his cheek. A dimple. As if the man didn't have enough swooning power over the female population. It transformed his striking, almost harsh, features into something warm and touchable.

"I find it very interesting," he murmured, "that I irritate you so much. Is it about the way I do business?"

"No," she lied.

"So it's personal."

She blinked nervously. He was close but not close enough to invade her space. Yet she could sense the warmth from his broad, impeccably suited body, the single-minded focus as his eyes freely roamed over her face, coming to rest at a spot dangerously close to her mouth.

She tried to swallow but it felt like dust clogged her throat. "I'm just here to do my job, Mr Vance."

"Really."

His scepticism irritated: it was obvious he trusted her as much as she did him. Still, she met his considering look with one of her own, willing calm into every inch of her humming body. "Yes. Shall we get back to your investment, Mr Vance?"

"Jake." In an echo of his movements in the Blackstone's basement, he pulled his phone out and checked the screen. "I need to know how the family interacts," he said as he pushed a few buttons. "I'm not going to invest in Blackstone's if they can't control their in-fighting. And then there's Matt Hammond, a man who's publicly and repeatedly voiced his hatred of Blackstone's and who now owns ten percent of the shares."

Holly paused, see-sawing between honesty and loyalty. This was another test. He already knew the answers but wanted to see how far she'd go.

Damn the man.

"You know the Hammonds and Blackstones have a long and tragic history," she said tightly to his impassive face. "Yes, Marise used to work for Blackstone's. Yes, she married into the one family Howard despised. And on her death—"

"Ursula's jewellery and diamonds went to Matt and Marise's son, Blake." Almost as if bored with the interrogation, he studied the passing traffic as they exited the Harbour Bridge. "But one diamond's still out there."

"Still lost," Holly conceded, stopping before she added, *just like James Blackstone.*

Lost.

A strange shiver brushed over Jake's skin, like the fingers of a dead woman grazing his conscience.

A lost diamond. A missing Blackstone.

The awful comparison sneaked into his head and lingered as he absently rubbed his arm where his so-called mother had dug in her fingers, the death grip from that frail hand suddenly sharp, astute.

Don't hate me, Jake. Her eyes had taken on a fevered

quality, wide in her sunken face. *I wanted you so much. I love you more than anything.*

And now here he was. Not lost any more. So why did he still feel like some shipwreck survivor adrift on the sea?

Two hours later, a pregnant Jessica Cotter Blackstone had met Jake and Holly at the back door to the exclusive Blackstone's Sydney store and guided them to a private showing room.

Holly shifted in her chair and recrossed her legs. Up until now, she'd always liked this room for its ample, airy space. But with Jake sitting so close, even the long glass-topped mahogany display table wasn't sufficient to ward off the strange little buzzes zapping her body.

She glanced to her right, to the huge photo of Briana Davenport above a display cabinet. Dubbed the Face of Blackstone's, the model was glancing into the camera over one shoulder, a sensual smile on her lips, drop diamonds shining from her ears, matching the sparkle in her gorgeous eyes. Holly had seen Jessica look at the picture when they'd first arrived, then apologetically at Jake. He'd merely shrugged, but Holly had watched the way his attention lingered on the stunning face of his former flame.

She shook her head. The man had dated practically every available, gorgeous socialite in Sydney. He was a confirmed bachelor. A confirmed serial dater, her all-knowing flatmate Miko would say with a toss of her jet-black hair. Jake had proved her rich man–supermodel theory in spades when he'd taken up with Briana. With the press alluding to marriage at one stage, it must have cut the man's ego deeply when she'd thrown him over for millionaire lawyer Jarrod Hammond who was also, ironically, Matt Hammond's brother. Jake had been suspiciously absent from the spotlight in the weeks that followed...unlike the Blackstones, with their undeserved trials and tribulations.

More than once her mind had lingered on the comparison between AdVance Corp and Blackstone's. Just like Howard, Jake Vance had started from nothing. But where Jake was a lone wolf, Howard Blackstone and his family had created a dream, nurturing it into the multibillion-dollar business it was today. Despite that success, people had loved to hate Howard Blackstone. There was that something in Jake Vance, too, something that made her quake. It was the same ruthlessness, the cold look in their eyes. Even Max, with his skilled ability to diffuse the most volatile of arguments, wasn't exempt from Howard's displeasure. And like Howard, once crossed, nothing short of total destruction would satisfy Jake Vance. She had no doubt if you incurred the man's displeasure, you'd know about it.

So what will he do to you when he finds out you're nothing more than a corporate spy?

Her heart, already pounding with nervousness, started to throb in earnest. *If he found out. If.*

Jessica finally returned with a velvet tray and Holly determinedly ignored the flutter of helplessness starting in her belly. Instead, she watched Jake, who was concentrating intently on Jessica as she explained the cutting process, the rarity of pink diamonds and alluvial deposits. When she referenced something in the store brief she'd prepared, he looked down at the document and Holly became all too well aware of his hair as it slid over his forehead. It was too long to be called a military cut, too short to be completely unconventional.

It looked clean. Shiny. She resisted the sudden urge to lean forward and sniff. Instead she remained still, only half-surprised that her breath quivered on the way in.

His tall, commanding presence, so supremely confident in an expensive dark grey suit, had her itching to scoot her chair back to the outer edges of her comfort zone. He might be an arm's length away, but she was too close to escape the aura that radiated from him like some kind of will-numbing drug.

Jake shook off the tiny prickles of sensation from Holly's scrutiny and deliberately focused on the tray of diamonds before him. As Jessica turned a huge yellow-stoned ring deftly into the light, it created a kaleidoscope of rainbow shards across the room. So this was the fuel for Howard's obsession. If he'd been hoping for answers in the multifaceted polished depths, he was disappointed.

"Blackstone's is famous for our candies," Jessica said, replacing the ring and picking up a blue-stoned bracelet set in silver. "Pale-canary to deep-sun yellow. Pinks, blues, greens. If I know Holly, she's already told you about our wares."

Jake zoomed back in on his too-silent assistant and directed his question at her. "How much are pink diamonds worth?"

He noted the way she shoved back her hair, the jerky movement containing an underlying tension. Yet her eyes were as sharp and clear as the gemstones he'd been viewing. "At a 2004 Sotheby's auction, a 351 round 1.23 intense purplish pink went for just over a hundred and forty-three thousand dollars a carat. Minimum bids started at a hundred thousand dollars a carat."

"So something like—say, the Blackstone Rose, would be…?"

"The four round trillion-cut diamonds were seven carats

each, the pear-shape center, ten. At the time it was worth millions. Today…who knows?"

The cool and matter-of-fact way she imparted that information intrigued him. He'd never known a woman to be so calm when discussing the glorious brilliance of a priceless gem. She'd been more into Blackstone history than what made Howard a dizzying financial success.

In the small space of a day she'd piqued his interest, both physically and mentally.

"Try it on." Jessica grinned at Holly, forcing Jake's attention back to the tray of diamonds spread before him like party trinkets.

When Holly smiled he got the feeling this was a familiar scenario for the two women. He watched her finger the blue sapphire solitaire, running her thumb pad almost reverently over the square gem on a gold band, surrounded by tiny diamonds. In the background, Jake heard Jessica recounting some statistics about diamond mining but, at this moment, Holly commanded his attention.

Slowly, sensuously, she slid the ring over her knuckle, until it came to rest at the base of her finger.

An image burst forth, unwilling, unbidden. Holly wearing that ring and not much else.

His throat suddenly became drier than the Great Sandy Desert.

"That's bad luck, you know," he murmured. Her eyes shot to his as he clarified. "Putting a ring on your wedding finger without a proposal."

She paused, obviously testing her retort, until Jessica answered with a laugh. "Don't tell me you believe in old wives' tales, Jake?"

"My mum swore by them."

Jessica's expression turned sympathetic. "I'm sorry about your mother."

He waved her apology away and instead picked up a pink diamond.

Holly quickly placed the ring back on the tray as her senses registered the faint teasing smell of Jake's cologne. She didn't want to look, shouldn't look, but somehow, she found herself engulfed in those intelligent green eyes. Too eagerly, her body leaped in response. Warmth started in the pit of her belly, heating as it unfurled and spread. *Oh, my.*

His eyes skimmed her face, betraying nothing but cool perusal. If she hadn't seen the spark of heat in his eyes that morning, she would've said he was a damn robot.

Do not think about that. Think about your mission.

She followed his movements as he picked up one stone, then another. Yeah, she was a regular Mata Hari all right, trying to uncover the deep dark secrets of Mr Midas Touch himself. As if she'd find anything that wasn't already in the public domain.

As if there'd be anything out there he hadn't already personally vetted and approved.

The problem was, she realised as they left the store, Jake was rapidly becoming so not what she'd expected. He'd greeted the heavily pregnant Jessica warmly, pulling over a comfy one-seater for her instead of the harder official viewing chairs. He'd silently flicked through Jessica's brief of the store, asked intuitive questions about the stones and the staff. And why had he wanted to see the diamonds? It didn't matter what a bunch of gemstones looked like. It was Blackstone's ability to make money that mattered. If selling cow dung turned a profit the man would be interested.

She stared out the car window, at the mounting peak-hour traffic. She needed to remember that Jake Vance was a ruthless man. She'd read about his famed decisiveness, his superior negotiation skills, all borne from his meteoric rise from the ashes following false accusations from Jaxon Financial's CEO. One interviewer in particular wasn't impressed by Jake's success, labelling him as "autocratic, cold and poisonously polite."

Jake had the ability to destroy people in so many different ways that it took her breath away. That should be enough to turn her off. So why did her brain have to act so damn... *female* when he was around?

As if sensing her thoughts, he glanced at her.

Their gazes clashed and for a second she felt a brief flicker of scalding heat before— Yep, there came the shutdown just before he returned to the brief.

Now he was just plain irritated. As if she was the last person in the world he wanted to see.

Yeah, I know how that feels.

Her phone suddenly rang, cutting off her thoughts.

With a soft groan, she noted the number. "I need to take this. Excuse me." Without waiting for Jake's acquiescence, she angled herself towards the window and took the call.

Minutes later, as her mother's bank manager spelled out the dire straits of her predicament, Holly's stomach dipped. The brief feeling of nausea was quickly followed by an irrational wave of injustice. Here she was, in the midst of almost obscene wealth, while her parents were struggling with the fallout of one stupid business decision.

The faint tinge of guilt roiled in her stomach as she clicked off the call. If only she hadn't been a typically selfish teenager, nagging her parents to sell… But now she had to be the strong one and take care of them.

Her breath came out in a whoosh. *I need to keep my job, which means spying on Jake Vance.*

She stared out the window, at the passing traffic along George Street, a constant reminder of the realities of who she was and what she'd done and what she needed to do to keep her reputation and her family safe.

Jake stared at the document on his lap until he realised he'd been reading the same paragraph five times. During her mystery call, he'd noticed her tense and bow her head. After a few hushed whispers, she'd shoved a hand through her hair and paused. He caught "money," "payment" and "default" before she finally hung up.

Suspicion arrowed through him like a bolt from heaven. He opened his mouth to say something but suddenly pulled himself short. Her shoulders were hunched in a position he'd seen too many times before. Defeat.

He caught a faint sound. A sigh? No. It was a shuddery intake, almost as if she were trying to draw strength on a breath but failing abysmally. That small vulnerability, hitting below the belt and tightening his chest in a fierce irrational rush of emotion threw him for a six.

Against all logical reasoning, he lifted a hand, but just as quickly, he forced it back to the brief with a thump.

His small movement shattered the air and Holly whirled. "Sorry about that." She shoved away a stray curl as the now-familiar polite smile spread her mouth briefly. "Where were we?"

"Your hair."

"What?"

He flicked a finger towards her head. "Your clip's come loose."

"Oh."

She yanked back her hair, a gentle flush spreading across the high curves of her cheeks. Jake couldn't hide his amusement, which faltered when a sudden unbidden thought flashed through his head. *How would she look, hair loose and spread out on my pillow?*

At the store, when she had picked up that blue ring, he'd seen a glimpse of something in her gaze. Longing. Wanting. As if she desperately needed but knew she couldn't have.

His attention flickered back over her face, taking in her profile, that small mole hidden from his view. There was nothing he couldn't have. Nothing he'd been denied.

Desire cleaved his gut, sharp and urgent. Despite the tight rein on his control, he smiled.

It was a smile bereft of humour. A smile full of grudging admission.

He wanted Holly. At least, his body wanted her and generally, what he wanted, he got. But this time…

After years of business decisions based on a combination of solid facts and honed sixth sense, his gut feeling failed him right now. And in the absence of that, he had to go with what his past had taught him.

Stay away.

"It's after five. I'll take you home," he said curtly.

She shook her head. "That won't be necessary."

"It's not a problem."

Holly crossed her arms with a soft sigh, realising arguing would be futile in the face of his cool determination.

Ten minutes later, they were in front of her apartment

building and he'd rounded the car to open her door. When he offered his hand, she hesitated only briefly before taking it.

Bad decision, she told herself. Bad, bad, bad.

After he helped her exit she just stood there, her fingers still engulfed in his. He commanded her attention, unwillingly, effortlessly.

If the May night air held a chill, Holly couldn't feel it. Instead, the heat of him sucked all the breath from her lungs, leaving her heart jumping merrily along in anticipation. He was staring down at her with those piercing, almost analytical eyes, their bodies too close for her comfort. For one insane second, the romantic in her imagined him leaning in for a goodbye kiss on the cheek but she quickly dismissed the fanciful thought with a blink. *Didn't stop you wanting it, though, did it?*

She eased her hand from his warm grip and just like that, the moment shattered. As he stepped back, the night air whooshed into the void, sending a shiver over her skin.

"What's your phone number?" he asked.

"Why?"

Amusement tweaked his lips into a shadowy smile. "In case I need to call you."

She felt the hot flush of embarrassment across her cheeks as she reeled off her mobile number and he punched it into his phone.

"Steve will pick you up at seven tomorrow. We'll be flying to an appointment in Lighting Ridge," Jake said, pocketing his phone. At her look of confusion, he added, "To check on a new complex I'm building."

"You don't delegate?"

"Some things I choose not to." He leaned against the car,

a nonchalant gesture that oddly suited him. "Have a good night, Holly."

Jake watched as she walked up the pathway to her apartment, her back ramrod straight, her hips swaying in that deliciously tantalizing way. When she unlocked the door, turned to him with a nod and disappeared inside, his smile fled.

It was time to find out just who Holly McLeod was.

Three

"The crisis center was your mother's idea," Holly casually stated as they boarded the Cessna on their way back to Sydney the next afternoon.

"Yes," he said, nodding to the flight attendant and handing him his coat.

"I'm sorry for your loss, Mr Vance."

He'd heard those simple words a thousand times in the past few weeks, yet instinctively he knew Holly meant them.

"My mother was committed to causes," he acknowledged as he eased into the black leather seat.

"So I heard. You must have been very proud of her." He gave a non-committal answer then said, "Better strap yourself in." She nodded and went to her seat further down the aisle.

Pride wasn't the first thing that came to mind when he thought of April Vance Kellerman these days. He'd buried her last month, what now seemed a lifetime ago. Unbidden, the past crowded his head with the suppressed memories his mother's shocking confession had stirred to the surface. An urgent, whispered confession that he'd put down to the pain-killers. The confession of a dying woman who'd been living a lie. One that had suddenly taken on malevolent form.

The only reason she'd confessed was fear—fear of being discovered. If Howard's investigator hadn't been so dogged in his pursuit, crossing state lines on the strength of specula-tion and hearsay to finally end up in Jake's hometown, he had no doubt he'd still be in the dark about his true parentage.

He balled a fist and thumped it gently on the cold glass window. Like water from a cracked cup, the resentment seeped out, leaving a deep, dark emptiness in its wake.

Everything he knew, everything he'd based his life on was a lie. Yet so many things, so many oddities he'd never questioned clicked into place: Why they'd lived like nomads, shifting across state lines. Why family was never mentioned. And the night-mares that had finally stopped when he was ten years old.

Jake sighed and allowed himself that moment of grief and guilt. The two powerful emotions mingled to form a hard black lump in his gut. If he took any more time, he'd be forced to look long and hard at every choice, every decision April had made that had shaped his life.

Reluctantly he acknowledged a simple fact: April's death had hit way too close to home. He'd already begun to reassess his life after her funeral, to silently question just who he was and what he was doing. The inevitable shadows of death had touched him deeply, the painful, scary vulnerability it wreaked forcing him to re-evaluate his ten-year plan.

That plan was close to completion: he had everything money could buy and then some. Everything the Blackstones had been born into, everything April had lacked. After this Blackstones fiasco was behind him, he could fully commit to the last on his list—get himself a wife and start a family.

He glanced back to Holly. She was staring out the window with a pair of headphones on, studiously concentrating on the tarmac as they taxied down the runway. And just like that, his whole body tightened, forcing a surprised breath from his throat.

With mounting irritation he silently admitted his plan to intimidate her—and by default, the Blackstones—with an overt display of wealth had backfired. He'd wanted Blackstone's to be clear on exactly who they were dealing with, and what he could do if crossed. But it surprised him how calmly she took everything in her stride, from the early flight in his top-of-the-line ten-seater Cessna to his subtle commands that had them winging their way back to Sydney a few hours later. She hadn't missed a beat, answering his blunt questions with accuracy, waiting patiently while he signed off on the multiplex center.

This girl from the bush fit right into his million-dollar world as if born to it. And she was tempting, his little Blackstone's assistant, with her snug business skirts and touch-me shirts. His groin ached in sudden painful remembrance of last night. She'd invaded his dreams and got under his skin in a way other women hadn't. It was part desire, part knowledge of the unknown. Was she a spy? Did she have an agenda? Perversely, not knowing excited him even more.

He scowled, looking but not seeing the runway flash by as they picked up speed and launched into the air with a flourish.

If he wasn't careful, his fascination would become a weakness. He'd been stupid enough to allow one woman to break his heart then let another destroy his trust. It wasn't going to happen again.

But damn, he wanted her. Probably, he admitted ruefully, because he shouldn't have her.

His phone rang then, dragging him from those dangerous thoughts.

"How did it go with the Blackstones?" said Quinn by way of greeting.

"How do you think?" Jake muttered, resting the phone on his shoulder while shuffling through the floor plans of the center he'd just inspected. "The DNA sealed it. And now I have a walking, talking Blackstone's billboard to keep tabs on me while giving the hard sell." He eased back in his seat and the leather squeaked in protest.

"Is she cute?"

"Does it matter?" Jake scowled.

"Which means she is."

"So?"

"A guy just needs to know these things."

The tension in Jake's shoulders relaxed an inch. "Right. You're getting soft in your old age, mate," he drawled, his attention fixed out the window, at the huge expanse of drought-stricken land rolling below.

"There's more to life than making money."

"Ahh, another piece of Quinn-wisdom. Next you'll be telling me 'all you need is love.'"

"Maybe all you need is your hot little Blackstone's billboard."

Jake snorted. "Forgotten Mia, have you?"

"Everyone else has. But hey, if you're happy dragging that baggage around with you—"

"I don't have baggage."

"Right." Quinn's frustration crackled down the line. "Lucy. Your stepdad. All those shitty little towns you grew up in. You've got a whole bloody wardrobe, mate."

"Yeah, thanks for that." Jake screwed up his eyes and rubbed the back of his neck. "While I have you here, is there any way of tracking down that missing Blackstone diamond?"

"I'll get onto it straight after I finish building my time machine."

"Smart-ass."

"Laser identification wasn't invented until the early eighties. You'd have a better chance finding Eldorado. And anyway, Matt Hammond…already…me…it."

Jake frowned. "You're breaking up."

The line went dead and with a soft curse, Jake hung up.

Suddenly restless, he rose to his feet and walked the few metres down the plane to where Holly was now studiously scribbling on a spreadsheet.

When he approached she glanced up and quickly shoved a folder across the papers, but not before he caught the heading on the top. Finances.

"A bit early for your tax return," he said mildly, and leaned against the back of seat, crossing his arms.

"I like to get on top of things." She met his eyes almost defiantly and changed the subject. "I've been organising your schedule," she said without preamble. "You've got a four-o'clock meeting with Kimberley, and I've asked our department heads for their last quarterly reports." She offered some papers to him. "I printed out the corporate structure, along with the contact numbers of key Blackstone personnel. After five I'll give you a proper tour of the building."

He stood there, filling the space too well, looking far too comfortable, Holly thought with chagrin. When he leaned in to take the documents, awareness suddenly hit. He smelled warm, musky and expensive. He smelled wonderful.

She surreptitiously glanced at her watch, trying to hide her nervousness, but he caught her look.

"Would you like to join me for lunch?"

His mild question hung in the air but she swore she could see a faint flicker of challenge in his eyes. Ruthlessly she ground out a stab of desire. "No, thank you."

He raised one brow. "Why not?"

"Because I brought my own."

"You'd rather brown bag it than have a proper meal with me?"

She paused, weighing her answer. "Yes."

His short chuckle surprised her. "It's just food, Holly. We'll use a Blackstone's restaurant. And talk business."

She tipped her head, considering him. "Hasn't anyone ever told you no?"

"Not if they wanted to keep their job."

She bristled. "You'd sack me for refusing to eat with you?"

"No." His answering grin did nothing to ease her tension. "Anyway, I can't sack you. You work for Blackstone's."

"And you want to eat with me…why?"

"Maybe I just want your company."

Holly gave an inward groan at the seductive smile stretching his sinful mouth. He might be gorgeous, but she forced herself to remember who he was. Her boss. At least for now.

Regardless of how she felt, she had to see this through.

It'd do no good to stuff this up, not when she'd been backed into a corner.

She gave a curt, imperious nod, not wanting to appear too willing. "Let me make a call."

An hour later they were guided to a private table at the back of Si Ristorante, one of Blackstone's first-floor eateries.

"I'm surprised you have time for lunch, given your schedule," Holly said as the waiter brought them menus.

"I always make time to eat. Good food and a bottle of wine predispose people to generosity. And I also have a weakness for—" his gaze skimmed over her face, settling on a spot a little left to her mouth "—gnocchi."

Flustered, she busied herself with pouring a glass of water from the carafe. "And do you always treat your employees?"

"Who said I'm paying?"

Holly snapped up her eyes to meet his amused ones, and for one incredible second it felt like the world had stopped spinning.

Silly girl, Holly thought dazedly as she looked into those emerald eyes, the edges creased with uncharacteristic humour. The man had a billion reasons to smile, yet not one press clipping showed him happy. Dark, brooding or scowling, yes. Smiling? No.

I wonder why.

"Did you always want to work at Blackstone's?" he asked casually, changing the heated direction of her thoughts.

"No." She took his lead and studied the menu too. "But jobs are hard to come by out west so I moved."

"Where are you from?"

She hesitated, contemplating the wisdom of giving too much information. "You won't know it."

"Try me."

"Kissy Oak." She flushed as his eyes focused on her lips for a second. "It's a small farming community a few miles west of Dubbo."

"A small-town girl," he said softly. "Did you leave any small-town boys behind?"

"Why do you need to know?"

"Just making small talk. Getting to know my assistant."

When he smiled with deliberate charm, Holly's suspicion deepened. The man obviously knew the effect he had on women. Just not this woman.

"Don't you know already, thanks to your crack research team?"

His expression turned shrewd. "Reports don't tell me everything."

She noted the pointed absence of an outright denial and crossed her arms, trying to keep a firm hold on her mounting irritation. "So *you* tell me."

To his credit, he looked her straight in the eye and said calmly, "You were born on the thirtieth of April, 1982 in Dubbo Hospital to Martin and Maureen McLeod. Your twin brother, Daniel, died two days later. Your parents owned McLeod Crop Dusting, serving the farming communities around Dubbo. When you were seventeen, MacFlight bought them out then went bust. You moved to the city, started at Blackstone's in Human Resources and have just finished a Blackstone's-funded degree at university. Your official position is PA to the Human Resources Manager but you're currently filling a temp position with PR. Your mother is living on a government pension and your father on disability."

Holly sucked in a breath as she shut the menu with deliberate slowness. How neatly he'd summed up the emotional
roller coaster of her life, explaining away the past nine years
without sensation or feeling. But she knew better. Jake
couldn't know the gut-wrenching hours at hospital, comforting her hysterical mother while waiting for her dad to come
out of intensive care following a stroke. Then the months of
expensive rehab, no longer covered by their expired health insurance. The day-to-day living expenses of food, electricity,
rates. She'd wrestled with the worry and stress every day
until it was a permanent throb of duty lodged in a tiny corner
of her heart.

She flushed when she was angry, Jake noticed absently,
watching the heat coloring her cheeks a soft shade of pink.
And unfortunately, he also realised that her precarious financial situation put her right at the top of his list of suspects for
the press leak.

She flicked her eyes away, sweeping the restaurant to study
the lunch crowd. But the calculated move couldn't detract
from the struggle he could see warring on her features.

He knew she was aware of his scrutiny. And when he saw
her fingers go to her earlobe and fiddle with the diamond stud
there, he smiled. She wasn't just angry. She was nervous.
Interesting.

"You were working while studying part-time at Shipley
University," he stated.

To her credit, she tempered her annoyance with a small
nod. "Business Management and Marketing."

"You were profiled in the university's journal as an exceptional talent," he said, "after handling that 'sex for grades'
scandal last year."

"That's right."

"So why didn't you take the university's job offer instead?"

Holly blinked. "Blackstone's paid for my education. Why would I take another job? Besides, the university is—" she paused, picking her words with care "—conservative. Dress code, morality clauses—"

"Blackstone's has a morality clause," Jake interjected.

"But only for employees working within the same department. And the pay is more, the opportunities to advance much greater. I also like working here."

His gaze became speculative. "Working full-time and going to university part-time must've played hell with your social life."

"No. I focused on work."

Jake nodded. "So what made you volunteer to assist me?"

"I didn't. I got seconded."

Ahh. Jake placed the menu on his plate. Despite her denials, she was pissed. Enough for a little payback? He did the math in his head. No. The leak had been going on since Christmas, which meant something had happened just before Howard's plane went down.

The waiter arrived to take their orders then, but after the man left, the silence continued.

Determined not to let the unnerving intensity of Jake's study affect her, Holly reached for the bread basket—at exactly the same time Jake did.

Her mouth dropped from the shock of their skin-on-skin contact, her eyes widening. To recover from that surprising little zing, she yanked her hand back.

And there it was again. Why couldn't she shake the feeling

that one day, somehow, if he had his way, they'd be more than boss and assistant?

"Can I ask you something?" she said suddenly.

He eased back in his chair and picked up the water goblet. "You can. But I might not answer."

"How long will you be here?" *How long before I can get my job back, when I can resume a normal life...and I can stop my stomach flipping every time you study me like I'm a particularly interesting puzzle that needs to be unravelled?*

His smile turned mockingly sensual. "In a hurry to get back to Human Resources?"

"No. I'm waiting on my transfer papers to PR."

He paused for a second, his gaze holding her defiant one. In the next, a grudging smile teased his lips.

Holly nearly groaned aloud. Oh, man. The warmth of that one simple smile scorched her like she'd been caught in the pathway of a comet. The heated aftermath spread from her fingertips to the bottom of her black Jimmy Choos, heat of a purely female nature. His smile, combined with the warmth in his voice, was deliberately calculated to disarm her. There wasn't a woman he couldn't charm if he put his mind to it. She'd already witnessed it with Jessica.

Bad, bad move. You don't even like the guy.

Jake watched her fiddle with the stud in her ear again. "You've got something to say," he said casually.

She stilled. "Mr Vance..."

"Jake. It's Jake."

"Jake." She paused, which only heightened the way his name sounded on her lips. Lips that were painted a luscious shade of berry, so very close to that little kissy-mole.

"Kimberley's brief said you're looking to invest in Blackstone's. But I thought AdVance Corp was all about…" She paused, searching for the right word.

"Conquer and divide?" Jake smiled thinly, toying with the stem of his glass. "Don't believe everything you read. I like to see what I'm getting before I invest, to decide if it's worthy of my time and money." At least, that part had started out true. But after last night, when he'd dissected the deeper implications for the tenth time, he'd realised one thing. He was a Blackstone. Just because he hadn't had the privilege of the name for the last thirty-two years didn't mean he should let a successful corporate entity crumble to the ground. He wasn't seventeen any more, running away from the shame of his past. The story wasn't going away and it was within his power to save this company.

Now he said, "I'm looking to expand my options. Blackstone's is an important part of Australian corporate history but has been floundering since January. It's a perfect choice."

"So you have no intention of breaking us up?"

Us. Not "Blackstone's" or "the company". *Us.* As if she was part of a family. His gut clenched. "Hadn't even entered my mind."

The doubt written so clearly on her face got his back up. "Afraid of losing your job, Holly?"

"It's more than just a job to me." She focused on straightening the already perfect cutlery. For one second, Jake thought about defending himself with the truth, but just as quickly reined himself in.

"You don't like me. Why?"

Her head snapped up, showing him a glimpse of something simmering just below the surface. Yet her reply was one in studied control. "I didn't think being liked would matter to a man like you."

"'A man like me'?" he said tightly. It didn't matter. It shouldn't. Damn. Why did her approval suddenly matter at all? "Let me guess. You think I'm just buying another failing company to carve it up and sell it off at a profit, ruining lives and families in the process."

"Are you?"

"That's not what I do."

"No?"

Her scepticism ratcheted his annoyance up a notch. "I've saved more jobs than I've destroyed."

He shouldn't care. Hell, he didn't. But despite that, irritation flared and he suddenly leaned forward, making her jump. "I've publicly refuted every crooked claim, every accusation. But rebuttals don't sell papers—bad press does."

He tightened his jaw, refusing the fury access before pulling back with a disgusted snort. "Go on, name a story."

"I don't…"

"Do it, Holly. Name your damn price if that's what it'll take."

She inched back in her chair as far as she could go before saying quietly, "The East Timor construction company."

"The press said I bought it out and sacked the workers, leaving thousands of families without income. They glossed over the fact it was actually a front for a terrorist group. I dissolved the company and built a school in the local village instead."

They both paused as the waiter brought their food. But as the man left, Jake said curtly, "Next."

"I…"

"You want to know. I'm telling you." He forced his expression into neutrality, revealing nothing. "Next."

She swallowed and suddenly his eyes were drawn to her throat, to the heartbeat that was undoubtedly thumping wildly in her chest. "Paul Bradley."

"My chief financial officer." He picked up his fork, spearing the gnocchi with curt precision. "I demoted him to my Hanoi office because he vocally opposed one of my takeover bids."

Holly's fear suddenly gave way to anger, giving her the strength to face his stare with one of her own. "'Cross me and you'll pay'?"

"Yes. I demand loyalty in my staff. I won't stand any bad-mouthing, especially when he was wrong. I had to make an example of him."

"Was Mia Souris an example too?"

As a dark scowl creased his forehead, she blithely charged on. "She was your secretary and made a mint with her story. Why haven't you made her pay, too?"

"What makes you think she hasn't?"

At her sudden silence, he said softly, "The last I heard she was working as a waitress in a London club, trying to escape the notoriety of her kiss-and-tell article."

He placed his fork on the plate and drew the napkin slowly, almost sensuously, across his mouth. "You are a surprising woman, Holly McLeod."

"Why?" She studied her chicken penne, wondering how she'd manage to keep it down when her belly was churning so much.

"Are you pushing my buttons to get reassigned?"

Astonished, she jolted straight in her chair. "If you're unhappy about my performance, Mr Vance—"

"It's Jake, for Pete's sakes!" His voice then became less harsh. "Say it."

She said slowly, "Jake."

"Much better."

She blinked at the warm languor in his deep voice. "I just want to do my job."

He studied her for the longest time, until she began to wonder if she'd left a bit of food on her mouth or something.

"So let's just agree to focus on our jobs, shall we?" he said softly.

She nodded, suddenly desperate for space. With a low murmur, she excused herself and headed for the bathroom.

While Holly washed her hands at the sink, Jake's suggestion played over in her head. It made perfect sense. Do the job she'd been blackmailed into doing, get what she needed and move on.

If he was here for just an innocent pre-investment visit, then he'd have nothing to hide, right? But if his motives *were* ulterior, then for the sake of Blackstone's, she'd be justified in finding out what they were.

But as she straightened her skirt and rechecked her lipstick, she noticed her worried frown in the mirror. Quickly she smoothed it out. *Yeah, just keep telling yourself that, Holly.*

Jake watched Holly make a beeline for their table but before she could reach him, an impeccably dressed man intercepted her.

She whirled, and her look of surprise, then disgust, registered so clearly that Jake slowly stood. As the man whispered something then glanced over to Jake, her expression smoothed.

She sighed, shrugged and made her way back to the table.

With a frown, Jake remained standing, unashamedly taking advantage of his height against the shorter man. A man who was standing close to Holly. Too close for Jake's liking.

Irrational anger tightened his muscles, shocking the hell out of him. Through his surprise he heard Holly murmur, "Max, this is—"

"Jake Vance," Jake supplied and offered his hand.

Max smiled and returned the shake. "Max Carlton, head of Human Resources."

Ten seconds and Jake had him summed up. Immaculately groomed. Subtly cologned. Even without his intel, he could spot an office player a mile off. It was something in the eyes, the way they shifted and moved, the expression a concentrated effort in politeness. Carlton was too polished, too smooth, and his smile was a blokey smirk that Jake found offensive.

"So how's Holly working out for you, Jake?"

Jake noted Holly's frown. "Fine," he answered smoothly, as if their topic of conversation wasn't standing right next to him.

Max smiled, a man-to-man grin that set Jake's teeth on edge. "My assistant's one of a kind."

"Didn't she move to PR over a year ago?"

Max's face tightened and he glanced quickly at Holly, who gave him an innocent shrug.

"A temporary position," Max conceded stiffly. "If Holly's work performance makes the grade, there could possibly be a permanent transfer."

Jake was so intent on Max's visible unease that he almost missed Holly's start of surprise. Then, with a smooth adjustment to his tie, Max said, "If you've got any personnel or staffing questions, just give me a yell. Holly knows where to find me."

Under a rock, no doubt. Jake caught Max's wink at Holly, who ignored it with a dark frown. But when Carlton's gaze deliberately roamed down her neck to rest on the gentle curve of her breasts, his eyes narrowed. Intimate knowledge or wishful thinking? Either way it didn't stop a lick of fury from sparking in his belly.

Slowly he forced his fists to unclench.

"So…" Max said, tearing his eyes away, "I'd better be going. Nice to meet you, Jake."

Jake glared at Max's retreating back. He had no right to be angry. What Holly did or didn't do on her own time was not his business. She was Jake's assistant, for heaven's sakes, not his lover.

Pity.

Shaking off the jolt that felt like fire on his skin—especially in one particular part—he turned to Holly. "Charming guy."

"Some people think so. I just need his signature on my transfer."

"After you finish with me," he murmured, suddenly taken by the way her skin flushed underneath her cool mask of indifference.

She nodded and finally sat, checking her watch. "Yes. And you have thirty minutes."

"Thirty minutes for what?" He grinned, unable—or was that unwilling?—to keep the suggestiveness from his voice.

She blinked, clearly flustered. "Until your conference call with New York."

He gave her full points for maintaining that composure as they finished their meal in silence. But deep inside, on a purely predatory level, his mind registered the undeniable heat of desire.

Fool. It wasn't his mind that wanted Holly. It was something much more primal.

And what Jake Vance wanted, he usually got.

Four

Jake left his meeting with Kimberley Perrini with newfound respect. Despite his reluctance, Kim still pushed the idea of bringing Holly into their cone of silence. "She was the spin behind the Shipley University scandal, not to mention some of our internal issues. We're lucky to have her," Kim had said.

Grudgingly he had to agree. And if the press started running with pictures of him at Blackstone's, he knew exactly where to lay the blame.

Meanwhile, his security chief was busy compiling a list of enemies and disgruntled employees and their possible sources within Blackstone's. Matt Hammond had been suggested then discarded. No proof, plus the man got his fair share of negative press, too. Shareholders? No, too much to lose.

So he was back once again to a person Howard had personally offended.

And that's where it got confusing. Holly had had no direct contact with Howard. Blackstone's had put her through university. Outwardly, she was passionate about and dedicated to her job. She genuinely liked working here. Yet she was broke and floundering under a mountain of debt, and could still afford rent, food, clothes.

Was she that good an actress?

A shot of heat started low and crept up his body. Hazardous, thinking about Holly McLeod. Because if he did that, he'd have to acknowledge how paper-thin his control was. Instead of quenching his fire, his suspicion only stoked the flames higher, creating a burning need that was slowly dominating his every thought.

You have to stop thinking about her.

With a sharp snap, he opened the file in front of him and focused on Ryan's scrawling signature at the bottom of the page.

Jake leaned back in his chair. Underneath the stubbornness, the pride, he'd sensed Ryan's private pain. Only a close family member could hurt so deeply, scar so indelibly. Ryan refused to toe the line, said what he felt.

There's a lot of me in him.

Jake couldn't go back and change the past. God knows he would've tried years ago. He'd even admitted as much to Ryan. *I can't be angry at the woman who saved my life, who raised me as best she could. Who loved me. A lot of kids don't even get that.*

He'd hit an unexpected nerve with that, judging by the look on Ryan's face. And when he'd offered up the signed statutory declaration, formalizing his verbal promise to keep Blackstone's afloat, surprise had rendered Ryan speechless.

Jake sighed, suddenly tired of justifying something he

himself couldn't explain. Hell, there were a lot of things that would send his legal department into a spin if they only knew. For instance, last night he'd made a nice little profit on the NASDAQ, an event that would've normally brought him the usual adrenaline rush of satisfaction and pleasure. So how come it felt…less than a total rush?

He stood and stalked over to the small kitchenette in the corner of the office, tapping out his impatience as the coffee machine slowly dripped out the expensive Colombian blend.

Finally.

He grabbed the pot, pouring a cup that was one of many that day, forcing away his doubts with the first scalding sip.

You're doing the right thing, keeping a professional distance from the Blackstones. Getting emotionally involved can only mean disaster.

He'd fix Blackstone's, turn it around. That's what he did. He needed to seal this deal, to finish it, so he could get back to his life. A life that suddenly gaped wide, filled with hours of solitary existence.

He frowned and made his way over to the window, staring down at the Sydney CBD. It had changed over the years. He'd been an angry teenager alone in a huge concrete metropolis—a dangerous, exhilarating place for a small-town kid with something to prove. Over the years, through many major developments—some he himself had engineered—Sydney had grown and thrived. It was physical proof of his enormous success. Proof he was no longer the rebellious, stupid kid from the bush.

He sighed. He'd worked hard and long for all he had, steadily erasing that deep dark place in his heart, in his memory. He'd been doing fine until a week ago.

He turned away from the view as he rolled his neck. He needed a distraction. Yet when he glanced back at the financials on the desk, the paper blurred before his eyes. He needed something…warmer.

In the past, sex had taken the edge off, had enabled him to refocus and re-energise. And suddenly, all he could think about was a smart mouth and a kissy-mole.

He shoved his cup across the desk and coffee sloshed over the rim. With a low growl of frustration, he rubbed at the spreading stain.

Damn Blackstone's and its employees. He slouched into his chair and swivelled back to the window, searching for the familiar angles of AdVance Corp past the metallic curve of the Harbour Bridge, but when he found it, a stab of unfamiliar doubt hit him in the gut.

That's stupid. Amateur. Irrational. He'd made billions. He regularly dealt with Middle-Eastern kings and oil barons, dined with the cream of society, both here and overseas.

You're so far out of their league, you're off the planet.

He squeezed his eyes shut, so tight that silver spots danced behind his lids. There was no way those old fears were going to psyche him out.

They're Aussie royalty, and you're just the bastard son of an alcoholic mother.

Jake clenched his teeth and shoved those insidious doubts back with a vicious curse. His stepfather had chipped away at his self-esteem for years, always there with a comment, a sneer, a put-down when Jake screwed up. "You'll be in jail or dead by eighteen, boy," was his favourite line. He'd finally stood up to the son of a bitch a week before he'd left, leaving the man with a black eye and a broken hand. Since then, he'd been on his own, determined not to depend on anyone.

And now, suddenly, he had these people relying on him to make the right decision. To save their family legacy. A family that had been stolen from him thirty-two years ago.

Bitterness tightened his chest, the acrid tension weaving up his back to finally settle on his shoulders like a heavy cloak. He remembered too many towns, too many faces, taunting, teasing. April's sad expression, her face once so pretty and alive, suddenly weathered way beyond her fifty-four years. A woman filled with demons, her own personal and painful reasons for keeping a child from his rightful parents. He'd tried to escape his past, little knowing it wasn't his to escape from in the first place, even after every million he made, every deal he brokered, which earned him the respect and security he'd been craving.

"Ready for the grand tour?"

Momentarily disorientated, he snapped his eyes up to Holly standing in the doorway with the ever-present notepad and pen. For a few seconds he allowed himself to drink in her neat little figure, the curve of her cheek, the way her eyes steadily met his perusal. And as he did so, the vibrating bitterness gradually seeped out, leaving him suddenly empty and icy cold.

With a nod of finality, he shut those thoughts down and rose.

An excruciating hour later, Jake's normally tight control was in tatters. They'd gone through every floor in Blackstone's and he'd spent precisely sixty-two minutes in Holly's orbit, her gentle fragrance alternately arousing and frustrating him. Her soft, animated voice had tripped over his senses, aided traitorously by the memory of that kissy-mole when her mouth curved into a smile. When she walked, he'd ashamedly found his attention riveted to those curvy hips, swaying one tantalizing step ahead of him.

And her smell… He'd breathed in deeply, guiltily, more than once. Since when had a woman smelled so damn good?

The only time he'd not been thinking about touching her was when they'd passed Howard's trophy wall. Photos of the man opening the Blackstone's store. At some formal function. Shaking hands with the Prime Minister, the Queen, four U.S. past-presidents.

Jake had barely been able to contain a sneer. Howard had loved putting his stamp on everything he owned, flaunting his wealth and power. Like the way he'd displayed it on Ursula's neck.

Disgust bubbled up and with a scowl he choked it back down. He was not like Howard, despite Kimberley's assertion.

"Let's move on."

He jumped at Holly's soft intrusion, only to have his body react on a more primitive level when his eyes focused on her curves once again. The grey pinstriped skirt moulded her hips, emphasising a defined waist and womanly hips. Her shirt was bright blue, making her eyes stand out, the elbow-length sleeves showing off long arms with a watch on one wrist, a simple gold bangle on the other.

Absently he'd wondered if she had on any makeup at all, given how fresh her face looked. How touchable it looked.

He shoved his hands deep into his pockets and nodded. He imagined Holly taking the news about his real identity with outward calm, a facade that covered up the fact she was a deep thinker. He'd noticed more than once the realities of her thoughts clearly mirrored in her expressive blue eyes.

No, not blue, more green. Like the complexity of shades in the deep ocean, where the—

His thoughts screeched to a halt. Since when had he obsessed about a woman's eyes before?

Yet despite his control, an unwanted ache started in his groin. An ache that couldn't be ignored when, an hour after the tour was over, Jake shoved his way into Blackstone's executive gym.

Instead of solitude, a stretching Holly on the treadmill confronted him, scattering all thoughts of a long hard run to clear his mind.

He stared. And stared. In short bike pants and a cropped sports top, she was gripping one tanned muscular leg behind her in a quad stretch, the white Lycra pulling tight across her breasts as they rose with her deep breaths. As his mouth went dry, she rolled her shoulders and her long ponytail dragged over her damp skin.

Her breath sighed out, quickly engulfing his brain, the part that was still functioning.

His bag dropped unheeded to the floor. She kept right on stretching, her shoulder blades flexing and contracting with the effort.

Swish of the hair.

Deep sigh.

He groaned, ready to beat a hasty retreat, but she must have sensed him because she whirled, pulling out her earbuds. She quickly dropped her leg and grabbed her towel, her chest rising as a trickle of sweat ran down her throat and disappeared in the cleft beneath her damp tank. He followed that journey, until he reluctantly dragged his eyes back up to meet hers.

"Leaving?" he murmured.

"Yes." In record time, she pulled a sweatshirt over her head then scooped up her bag, quickly heading for the door.

He just stood there, the air as she hightailed it past him yawning cold and empty. Then he heard the door click with finality.

As the gym doors closed behind her, Holly wrapped her arms around her body to ward off the chill. *Escape first, then put on your track pants.* She thought she'd nearly succeeded until Jake appeared beside her.

"Yours," he said gruffly, holding out her iPod. She paused, glanced at his hand, then up at his face. A blank, stern face devoid of all warmth.

She slowly took her iPod and couldn't help but notice he relinquished it without making skin contact. "Thanks." She turned back to the elevator, repositioned her bag on her shoulder and stared at the ascending floor numbers.

When he remained still, she shot a quick look in his direction. "Working late?"

"This is early for me."

She smiled thinly but said nothing.

"But…?" he prompted.

"Don't you ever take a day off?"

He shrugged. "Too much work to do."

"What's the point of making all that money if you can't enjoy yourself?"

He frowned. "I'm not unhappy with what I've achieved, Holly. Money doesn't make you miserable."

"No. People do that all by themselves." The elevator doors swung open, signalling the end to their strange conversation. But to Holly's surprise he followed her in. The doors swished closed and in the next second, he pushed the stop button.

"And to answer your question, I enjoy myself plenty."

She stilled, her breath rattling around, too harsh in her throat, her heart beating too loudly in her chest. She looked at him, noting his narrowed eyes, the sudden tension in his body as it practically sizzled…not with anger but something else, something indefinable that he struggled to contain.

Apprehension chugged through her body, leaving her immobile. Wasn't he supposed to be ice cold in the face of adversity?

Then he fixed on her mouth and she felt a hot flush start in her belly and fan upwards. She parted her lips, the air in her lungs thickly seeping out. Was he actually thinking about kissing her?

He moved quickly, so smoothly for a man the size of Ayers Rock that it took the rest of her breath away. Or maybe it was the kiss stealing all her will to function properly. It froze her limbs, stuttered her heartbeat. Erased all the memories of other kisses that had come before.

When his hot mouth covered hers in deep possession, his hands buried in her hair, preventing escape, a low groan escaped her. The kiss, the sheer power and force of it, stole her will, along with any denials she may have entertained. All that existed was Jake and the force of his kiss, the utter command of his lips sliding over hers and his tongue invading her mouth.

She took a deep, shuddering breath as her eyes fluttered closed. His smell was so different from anything she'd experienced, the heat, the passion. When his hands cupped her face, holding her in place, Holly kissed him right back.

* * *

It did Jake in, finally having her lush mouth beneath his, that tiny mole teasing the corner, his to kiss. The mole that had distracted him time and again for hours on end.

Her skin scorched him, as if a furnace burned just below the surface. Suddenly the desire to have her naked, to be against the rest of that silken skin, crashed into him.

His hands were under her sweatshirt and he hit what he was seeking—hot, damp flesh. But like an addict craving more, he wasn't satisfied with the mere touch of her skin, the feel of her rib cage under his questing hand. He wanted—needed—more.

With his blood pounding thickly in his veins, the ache in his groin an almost unbearable tightness, he found the edge of her tank top and eased his way under to the gentle curve of one breast.

Her sudden gasp snapped him back to reality, and he wrenched his mouth away from the temptation of hers.

What the hell are you doing?

From a great gaping distance he heard Holly's breathless question, thick with passion.

"Jake?"

She'd never know how difficult it was to withdraw from the pleasures her body promised. How much he ached to succumb to the raging passion that forced beads of sweat to run down his back.

Desire grabbed at him, yanked and twisted his brain until he was left hot, hard and frustrated. But with a shuddering sigh, he withdrew and stepped back, the cool air rushing into the gaping chasm between their bodies.

"Pull your shirt down," he said, knowing it came out more

harshly than he intended when the light of desire flickered and died on Holly's face.

Self-disgust filled him, quickly followed by guilt. He'd lost control. For the first time in years he'd lost it.

He wanted to reach out to her, offer some kind of apology, but if her crossed arms and steely back were any indication, he'd have a better chance of flying to the moon.

Slowly, he released the emergency stop button and with a sudden jerk, the elevator started up. "I'll take you home."

She shot him an incredulous look. "I'm not your responsibility, Jake. I can catch a cab."

"Look," he said slowly, turning to her. "We…"

"Jake, I understand." She refused to meet his eyes as the elevator doors slid open. "It's not a big deal."

Jake stared at her retreating back, the words stuck to the roof of his mouth. Not a big deal? So how come he suddenly felt the urgency to taste her right now? To have those shapely legs wrap around his waist and feel the erotic glide as he buried himself deep inside her?

Dammit. Now he was hard again.

With a soft curse, he pressed the basement button before he did something even more foolish than what he'd just already done.

As the morning sun crept cautiously into her bedroom, Holly lay staring at the ceiling. What on earth had possessed her to kiss Jake Vance? The implication sent a wave of cold reality over her hot skin. They'd been about to… She shook her head. And how she had wanted to. Still wanted to.

It shouldn't be. He stood for everything she despised, everything that had taken away her family and forced her into this spying role. But when she tried summoning up righteous anger all that emerged was an overwhelming mesh of confusion. It happened every time he glanced her way, ran that frankly sensual gaze over her face, let it linger on her mouth.

Despite her best efforts, she was acutely interested in him. How could she be so attracted if he was truly the bad guy everyone was intent on perpetuating?

You're an intelligent woman, Holly McLeod. Apart from one obvious glitch, you can tell the good guys from the bad. Yet Jake was a study in extremes. Corporate raider or saviour? Genuine attraction or predatory lust? He'd gotten her so wound up she didn't know what to believe any more.

Deep in thought, she walked slowly into the bathroom, and by the time she'd fixed her makeup and left for work, her bad mood had been replaced by the day's schedule.

She walked into Blackstone's foyer with a sigh of relief. With coffee in one hand, handbag in the other, she'd survived the early morning bustle of George Street and a sharp biting wind that had determinedly yanked at her coattails. But after she pushed the elevator button and the doors opened, her luck ran out.

Jake Vance. In the flesh. In the warm, heated, taut flesh that she knew felt, smelled, tasted divine.

"Good morning, Holly."

The warm intimacy of his voice, combined with the small interior swamped her, leaving goose bumps on her skin.

"Good morning." She repositioned her cappuccino while hitching her bag on her shoulder.

As the elevator sped smoothly upwards, she surreptitiously eyed him. Twice she started to say something, and twice she hesitated, swallowing the words on the tip of her tongue. Surely he'd say something about last night, even just to set her straight with a familiar *It didn't mean anything. Let's just keep things professional.*

Yet he remained silent, reading his newspaper in complete and utter concentration. As she stared at his firm grip on the pages, her brain flashed back to last night, to this same place, to those long skilful fingers. The way they'd teased. The way he'd touched her as his tongue had eased inside her mouth.

She swallowed a shocked gasp, snapping her focus back to the doors.

"Do you have anything specific on the agenda today?" She forced cool professionalism into her voice. Unfortunately, her idea of broaching a business-related topic only effectively made her the center of his attention.

His slow perusal of her was thorough and hot. She tried to ignore it but on every level, her body tingled with the attention. Instead she determinedly stared at the ascending numbers. *Surely if you don't look at him, he'll lose his effect. Like a solar eclipse.*

"I have meetings," he said. "Look, Holly. About last night."

And here it comes. Holly shook her head, hot embarrassment flooding her cheeks as the doors slid open. Quickly she strode out, escaping the warm intimacy that reminded her of last night. He followed closely. "You don't need to—"

"It was—"

The both paused awkwardly as Holly unlocked the glass door until she blurted out, "It doesn't matter. Really."

His eyes narrowed, darkening. "Doesn't it?" he challenged. "I think it matters more than you want to admit."

"How would you know?" She tried for nonchalance as she walked in and placed her coffee carefully on the desk.

"Because I know how to read people. You were an eager participant in that kiss."

She flushed. "Is that how you win—by figuring out what people want then turning it against them?"

"I present them with an offer they can't refuse."

On another man, the arrogance would have forced a sharp, scornful rebuttal from her lips. On Jake, there was no egotism or conceit. It was simply a statement of truth.

She tipped her head. "So there's nothing you've wanted that you couldn't have."

Danger. She sensed it the very moment Jake's eyes darkened. The air seemed to thicken, and the seconds ticked by on the clock so loudly they echoed the beat of her heart as it upped tempo.

"I still have…things I want to achieve."

She finally dragged her eyes away, unable to bear the intensity in his any longer. It was like a promise, a weird prediction of the future, of her and him together. Completely.

"What about a wife? A child to leave all your wealth to?"

"Eventually." A stab of emotion, totally unexpected, tightened his jaw for one brief second. Then he blinked and his signature expression of cool blankness took over.

So he had thought about that. And letting her know irritated him, for some reason. Why? Did he view it as some kind of weakness? Or… She swallowed a small guilty breath. Did Mia's betrayal still affect the unfeeling Mr Midas Touch?

After he closed his office door, Holly suddenly realised they'd both avoided discussing the implications of last night. And that non-closure worried her.

Five

Any normal girl would be out on a date Saturday night, Holly muttered to herself as she walked into Blackstone's, bravado propelling her forward. Not at work, spying on her boss. Not sneaking around, trying to uncover Jake's big plot to bring down Blackstone's.

As the elevator sped up to the top floor, Holly recalled the past hour. Kimberley had offered her two tickets to the Alex Perry fashion show at the Powerhouse Museum as compensation for pulling her from the preparations. Sitting through the traditional bridal theme closing with gorgeous women strutting about in stunning white gowns wasn't exactly what Holly had in mind to occupy her thoughts. Then she'd spotted Jake in the front row and her evening had suddenly ratcheted up in the interesting column.

He was seated next to one of Blackstone's prominent shareholders, engaged in deep conversation, when some sixth sense must have told him he was being watched. He glanced up and pinned her with his dark gaze.

Her clothes had suddenly felt constrictive. She may as well have been naked sitting there, the off-the-shoulder wrap-around designer blouse providing absolutely no coverage whatsoever.

He had no right to stare at her like that. And less right to make her feel…hot. Bothered.

Aroused.

She rose quickly, murmured something about fresh air to Miko, her surprised flatmate, and made her way to the exit. Strobe lights flashed behind her, loud music throbbed low and sensual, but she kept right on walking—even when she realised that Jake had a perfect view of her backside clad in skintight black velvet hipsters. Another brilliant decision gone horribly wrong.

She was waiting in line at the open-air bar, eyeing the congregation of smokers on her left, when a man broke free from the group and strode over.

Max.

A wave of cigarette smoke reached her before he did and burnt her nostrils. She barely suppressed a cough of distaste as he crossed his arms on the bar next to her, bumping his shoulder into hers.

"What are you doing here?" she said and angled away.

"Socializing. Having a few drinks. Keeping an eye on you. You've been avoiding me."

Ignoring his oh-so-charming smirk, she reached for her glass but quickly recoiled when Max reached it first.

He frowned. "Holls, don't be like that."

She just scowled and pulled the glass back, wine slopping over the rim as she resisted the overwhelming desire to clock him with it.

"Jake's getting to you, huh?"

She gritted her teeth, praying for control. "Haven't you got someone else to blackmail, Max?"

Max laughed an unpleasant bark. "Watch it, Holls. It's not just me who's got something to lose here."

"*You* were the one sleeping around. *You* were the one who offered me up as Jake's assistant. And you—"

"And you were the one who didn't say no to sex on my desk. We had a good time, Holly. Admit it—you got off on the whole 'secret and forbidden' thing."

Disbelief rendered her speechless. She didn't know what was worse, her raging stupidity for ignoring Blackstone's morality clause, or her naivety for thinking she'd be any different from the rest of Max's women.

It was those innocent choirboy looks, complete with a mop of golden curls that made Max Carlton such a hit. The men liked him for his after-hours drinks and blokey talk about football and women. The women were flattered by his charm and good looks. And to her surprise, there'd been a spark of interest despite the unofficial gossip. He was an attractive smooth-talker and everyone knew it, especially Max Carlton.

So you fell for it and now he's got you over a barrel. Way to go, Holly.

"What do you want?" Before she could blink, he took her arm and steered her across the courtyard to a dark corner.

She wrenched from his grip, her breath coming quick and angry. Thank goodness for public places. Past him, she noticed the caterer's tables, the half-dozen people setting up for the hungry masses.

"What have you found out?"

"Nothing," she said, disgust clogging her voice. "Jake Vance is above board on this one."

Max smiled thinly. "We're talking about the same guy, right? Men like Vance don't just waltz into a company with good intentions. They destroy them."

"He's not here for a takeover. And I'm sure Ric or Ryan would have—"

Max snorted. "They're too busy playing happy families. Vance has 'em fooled. Listen." He stepped closer, an intimidating figure in the half-shadows. "I've got a good thing going at Blackstone's and I plan to keep it that way. Just get me proof of Vance's intentions. After I get compensated by the board—"

"You'll sign off on my permanent PR transfer."

"Yeah, sure." He reached out to touch her cheek but she flinched. He narrowed his eyes. "Make no mistake, Holly. If you blab, I'll take you down with me. Whom do you think the board will believe?"

Then he swiftly tipped the glass of wine down her shirt. Holly choked off a squeal and jumped back, too late. The dark wet stain spread rapidly over the chiffon, dripping down her front.

Max looked nonplussed. "Jake's busy chatting up the models. Go back to the office and change. And check out his desk."

The elevators pinged open, startling Holly into the present. The insides of her mouth were arid and scratchy. It was all about Max—his job, his comfort. No thought as to how this corporate espionage went against every decent bone in her body.

She tamped a lid on her emotions. Panic had never solved her problems before; it wouldn't now.

Slowly she walked out, unlocked the glass doors then closed them behind. She'd worked late and on the weekends before, which meant the security guy had suspected nothing amiss. She'd strode into the building with her head held high, even tossing him a wave as she walked over to the executive elevator. But now, standing stock still inside the darkened office, trepidation fluttered in her belly.

"Just get changed and leave," she muttered to herself. "You can stall Max another couple of days."

Bolstered, she turned on the desk lamp and laid her key card on the filing cabinet. She checked the hallway then plucked a shirt from her locker and swung open Jake's office door.

She changed in the shadows, and just as quickly, she scanned his desk. The brochures she'd finally managed to give him lay open on the top. She glanced at the financials in his in tray.

No. You can't.

Yet what could she do? It was either help Max or get fired. Despite her desperate need for the money, she genuinely loved working here. She'd carved a niche, made friends and garnered the respect of her colleagues. She prided herself on working hard and being professional, and Kimberley, for one, had noticed that.

So professional you breached your employment contract and had sex with your boss.

She swallowed, fighting with nerves until finally she made a decision. With a determined slant to her mouth, she strode around the desk and tried the drawers. Locked. She shuffled through the papers, flicked open the folders but came up empty-handed.

Holly paused, her mind buzzing. Or perhaps it was the

subtle hint of cologne, all male and all Jake, invading her senses that sent a shock of remembrance through her brain.

Jake's mouth, warm and needy on hers.

Her breath shook on the way in. She stilled, listening in the stillness to the guilty beating of her heart.

It was then that two things caught her attention: a tiny green light coming from the phone recharger on the edge of his desk. And the soft swoosh of the glass door opening in the outer office. He'd come back for his mobile phone.

Panic clogged her throat. *Think, think!* With a held breath she quickly stepped from behind the desk and undid the buttons on her blue silk shirt. It hung open, showing a glimpse of her black satin bra, when Jake opened his office door.

She didn't have to fake a gasp as he swung the door wide. When he zeroed right in on her cleavage, she breathed a sigh of relief. Her smokescreen had worked.

"I spilled wine on my shirt," she hurried to explain. Yet when his eyes dragged over her skin, leaving it practically sizzling in his wake, she self-consciously tugged at the shirt-front, realising the danger of her situation.

His hand stilled on the door handle. Light spilled around the frame, silhouetting his body in stark relief. To her chagrin the shadows also hid his expression. It didn't hide the deep timbre in his soft statement, however.

"Really."

She gestured to the windows covered with blinds. "Your office has coverage. I had a spare shirt in my locker…." She began buttoning it up, suddenly feeling stupid and exposed.

"You left the closing show early?" she asked unnecessarily.

"So did you."

He moved, walking into the small pool of light from the

desk lamp. Shadows slashed across his face, illuminating the darkness and light of his features. An elegantly straight nose. The dark hooded brows. The angular cheekbones combined with a strong, almost glacial jawline.

"Are you really here to change your shirt, Holly?"

"I...I..." *Think, Holly!* Yes? No? Arrghh. Seeing her hope fading gradually away, she leaned back, bumping her bottom on the desk. That small movement commanded Jake's eyes back to her open neckline, lingering. As his eyes dipped into a frown, she caught something else in their depths. Desire.

She held her breath as the room spun.

He drew out the words softly when he spoke. "What are you doing, Holly?"

"I..." Panic had rendered her voice husky, and she cleared her throat before adding lamely, "My shirt."

She tried a smile on for size, one that faltered when he remained silent. *Oh, for heaven's sake!* She drew herself up with all the courage she could muster, fully prepared to walk out if only her legs weren't about to buckle under the weight of her trembling body. She even started forward, getting to within a metre of freedom, but instead of standing aside he remained rooted to the spot, a huge immovable mountain of brooding male.

"Excuse me." She stepped to the side, attempting to boldly brush past. That proved to be her first mistake.

He grabbed her arm, stilling her departure. She opened her mouth to protest but, in doing so, glared up at him. Her second and fatal mistake.

His green gaze blazed down at her like a newly stoked fire, the muscles on his face tightening, his jaw straining with effort.

Retreat proved an impossibility. She'd irrevocably invaded

his comfort zone. Her blood buzzed as he stood there, ramrod straight, her arm firmly in his grip. Her skin burned from the contact, the silk no barrier for his scorching heat. Undeniable tension unfurled from his body as their eyes clashed, warring like two familiar adversaries. He shifted and Holly held her breath. Was he going to…?

When he gave a ragged sigh and abruptly let her go, turning away to shove a hand through his hair, she muffled a small moan of perverse disappointment. She didn't realise he'd heard it until his taut body stilled.

It was as if everything was caught in a freeze frame. The tension in the air practically crackled.

She knew the exact moment he crossed the unspoken line between chaos and control because everything happened all at once. Suddenly. Unexpectedly. With an oath he whirled and crushed her in a deep, punishing kiss.

He ground his mouth into hers, demanding acquiescence, and amazingly, she gave it to him. Heaven help her, she wanted this. Their tongues tangled as a fierce and frenzied passion swelled up inside her. With her damp body plastered to his, his heat quickly soaked through her shirt, sparking off a desperate desire to have him inside her, here and now.

He was made for pleasuring a woman, she realised dazedly as his mouth moved down to her neck and sucked gently. Every touch, every hot breath elicited her abandoned response—a groan, a gasp, a sigh. He approached the task of pleasing her with complete and utter focus, every move determined and skilled. Unlike other men, he seemed finely attuned to her body, knew exactly what to do to have her trembling.

Through a red-hot daze, Holly felt cool air on her body and realised her shirt was on the floor. Before she could take a breath, he'd backed her up against the cold glass door. Freezing glass on her back, hot Jake at the front. Hot and cold. Just like the man himself. So intensely passionate yet so cool in the boardroom. His expression was a study in tight control as he hoisted her legs up and wrapped them around his waist.

They spent long, aching minutes like that, Jake supporting her weight as he took his time to feast on her, placing scorching kisses along her neck before returning to her mouth. When she thought she'd pass out from pleasure, he grasped her bottom and turned, easing her onto the edge of his desk.

Passion nipped at Jake's self-control as he dragged his hands down her back, over the curve of her sweet butt that had teased him with her fashion-show exit. The velvet rubbed erotically against his palms and he pulled her against his throbbing groin, pinning her to the spot. She offered a muffled groan against his mouth and kept right on kissing him.

Heat exploded, consuming his body in a flaming inferno as he eased his fingers under the waistband of her pants. With her hips thrust forward, he bent her back over the desk, palming her stomach as their mouths and tongues tangled in damp seduction.

Papers scattered to the floor, followed by the thump of a file. She propped her elbows on the desk, bracing herself, which allowed him to ease his knee between her legs.

She felt so good. Tasted even better. But he wanted more.

He quickly found her zipper and in a nanosecond, his hand dived in to cup the warm curls between her legs.

She gasped beneath him and for one gut-wrenching second, he thought she'd balk. Amazingly, though, she parted her legs and drew him down for another kiss.

Color burst behind his eyelids as he let out a shuddering

groan. In one determined movement he slipped his finger into her wet, hot core, and with that, his world shattered in a thousand pieces.

Holly was consumed by scorching heat, every one of her cautious warnings reduced to ashes beneath his masterful hands. Her breasts throbbed as they slid against his chest, a wall of hot, tempered steel beneath his sinfully luxurious shirt. His tiepin rubbed against her bra, creating an erotically painful friction that pebbled her nipples. And below that incredible sensation came another—the intimate stroking of his finger, buried deep inside her.

Oh, my.

His mouth left hers, leaving a hot trail of wet kisses from her sensitive collarbone before finally coming to rest on her breast. There, he tongued her nipple through the bra, teasing it, while with one slow deliberate movement, he eased another finger into her.

It took all of Jake's self-control to pause right there, to feel the deep pulse of her muscles surrounding him, to hear the soft mewling coming from her lush mouth and not completely lose it. Ferocious desire scorched every vein, every nerve ending of his body. His groin was harder than granite, straining against his pants, desperate to bury inside her. Meanwhile, blood thundered in his brain, blocking all rational thought. A thick groan welled up in his throat as he clawed for control.

Beyond the sound of his harsh, ragged breath came her soft gasps. "Jake, please…"

She squirmed under him frantically, clenching her muscles around his fingers. He squeezed his eyes shut, commanding his body to remain in control, even as his groin throbbed hard and hot.

"Jake!"

Her plea undid him and with a curse and a prayer, he continued, plunging deep into her wetness then easing out slowly as she hissed in pleasure. He gritted his teeth, trying to block out her deep sighs of satisfaction, the way her lips moved over his, nibbling, wanting. *I can't...can't...*

And then she gasped. Her whole body stilled in tense, expectant pleasure. He watched her eyes widen, pupils dilate with arousal, her mouth round in a shocked little *oh*.

Knowing she was powerless to stop the hot waves of release crash over her, Holly shuddered. She clung to him, feeling her heartbeat thunder away in her chest, matching the heavy thud of his as she pressed her face to his chest.

Soon, too soon, her breath slowed, yet still he held her. She allowed herself the fantasy, squeezing her eyes shut and deliberately forcing her doubts back from the edges of reality.

But eventually she felt his hands pressing gently on her shoulders, his tension straining as he withdrew. Was it regret tempering every ounce of his body as he stepped back and turned away? Cold air rushed her skin, bringing clarity to her thoughts. *What the hell had she done?*

"I'll take you home," he finally said, his back to her.

"You don't have to."

He didn't look at her, just remained a silhouette, his jaw clenched in the dim light. "I do. Get dressed."

His soft command landed like a cold slap of reality on her hot cheek. She struggled with her shirt, embarrassment flushing her neck. If that weren't enough, she realised that she'd have to face him Monday. And the next day, and the next. Instead of a spy, he probably just thought she was unprofessional and easy.

That thought made her want to throw up.

The ride was mercifully quick, considering it was close to one in the morning and the whole of Sydney seemed to be on the road.

The car stopped and Jake glanced over at her. Her eyes looked glassy and tired. He shook his head. Sobering up, most likely.

He led her to the door, let her fumble in her purse for her keys. When she swung it open, he followed her inside.

"Thanks," she mumbled politely, and headed straight down the slate-floor hallway.

He watched the gentle sway of her hips for agonizing seconds, mesmerised by the way the velvet cupped the rounded cheeks of her butt. With his groin still throbbing, he whirled and forced himself to focus on his surroundings.

The living area was to his right, a large L-shaped space with a huge wide-screen TV and accompanying electronic gadgets. A dark blue corner couch sat against the wall, while a few side tables, a display wall of books, photos and awards filled the space.

He walked in, picked up a trophy and eyed the inscription. *Miko Tarasai—2007 Sydney University Netball Championships.*

She had a flatmate.

He turned and cast an eye over the photos—shots of a Chinese family against the backdrop of Hong Kong. The same young girl with a Labrador. A very young Holly and an old couple—her parents, judging by the similarities—posing in Akubras and leaning against an old gum tree.

Jake turned and walked down the hall. In the dimly lit kitchen he saw Holly open the fridge and search around inside.

"You own this place?"

She jumped at the sound of his voice. "Don't you know that already?"

"No." He waited for her to emerge but, after a few seconds, said softly, "Are you going to freeze to death to avoid looking at me?"

With an aggrieved sigh, she slammed the fridge closed, a half-empty bottle of something dark and red in her hand.

"Don't you think you've had enough?"

She scowled. "It's grape juice. Please go home."

"Not until I know you're OK."

With a sarcastic slant to her mouth, she held out her arms then pirouetted. "See? I'm in one piece. Now leave."

"Holly, we should talk about what happened." He hesitated and as he watched her, the flush on her cheeks began to grow.

"You don't need to say anything."

"It was just something that—"

"—happened," she finished for him.

"Yeah." *Something incredibly hot.*

"We're two professional people. It was a…" She faltered as his scowl deepened. "A lapse in judgement. Let's concentrate on our jobs and forget this happened, OK?"

Forget a tornado hadn't just swept into his life and turned it upside down? Jake wanted to interject, but the expression on her face was nine-parts resolve, one-part vulnerability. She needed him to agree.

"I'm hoping I can rely on your discretion," she continued, confirming his suspicions. "And I hope you won't tell the Blackstones about this. I signed a morality clause and—"

"I'm not your boss."

She blinked. "Technically, no. But Legal could interpret it differently."

If her look of apprehension hadn't swayed him, the gentle beseeching in her eyes did. He'd never had a woman plead with him before over something so innocent.

Right. There was nothing innocent about what they'd done, what they would've done. What he really wanted to do.

He felt his body stir again and cursed himself long and hard.

"You have my word," he said with a nod.

As if she'd been holding her breath, the tension in her body flooded out. And when she gave him a grateful smile, he watched her little kissy-mole move with the curve of her lips.

He muffled a groan. It was a smile that was all about thanking him, not turning him on, yet amazingly it achieved both. It flared in his memory, reminding him how she'd felt beneath his mouth, surrounding his fingers.

"Well, it's late," Holly said lamely. Something had changed, something dark and hot in the dim light of her kitchen as she shifted her weight from foot to foot, willing him to go. Yet her mother had taught her to be polite, so like a good-mannered girl, she waited for Jake to be true to character and leave.

He didn't.

A breeze sprang up, carrying with it a tinkling sound from the balcony. He glanced across to the closed doors. "Wind chimes?"

She said slowly, "Yes. My flat mate is Chinese. She's into feng shui."

"She decorated the flat."

"No, actually I did. She just approved the final colors and furnishings. It's her parents' place."

"You have an eye for color."

"I wanted to be an interior designer, but—" She paused. *You want him to leave, not engage him in further conversation.*

"Couldn't afford the risk?" he said casually.

"You know I couldn't. I needed a steady job."

Instead of rising to that, he pulled the sliding glass doors open an inch, letting the cool wind blow in.

She sighed. "Are you staying to discuss my decorating skills?"

"Maybe I just like your company."

She drew in a sharp breath. "Are you enjoying this?"

"Enjoying what?" He cast an eye over the rolling dark clouds outside, then back to her.

"This…uncomfortable moment."

"Is that what it is?" he murmured. "Just 'uncomfortable'?"

She drew back, painting an invisible barrier around herself. "It's late. Good night, Jake."

The scowl bloomed across his face, confusing her. But before she could even try to interpret that, he nodded. "Good night."

One second he was there, the next he was gone. After she heard the door click, the tension in her limbs rushed out like air from a balloon. With a soft groan, she dragged herself over to the balcony, slumped into the patio chair and drew her knees up, allowing herself to wallow in the moment of self-pity.

Why couldn't she ever learn from her mistakes? First Max, now Jake. How foolish could one woman be when it came to matters of the heart? She'd not only put her job in jeopardy again with a stupid lapse in judgement, but she'd also failed Max's ultimatum.

One second, then two and she breathed deep. No way would she let this beat her…let Max beat her. On Monday she'd confess Max's blackmail to Kimberley, plead her innocence and throw herself at her mercy. On Monday she'd be strong and face her mistakes head-on.

And what of Jake? Was that a mistake too?

She allowed herself a brief memory—the searing heat of his mouth, the exquisite torture of his hands, the burning desire in his eyes.

She swallowed, her throat as dry as parchment. How much would he want her if he knew the truth?

Six

Kimberley Perrini arrived ten minutes early on Monday for her emergency meeting with Jake, taking a seat at the small conference table in his office. Holly had always admired Kim for her forthrightness, her resilience and the poise she'd retained in the face of the whole Blackstone's scandal these past few months. As usual, she was impeccable in a dark green business shirt and long, tailored skirt, despite the touch of worry in her eyes.

"Jake isn't running you too ragged, I hope?" she inquired.

Ragged? Holly's pulse hitched. "No."

"The man is quite…" Kim trailed off, looking thoughtful "…intense."

Holly merely nodded, not trusting herself to speak. Thanks to last night, she knew more about him than she'd thought possible. Intimate things.

It was bad enough trying to maintain a professional work-place without letting Saturday night take over her brain. He'd invaded her dreams, hot, erotic ones that forced her awake in a tangle of sheets and a throbbing between her legs.

"This assignment won't be for much longer," Kim was saying. "We miss you in PR."

"I miss it too." Holly rose, retrieving a document from the printer while trying to squelch her thoughts. "Listen, I need to talk to you about something…" She trailed off as Jake, then Ric Perrini, walked in the door.

"Later, OK?" Kim was already turning away and Holly could do nothing but nod.

As Jake strode past with a murmured greeting, her body betrayed her. Her heart began to pound and her skin tingled. She glanced away, only to catch the intimate look passing between Ric and Kim, followed by a small smile on Kim's lips and the answering gleam in her husband's eyes.

They were in love. Despite their tumultuous past, they were deeply, head over heels in love. Holly barely had time to swallow her envy before Ryan strode in, shattering the moment.

"Have you seen this?" Ryan shoved the financial section onto the conference table as Garth entered and closed the door. The heading Takeover At Blackstone's? blared out in bold type.

Jake shrugged. "The shares are stable."

"For now," Ryan replied, unconvinced.

"So some people have seen me about. It was bound to happen. We all know it's no more true than Briana Out, Mystery Woman In."

Holly flushed as all eyes turned to her. With his ex Briana Davenport, taken by Jarrod Hammond, did the press think *she* was Briana's replacement? She glanced at Jake, whose mouth was curved in irony. Unable to look away, she focused on those lips for seconds longer than necessary.

Lips that she had imagined last night, kissing her in places she'd never think could react to such soft contact. Expert lips, warm and welcoming and completely open to taking their kiss further. Dangerous lips. Dangerous fingers.

Focus!

"Who? W-where?" she said, stammering.

"Us, in some gossip magazine. Seems we now have a personal relationship. First diamond shopping, then lunch. Who knows where it may lead. Perhaps an office liaison?"

He was mocking her. That green-eyed devil was actually mocking her!

"Which is a good lead-in to this meeting," Kim said smoothly, turning to Holly as they were all seated. "We've recently found out and proved that Jake is actually our missing brother, James Blackstone. We've also agreed you need to know the truth behind Jake's presence at Blackstones."

Holly hesitated for a heartbeat, filling the silence with a slow intake of breath. "I'm sorry, did you say—?"

"Yes," Jake interjected calmly.

She felt her mouth sag but recovered quickly, snapping it shut so hard she felt her teeth click. Stunned, she looked from Kim back to Jake, only to come up against a familiar brick wall. She took a deep breath to calm herself.

"You're really James Blackstone?" she said on a breath.

Man, did Max have it wrong. Now things made complete sense—why Jake wanted to know about the company, the nagging familiarity in his emerald eyes, so like Kim's and Ryan's. And why, even as Jake Vance, that irrefutable Blackstone aura of entitlement and power shone through.

There was so much she needed to ask. But as she floundered, gathering her thoughts, Kim said, "I don't need to tell you we're expecting the utmost confidence on this issue, Holly."

Holly nodded mutely, firmly suppressing her curiosity. "Of course." Nonetheless, her eyes still made a beeline for Jake, who was watching her with an intensity she found acutely disturbing.

"Everyone tells me you're an expert in spin," Jake said now, his eyebrows raised questioningly.

"Well, I…" She forced her voice to steady. "There've been no complaints."

Kim said, "At my request, Holly's prepared something we're sure will combat the negative press."

Holly breathed in, focusing on the presentation in front of her. With a confident flick, she opened it. "A charity ball with a combined auction." She surveyed the Blackstones, who sat silent and thoughtful. "We approach retailers for donations— a romantic cruise, Blackstone jewellery, a weekend retreat, gift packs, LCD TVs, that sort of thing—then the guests bid on them. I drafted a press release," she said, pushing a page over to Jake. "I also thought we could explain Mr Vance… uh…Blackstone—"

"Vance," said Jake calmly, taking pity on her.

She flushed. "—Mr Vance's presence by auctioning off a two-week apprenticeship at AdVance Corp."

"Which means what, exactly?" Jake said.

"The highest bidder gets to be your apprentice for two weeks, accompanying you to meetings and learning the ins and outs of business from your unique perspective."

His smile was sceptical. "And you think people will bid on this?"

"Of course. My other idea is a bachelor auction—"

"No."

She stopped and, in the silence, handed out her proposal to everyone. Finally Garth said, "What about preparation time?"

"We've organised other events in less," Holly said. "We'll use the Grand Ballroom downstairs, of course. Kim and I agreed on the last Saturday night in May."

Garth looked thoughtful. "That's under three weeks away. You'd need to get the announcement out tomorrow, especially in light of today's paper."

Kim added, "We'll time our publicity push to generate positive spin leading up to the ball."

"But what of the bigger problem?" Garth fixed Jake with a steely look. "I've been talking discreetly with our shareholders and the message is the same. As a family company with long-standing investors, Jake's business reputation is not the only thing that worries them."

"I can't help that," Jake interjected.

"Ahh, but you can. That construction company takeover you brokered last week didn't help, especially when their chief accountant jumped from the window."

"It was the second floor. He lived," Jake said calmly, ignoring Holly's gasp. "And the man was being charged with bribing a local politician."

"But my point is—"

"Your point means curtailing my business transactions. No."

Everyone paused, letting that sink in until Ric said, "Maybe there's another way. A more press-friendly way of creating a positive buzz—above and beyond the charity ball," he added, nodding at Holly.

"I've done a timeline to chart strategic points for maximum

impact—release of the invitation list, the donors, the theme," Holly said, her mind working quickly to incorporate the revelation of Jake's true identity. "We can hint at an 'important announcement' that will be made at the night's end."

"Why at the end?" Jake asked.

"Because the evening is about the charity auction, not the Blackstones. And it ensures everyone stays to bid. We don't want guests leaving halfway through."

"I don't think that'd be a problem," Ryan said smoothly. "Can it be pulled off in time? And will it work?"

Holly gave a confident nod. "Short of a Blackstone wedding, the press will see through any other attempt to garner favourable publicity."

Ric smiled thinly. "Not planning marriage, are you, Jake?"

As everyone murmured in amusement, Garth said, "That's not a bad idea." All eyes swung to him, but he merely shrugged. "As I was saying, our shareholders aren't just intimidated by Jake's business persona. They're distrustful of a single man in his mid-thirties who hasn't formed any significant romantic attachments. A wedding, even an engagement, is the kind of event that brings people together, as you well know. It's a confirmation of love, honour and commitment, which generates a warm fuzzy glow with the public."

From the sudden drop in temperature, Holly knew everyone was holding their breath. She told herself not to look at him. But Jake was like a car crash; you couldn't *not* look.

When she finally gave in to temptation, she fully expected to see a mask of righteous fury, all tight lines and muscle. Instead, his face was blank.

His game face. She'd seen it when he'd met Max, when she'd quizzed him about his intentions. He kept his thoughts firmly under lock and key. When he finally did speak, the room practically vibrated with restrained anticipation.

"Certainly, marriage is on my ten-year plan."

"Jake, it's not—" Kimberley began. "What?"

"I'll think about it."

After a stunned silence, discussions finally moved on to the charity ball, but Holly couldn't drag her eyes away from Jake. When he wasn't looking, she stared at him, only to be caught not once, but three times, by his mocking green gaze.

Just when she thought she had him pegged… She'd fully expected him to blow that idea out of the water, not to actually consider it. But of course. As she quickly handed out the estimated costings for the ball, she shook her head. He had a ten-year plan. He'd approach finding a wife just like any other business deal. He'd want the best—breeding, looks, class. A privately schooled daughter of some brain surgeon, or a minor royal with centuries of hyphenated ancestors.

As if sensing her mounting turmoil, Jake glanced at her. The small conspiratorial smile teasing his mouth incensed her even more.

Damn the man.

For the next thirty minutes everyone added to Holly's proposal. They all agreed it should be a glitzy, glamorous black-tie event specifically designed to raise awareness of Australia's over-stretched rescue services, and all proceeds would go to AusSAR, the national search and rescue organisation that had led the search for Howard Blackstone's downed jet.

When the meeting finally broke up, Holly quickly gathered her paperwork and was first out the door, desperate to focus on work and not other, more dangerous thoughts.

Jake was James Blackstone. Practically Australian royalty. So out of her league.

She stopped her errant thoughts. Since when had she started to entertain those feelings?

"You and Jake should discuss his press statement," Kim said as she emerged from the room and handed her a piece of paper. "And here's a few more people to add to the guest list."

Holly glanced down at the paper. "Matt Hammond?"

Kim nodded. "Yes. We've got Jake back." She looked pointedly at Jake, who was in discussion with Ric and Ryan at his office door. "It's time to start building some bridges and bring this family together again."

Holly followed Kim's eyes and at that precise moment, Jake looked straight at her. Their gazes immediately locked, held. And in that breathless moment, her skin began to heat, like smouldering embers of a furnace stoking back to life.

His study of her felt different. *She* felt different. More aware of the sensual slide of her shirt over her skin, the way her breath faltered on the intake before coming out in a sigh. The way his eyes, full of exquisite knowledge, skimmed the parts of her his hands had touched. Of course, if she were interested, she'd be preening about now.

No, you're not interested. You are so not interested you'd have to drive across the Great Sandy Desert to even find the signposts telling you where interested was.

Yeah, and his kisses were the worst thing you've ever experienced.

As she stood there arguing with herself, she could feel the air suddenly charge with expectation. The interest and heat in his eyes morphed into full flame, his mouth curving in an intimate smile.

Photos never did him justice. Not that strong jawline, the noble Gallic nose, the high brow. And those intelligent emerald eyes that could make her knees buckle with just one hint of a smile. The smile that transformed his entire face right now into something breathtaking.

"Holly, the press statement?" Kim was saying.

Holly ripped her attention away from Jake, only to light on Kim's amused face. She blinked and picked up a notepad, effectively ducking the woman's shrewd eyes. "You're not handling it?"

"I'll take a look at it, of course. But I trust you with this. Just run everything by me before you release anything."

Holly nodded as guilt flooded in. Yes, Max was blackmailing her, but she'd gotten herself in that position. It didn't matter who was right or wrong; the moment she admitted her guilt, there was a good chance she'd be fired. Worse, the Blackstones had invested in her, had trusted her yet she'd betrayed them. How could she admit that failing to Kim, someone she admired and respected?

She couldn't.

"Time will be tight leading up to the ball," Kim said, "so if you need help, just ask." She paused then said, "You needed to see me about something?"

Holly thought quickly. "Did you want to view the decorations, choose stationery…?"

"If you need a second opinion, I'm happy to give one," Kim said, moving towards the door. "But it's your baby, Holly. I know what you're capable of, so just wow us, OK?"

Holly was rooted to the spot, staring at the glass door as it slowly closed. Kim's supreme confidence should have made her ecstatic. Instead, it wounded her in a dozen tiny cuts.

With a steadying breath she whirled, refusing to let worry control the moment. She'd been entrusted with this so she was going to make damn sure it was a success.

With purposeful strides, she walked into Jake's office. He was refilling the coffee pot, his controlled movements a study in efficiency. She halted as he glanced up, every muscle in her body stilling as a welcoming smile spread his sensual mouth.

Her insides did a weird little flip as she returned his smile, feeling like a teenager, all breathless and jittery around her first crush. Even the childish words "James Blackstone is smiling at me!" ran through her mind until she gave an inward groan and chased them away.

"We need to talk about your press release."

Abruptly his expression cooled. "I have another meeting."

"I understand," Holly said, reluctantly matching his business-like tone. "But we need to make time for this."

"I will. Just not now."

She ignored his curt warning. "Let me at least make a start, like some personal background to go on."

With a scowl, he leaned back in his chair and fixed her with that cool, calm stare. It was almost as if he was trying too hard to remain emotionless, to show her that this didn't matter. But deep down, she knew it did. She knew that men like Jake possessed an almost demonic drive to succeed. The key to success was often found in their past—what they did and didn't have. What they lacked. What they desired most.

"Your mother was a single parent?"

"Yes."

"And?"

In the silence, Holly met his stare unflinchingly. "You have to let me do my job, Jake." She stopped, unashamedly wallowing in that small rush of intimacy she felt from simply speaking his name. "Just tell me whatever you feel comfortable with."

He seemed to debate his answer. With deliberate care he admitted, "Nothing about this makes me comfortable."

"So let me help you," she said gently. "We just need enough info to pre-empt all those intrusive questions. Like, how did you find out you were James Blackstone?"

"What happened with Max Carlton?"

She blanched. "We're talking about you."

"And I'm talking about *you*." He leaned back in his chair. "Why should I trust you when you're hiding something?"

Panic forced her into silence. Just what did he know? Had he seen her with Max at the fashion show? Had he somehow dug something up with his team of investigators and bottom-less funds?

He watched her like an animal studied its prey, as if with one wrong move or word she'd be history. Yet memories of Saturday night thundered between them, and just like that, the air turned from strained reservation to electrically charged.

She shoved her chin in the air and forced calm into her voice. "There's nothing going on between me and Max."

He leaned back in his chair, his smile full of male knowledge. "See, there you go again. Lying to me."

She arched her brow. "How do you know?"

"You've got a tell."

"A what?"

"A tell—a facial tic, like a giveaway sign. Cops and lawyers use it. So do conmen. I've studied a few techniques myself."

"Is that why you're so good at winning?"

"That and making sure people can't say no."

Holly crossed her arms. "So what is my 'tell'?"

"Your eyes," he said softly. "They widen a little, and your focus shifts away, dropping to my shoulder or just past my ear."

"Maybe I find your ear fascinating."

His short bark of laughter surprised them both. As she stood there, a reluctant grin on her lips, her heart did that weird little jump again.

Her pen dropped from her nervous fingers and she bent to retrieve it, panic closing her throat. *You want him. He can't know.*

Like a strange rhythmic tattoo, she repeated the mantra in her head until her senses spun from the realisation. With steely determination she straightened, forcing it from her mind.

If you don't think it, he can't read it on your face.

Still, he must have sensed something, because his eyes narrowed curiously.

"Tell me about your childhood," she asked, desperate to deflect his focus. "Where did you grow up?"

With a look that told her he knew what she was doing, he said, "When I was ten, we settled in Tanunda, South Australia. April remarried when I was fifteen."

"Were you happy?"

"Are teenagers ever happy?" When she frowned, he sighed. "Did we have money? No. Life was tough. We moved with whatever seasonal work my mother could get, which always made me the new kid at school."

"I can imagine."

"No, you can't," Jake bit back harshly as the memories tumbled in like a burst dam. "You're from a small town where everyone knows you, where your family has roots, standing in the community. You probably know the bank manager by name and invited the neighbors around for barbeques on the weekend." Unable to contain his agitation any longer, he whirled to face the huge windows. "You weren't called the bastard son of the town's drunken whore."

Her sharp intake of breath sliced at him, bringing fresh pain to the surface. He shut his eyes, forcing the memories back where they belonged.

"I need to be across town in half an hour," he said curtly. "We'll discuss this later. Just…" He waved a dismissive hand, "Just write up what you know and leave the other bits blank. E-mail it to me and I'll fill in the rest."

He then turned to the papers on his desk, riffling through them with single-minded concentration, even as he sensed Holly still standing there, radiating with frustration.

A moment passed, then two and Jake finally looked up. "Is that all?" he queried softly, forcing his expression to reveal nothing of his inner turmoil. Inside, his jaw ached from clenching it so tightly.

Go. Just go.

A look passed over her face—part sorrow, part pain. Before he could say anything, she nodded.

"That's all for now." And she turned and walked out.

At five-thirty Holly sat in Jake's car, being taken to goodness knows where. She twisted the earring around in her lobe, staring out at the passing traffic. Max had called to demand an update, which had forced her to acknowledge their plans for the ball. When he'd sneered, "How noble," it gave her a small perverse satisfaction to say swiftly, "I have work to do. Gotta go," and hang up on him.

Thankfully the ball preparations had then commanded her thoughts elsewhere, away from Max, from her situation. The

Blackstones had placed an almighty trust in her by revealing Jake's identity, given the tenuous grip they had with privacy right now. How could she possibly destroy that trust?

Worry sawed at her composure, leaving her raw and confused. She needed to stall Max until after the ball, after she'd proven her loyalties lay with Blackstone's. Only then could she come clean and get rid of the menacing threat hanging over her head.

She glanced at a silent Jake…James. *James Blackstone.* Sheer amazement had waylaid her at inopportune times during the day. She'd wanted to ask him a dozen questions but hadn't seen him since their press release discussion. Of course he had other things to do, important meetings to attend, small countries to buy out. He wasn't avoiding her.

At least, now he wasn't.

"Tell me again why I couldn't just catch a cab home?" she said as the peak-hour traffic crawled by.

"You saw the reporters outside Blackstone's." She wasn't sure if his sympathetic glance was real or a put-on. "As my rumoured love interest, you *are* news now."

"And me in your car helps how? You *have* read that little article on page ten of today's *Telegraph*, haven't you?"

He waved away her concern with an imperious hand. "We both know you're not having my baby. Unless—" his eyes turned mischievous "—you want to."

She blinked, cramming down the sudden fluttering desire that flared in her belly. "Jake…"

"Relax, Holly." He dismissed her shocked look. "You want my undivided attention for this press release. I'm giving it to you."

Fifteen minutes later, passing through no less than two security gates that required key card and password access, then another keypad at the complex doors, Holly stood in the middle of Jake's elaborate Pyrmont Bay apartment in silent awe. As if sensing her keen interest from the moment she walked in, he'd given her the cook's tour. From the entrance she stepped into an open-plan living area featuring a large fireplace at the far end flanked by two curved couches. To her left was the modern kitchen. His office space was separated by a glass wall. She'd walked down the two steps to the sunken entertainment area, which boasted a massive plasma screen and two single reclining lounge chairs. Beyond ceiling-to-floor windows, a balcony offered a magnificent view of Pyrmont Bay and Darling Harbour.

To her relief he'd nodded to the staircase and said, "Bedroom, spare room and bathroom."

She looked around. The place simply screamed rich single guy. She didn't even notice that Jake had turned on the TV until she saw her face plastered on the six-o'clock news.

"Are you seeing this?" she said softly as he walked past her into the kitchen.

He retrieved a bottle of wine from the fridge. "I caught the midday news."

She stared as he grabbed a corkscrew from the drawer, his nonchalance only cranking up her irritation. "So what are you going to do about it?"

He glanced up at the screen, then back to the cupboard where he removed two glasses. "I'm flattered you think my powers extend to bringing down the world's oil prices."

She scowled. "I'm talking about us. Us. On the news. Having a love affair."

His throwaway smile curled Holly's toes. "We're having a love affair on the news? How Paris Hilton of us."

She took a deep breath and sent a small prayer heavenwards. "Is this funny for you? We're the lead story and that doesn't bother you?"

"No. We're both single, responsible adults. Why should it bother you?"

"Because it's dragging Blackstone's into the limelight again. It's intrusive and inflammatory and they've been through enough."

His expression became astute, as if she'd said something vitally important. "But it's not about them. It's about us— Holly and Jake's clandestine office romance."

She opened her mouth to argue but quickly snapped it shut when realisation dawned. "It's good publicity. For once, the headlines are positive."

"You got it in one."

She perched on the arm of a lounge chair and toed off her heels. "Great. At least they haven't found out where I live." But the look on his face plummeted her scant hope. "You're kidding me."

"Sorry." He offered her a glass and she took it, downing her first gulp of expensive crisp Riesling. Miko's father was going to be pissed. The Tarasais were very private, very conservative…

She abruptly stood. "My parents. They'll freak if—"

"Already taken care of."

"How?"

"I sent a discreet security detail this morning."

Stunned, she sat back down on the couch with a shake of her head. "I can't let you—"

"Sure you can." Even as he casually leaned against the wall, his eyes remained watchful. "You didn't e-mail me your draft release."

With a soft sigh she rubbed her temple. "Because there are too many gaps. I still don't know how you found out you were really James Blackstone."

"My mo— April confessed before she died."

"I see."

Jake shot her a look. "It wasn't a guilty conscience, if that's what you're thinking. Someone in her old town had contacted Howard's P.I.s, and she wanted to tell me before the shit hit the fan."

"So she was protecting you."

His derisive snort came out half-hearted, giving her hope. She tried again. "What was the first thing you bought when you made your first million?"

"Why?"

It almost made her want to weep at the distance in those expressive eyes. "Just go with me on this."

He paused, as if weighing her intentions in that simple question. "A town house for my mother in Lilyfield."

He gave her his back then, turning to the expansive view of the bay. Yet she could see his face mirrored in the smooth glass, the naked emotion twisting his features until his reflected gaze landed on hers. Their eyes held breathlessly for one second, then two…then his expression eased.

He turned back to her and crossed his arms. "She was sick for a long time," he said softly. "Liver cancer, even though she'd stopped drinking years ago."

"But she took good care of you?"

"As best she could. Until I could take care of her. She…"

He paused, and in that small hesitation Holly sensed something, something deep and painful enough to bring a falter to his steady voice, something that still continued to eat away at him.

She watched him rub the bridge of his nose, his eyes dark with remembrance.

"I asked about my father once," he said quietly. "I was about eight. She told me her last boyfriend was abusive. I never asked again."

Holly stilled, the air so motionless she could almost hear the dragging reluctance as he continued.

"I was fifteen when she married John Kellerman. The guy was a nasty piece of work, always drinking, always abusive. I couldn't figure out why she'd stay with someone like that."

"Maybe she wanted to give you stability."

He fixed her with an astute look. "Well, it royally backfired."

It hurt her heart, the sudden and instant vulnerability this man displayed. For all his control, all his power, he was felled by something so simple, yet so complex.

A mother's love.

She glanced at the TV screen, which flickered with images of a devastating south-coast rainstorm. So furious and powerful. Yet when everything was over, devastation and vulnerability.

"You can trust me, Jake."

He straightened, a shutter descending over his features as he abruptly changed the subject. "Are you hungry?"

Through the simple meal of steak and grilled vegetables that he refused help to prepare, he dropped cryptic personal tidbits that were short on emotional detail. It was as if by leaving out embellishment, he could remain detached from it all, a bystander just reeling off the facts. By the end of dessert—a decadent vanilla toffee-chip ice cream—she knew that Quinn's mom had taught him how to boil perfect spaghetti, that he'd invested in nearly every country in the world and that he'd broken his nose twice.

"You'd never know," she said, eyeing his profile as they took a seat on the lounge before the fire.

He ran his finger down the bridge almost absently. "I had it fixed."

"Really?"

"My only concession to vanity," he admitted with a small smile.

Vanity or trying to fix the past? Under Holly's probing gaze, he remained silent until she said softly, "When?"

He met her eyes unflinchingly. "After my stepfather broke it."

She swallowed, emotion clogging her throat as she broke eye contact and glanced around his expansive apartment. It was then she noticed the small array of private objects gathered atop a bookshelf.

"Tell me about those."

She noted the way he studied the items, and instinctively she knew he could catalogue them blindfolded.

Finally he said, "The black stone is from Bells Beach, my first visit. The key is from my first car, a Holden Torana." His smile flickered.

"A list of firsts," Holly murmured. "The boarding pass?"

"First overseas flight." He nodded to one of the two framed photos. "Quinn and I flew to Africa to inspect the diamond mines."

"Must have been a good trip."

At his quizzical glance, she supplied, "You're smiling. You don't do that often."

"Don't I?" he replied absently, his gaze going back to the other photo, older and grainier.

"You and April?"

"Yes. She…" Jake stopped, remembering the brief moment of happiness all too well. "I was eleven. She'd just got a cashier's job at the local 7-Eleven store and we'd gone to the games arcade to celebrate." The seasonal fruit-picking gig had dried up when the rain had, leaving them with barely enough money to eat, let alone feed his mother's alcohol habit. When she'd realised it was either the drink or food for her son, she'd stopped cold turkey.

"Tell me more about her."

At her soft probing, Jake felt a well of trepidation lodge in his gut. "Until I was about ten, we moved a lot. Now I know why." Seeking the comfort of movement, he stood, turning to face the window displaying Sydney's cloudy night sky. "Howard's housekeeper and her boyfriend were named as the kidnappers."

"Yes. Two months after you disappeared, the cops found their bodies. Everyone believed James drowned in that car," Holly said behind him.

Jake nodded curtly, battling with the sudden claustrophobia as he focused on his reflection in the spotless window. "April rescued me."

"Why didn't she turn you in to the authorities?"

Jake closed his eyes as the demons struggled within. "It wasn't that simple. She was on the run from an abusive boyfriend and still suffering the loss of her own baby a year ago. When she pulled me from the car it was like God had given her another chance. At least, that's the way she saw it."

"So she deliberately kept you."

Jake turned at the lack of emotion in Holly's voice. "Yes."

"Didn't she know who you were? That there was a

mother and father out there grieving for a child they thought had drowned?"

Jake's throat constricted. Determinedly he forced the memory up, as if confronting it would somehow negate the fear. Foul-smelling dirty water rushing in through the car window. Him screaming and beating his small fists at the door. Choking, crying.

And then a saviour.

April Vance. His mother for the past thirty-two years of his life. A life that had been ripped away, a potential fishbowl for the world to view and inspect.

"She risked her life to save me."

"That must have taken courage." Holly stopped all pretence of mentally cataloguing his story now. The urge to grab the pad and pen from her bag, gone.

"Yes."

The look on his face was stark. A great man suddenly vulnerable and raw, Holly realised. And past that, she could see reluctance…and embarrassment. He was a man unfamiliar with discussing his deeper feelings, with showing emotion.

Holly's heart ached for him, for the pain of his youth, for the still-to-come scrutiny that he'd have to weather. And on the heels of that came the sudden overwhelming desire to alleviate his pain, to share some of the burden.

Her voice was small when she spoke. "A big-shot buyer promised to bail out my family's company when we got into financial difficulty."

He turned, studying her face carefully, searching for a deeper meaning behind her sudden revelation. Determinedly she continued, "Instead, they bought us out then liquidated. Sacked everyone. Twenty families couldn't afford to feed their children, marriages fell apart, people had to sell their homes and possessions. Some had to leave the town where they'd lived all their lives."

"And you were one of them."

"We stayed. Many didn't. When Dad lost the business, it was the end of him. He just…" she hesitated, pausing to analyse the once-painful memories. "He gave up. The workers blamed him and pretty soon he did, too. I blamed myself."

His eyes turned razor-sharp. "You were seventeen, just a kid."

"I nagged him to sell because I wanted to go to university." She let the remnants of bitter frustration hover in the thick air, waiting for it to dissipate into the silence. After it slowly faded away, she sighed. "After Dad's stroke, Mum gave up too. Their living expenses and medical bills were astronomical—" And her responsibility. The reminder ground the rest of the words to dust in her mouth. "Sorry, I got off track. We were talking about you."

But with a sinking heart she knew the moment was gone. Jake's expression had reverted to his signature control, albeit with a tightness bracketing his mouth.

"It's getting late. I'll get Steve to drive ahead, make sure the press have gone from your place. Do you have enough to draft something up?"

She nodded, knowing there'd be nothing else this evening.

Later, in Jake's car, when she finally had a chance to make sense of her uncharacteristic confession, a terrifying thought began to bloom. With a soft groan, she put her forehead on the cool glass.

Oh no. You can't. Are you actually having feelings for Jake Vance?

Seven

On Wednesday, Jake took a left turn and drove into the exclusive suburb of Vaucluse, then clicked off the ten-o'clock news. As predicted, there had been a flurry of activity following yesterday's press release of the charity ball, with both Blackstone Diamonds and AdVance Corp fielding interview requests for the past hour.

He'd never cared for subterfuge or smokescreens when it came to business, yet he understood the necessity behind it all—protecting Blackstone's bottom line. To their credit, Holly and Kim had done a skilful job of appeasing the public, spending the whole day with the press and on radio, generating interest in the ball and expertly diverting any negative questions.

Behind the steering wheel of his brand-new dark blue Presara, he glanced out the window, noting the barely visible Vaucluse mansions from the road. He counted off the numbers, searching for the right one that would signal his impending meeting with Sonya Hammond.

It was not in his plans, this "getting to know the family" stuff. At least Ryan and Ric had kept it to a minimum, focusing instead on his intentions for Blackstone's. Kimberley had been more of a problem, with her gentle probing and bulldog stubbornness. In that respect, she was like him, a comparison that sent a wave of weird déjà vu scuttling across his skin.

There was no good reason he needed to meet Sonya. Baring his past to scrutiny made crawling over hot coals a more appealing prospect. But despite all his logical reasons why not, there was one big why.

He wanted answers. He needed them. And the not knowing felt like a hole burning away in his gut.

He needed to know about Howard—and not just what the papers reported. He needed to know about his real mother, and whether she'd truly been as miserable as he'd assumed.

So he'd finally agreed to this meeting, much to Kimberley's surprise. "If you hurt Sonya, your life will not be worth living," she'd stated mildly, her glittering emerald eyes hard like the jewels she promoted. He'd merely nodded. Over the past few days, first Ryan, Ric, then Kim had dropped tidbits about Sonya Hammond. They considered her more than just Ursula's sister, more than the mother of Danielle. She was a mother-figure, one who was loved and cherished, who was the backbone of the Blackstone family.

He finally reached the end of the road. Dead ahead lay a set of huge iron gates, accompanied by a discreet security camera on the left. The gates swung inwards without a sound, giving off a final click after he drove through.

It wasn't until he'd exited his car and stood in front of the huge three-story mansion that a wave of apprehension nearly knocked him flat.

Oh, God. The house.

With his eyes he traced the lines of the building, lingering on every window, every angle of the smooth white cement render.

The dreams had mercifully stopped years ago, but now he forced himself to remember the fragments—a large white house with a million rooms, enough for a small boy to hide from a laughing woman with loving eyes. But they weren't dreams, he realised now. They were memories. Memories of this house, of his real mother.

For one incredible second, he was catapulted back in time, back to where his mind jumbled with familiar smells, familiar sights. The sharp, salty tang of the ocean. The warm, grainy sand between his toes.

A hug, the sound of gentle laughter.

He rocked on his heels, fear icing his feet as he struggled, standing there on the expensive parquet driveway, the huge haunting house looming ahead.

Yet amazingly, underneath the panic, a tiny sliver of relief bloomed. Relief that, however far-fetched it sounded, he finally knew he wasn't crazy.

He forced himself to focus, concentrate, to walk forward to the house.

Just like last week, when he'd been hovering on the threshold in the foyer of Blackstone Diamonds, he regrouped. This wouldn't beat him. He'd spent nearly all his life fighting something, from playground bullies to his stepfather, from workmates to competitors.

He was determined to focus on business but this family stuff was freaking him out. His jaw ached from gritting his teeth. This would not beat him.

So why was he so bone-tired from fighting?

He dropped his head, staring at the stonework as a flood of eerie emotions swamped him.

He was the eldest son of Howard Blackstone. Maybe this was where he belonged.

With a determined slant to his shoulders, he walked the small distance between familiarity and the great unknown. But before he could press the doorbell, the door opened and an elegant woman stood before him.

She was immaculately groomed, from the top of her regal head with its pulled-back brown hair, to the blue cashmere sweater and tailored beige pants, to the tips of her brown pointy heels.

A queen, fit to head the Blackstone dynasty, was his first thought. And when he took in her face, he was struck by the warm, welcoming expression, completely at odds with her majestic composure. Then she enveloped him in a generous embrace and his polite greeting fizzled on his tongue.

"James," she whispered as she squeezed him tightly. "You're finally home."

In stunned silence he felt her tremble as she hugged him. For one second, he hesitated. Should he step back? Refuse to come inside? Maintain that crumbling wall of cool politeness he'd reserved for the whole Blackstone clan?

Should, should, should...

The choice he finally made shocked the hell out of him. He embraced her back. And somehow it felt right.

* * *

It was after ten on Friday night, after Jake had negotiated a deal with a New York property development company, that he finally gave his meeting with Sonya a critical going over.

He'd expected the meeting to take an hour, tops. His goal had been to find out what Howard was really like, get a sense of his dead mother, discuss family dynamics. Instead, four hours later he was still there, listening in silent fascination as Sonya recounted personal memories of the Blackstones.

When Sonya had given him a tour of the mansion, he'd finally had an explanation to his haunting dreams. She'd also provided greater insight into Ursula and Howard. Especially Howard.

But for every positive, there were a dozen major character flaws. Howard was a horrible human being, of that he'd had no doubt. The kind of person who collected mistresses then tossed them away like a petulant child with a broken toy.

His fists clenched. There was no way he was like that bastard.

"Did you have a good life, Jake? Were you happy?"

Sonya's soft question, her calm warmth, had undone him. For one horrifying second, he thought he'd break down and blubber like a newborn. Instead he'd forced a smile and replied, "April loved me. That's better than a lot of other kids."

That part was true. He'd wasted his teenage years blaming her for every setback, every disappointment. After he'd clawed his way back on the stock market he'd finally had a chance to right things.

"And what of a family of your own?" she'd asked him. "A wife, children?"

For the second time in as many days, a sudden aching desire slammed into him, astoundingly intense. Everyone close to him had paired off, like partners at a dance and he'd been a last-minute invite. Meanwhile, he'd been trying to fill the void with material things. It was only now he realised he'd been digging in vain.

He needed…something more. Something like he'd glimpsed on Ryan's face. Something he sensed from Kimberley and Perrini.

Unity. A partnership. Trust.

Through the frustration, the desperate want, he kept coming back to the one woman who'd gotten completely under his skin. One who didn't care how many millions he made. One who challenged him, both verbally and mentally, who had tugged violently at his self-control for the first time in for ever.

He walked into the kitchen, the polished floor shockingly cold to his bare feet. After grabbing coffee from the counter he drank deep, the scalding liquid flaming his throat.

He tried to quench a thirst that had nothing to do with his burning desire to make more money, to scale that tentative tightrope of success. Instead, erotic images, like exploding firecrackers, shot through his mind, emptying it of rational thought. He gave himself a mental shake and tried to concentrate on the deal he'd made two hours ago, but all he could think of was a pair of languid eyes and a kissy-mole near the corner of a luscious mouth. How that mouth had tasted beneath his, all warm and wet and pliant. How it would feel on his body, trailing hot kisses over his chest, down his belly, taking him willingly and deeply…

He'd wrenched himself from the fantasy too many times in the past few days. The last time he'd practically bitten off his broker's head. Now his mind whirled as he gave it free rein, his entire body humming with pent-up tension. He could practically feel her beneath his hands, taste her.

Smell her.

With dawning realisation, the denials he'd been wrestling with fell away like dirt washed from a submerged precious stone. He understood one thing with perfect clarity—he wanted Holly.

So what was stopping him?

"Go away. And no comment!" Holly's husky post-sleep growl came crashing over him through the intercom, and suddenly the wave of purpose that had carried him to her apartment drowned in hot desire.

"It's Jake."

She cursed softly. "Do you know what time it is?"

"It's—" he checked his watch "—ten minutes past eleven."

He heard her sharp intake of breath as she battled for calm. In gleeful anticipation, he wondered if she'd win.

In his mind's eye, he envisioned her jumping up from the bed in a flurry, throwing off the blankets, her hair in disarray. Her bare legs hitting cool air and goose-bumping her skin. Her nipples pebbling beneath some kind of red satin nightgown, one thin strap slipping gently off a shapely shoulder.

"What can't wait until Monday?" Holly was saying, her tone indicating she'd already repeated herself while he'd been halfway to fantasy land.

"I need to ask you something."

Holly rubbed her eyes and caught her sigh before it escaped. *Jake Vance needs me.*

She nearly laughed aloud. *Yeah, he really needs me like*

this. She took in her yellow oversize T-shirt and shorts, dotted with huge red hearts.

"Holly, can you just let me in?"

In answer she jabbed the button, grabbed a robe then shuffled to the door, opening it as he emerged from the dark pathway into the porch light.

"You've been working?" She eyed his business attire, her gaze coming to rest on the neckline where he'd loosened his tie.

"And thinking."

"Ahh."

"What?"

She heard the irritation in his voice and smiled. "Too much thinking'll do that." She walked down the hall then turned into the dimly lit kitchen. "About what?"

"I have a proposal for you."

"Which is?" She tightened her robe then glanced up, only to find him looking at her with that single-minded focus. She smiled to cover her nervousness. "What?"

"Marry me."

Eight

"Are you out of your mind?"

His smile petered out. "Not exactly the answer I was looking for."

"You're seriously going to go through with Garth's suggestion? Get married for the sake of Blackstone's?"

"No. I've given this a good deal of thought."

"You obviously haven't!"

"Yes, I have," he countered, eyeing her as she stopped pacing to glare at him. "A wife has been on my list for over a year."

Holly felt her jaw go slack. *Of course it has.* "Why me? Aren't there a dozen other women you could pick from? Supermodels, socialites…"

"I picked you."

Holly's skin prickled in excitement at his possessive declaration. She stubbornly forced it down. "Why?"

"Holly, let me lay this out for you. What I'm proposing is a business deal, pure and simple."

She narrowed her eyes. "What?"

"Hear me out. Romance, love, is unpredictable at best. I believe in attraction, lust. Sex." His eyes darkened as they settled on her lips. "I don't believe there's a power that conquers all. That's just too..."

"Optimistic?"

"Unrealistic," he corrected.

She blinked, weighing his words carefully. She had to know. For some perverse reason, she just had to. "You've never been in love?"

"Once. It didn't amount to much."

The cold cynicism slanting his mouth took her breath away. "With Mia?"

Jake's lip curled in barely hidden contempt. "No. Quinn's foster sister, Lucy."

Lucy? Holly blinked at the unfamiliar name. "So you'd settle for a bought wife."

"I'm not settling. You're everything I need in a wife. I'd be a fool to pass up the opportunity."

Indignation tightened her jaw. "How clever of you. And what do you have that I could possibly need?"

"Money." His eyes turned deadly serious. "I can clear all your debts, buy back your family home and pay respite care for your father." He named a dollar amount that staggered her.

"You..." she breathed, as reality washed over her in an icy wave. This was the kind of man he was. The kind of man who kissed like an angel, had the face of a living god. And who made deals like the devil.

"Your family needs you, Holly. Which means *you* need *me*.

I'm offering you a business deal and you should give it the attention it deserves."

Her heart contracted painfully in her chest. "Marriage is not a business deal. For your information I have other ways of finding that money. I don't need to marry you to get it."

"Really?" He narrowed his eyes, calling her bluff. "How?"

"That's none of your business."

"Does it involve Max Carlton?"

She flushed furiously. "No!"

"Blackstone's?"

"Why would it involve…" She blinked in sudden clarity. "You think *I'm* the press leak?"

Her disgust was so palpably raw, so instantaneous that it shamed him. Her response irrevocably proved her innocence. But despite that, one thought still niggled. "No. But there *is* something going on with you and Max."

She swallowed, her eyes darting past his shoulder. "He was my boss." She looked defiant. "End of story."

Liar. "So why not take my offer?"

Frustrated at her stubborn silence, he crossed his arms. "Fine. Let your parents lose their house. Have them floundering around in debt for the rest of their lives. And keep right on using most of your pay packet to support them."

The hurt in her eyes cut deep but he was too wound up, too hell-bent on getting her capitulation, to let that stop him now.

"You…you…"

"It's the truth. What we have is simple. You agree to be my wife and weather Blackstone's through this mess and I will compensate you so you can set your family up for life."

Holly slowly shook her head, backing away from him. The enormity of this situation, the implications, fluttered around in her head like swarming butterflies. "I can't think right now. I…" She swallowed thickly. "I need you to leave. Now."

"Holly."

She crossed her arms, aware how futile her defiance was in the face of his iron determination. "You can't force me into this. I need some time."

He searched her eyes, but she steeled herself to reveal nothing. "Don't take too long," he finally said. "I'll be expecting your answer." And with that he turned on his heel and walked out.

An hour later, Holly lay on her bed and glared at the ceiling, phone in her hand.

Despite the time, she'd called home to restore some of the balance to her careening thoughts, to touch a piece of stability that had been sadly missing since Jake had shown up. When her mom had answered, a wave of longing washed over her. Through the brief conversation Holly couldn't help but think how different everything would be if she was finally free of the weight of debt.

She loved her family but was so weary from being the sole responsible one. Her father couldn't help his condition, but her mother… Her chest tightened, hating the way her thoughts were headed. The term "enabled dependency" fit her mother well. She'd simply given up trying to cope and now Holly bore that burden alone, taking charge of the bill payments, buying groceries, scheduling her father's gruelling rehab. The exhaustion ate into her very bones, bringing forth a deep ache to her muscles.

The engaged signal buzzed in her ear, dragging her back to the present. With a tight throat, she cradled the receiver.

Rolling on her side, she shoved her cheek into the pillow. Pride and honour were two qualities she'd gotten from her dad. From her mum, it was a sense of integrity, a strong and deep respect for family. You stuck by them, no matter what.

She squeezed her eyes shut as uncertainty and fear battled for top honours, yet she had to consider all her options. It didn't change her situation with Max. In fact, it would only make it worse. Heaven knows what he'd do with no leverage against her. But that only made her more determined to extricate herself, to prove her innocence. Damned if she'd play a helpless damsel and let Jake fight her battles. But everything else had changed with one cool proposal. She had to do *something*, anything to save her family.

Jake Vance wants to marry me. The prospect excited as much as it petrified her. She swallowed thickly, shoving an errant curl off her cheek. Was it selfish to actually want this? That despite how concrete her marriage beliefs were she still thrilled at the prospect of having Jake all to herself?

She punched the pillow. He'd seduced her with his mouth and hands, then unknowingly elicited her compassion with his expertly covered wounds. Jake had changed everything, and despite her fervent wishes, she couldn't turn back time.

So if he could enter into this union with business-like clarity, so would she.

As the cab drove her to Jake's apartment complex, she glanced at her watch—one in the morning. Not too late for Jake, who was probably negotiating another million-dollar deal at this very moment. Which was why she was so surprised to hear his husky, sleepy growl after the reluctant security guard had buzzed the intercom.

Her thoughts were confirmed when she walked up the flight of stairs and found him framed in the doorway, waiting for her. She eyed his pajama bottoms, deep creases still indented in the fabric. They were new.

He must sleep in the nude.

She swallowed. Her eyes travelled over the smooth, broad chest, tracing the generous dip and swell of muscle before ending at his shoulders, one of which was leaning on the doorjamb.

"Can I help you?"

His words were mild but his expression was something else entirely. Holly felt the warmth spread from her neck. Another kind of heat—intimate heat—curled in her belly and fanned out. "We need to talk."

He shifted his weight, his arm slipping from the frame. "Come in."

She walked past his half-naked body and only just stopped herself from breathing in deep. Instead she straightened her back and kept going, finally stopping by the fireplace. Heat licked over her body, almost as if trying to ease her apprehension, assure her the decision she was about to make was the right one.

He just stood there, looking rumpled and touchable and so male that she wanted to run her hands over him to make sure he was real.

She crossed her arms. "Is this some strange boardroom game? Revenge against the Blackstones?"

"If I wanted to do that, I'd also want to see those share prices fall. Which I don't."

"Are you sure about this?"

"Isn't that my line?" His eyes creased with humour.

Unbidden, her lips quirked. "I won't quit working."

"I don't expect you to."

"Where will we live?"

"Howard's mansion is now mine."

Rattling around in that huge place…all those rooms… She shook her head. "What's wrong with here?"

He grinned. "Nothing, if you don't mind sharing my bed. I've only got one bedroom."

Holly blinked and flushed, her limbs suddenly becoming languid. "I don't want the press ambushing me at home, taking photos of me collecting the morning paper, digging through my garbage." Her face soured. "Miko's a private person and I won't do that to her."

"Then move in with me." Before she could voice the firm refusal teetering on her lips, Jake cut her off. "You've seen the security. You'll be completely protected."

A shiver tripped down her spine at his supreme confidence. *But who'll protect me from you? Who'll protect…*

"My parents." She stared in sudden acute awareness. "They'll be—"

"They'll be fine. I'll do what it takes to keep them out of it."

Holly's heart contracted painfully. "You're assuming I've said yes."

He crossed his arms. "Haven't you?"

She closed her eyes for a brief second. Where was the romance that she'd dreamed about since she was a little girl? The bended knee, the shaky question from love-filled eyes?

She tamped down her disappointment. *Get a grip, Holly. That's a fantasy. A romantic, unrealistic fantasy.* "I'm saying yes."

"I'll get the contract drawn up." He picked up his phone, punched in a few numbers and issued some orders.

So that's how it was done, Holly thought dazedly. One call, a couple of words and her whole life was irrevocably changed.

The enormity of what she'd just agreed to stunned her so much that she never saw the kiss coming. But in the second that it took for his lips to briefly brush hers, she'd wished he'd never made the effort. It was cold, chaste and very, very business-like.

"To seal our deal," he murmured before withdrawing, taking the heat from his bare skin with him.

You're about to enter into an arranged marriage purely for altruistic reasons. Of course the kiss would be passionless.

So why did she find herself yearning for another, the same one that had stolen her breath with its will-sapping intense heat?

"We'll tell the Blackstones on Monday," Jake said.

Holly paused. "About that. I'd like to keep the details of our arrangement private."

"You want us to fake it?"

She tilted her chin up. "If the truth stays with us, then there'll be no leak. And I need to tell my mum before some reporter splashes it all over the papers."

That sobered him. "You're right. Our success depends on maintaining the charade of romance."

There was something in the way he said that, a definite curl to his lip. "You think romance is a charade?"

"I believe in making logical decisions, not emotional ones. So I'm assuming we have a deal?"

A deal. She dropped her gaze to avoid Jake seeing her dismay. They were so different, so incompatible. Marriage was the culmination of her adolescent romantic aspirations, her fantasies of having it all—a career, a husband and someday, children. Instead she'd made a deal with the devil.

What on earth was she thinking?

It was the look in his eyes, so cool, so business-like. Surely there'd been a time when he'd been a young boy in love, full of hopes and dreams for the future?

She jumped as his firm hand tipped her chin upwards. "Getting cold feet already?" he murmured.

"I have terms." His eyes narrowed and he let her go as she continued, "The full amount you offered needs to be transferred to my account as soon as possible."

"Done." He nodded.

She swallowed. "And I need you to be faithful."

"As in…?"

"No dating other women, no photographs, no cheating. No gossip. It might be a sham marriage, but my family will not suffer for it."

Jake watched the way she tilted her head, proud defiance shimmering in her honest blue eyes.

She'd been the subject of gossip before, first after the Mac-Flight takeover, then the Shipley scandal. He knew she abhorred it.

Which meant, beyond a doubt, that she wasn't the press leak.

When he nodded, the tension in her face ebbed. "How long before we'll see an upturn in the Blackstone shares?" she asked.

"A few weeks, maybe. A good year before it stabilises."

"So that's my stipulation. A year after our wedding date, I'm free to seek a divorce."

Jake raised one eyebrow. "Don't you mean an annulment?"

"An annulment is only if we don't have sex. Oh."

On the tail end of this grin, Holly's face heated.

"Are you planning on having sex with me, Holly? Because

if you are," he continued slowly, obviously enjoying her look of shock, "then I'd be more than willing to accommodate you. Considering my vow to remain faithful for a whole year."

Holly opened her mouth but nothing came out. Until… "You are the most arrogant, conceited—"

He reached out and silenced her with a practised kiss.

The kiss was different again. Not the cool, perfunctory one of seconds ago. Not the punishing one of Saturday night, full of anger and barely leashed frustration.

No, this one was a lesson in seduction, a leisurely exploration of her mouth, designed to specifically arouse.

A guarantee of things to come.

He nibbled her bottom lip as his strong hands cupped her face. Gently, he took his time, increasing the pressure and intensity until desire began to thump in her blood and her eyes fluttered closed.

This was more like it.

She settled up against him willingly, wanting to feel him, to melt into the hot promises his kisses offered.

It amazed her that her body responded to his so surely, so completely. But it was thrillingly, terrifyingly wonderful.

"Stay."

She groaned at his soft command. She attempted to swallow, but her throat was suddenly thick. Instead she looked away, trying to hide the desperate desire no doubt written on her face. For all her hesitation, all her fears, the look in his eyes was real. Her body tingled.

"I can't."

"Can't or won't?"

She closed her eyes as his soft breath ruffled a curl across her cheek and his insistent arousal pressed firmly against her belly. "I can't. I'm going home tomorrow. It's Mother's Day on Sunday."

She felt the exact moment he withdrew. A withdrawal that had nothing to do with his physical position and everything to do with his mindset.

He nodded curtly, running a hand over the back of his neck. Fascinated, Holly watched the corded muscle in his arms flex and release. "You can take my jet."

"Your…?"

He smiled without humour. "Get used to it, Holly. Steve will pick you up in the morning and fly you home. No arguments."

Nine

Late Sunday night, Jake was there to meet her after the plane touched down at the private airstrip. Holly couldn't stop the thrill of pleasure bubbling up at the sight of him. There was no doubt he was a powerful presence in the boardroom, but now, dressed in jeans, emerald sweater and a black leather jacket, that power kicked over into crazy-dangerous territory. It took all her control not to reach up and run her palm over his five-o'clock shadow, to feel the rasp of skin on skin.

It was an ominous portent that excited yet terrified her.

"I told my parents," she said as the car sped them through the clear, cool night. Her lips tilted briefly, as she remembered her mother's excited face, one that had paled then flushed in shock when she realised just who her son-in-law was going to be. Holly even thought she'd seen a flicker of emotion in her father's well-worn face, a face devoid of expression for so many years. "She wants to meet you."

"Of course." Her surprise at his quick acceptance must have shown on her face. "What?" He studied her carefully. "You don't want me to?"

"No. Yes." She untied her tongue. "That is, if you want to." He nodded. "I want to."

A moment passed between them then, a deeply intimate moment that Holly seized like a desperate woman, tucking it away.

Then he looked away and the moment was gone.

When she returned to the view, she frowned. "This isn't the way to my place."

"The press are still sniffing around. We're going home instead."

Home. She barely had time to be annoyed at his autocratic assumption before they were there. When she reached the doorway to his apartment, her legs were leaden with trepidation. At his enquiring look, she shook away the anxiety and stepped over the threshold, shrugging off her jacket and hanging it on the coat rack.

She was going to be living here and Holly couldn't quite believe it. He was James Blackstone, heir to untold wealth and fortune, holder of extraordinary power. But he was also a man—an amazing, strong, complex man who would soon become her husband.

"First room on the left," Jake called as she mounted the stairs. With a sigh she dumped her bag near the brand-new double bed, the sigh ending in a little gasp as she walked into the ensuite.

It wasn't the gorgeous clawed marble bathtub that surprised her, nor the clean blue-on-white tiling or the skylight that twinkled in the dim light. It was the toiletries lining the elegant vanity—brand-new versions of her moisturiser, her cleanser, her hair mousse. She blinked and smiled, then turned on the shower.

She moved into his spare room silently, but Jake felt her presence more keenly than ever before. When he came up to ask if she wanted coffee, he saw that she hadn't touched anything, not even rearranged the chairs or removed one book from the shelf, yet it was as if her essence had seeped into every piece of furniture in his apartment. The faint, fresh smell was everywhere now, not just at work or in his car. She'd not only invaded his thoughts, but now she was in his space and it suddenly felt like nothing was his any longer.

It felt comfortable.

With coffee cup in hand she settled on the far corner of his couch. She was barefoot, dressed in jeans and a dark blue sweater in some soft material that clung to her curves, and the intimacy of having her in his place, on his couch, speared him low.

Yet the intimacy was tempered with a small but definite amount of tension. He watched her carefully over the rim of his cup, noting the way she fidgeted with her hair. Hair that wasn't tied up in a ponytail, he noticed. It fell around her shoulders, shiny, curling at the ends, demanding to be touched.

"When we visited Daniel's grave on Sunday…there was a new headstone. You didn't have to do that. Thank you, Jake."

He quickly shook himself from the fantasy. "It just seemed like the right thing to do."

"With money so tight, we couldn't afford a decent one."

"I know."

He nodded then cursed inwardly at his lame response. Instead of taking guilty pleasure from the heartfelt gratitude shining her eyes, he should be saying something, doing something…

And then, in a wave of singular clarity, he knew exactly what needed to be said.

"I used to have nightmares."

Holly stilled, unable to move for fear it would jinx the moment. "About?"

"Driving when it was teeming with rain. I can hear the sound it makes on the roof right before we plunge headfirst into a river. I hurt my neck from the whiplash."

Holly held her breath and her head began to spin.

"The water…is dark and foul." His voice came out husky and raw, almost like a great pain seeped from his heart. "It leaks into the car from the broken front window. I bang on the windows but can't get out. I try and try but my hands start to hurt and—" He voice faltered and suddenly there was silence.

It shattered the intimacy so suddenly that Holly reeled from the shock.

When he finally spoke, her chest ached at the cool distance in his clipped tone. "I'm sorry. It's late. You should go to bed."

She watched him stand abruptly while her heart pounded in her throat. There was no way she could sleep now, not with what he'd just said running crazy circles in her brain. He'd given her an amazing intimacy, more intimate than that night in his office, when his lips had been on her mouth, his fingers buried deep inside her.

This powerful, proud, untouchable man had shared something. Which meant she'd discovered a little part of his soul, too.

That thought thrilled her, almost too much.

"No. Stay with me."

Jake was frozen to the spot for one long second, then slowly he turned.

"Stay with me," she repeated, stepped forward to press her body against his, ending his denial on a groan. Her chin tilted up, the look in her eyes pure wanting.

She wanted him.

"Holly—" With a soft curse, Jake relinquished the thin grip on his control.

Like a man deprived of water for weeks, he covered her mouth with his, drinking deeply of her warmth, her compassion.

When her tongue slipped gently between his lips, a low growl of possession erupted from deep within. He crushed her up against him as if he could absorb her directly into his skin.

He wanted to be buried in this woman's passion. Now.

In one swift movement he lifted her in his arms and strode purposefully out of the room, her arms wrapped around his neck.

Mere seconds—or was it a lifetime?—later, he shouldered open the bedroom door and laid her on the bed, his attention never leaving her face as he stripped. Reclining on bent elbows, she watched him with a knowing smile, all tease and promise. All woman. Her eyes grazed over his skin, an erotically charged caress.

Arousal came on hot and strong.

"Strip."

His harsh command sent a thrill of anticipation through every nerve ending in Holly's body. She did, and in record time she was standing there in only a pair of white bikini panties and a matching push-up bra.

When she reached behind for the clasp, he grabbed her arms and shoved her back on the bed.

"Leave it."

And then he was covering her, his long, lean body of granite muscle and hot flesh easing up then settling into her dips and curves.

They fit perfectly.

His hand covered her breast, her nipple eagerly tightening under his smooth caress. With a guttural growl, he gently eased the satin down until both her breasts spilled over the top, a delicious display for his hungry eyes.

Cupping her soft flesh, he took his time, tasting first one, then the other. His mouth and teeth grazed the hard little buds, sucking them into peaks, before pulling back and blowing gently on the swollen nipples.

Ribbons of exquisite sensation wrapped her entire body, swaddling her tingling flesh. His hands were built for loving, for pleasure. And she revelled in it until the throbbing between her legs became unbearable, and she squirmed, needing to find relief.

All she found was his hard arousal nudging at her belly.

She groaned. "Jake, please."

He looked up at her with a wicked gleam in his eye, his mouth still surrounding one breast, teeth grazing, tongue flicking. She couldn't bear it any longer!

Then, finally, he said, "Since you asked so nicely…"

With hot need throbbing away in his veins, Jake reached down and dragged aside the damp fabric of her panties.

He heard Holly gasp, an erotic sound of excited eagerness. *Not yet, my love. Not yet.*

When he placed his mouth to her hot damp curls, she

nearly bucked right off the bed. With a firm hand he grasped her hips, holding her in place. And then slowly, sensuously, he proceeded to love her with his tongue.

For a million seconds Holly couldn't breathe. She was one raw nerve, tingling and hot from Jake's mouth, from his breath fanning the fire between her legs, from his soft tongue, licking, caressing the tiny bud that made her quiver and shudder every time he rolled over the sensitive flesh.

She wanted to faint from pleasure. Instead she screamed as the desperate flood of release crashed into her body, drowning her in a wave of ultimate bliss.

Before she could recover, Jake had eased up beside her and was kissing her, her salty taste shockingly intimate on his lips.

She drove her fingers in his hair, revelling in the silky smoothness, joyous that he was all hers to touch, to taste. She wanted to do all that and more, to show him that if he'd only let her, they could have a real future together.

"Jake," she whispered, her breath ragged when he finally, gently, eased his finger into her tightness, still wet from her climax.

Jake clenched his jaw, trying desperately to cling to control, even as he felt it slipping away. With gritted teeth he reached for the nightstand, cursing as he fumbled with the condom packet before she impatiently shoved his hands away and completed the task in record time.

Finally he poised above her, devouring the sight of her peaked nipples, the hot passion in her eyes. With a shuddering breath and a fervent prayer, he plunged deeply.

Colors swirled behind his eyes, creating a maelstrom of sensation. He felt the hot slickness of her muscles surrounding him, the eagerness in her lips as their tongues mingled in erotic mimicry. She smelled divine, an innocent scent mixed with the musky decadence of sex.

She whimpered, almost as if the feeling was unbearable. Yet still her hips rose to his, meeting him stroke for stroke, urging him on. Her gasps as he drew back nearly did him in, but he forced his body to maintain a steady rhythm inside her.

He was on fire, the flames licking at every inch of his skin, pulsing and throbbing.

But he wanted more. Needed more.

He grasped her legs, wrapped them around his waist and plunged deeper.

Holly's eyes opened wide. She realised she was gripping his shoulders, clinging to him the way a drowning victim clings to a life raft. His face was a study in erotic intensity. Those green eyes glowed, full of blazing desire and heat. The muscles in his taut jaw eased and tensed with every soft moan of pleasure he dragged from her.

When he took one nipple in his mouth, grazing her with his teeth, she lost it.

Release, long and loud, erupted from her lips. Through her climax she felt him shudder, as he too, finally took his pleasure.

Much later Holly lay on her back, Jake's rhythmic breathing on her nape, his hand curled possessively around her breast. With a slow, shuddering breath, she let the tumbling emotions wash over her, a blissful wave that paradoxically thrilled and frightened her all at once.

There was no way she could deny it. She loved him.

Jake muttered in his sleep, his hand moving gently over her skin. Her eyes widened as her body leapt to life underneath his touch.

Even now she wanted him. Again.

Slowly, almost teasingly, his palm began to move over her nipple.

She drew in a trembling breath and squeezed her eyes shut, only to hear his rumbling chuckle.

Her eyes snapped open to meet his, and she encountered the smoky desire in those emerald depths.

Later she'd sort through what this all meant. Right now she turned to cover his grinning mouth with her own. Right now this powerful, proud, amazing man wanted her.

"Engaged."

Holly nodded as Kim stood from behind her desk and repeated the word again like an incantation. "That was…" Kim hesitated then looked Holly straight in the eyes and said carefully, "Sudden."

"Sometimes you just have to seize the day." Jake took Holly's hand, nearly startling her, and smiled.

Holly swallowed, caught up in the glow of that one simple action, the way Jake's face transformed into something that stole the uncertainty from her lips. How good an actor was he?

She returned his smile, which he took in his stride, squeezing her hand in acknowledgement.

"Well, Jake is nothing but unpredictable," Kim finally said, walking over to place a congratulatory kiss on Holly's cheek. When she pulled back she scanned Holly's face, her eyes radiating concern.

Holly offered a smile and met her look head-on. "Given the time frame, we should announce it a week out from the ball."

At Kim's silence, Holly added hastily, "You've seen the

media with this. We want the ball to get as much publicity as possible before diverting attention elsewhere."

Kim nodded and sat on the corner of her desk. "OK. I've e-mailed you the final guest list, so after the invites go out, you can make that public. If you need anything, let me know."

"Thanks." For one second, she thought Kim would add something more, but instead, she let them go without further interrogation.

"Do you think she bought it?" Jake asked her as they walked down the corridor to their office.

"Probably not."

"I wanted to tell her the truth."

"No."

"Why not?"

Holly walked through the glass doors, her back straight. "Because it's embarrassing, OK? Normal, well-adjusted people date, fall in love and get married. They don't coldly sign a contract for mutual gain."

He smiled at her indignation. "You're one of the most normal, well-adjusted people I've met, Holly."

"Am I?"

She didn't need to be a mind reader to work out just what was going through his head as they stood there. She blinked slowly, desperate to hide her expression, but her body betrayed her. She felt the heat bloom across her cheeks, spreading languorous warmth into her limbs.

Just when she thought he was about to say something, his phone rang. He flipped it open, said, "I'm on my way," and dropped a perfunctory kiss on Holly's cheek before he strode out the door.

Her fingers traced the rapidly cooling warmth where his

lips had just met her skin. The smallest remnants of a tingle forced her heart into a loping thud-thud.

She'd been dismissed. And just as quickly, her heart began to pound in irritation.

She tried not to let it get to her, to focus on the ball preparations, but like a nasty, annoying itch she kept returning to the irritation. Was this an indication of things to come—an abnormal marriage, made from an abnormal deal?

She'd be a professional wife, all show and smiles, Jake's escort to all the proper functions. There would be no intimacy outside the public eye, no sudden romantic gestures, no happy-ever-after dreams that she'd envisioned all her teenage life. No promises of everlasting love.

Why should that upset her?

She squeezed her eyes shut and breathed deeply. *You need to get real, Holly. That's not going to happen.* There'd be no physical contact, unless she told him she wanted it, like last night.

She jolted, her eyes snapping open.

Oh, she wanted it. Badly. But could she walk away after a year was over?

Enough. You need to focus on the here and now. With a determined straightening of her shoulders, she reached for the phone and dialled.

"So what's the big secret?" Jessica asked after they'd both collected their lunches and taken a seat near the sun-drenched windows overlooking busy George Street.

"Why do you think I have a secret?" Holly glanced around the Blackstone's cafeteria before biting into her chicken salad sandwich with gusto. Jessica's eyes followed hers.

"That's the only reason we're here at two o'clock, long after the lunch rush. Why you chose this table, away from everyone else…" She dropped her voice low. "You're not pregnant, are you?"

Holly nearly spat out her food. In a flurry of coughing, she grabbed the bottle of water as Jessica gently patted her back.

"No," she finally choked out.

"Well, it has to be something big to warrant this sudden meeting. Not that I don't enjoy our infrequent lunches," Jessica said quickly. "But I know you're flat out with this ball, and handling Jake Vance can't be a walk in the park." She picked up her spoon and dipped it into her pumpkin soup. "How's that going, by the way?"

Holly hesitated, telltale heat prickling her skin. "Busy."

Jessica smiled. "It's OK, Holly. Ryan told me."

He did? "How does he know?"

Now it was Jessica's turn to be confused. "About Jake being James?"

"Oh."

"What did you think I meant?"

Holly took a bite of her sandwich to stall. Jake had been at AdVance Corp all day and whether she wanted to admit or not, she'd missed him. Her thighs tingled at the memories of last night. How he'd made her feel. It had been simply… amazing. He certainly had the Midas touch when it came to pleasing a woman. And he was all hers for a whole year. That thought sent a decadent thrill through her.

A year. Twelve months. Fifty-two weeks. Three hundred and sixty-five days.

She focused on the tabletop and took a thick swallow. No. It wouldn't be all Jake, all the time. He led a busy life that centred around making money, not keeping a wife happy. She was purely there to bolster Blackstone's standing and she had gone into it willingly, with eyes wide open.

"So that's it."

"What?" She refocused on Jessica, who was now grinning like an idiot.

"You've got a thing for Jake Vance."

Denial teetered on the tip of her tongue, the second before she realised that she needed Jess—in fact, everyone—to believe she and Jake had fallen madly in love in less than two weeks.

"Well…"

Jessica leaned in conspiratorially. "I saw that look. Your insides went all gooey just thinking about that six-foot-four hunk of corporate muscle."

"Power does not turn me on," Holly said primly, picking out a piece of tomato from her sandwich.

"Well, must be those eyes, then. That face. Hmm…have you kissed him yet?"

"Jess…" Holly squirmed in her seat.

"You have! I knew it. Tell me."

Holly took a breath and said slowly, "It's a bit more than that."

"Ooh, a scandal!"

"He asked me to marry him."

Jessica's spoon clattered to the floor. "No."

"Yes!" And despite herself, she felt the wide grin from ear to ear.

Jessica grabbed her hands, her joy evident. "This is wonderful! I'm so happy for you!"

At last, a reaction that was worthy of such a life-changing event. A rush of relief flooded her, easing the tension from her spine. "Thank you."

"I thought I saw something between you two at the store," Jess teased. "Have you told your parents?"

"Yesterday. I don't think Mum can comprehend it. She asked when Jake was coming to visit."

"That'll be a culture shock," Jessica murmured.

An understatement, Holly thought as Jessica started on which bridal magazines to stock up on, who would be available to cater, decorate, design. And for once, Holly shoved away the gloomy realities and instead let Jessica's excitement buoy her.

Ten

It was 6:22 p.m. when Holly walked out of Blackstone's delivery entrance to hail a cab. She knew the exact time because she'd been fiddling with the full-color screen of her brand-new mobile phone prototype that Emma in Design had thrust upon her earlier.

"Five megapixel camera, voice recording, Internet access… encrusted with Blackstone diamonds, of course!" the girl had enthused.

"How much is it worth?" Holly had breathed, fingering the stone-studded buttons.

"This one's only a prototype. The stones are CZs instead of real diamonds. It's for the woman who has everything."

Now Holly grimaced as she scrolled through the function buttons. Was she officially a woman who had everything?

Well, you do have Jake Vance. Most women would kill for that.

She nearly dropped the phone when someone suddenly grabbed her arm.

"Max! What are you—" She snapped her mouth shut at the dark anger contorting his face.

"I've been hearing things, Holly. Interesting things. About you and Jake Vance."

He furtively glanced about, alerting her to the fact that the dock was deserted. She was alone with Max in a darkened alleyway, away from prying eyes. She swallowed her apprehension and hoisted her bag on her shoulder.

"What things?"

A sharp wind blew past and he shoved his hands in his pockets. "How you and he are getting along a little too well."

"So?" She blinked. "The papers are full of that stuff. Doesn't mean they're right."

"Oh, I know the difference between fact and fiction." He gave her a devious grin, full of malicious intent. "I have proof."

Holly's mouth went dry. "Proof?"

"Does Wednesday night, executive elevator, ring any bells?"

Holly's heart swelled up, pounding in the back of her throat. Through the shock she saw Max smile. "Funny, I'd never peg Vance for a ten-minute guy. But then, I have intimate—" his eyes swept her body appraisingly "—knowledge of you. He probably couldn't control himself."

Shock yielded quickly to anger. "What do you want?"

"You focusing on our deal," he snapped. "Vance has been meeting secretly with the board and the Blackstones. The bastard's trying to get proof so he can fire me. And if he does, I'll bring you down, Holly. Don't doubt that. All it takes is one phone call and you'll have a dozen reporters on your doorstep."

"I already have," Holly snapped, her heart skipping a beat. "What else can you say that hasn't already hit the papers?"

Max rocked back on his heels, a triumphant gleam in his eyes. "Oh, I reckon the public would be interested to hear all about our little liaison. Especially now that you and Vance are bedmates."

The sharp crack of her palm meeting his cheek echoed in the cold air. The imprint of her hand slowly reddened before Holly's disgusted eyes, her shock only confirming what Max already knew. He barked out a triumphant laugh, a horrible "gotcha!" sound at her look of horror.

"It's funny—you getting cozy with the same guy who's blocking your transfer."

Max's verbal bomb exploded deep inside her. As she numbly shook her head, he shrugged. "When I asked Kim for an update, she said Jake put a hold on your transfer indefinitely."

"I don't believe you!"

"Go ask him. Oh, and that slap will cost you, babe. You and your boyfriend. Ten thousand to start. Or I'll release the tape to the papers."

The press. Oh, my…

The pieces suddenly fell into place with a resounding click. "You!" she said. "*You're* the press leak."

He gave her a slow, controlled clap. "Well done, Holly. My own secretary the first to figure it out. Pity you can't do anything about it."

"Why, Max? You have a good job, an excellent job. What on earth made you betray the Blackstones' trust?"

He gave her a scathing look. "Howard Blackstone thought he was so bloody untouchable with his boardroom politics and holier-than-thou kids. The man had a string of women yet he had the nerve to include a morality clause then lecture me on personal ethics, to reprimand me for sleeping with his staff. It was none of his bloody business."

"So you leaked stories to the press to get back at him. The plane crash. Kimberley's wedding…"

"Yep. And soon the sordid details of Holly and Jake's little affair." His eyes gleamed. "It'll be the lead on every news channel in the country, possibly even the world."

"Unless Jake pays up."

"Unless he pays up. And you, babe," he added, his expression turning triumphant, twisting his features into a snarl, "are my leverage."

Jake knew the moment Holly turned up on his doorstep that something was wrong.

"Why are you blocking my transfer?" she gritted out as she strode inside.

He closed the door with a gentle click then pointed the remote at the television. The split screens flickered off.

"Who told you?"

"Max."

"Ah."

"So? Is it true?"

"Yes."

She shot him a look of pure venom laced with haughty pride.

"Why? Why would you do that?"

"Why are you suddenly concerned about what that man says?"

"Because I've just spent ten minutes listening to his demands. And don't change the subject. Why—"

"What demands?"

"He has a security tape of us in the elevator."

"I see."

The angular lines of his face tightened and she breathed in quick, sharp. "He's also the press leak."

She waited for rage to explode, but all she got was a raised eyebrow. Jake said, "That I suspected."

She blinked. "You did?"

He nodded. "I've had him under surveillance. And I've been meeting with the board outside Blackstone's. It's amazing what people will let slip when they're relaxed and on their own turf." He reached for the phone and dialled.

"What are you going to do?"

"Get him arrested."

After a few minutes, he hung up and swung to face her with a considering look. "Is that all?" he asked softly.

She blanched. "Why?"

"Because a tape of us does not make for a huge scandal, considering we're now engaged. What else does he have on you?"

She tried to swallow past the lump in her throat. "Does it matter?"

"It matters."

She closed her eyes briefly then opened them again, meeting his steely gaze without flinching. "When I was working for Max I slept with him, OK? I breached my morality contract. A dumb, stupid thing to do. Then I put in for that temporary PR job and thought he'd let me go but…" She trailed off in the face of his cool silence. "You knew, didn't you?"

"Max enlightened me about your relationship when I fired him yesterday."

"He—" Holly swallowed a thick wad of disgust in her throat. "Did he also tell you he was blackmailing me to spy on you?"

"No." It wasn't the matter-of-fact way he'd said that one small word; it was the flash of suspicion crossing his face. "Did you tell him anything?"

Her heart plunged. "If I said no would you believe me?"

Doubt was quickly replaced by a cold, remote expression, so eerily familiar that it cut her more surely than Max's threats ever could. "So why bother asking? You've already made up your mind."

His uncertainty in her innocence wounded her to the core. Hadn't she gone against every deeply held belief she had and said yes to a marriage, even when she knew it'd only end in failure a year from now? Didn't he realise how much it had taken for her to say yes?

You love him.

At that tiny spark of realisation, her whole body leapt with joy. But just as quickly, pain sent it crashing to the ground. No. She couldn't. She wouldn't. How could she fall in love with a man who would never return it? A man who thought marriage was just another requirement to tick off on his to-do list, who had brokered it to save a company?

A company you love, her conscience niggled. A company where you felt you belonged, working with people whom you've come to like and respect. But all that didn't mean squat, not when Jake was standing right there, waiting for her to say something, as if daring her to prove her wild claims.

Slowly she withdrew the mobile phone from her coat and gently placed it on the kitchen bench. "I'm not lying, Jake. Here's your proof."

Her dignified exit was foiled when he grabbed her arm before she could reach the door.

With a sharp hiss she twisted, only to still at the serious look in his eyes. "Stay. Let me hear this first."

"I'll be out on the balcony." Craving the cold, sharp bite of air, Holly opened the sweeping glass doors and walked outside. Behind her, in the cavernous silence, she could hear her tinny voice as Jake played back the recording of her and Max in the alleyway.

Ten minutes later Jake had managed to put a lid on his simmering anger as he crossed the threshold to the balcony. The sight of Holly framed against the darkening storm clouds stopped him short. She was propped against the railing, her forehead resting on her arms as they hung limply over the edge. It was the stance of someone close to defeat, to complete and utter exhaustion.

In the blink of an eye, his anger dissipated, whatever details he'd been about to demand escaping his lips in a small sigh.

"Why didn't you come to me with this?"

She raised her head abruptly but didn't turn around. "It was personal. What we have is purely business."

A band of something he couldn't define tightened around his chest.

She turned then, crossing her arms. "So you believe me."

Lord, she unmanned him with her searching eyes. He swallowed. "Yes."

The intensity of her relief surprised him. Yet it also revealed that she needed him to believe she was innocent, that his trust meant something to her.

He'd never thought that one person's opinion could count for so much, could affect him so profoundly. And in that moment, pleasure swamped him.

"Max said you were refusing to approve my transfer."

Her soft statement, devoid of accusation, sent a shot of guilt along his spine. "You've heard the expression, Keep your friends close, your enemies closer?"

"Jake. I'm not—"

"I sensed something going on between you and Max, something you were hiding." He dragged a hand through his hair then rubbed the back of his neck, pausing to warily eye her. She remained still, her expression shadowed by the cloudy night sky. After a brief hesitation, he said brusquely, "I promised the Blackstones I'd find their leak."

Guilt tore at Holly's conscience. Jake was so used to running his own show that explaining himself was obviously foreign to him. It showed in every line of his scowl to the harsh gruffness of his voice.

"I'm sorry," she said, "but I needed to save my job. For my family." She stared across the water, at the dancing lights of Sydney. "I know it's no excuse but—"

Jake covered her cold hands in his. To her amazement the simple touch exuded comfort.

"You're a strong woman, Holly," he said at length.

"Not out of choice."

His eyes met hers in gentle acknowledgement and Holly held her breath, one second, two, before voicing the question teetering on her tongue.

"Tell me about your mother."

He abruptly broke eye contact. For one unbearable moment Holly thought he was going to shut her down. *Don't, don't, don't. Tell me because you want to, Jake. Not because you have to.*

When he finally spoke, his voice was so low the air practically vibrated. "April drifted with the seasonal work—fruit picking, mostly. Then cash-in-hand stuff like cleaning and bar work. I remembered being on the road a lot, different houses and rooms, YMCAs, lots of take-away places.

"One time I asked why we always had to leave." He sucked in a slow breath as though the admission pained him. "I can still hear her voice, see the sadness in her eyes, almost as if she were ashamed. 'Because I'm afraid of what will happen if we get caught,' she said. I assumed it was about her abusive boyfriend. We finally stopped running when I was ten."

"South Australia."

"Yeah. In a town that never fully accepted her." Jake remained silent for the longest time, torn between the wisdom of keeping silent and the desperate need to finally have done with it. With clenched fists he took the first terrifying step and forged on.

"By the time she married, I was uncontrollable, on the path to a criminal record. Maybe she needed to be loved. Maybe she thought I needed a father figure—who knows. So she married an abusive drunk who spent all their money on cigarettes and liquor."

"So you left home."

He nodded. "I was a frustrated, angry kid, desperate for a place to belong. I felt...alone, like a stranger in a foreign country. Like I was destined for something else. No one understood that, least of all April. We argued about me leaving. I didn't want to be her only reason for staying sober. And I couldn't save her unless she wanted to be saved. So I left.

"I ended up in Sydney with three dollars to my name and a chip on my shoulder the size of a skyscraper. After the small-town gossip, the city was a relief. A huge, concrete metropolis of anonymity. Without any money, I was taken in by Quinn's parents, into their halfway house in Newtown."

"Where you met Lucy."

He nodded. "We were together for seven years, until the whole Jaxon Financial thing. It took all my money to clear my name, and suddenly she didn't want to be with someone who was broke. Recovering from that betrayal was one of the hardest things I've ever done."

Her hand on his arm was soft, the touch reassuring. It unmanned him.

"Then came Mia."

"Yes." His mouth twisted. "My assistant who lied and cheated."

"Did your mum know where you were after you left?"

He swallowed and closed his eyes. "Not for ten months."

"Oh, Jake."

Her abject sadness pierced his heart. "Believe me, it's not something I was proud of."

"But you eventually made it up to her. That counts for something."

He pressed his fist to the cold metal, trying to grind out the fresh pain welling in the old wound.

As Holly watched him standing there, a solitary figure surrounded by wealth and success, struggling with his inner demons, her compassion took an abrupt detour, morphing into something warmer, deeper. Scarier. It bloomed slowly, cautiously in the corner of her heart she'd reminded herself never to relinquish until she was positive she couldn't be hurt again. But her emotions were far from listening to reason. Her heartbeat quickened, her breath became shallow, her skin heated.

Here was a man who desperately needed to be loved. His

eyes might radiate coldness, a calculating coldness that fooled most, but not her. In every stern line on his granite face, every steely tension in his muscles, she knew.

It would take a special woman to break through that tightly leashed control. She knew what she was up against—the ghosts of women past had not been kind to Jake Vance. They'd made him who he was—distrustful of emotion, determined not to take risks.

She nearly laughed aloud. His whole life was about taking risks...except when it involved love.

Oh yes, he was a long shot. But what did she have to lose? Her heart? No, he already had that. But if she didn't at least try, then she'd never know.

"I have something for you," he said softly, shattering the silence.

She waited as he dug around in his jacket pocket. When he produced a velvet box Holly felt the breath catch in her throat.

She took it, eased open the lid. And gasped.

She recognised the ring from the Blackstone's store—a simple square-cut sapphire on a plain gold band, surrounded by tiny diamonds.

When she finally met his eyes, the uncharacteristic uncertainty on his face stunned her.

"I know it's not exactly how you thought this moment would be, Holly, but—"

"It's perfect. How did you know?"

He smiled an odd, almost gentle smile. "You stared at this ring for far too long."

She smiled back, and despite the reality of what she'd agreed to, emotion clogged her throat.

He must have sensed that because, with a barely hidden

flash of alarm, he removed the ring from the box, grasped her hand and slipped it on.

A perfect fit.

His hand lingered on hers, yet when she looked up at him, he'd erected his wall so quickly that Holly could almost see it going up brick by brick. And it was so expertly made that it made her want to weep. How could she ever break that thing down, when it had taken him years to construct and perfect it?

By showing him with the only thing that felt true, that temporarily dismantled all his defences, all his barriers.

She took a deep, shuddering breath before she leaned in and kissed him.

Eleven

The remaining days leading up to the charity ball passed in one big blur. Holly felt as if she were walking on air, as if sheer joy radiated from her like a tiny sun. First Jessica, then Kim, had commented on her "bridal glow," a comment that brought an embarrassing flush to her cheeks.

As expected, their engagement announcement the week before had prompted an almost obscene amount of publicity. Blackstone's had been inundated with requests for interviews, photo shoots, exclusives. And every time, Jake had told her to refuse them. Their silence only exacerbated the mysterious secrecy surrounding their initial announcement, which, from a publicity point of view, couldn't have been more perfect in its timing. Instead of takeovers and Jake's chequered past, the papers were now speculating on wedding dresses, honeymoons and whether the charity ball was really a cover for their secret wedding reception.

As Jake had promised, Max was charged with multiple contract violations and issued with a gag order. "Along with some subtly aimed threats," Kim had confided to Holly. To Holly's amazement, she and Kim had quickly formed a strong bond, sharing more than just business-related topics as they worked towards the impending date of the charity ball. Jessica had also made a habit of lunching with her every Friday, which touched Holly more deeply than she wanted to admit.

It was bittersweet, this sudden and immediate acceptance into the Blackstone clan, yet she refused to dwell on the wider implications. For once in her life she wasn't planning, scheduling and budgeting for the future, and she discovered she actually liked the feeling of not knowing what the future held.

At least, most of the future, anyway.

Jake was in meetings all day, either at Blackstone's or AdVance Corp, and when he finally came home, he sequestered himself in his office.

Despite her disappointment at being unable to publicly lay claim to him, to show him off in a burst of uncharacteristic womanly pride, the nights more than made up for it. They made love with a deep explosive passion, almost desperate in its intensity. Afterwards, in the dark, Jake revealed scraps of what his life had been like, how he'd come to scale the dizzying heights of the corporate world. She treasured those moments, storing them deep inside, knowing how much it took for this intensely private man to open up, even a little.

It meant hope, however meagre.

Many nights the words *I love you* teetered on the tip of her tongue, but she always ended up swallowing them. Yes, she desperately wanted to tell him how she felt. But she was also afraid. Afraid it would further add to what was already a complicated situation. That he wouldn't believe her and she'd drive him away.

Afraid she'd lose whatever little he offered her.

So instead she showed him. With her body, her hands, her lips, she showed him how desperately she loved him. It had to be enough for now.

And all too quickly, the night of the charity ball rolled around.

Jake was on the phone when Holly returned from her hair appointment. He caught a brief glimpse as she darted up the stairs, and when he'd followed her into the bedroom, found the ensuite door firmly closed, her "don't come in!" full of warning when he'd rapped on the door.

"I'll be in the kitchen," he replied through the door, glad he was already dressed.

He was staring out the kitchen window at a glittery cruise ship in the harbour when he sensed Holly behind him. Then he turned, and all brooding thoughts fizzled from his brain.

She was dressed in a white clingy creation, the vertical pleats emphasizing the gentle curves of her body. With her hair pulled high and back, curls cascading over her shoulders, she looked like some Egyptian goddess. The gauzy material draped across her breasts almost lovingly, and it was held up by small shoestring straps, leaving her arms bare. Beneath his unabashed staring, goose bumps spread over her skin.

"Is my dress OK?" She nervously tugged at the neckline, tweaking the fabric into place.

"You're more than OK."

Amazingly, after everything they'd done together, after every body part he'd teased, kissed and caressed, she blushed. He'd never get tired of seeing her blush.

Holly swallowed, suddenly breathless and more than a

little hot. It was as if he wanted to rip off her dress right then and there. And heaven help her, she wanted to let him.

Instead, she let her gaze roam over her husband-to-be. Jake had flaunted the black-tie requirement, instead choosing a black suit with a long dress coat, a pale green shirt and emerald cravat.

Under her careful study he grinned. "Acceptable?"

"Definitely. Me?"

"You're beautiful."

She swallowed, shifting her weight from one foot to the other. "Th-thank you."

He reached up, almost as if he was going to touch her cheek. She noticed a hesitation that revealed more than any words could.

Doubt swamped her. She'd spent the better part of the day with Kimberley and Jessica, first nailing down the last minute details, then being completely pampered with a half-day intensive makeover at Double Bay's exclusive Angsana Day Spa. Buoyed by the anticipation of the coming night, Kim had expressed her future vision for Blackstone's. Despite Holly's joy that Jake was included in those plans, Kim's predictions only served to exacerbate the glaring differences between her and the Blackstones, widening that chasm even more.

Now Jake's palm on her cheek seared her skin, branding her for ever. "I need to tell you something."

She leaned in to the touch, reveling in the gentle intimacy. "Yes?"

"Ric is going to announce our joint chairmanship tonight."

Holly eased away with a confused smile. "You and Ric will be running Blackstone's together?"

Jake nodded, absently running his thumb pad over the

curve of her cheek. "That's why I've been in all those meetings. He and Kim are building a house and want to start a family. He's had a shift in priorities."

"I see. That's...wonderful." It was. Really. The implication for Jake was huge. It meant he was a trusted family member of the highest standing. Yet all she could think of in the glow of his deep satisfaction was the growing canyon between them. This was just another small detail to glaringly highlight they were two completely different people.

She smiled brightly to cover up her burgeoning sadness then glanced at her watch. "We'd better go."

He nodded and placed a hand on the small of her back to lead her out the door. It was a warm brand of possession, one of such erotic simplicity that it made her insides ache. It felt as if every inch of her skin was aware and craved his touch, as if she couldn't get enough of it. As if she hungered for it.

Yet as she stared at him, all she could think of was how good he'd felt under her fingers, her lips. How much she wanted to lean over and kiss him.

How much she loved him. And how desperately she wanted to tell him, despite how it would irrevocably change everything.

They arrived at the ball amidst a press frenzy. The flash and pop of cameras lit up the red carpet like Oscar night, the air peppered with paparazzi calling out commands, eager for everyone's attention.

Holly stared out the car window and took a deep breath.

"Ready?" Jake murmured beside her.

She simply nodded.

As he exited the car an excited buzz went up from the assembled crowd.

Opening her passenger door, he extended his hand. The confident smile on his sensuous mouth set her nerves fluttering again, but for an entirely different reason. "Smile, Holly. We're engaged, getting married, and it's the best night of your life."

He'd never know she didn't have to fake it. She shoved all her niggling doubts firmly aside and smiled back at him. And then she firmly entwined her fingers in his, gathered up her skirts and stepped out into the waiting melee.

"Jake! Jake! A shot of you and your fiancée!"

"How does it feel to be finally getting married?"

"Have you set a date yet?"

"Holly! Who's going to be designing your wedding dress?"

The roar of the press, the flash of cameras came at her like a wave. She lifted a hand to shield her eyes, but Jake grabbed it and whispered, "Hand down. Smile as much as you can. Wave to the people. And pretend you're excited to be here."

"But I can't see!" she replied through a clenched smile.

"I know." His fingers tightened around hers as he waved back to the crowd and grinned. "It'll be over soon."

When he swept her into Blackstone's Grand Ballroom, the sudden noise drop made her ears ring. But in the next instant, she gasped.

The room was fit for a royal reception: dark purple velvet drapes edged with gold spanned the wide length. On top of white Grecian pillars sat huge golden decanters, pouring out black branches sprinkled with fairy lights. On the ceiling strings of tiny lights winked and sparkled, swooping low to meet the huge chandelier in the middle. Like an expensive diamond caught in the lights, the room shone—an apt backdrop for a Blackstone ball.

Yet after Jake's initial assessment, the room could have been knee-deep in desert sand for all the attention he gave it. Instead, he was mesmerised by Holly's satisfied smile on her dark pink lips, the kissy-mole creasing upwards.

Like a man suddenly wakened from a dream, he couldn't stop staring at her. Her profile, the way the shiny curls brushed the curve of her shoulders, his to touch if he so wished. And when she turned to look at him, pride glowing in her face, all at once a slow smile spread his mouth.

He could see the pulse beat in her throat, too great a temptation.

With a stubborn set to her jaw she looked right into his eyes and lifted her brow, a female imitation of his boardroom stare down.

I dare you.

He leaned in to kiss her, a kiss of such slow tenderness that something bloomed deep in his belly, something warm and protective and totally crazy. As he gently explored the shape of her mouth, his whole body began to vibrate.

"Aren't you going to introduce us, Jake?"

Holly started at Jake's soft oath, seeing the frustration tinge the edges of his expression, and smothered a chuckle.

Then she turned to the stunning blonde in a show-stopper strapless red dress, diamonds shimmering along the deep slit that rode high on one long tanned thigh. She needed no introduction to the woman labeled the Face of Blackstone Diamonds.

Briana Davenport.

"Briana." Jake kissed her lightly on the cheek, nonplussed when her date gave him a once-over, possessiveness clear in his blue eyes. "So you're the lucky guy who managed to land Briana."

"She picked me. And it looks like I'm not the only lucky one." He gave Holly a smile before shaking Jake's hand. "Jarrod Hammond. Congratulations on your engagement."

"Thanks. You're Matt Hammond's brother, right?"

As the men launched into a low discussion, Briana smiled at Holly and rolled her eyes. "Men. Remove them from the workplace and they still manage to talk about it. That's a gorgeous dress, by the way."

Holly returned Briana's genuine smile gratefully. "Thank you. I nearly tripped over the train three times."

Briana laughed. "Your first public outing is going well."

Holly grimaced. "I wish I was more like Kimberley, all grace and presence."

Both women's eyes landed on Kim, a vision of elegance in a black strapless floor-length creation, as she led the conversation in the circle of Blackstones.

"They all look fabulous, don't they?" Briana whispered. "Kind of regal. Almost perfect."

A perfect fit for Jake.

Her stomach dropped to her knees. *You knew what you were getting into. All the signs were there.*

According to Kim's vision, Jake would eventually take over Blackstone Diamonds and all that entailed. More money, more power, with a family who'd been denied to him for so long. Who did she think she was to demand his attention from all of that?

She closed her eyes for a brief second as pain ratcheted through her. How could she possibly let Jake go when their time was up? Yet she couldn't go back to her normal life as if nothing had happened.

She'd have to leave. Not just Blackstone, but possibly the

country. At least until the attention died down. There was no way she could remain here, feeling his presence in the halls, possibly even seeing him again.

Love wasn't in his plans, he'd made that perfectly clear. He needed her to see this deal through professionally, unemotionally.

She knew she was deathly scared, and in ignoring the deeper implications, she chose to protect her heart, to keep it intact so she could survive the rest of their time together. Self-preservation. That's what it was. And as much as she wanted to crawl into a tight ball and weep with the injustice of it all, she ignored it. Jake had been through enough, everyone had.

This was her gift to him.

As Holly watched, Ryan Blackstone said something to his wife and passed a gentle hand over her rounded belly. Jessica laughed, glowing in a shimmery silver halter-top gown.

An unexpected wave of longing smashed into Holly, freezing the smile on her face. Stunned, she blinked, glanced away…only to clash with Jake's all-seeing eyes.

She stiffened, desperately trying to dredge up a nonchalant smile to cover the raw emotion but failing abysmally. He wasn't just looking *at* her—he was looking deeper than that. His dark eyes glittered with something she couldn't quite fathom, something almost intimate and tender.

She held her breath.

"I don't believe it," Briana whispered. Holly followed Briana's shocked gaze and saw a tall man, resplendent in a black tux, standing apart from the crowd, flicking through the auction catalogue with a scowl on his handsome face.

"Matt Hammond," Jake said softly before taking Holly's hand in a firm grip and striding forward.

In a confused haze Holly kept up. Matt Hammond, Kimberley's ex-boss, Briana's brother-in-law, the widower of Marise. A man so committed to keeping the Blackstone-Hammond feud alive that he'd refused the ball invitation point blank when she'd called to confirm he'd actually received it. The man now in possession of four of the missing five Blackstone diamonds.

The closer they got, the more Holly felt trouble brewing. It wasn't anything overt, like Jake's commanding presence, more like a dark shroud of pain and betrayal covering the other man's impeccably dressed shoulders.

"Hammond," Jake said.

"Vance."

The two men shook hands and Holly was introduced, Matt acknowledging her with the barest of nods.

"What changed your mind about the invitation?" Jake said without preamble.

"Curiosity. I heard a rumor about some special announcement tonight." He flicked icy-cold eyes across the assembled throng that buzzed with the low throb of conversation and excitement. "And I wanted to see just how deeply the Blackstones had dug their claws into you."

Jake gave him a thin smile. "Wound-free, so far."

"Really." When Matt's gaze settled on Holly, she felt the shiver all the way up her spine. She bore the brunt of that deep, slow-burning anger with outward calm yet instinctively sought the warmth of Jake's hand. Without hesitation, he linked his fingers in hers.

Matt shifted his stance as a flash of something tightened his features. She'd thought Jake had a closet full of demons, but Matt Hammond had a thousand more.

"Quinn tells me you're looking for the last Blackstone Rose diamond," he said curtly.

Holly knew Matt Hammond had hit a nerve when she felt the tension vibrating through Jake's body. But she also knew his face would betray nothing. Still, she gave his rigid hand a reassuring squeeze, to let him know she was there if he needed her.

"That's right," Jake said.

"It's not yours to find."

"So?"

"So back off."

The air suddenly bristled palpably. Holly held her breath. For seconds—or was it minutes?—the two men faced each other off, not exactly adversarial yet worlds away from being friendly. Around them, people chattered, laughed, drank and ate, but the glittery event felt strangely muffled and dull around the edges of this small standoff.

Then, amazingly, Jake squeezed her fingers and in the next moment she felt his body relax.

"Only because you asked so nicely. And now, if you'll excuse us?"

Jake turned and, with a conspiratorial smile at Holly, drew her away.

"What was that about?" she whispered, pausing for the photographer before giving Jake her full attention.

"It's about knowing when to pick your moment, my sweet." He nodded over to the stage, to where Kimberley was adjusting the microphone. "The auction's about to begin."

"...and so, we have pleasure in introducing you to our eldest brother, James Hammond Blackstone."

There was a brief second of total stunned silence, a second in which Holly held her breath and tightened her grip on Jake's hand as they stood in the wings. But in the next instant, he smiled down at her, released her fingers and walked out onto the stage.

From behind the curtains, Holly dragged her eyes from his commanding figure to scan the crowd. The official photographers were going wild, snapping pictures of Jake, of the official handshake with a smiling Ric, of Jake accepting Kimberley's hug with practised ease. It was only when he came to Ryan that she saw him falter, a brief question in his face. Ryan nodded and instead of taking Jake's proffered hand, enveloped him in a hug.

Tears pricked behind her eyes, her heart swelling.

"Thank you all for your generous support tonight," a flushed Kimberley finally said over the din. "Please stay and finish the champagne. For those of you leaving, travel safely."

As they all left the stage, the noise level rose in one raucous wave, followed by flashing cameras exploding like tiny stars. Then the curtains abruptly fell, plunging the stage into muted normality.

When Jake spied Holly on the outskirts, fiddling with the tiny drop earrings in her lobe, his heart did a strange flip. She accepted everyone's congratulations with gracious aplomb, and when she looked up and spotted him, he echoed her heartfelt smile with his own, one of such unadulterated pleasure that he could see her flush from where he stood.

He devoured the space until she was in his arms. Slowly, deliberately, just because she was his and he could, he pulled her up against his length and kissed her. The truth of that kiss, the deep emotional connection they'd shared the past few weeks, floored him. Unmindful of where they were, he let his mouth leisurely roam over hers, pausing at the edge to lavish attention to that kissy-mole. Against him, he felt Holly stir, felt her warm sigh spill over his jaw, and just like that, he was ready.

"You need to stop," she muttered even as her neck tilted to give him better access.

He glanced across the room, to where the Blackstones were in animated discussion. "Can't stop."

Gently she placed her hands on his shoulders. "Must."

"Can't. Holly," he warned, stilling her. "Give me a minute. Unless you want everyone to know exactly how much I can't control myself."

As realisation heated Holly's cheeks, she felt the gentle rumble of Jake's chuckle, one full of intimate knowledge. And just like that, a deep, bone-jarring ache hit her. She wanted to spend the rest of her life with this man. She wanted to be the one to make him smile. To have his babies.

She blinked. What if that had already happened? They'd been using protection but nothing was foolproof. How could she justify leaving if Jake's child grew in her belly?

"You can turn around." His warm breath across her cheek jolted her back to the present. "We'll finish this later." His eyes held so much promise of pleasure to come that it made her forget every misgiving, every doubt.

At least, for tonight.

Twelve

Jake lingered in bed, unwilling to leave the warmth of Holly's soft, naked body. In truth, there was no place he'd rather be than here.

He reached for her, gently waking her with warm kisses. He loved the way she woke, all sleepy eyed and confused. As if she wasn't entirely sure she should be here, as if she'd emerged from a dream.

It was his dream—big, bold and erotic.

She blinked, twitching her nose as the delicious smell of hot coffee permeated the air.

"Morning," he muttered against her cheek.

She stretched, her curves moving in delightful torture against his growing arousal, and he felt her smile. "Is that coffee I smell?"

"Maybe." He nibbled her earlobe, grinning against her

neck as she shivered. In the next second, she leapt up and grabbed her robe, swishing it around her gloriously naked body with a laugh. "I'll be back."

He flopped back on the bed with a mock sigh. "Don't drink it all. And bring me a cup!" he called as she padded out the door.

An unfamiliar languorous warmth spread over his body, seeping into his bones.

He was…content. Happy.

Damn, he was ecstatic. For once, he felt like he belonged.

He'd been working hard these past few weeks, driven by the unfamiliar compulsion to convince the Blackstones of his commitment. He knew they were the kind of people who judged by deed, not words, so he'd personally ensured that Max Carlton was no longer a threat, that his mates on the board were quietly handed an ultimatum to leave or face criminal charges.

Instead of dark apprehension, he was surprised to feel relief. Relief it was all over, finally. He felt confident, almost optimistic, about the future. A future that hadn't felt so right until now. Until Holly.

He'd been missing something…something that began with a kiss and burnt bushfire hot when he and Holly made love. A flame he'd been determinedly ignoring in order to focus on the Blackstones.

The truth hit him like a speeding truck. What he'd been missing out on all those years while clawing his way to the top was family.

Yes, he'd had Quinn's family, but despite the glorious welcome they'd always given him, he'd always felt on the fringe, an outsider looking in. He'd been blessed with April.

She wasn't perfect or of his flesh and blood, but a generous, supporting woman all the same. One who loved him completely, who'd been prepared to do anything for him.

The power of a parent's love for a child was real; it was tangible. The kind of love Holly had for her mother and her father. The kind of love he wanted to share one day with his own child.

The object of his thoughts now stood in the doorway, fully dressed, a sheaf of papers in her hand.

"What, no coffee?" His teasing grin fell at the tight look on her face. His eyes went quickly to the papers. The prenup.

"When did you get these?" Her voice was light, almost calm.

"A few days ago."

"I need to sign them, yes?"

No. He sat up and nodded. With an odd, dignified composure, she made her way over to the bedside table, picked up a pen and signed with a flourish.

"Aren't you going to read it?"

She straightened. "I'm sure you've addressed every contingency, Jake."

He frowned as she walked over to the door. "I need to make sure the ballroom's been cleared plus Briana invited me to lunch later. I might not see you until tonight." She gave him a fleeting smile, devoid of warmth. Then she was gone.

What the hell had just happened?

He threw off the covers and grabbed the prenup. If she'd only just read it, she'd realise he wanted her for longer than a year. If fact, he was so confident about their deal that he'd actually made an allowance for babies resulting in the union.

It was all there, in black and white. Clause 22A paragraph C…

He paused as realisation suddenly hit, then groaned long and loud.

You fool.

With tears blurring her vision, Holly grabbed her handbag then slammed out the front door. Did she really think she could change this man with a bunch of kisses and a few nights of passionate lovemaking? He may have the Midas touch but no amount of gold could turn this marriage into a real one.

She stumbled and a strong hand yanked her up short. She whirled and came face-to-face with Jake, dark exasperation clouding his features.

"What are you—?"

"We need to talk."

"I'll be late." She pulled at his grip but her strength was no match for his. She had no choice but to follow him back into the apartment.

After he slammed the door behind them she backed away, crossing her arms. "What on earth are you doing?"

"I changed my mind. People do that sometimes."

But not you. Holly swallowed. "OK."

He took a breath, releasing it in a rush. "Is this about me co-chairing Blackstone's?"

Her chest contracted painfully. "No. This is a big thing for them, Jake," she said softly. "It means they trust you. You're truly a Blackstone now and all that entails."

"And what about you?"

"Is being a Blackstone something you want? Wait." He held up a hand when she opened her mouth. "For one second, forget about our deal—the money, the press. What do you really want, Holly?"

Fear rioted through her. She took a deep, shuddering breath meant to give her strength. Instead it robbed her of all rational thought.

"The party—those people…I'm just a country girl who still believes in love and you…" She waved her hand in his direction. "And now with the added weight and prestige of the Blackstone dynasty, where does that leave me?"

"You think we've made a mistake."

"Yes, I do." It was out there now, no going back. "I'll…I'll pay you back—"

He blinked, clearly taken aback. "Don't be ridiculous."

She forced herself to rise above the hurt and resentment. She'd pretended she could handle this maturely, but the truth was stark. She'd given her heart, and nothing short of his in return would have satisfied her. But he didn't offer it. Jake had been nothing but honest with her, laying down everything clearly and succinctly. She'd gone into this with open eyes and now she was the one wanting to change the status quo. He probably felt pressured and she couldn't blame him.

Her heart plummeted to her feet. "So it's just me you don't want."

Escape. Run. The fight or flight response snaked low in her belly and Holly shifted her weight, her calves aching from her hesitation. The air seemed to throb with life, the silence growing louder as he stared at her.

Then he smiled, shaking his head.

Her icy fear instantaneously melted into irritation. "You think this is funny?"

"I'm not laughing at you, Holly." He reached for her but she slapped him away, taking a step back for good measure. "And *I* thought I couldn't read what was right in front of me."

At her fierce glare, Jake's amusement dropped like a stone in water. A thousand unsaid words jumbled about in his head, none of them clever, none of them sane. He took a steadying breath to prepare himself. Still, he didn't know what to say.

The billionaire negotiator suddenly lost for words. Quinn would laugh himself silly at the irony.

Finally he spoke. From the heart. "Even when I left home, after I made my money, lost it, then gained it again, I always felt something was missing," he said slowly, picking his words with care. "Even with all the answers, there's…" He struggled with the admission before finally saying, "There's a hole. For years I thought it was guilt because I couldn't change the past no matter how much money I made." He allowed himself one moment of grief before shoving it away into the past, where it belonged. It was time to focus on the future.

"But now I know it's something else." He studied her keenly, trying to get handle on her thoughts. Her head was bowed, eyes focused on the floor, fingers threaded together in front. A lonely picture of defeat.

He nearly groaned. She unmanned him. He'd put those doubts in her stance with his stupid hesitation. Not any more.

"You asked where it left you. It's here, as my wife. Let me finish, Holly," he growled when her eyes snapped up and she opened her mouth. "Yes, this started out as purely a business deal. But right here, right now—" He broke off, took a shaky breath. "You touch me on a deep level, a level that includes both my head and my heart, in ways I never thought possible. Yes, my past was tough and shaped me into who I am today. But that's not who I am inside." He finally took her hand and placed it on his chest, and his throat clogged with emotion. "You saw that."

She closed her eyes briefly, as if his words pained her. But when she opened them, he was blown away by the love shining in those blue depths.

"I want you as my wife, my friend, my lover. I don't need the Blackstones to feel like I belong because I know I already do with you. I love you."

Holly couldn't breathe, couldn't move. The look in his eyes was so bare, so raw. So desperately needy that it made her want to cry.

She felt the telltale prick of tears behind her eyes. And when a sole tear slipped silently down her cheek, Jake reached out and caught it with one finger.

Slowly she smiled, joyfully throwing herself over the abyss. "I love you, too, Jake. Always. For ever."

They came together in a kiss, a tender kiss that gradually turned from gentle to aching in the blink of an eye.

Jake finally pulled back to search her face. "I want what Kim and Ryan have. A family, a future. A place I belong." His voice dipped lower, almost breaking. "Babies."

The love blazing from her eyes floored him. Humbled him. And filled him with so much joy that he felt like shouting it from the rooftops.

She was his. Now. For ever.

"Are you going to kiss me again, or what?"

He laughed and as he bent to accede to her demand, muttered, "I love you, Holly."

Her contentment seeped out against the gentle pressure of his lips, the promise of more, much more, to come.

Much later that day, Holly lay beside Jake, her fingers entwined in his in the cool silence. He'd finally unplugged the phone after the third call from his office and the second from first Kim, then Ryan. She sensed he'd detached himself but knew she only had to touch him to bring him back to her.

She knew his demons, knew them and still loved him for it. She squeezed his hand, glanced up at her husband-to-be and basked in the realisation that he was finally hers.

The gentle beep of Jake's mobile permeated the air but he ignored it, instead saying, "Kim told me she'd talked to you about Max."

"Mmm." Ridden with guilt, she'd finally confessed her involvement last night. "You know what she said? 'If you'd come to me, I'd have believed you.'" Holly shook her head. Kim's blind acceptance of her innocence in the spy plot still stunned her.

The rumble of Jake's laughter filled the bedroom. "Man, we don't need anyone to complicate our lives. We do that all by ourselves." He dodged Holly's nudge. "Kim also asked me to help mend the rift between the Hammonds and the Blackstones."

Holly paused, recalling the look on Matt's face last night following their revelation of Jake as James. Betrayal? Anger? "It won't be easy. Matt Hammond is—" she searched for the right word "—very committed to his bitterness."

"I live for a challenge."

She laughed. "Don't I know it."

He lifted himself up on one elbow, studying her intently. "Are you ready for this— For the entire country to finally know the complete details about the Blackstone Baby?"

"For as long as you want me, Jake Vance."

"Jake Blackstone," he corrected, before placing a gentle kiss on her lips, a promise of things to come. "And that would be for ever."

* * * * *

JEALOUSY & A
JEWELLED PROPOSITION

YVONNE LINDSAY

New Zealand born to Dutch immigrant parents, **Yvonne Lindsay** became an avid romance reader at the age of thirteen. Now, married to her blind date and with two surprisingly amenable teenagers, she remains a firm believer in the power of romance. Yvonne feels privileged to be able to bring to her readers the stories of her heart. In her spare time, when not writing, she can be found with her nose firmly in a book, reliving the power of love in all walks of life. She can be contacted via her website, www.yvonnelindsay.com.

This book is dedicated to Gordon, Morgan and Tegan, for your patience, understanding and support through every stage of the continuity and beyond. Thank you. I love you guys so much.

One

He was alone.

Matt Hammond punched in the code that gave him access to the inner sanctum of House of Hammond and realised being alone was the one true constant in his life these days. Even Lionel Wong, the backbone of the business and usually the last to leave each evening, had gone home. Matt paused in the silence and drank in the satisfaction that came from being here.

It always felt like coming home. A feeling he'd come to look forward to during his all-too-frequent forays overseas in the past few months.

He dropped his briefcase on his desk and slumped into his high-backed leather chair. Weariness pulled at every cell in his body, but he refused to acknowledge it, or the hollow emptiness that dwelt in his chest. It'd been a helluva six months so far. Just when would life let up? He brushed the question aside. He had no time for the inanity of rhetoric right now. Each day brought its own challenge, and he would meet every one of them and win. Winning was just about all he had left.

He snatched up the collection of messages his secretary had left in the centre of his desk, a frown scoring two sharp lines between his eyebrows as the same name appeared again and again.

Jake Vance. Or, in his other persona, James Blackstone—the famous Blackstone missing heir finally returned to a glorious welcome home.

With a reflexive crunch of his fingers, Matt reduced the messages to trash and ignominiously launched them into the wastepaper basket.

He had no desire to speak with a Blackstone, whether he bore that name by choice or otherwise. The family was responsible for more misery than he cared to acknowledge. Traitors or thieves, every last one of them right down to Kimberley Blackstone. Perrini, now, he corrected himself. Hers had been the bitterest betrayal of all. He'd expected more of his cousin. She'd become his right hand in the business over the past ten years, but in the end she'd been just like her father. A Blackstone to the bone. And to think she'd believed the rivalry between the Hammonds and the Blackstones could be mended.

The slow rage that constantly burned deep within him fought to rise to the surface, but with his inimitable cool control he tamped it back down. There would be

satisfaction. Everything the Blackstones had done—
and the list was extensive—would come home to roost.

Matt leaned back in his seat and steepled his fingers
under his chin. It wouldn't be long now and he'd be the
one pulling Blackstone strings. A Hammond in control,
as it should have been before Howard Blackstone
stripped the family of its Australian assets with his un-
scrupulous methods. Blackstone had made his fortune
by taking what he wanted, particularly from the Hammonds, but he'd dealt one hand too many when he'd
taken Marise. Matt had sworn on the man's grave that
he would pay and he would. Despite the glitch in his
plans when Vincent Blackstone had refused to sell out
his share holding to Matt back in February, there was
nothing the Blackstones could do to stop him now.
Matt's people had painstakingly approached minor
shareholders with enough incentive that he was now
very close to success.

He gave his desk another cursory glance. Still no
message from Quinn Everard. He'd expected by now
that the gem broker would have a solid lead on the last
of the Blackstone Rose diamonds. Perhaps Everard's
contacts weren't as efficient as he'd believed. That was
the trouble with stolen property. It was difficult to find.
Especially property that should have been a part of
Matt's family's heritage and not tainted by the Blackstone name.

With a sigh, Matt leaned forward and popped open
his briefcase to remove a contract from inside. A faint
hint of a smile played around his lips. Success. With the
agreement of the New Zealand Pacific Pearl distribu-

tors now in his hands he could fine-tune the launch of the Matt Hammond Heirloom Range of jewellery.

His own signature range.

He'd been working hard for months on developing the line of reproduction antique jewellery, and finally it would come to fruition. A man had to grab his pleasures where he could, Matt reminded himself, especially in a life like his that had seen precious few of them in some time.

Speaking of pleasures, this little foray into the office on his way home from the airport had cost him the pleasure of putting his son, Blake, to bed. Matt flicked a look at the Patek Philippe watch his father had presented to him on his twenty-first birthday and grimaced. Yeah, it was definitely far too late to catch Blake. But there was always the morning.

No matter how empty his marriage had become before Marise's departure to Australia, at least it had left him with his son. The void around his heart squeezed a little tighter. Had his dead wife had the last laugh on him after all? No, he didn't want to go down that route. He didn't want to even consider that Blake was not his own. As an adopted child himself he knew it shouldn't matter. Love and care and upbringing created the bonds between father and son, not just blood. But the question continued to prickle, like a fine metal filing wedged under the skin.

Was Howard Blackstone Blake's real father?

The thought made his gut clench. Marise had always been fascinated with the Blackstone family. But her death five months ago, as a result of the plane crash that had also taken the life of the Blackstone patriarch, had raised more questions than answers. Questions like what the hell was she doing with Howard Blackstone in the first place? Matt knew Blackstone would have relished rubbing his nose in an affair.

He wrestled once more with the anger that threatened to boil over. Howard Blackstone. It always came down to him. But no more. By the end of the month Matt's plans would reach their ultimate conclusion and he would exact his ultimate revenge.

He got up from his chair to file the new contract, dictated a short note to his secretary and headed off for home. Tomorrow was another day. He still had the night to get through and it would be long and lonely enough.

Subtle garden lighting spread pools of gold over the rain-washed driveway as Matt turned in through the iron gates that led to his family home in Auckland's exclusive Devonport. At least the paparazzi were no longer camped at his front gate. Five months ago he'd barely been able to move without having a camera or a microphone shoved in his face. Now the furore over Marise's and Howard Blackstone's deaths had all but died away, but the bitterness still lingered.

The formality of the gardens that lined the drive had once been his mother's pride and joy. Matt still questioned his parents' decision to move to a nearby assisted-living complex after his father's stroke. Goodness knew the house was large enough for them all and modification of a suite of rooms for his parents would've been simple enough. But they'd been insistent it was time he took over the property for his family.

Some family. A wife who'd been homesick and un-settled almost from the day of their marriage and who'd abandoned their vows and their child without so much as a backward glance. Matt could never forgive her for walking out on them the way she had—and especially not when she'd gone straight into the arms of Howard Blackstone.

The garage door slid open at a touch of a button and Matt pulled his Mercedes-Benz SLR McLaren into its bay, the rumble of its powerful engine fading as he turned the motor off. To one side still sat Marise's Porsche Cayenne. He really had to do something about getting rid of the Cayenne. Since she'd gone, he'd done little more than take it round the block once a month, preferring to use his other car—a Mercedes sedan—when taking Blake out. But like other less urgent things, dealing with the Porsche had to wait until he was ready. More important matters pressed on his time right now.

He'd told Rachel, Blake's temporary nanny, to use the thing. Marise had, after all, insisted on the vehicle for Blake's safety on the road, but Rachel had preferred to use her mother's smaller hatchback, arguing that in his child restraint Blake would be just as safe. She'd even gone onto the Land Transport Safety Authority Web site and printed the crash reports for her make and model of vehicle to prove her point. Eventually it'd been easier to give in to her demands.

But Matt knew from past experience, giving in to Rachel Kincaid's demands was a weakness that spelled trouble with a capital 'T'.

The interior of his home was softly lit, quietness all

pervading. He made his way along the passage towards the stairs with the intention of checking on Blake. He could have negotiated every room in the dark; there was no need for Rachel or her mother—his house-keeper, Mrs Kincaid—to have left lights on for him.

A small noise as he passed by the living room attracted his attention. His eyes alighted on a sleeping form spread out on the large couch. Rachel. Her rich nut-brown hair was pulled back in a plait, but tendrils had escaped to kiss the rim of her heart-shaped face. Like this, she looked about ten years younger than the twenty-eight he knew her to be. In fact she looked little different from the determined tomboy who had followed him and his brother, Jarrod, around as often as her mother had allowed it while they were growing up. Nothing like the suddenly sophisticated young woman he'd escorted to her high school graduation dance on the night that had seen her graduate to new levels of maturity beneath his touch. He'd betrayed her innocence, he reminded himself, forcing his wakening libido into submission, and he'd betrayed her trust. It wouldn't happen again.

She stirred again, as if aware of his scrutiny, then settled back into the plump cushions of the sofa. Her sweatshirt slid above the waistband of her jeans and slightly twisted across her ribs, showcasing the lush curves of her body. Her lips were soft and full, slightly parted as if awaiting some fairy-tale prince to come and wake her from her slumber. Matt clenched his jaw uncomfortably. What was he thinking?

Rachel Kincaid was his son's nanny, no more, no

less—and he was certainly no prince, fairy tale or otherwise. What happened in the past was a mistake best forgotten and filed back into the recesses of his memory. What he needed to do now was rouse her and send her home. Goodness knew what she was still doing here, anyway. Mrs Kincaid lived in her own quarters—a self-contained unit at the far end of the house—except for the times Matt travelled overseas. On those occasions she'd stay in one of the upstairs guest rooms so she could keep an ear out for Blake. It hadn't been necessary for Rachel to live in, and that was just the way he liked it. It was unsettling enough to have her in the house by day, but to have her live in? That would definitely stretch the bounds of sanity.

He reached forward to give her a little shake but hesitated with his hand in the air over her shoulder, the warmth of her body a tangible thing in the air between them. At her side Blake's even breathing could be faintly heard on the baby monitor. It suddenly occurred to Matt that Mrs Kincaid's quarters had been in total darkness when he'd pulled into the driveway. Strange.

Matt let his hand drop to Rachel's shoulder, his shadow crossing her face. She stirred and her eyelids flicked open. Her hazel eyes, initially unfocussed, sharpened suddenly as she realised he was there. Matt pulled his hand back, telling himself it was not regret that trickled through him because his touch had been so brief, but relief instead.

"You're home."

There was an accusatory note in her voice that set his hackles up instantly.

"So it would seem," he answered coolly.

"Blake was upset you weren't here at bedtime, like you promised," she persisted in the same tone of voice.

"My flight was later back than anticipated and I had to go into the office from the airport." Damn, he didn't answer to her, so why did he let her make him feel so darned guilty?

"Really? 'Had to,' Matt? On a Sunday night? You've been gone since the middle of last week." She pushed herself up from the couch and stood up to him, her five-and-a-half-foot frame no match for his six feet. "What was so much more important than spending time with your son? You forget, he's just a little boy—not even four years old. He needs his father."

"I forget nothing, Rachel." For a moment the air between them thickened, his words taking on a double entendre that related more to the spectre of the past that hovered broodingly between them than the present. Matt made a sweeping motion with his hand, as if to brush away the words he now wished unspoken. "Go on, head off. Start later tomorrow. I'll get your mum to see to Blake in the morning."

He reached for the baby monitor on the couch and switched it off. He had one in his master suite downstairs. Since Marise had departed for Australia at the beginning of December last year, he'd become attuned to the noises Blake made through the night. His fatherly instinct had sent him flying up the stairs to the boy's room at the slightest indication of distress before Blake could even wake properly.

"That's the problem. She can't."

Matt stilled. "What do you mean?"

"I left a message on your cell phone," she said with growing irritation, evidenced by the tension around her full lips. "Mum's been called away. Her sister, down in Wanganui, had a fall today. She's really shaken up. Mum flew down to help her."

The ramifications of Rachel's short speech hit home hard. No Mrs Kincaid? That meant…

"So I'll have to stay in house." She continued, oblivious to the silent clamour of denial in his head. "I can stay in Mum's apartment, or one of the rooms upstairs. I think upstairs would be best, given your erratic hours lately."

Matt fielded her pointed glare. "How long?"

"What?"

"How long is your mother going to be in Wanganui?"

"We don't know yet. Aunty Jane is quite a bit older than Mum, and rather frail. Hopefully we'll get a better idea in a few days."

"A few days." Matt repeated the words flatly. He could cope with a few days.

"Well, we'll know in a few days. It could be longer." She put up one hand to stifle a yawn. "Before I go, there's something else I need to talk to you about."

"Can't it wait?"

"Not this, no." She fidgeted slightly, pulling her bottle-green sweatshirt down over her hips and smoothing the fabric.

The movement drew his attention to the tiny span of her waist and the generous flare of her hips. She was dynamite in a tiny package, all right. A forbidden package, he reminded himself sternly. As forbidden now as she'd been the night of her high school graduation ball.

But that hadn't stopped you then, a cold, sly voice reminded him.

"What is it?" he snapped, irritated by his own inability to tamp down the curl of desire that snaked through his body at her mere presence.

"I'm worried about Blake." She hesitated, chewing slightly on her lower lip, clearly reluctant to continue.

"Worried? In what way exactly? Is he ill?" His hand clenched around the baby monitor; the plastic casing squeaked in protest.

"No, he's fine. He's over that cold from last week. Look, I really don't know how to put this any other way so I'll just come straight out with it. You have to make more of an effort to spend more time at home with him."

"I'm doing what I can," Matt ground out.

"It's not enough. He's become too attached to me of late. Surely you've noticed."

He had noticed, and it had hurt that when Blake had taken a tumble off his little bike on the back patio the other day, he'd run straight past Matt and into Rachel's comforting arms.

"It's only to be expected. He's lost his mother and I've had to be away a lot lately. He'll come right." They all would, in time.

"Matt, he's started to call me Mummy."

The words sank in with the weight of a sinking destroyer.

"He what? And you're letting him?"

"Of course not! I correct him all the time but he's

a stubborn tyke, you know that. He's just like you in that respect."

In that respect, yes, but in others? Blake's colouring was nothing like Matt's own sandy-blond hair and grey eyes. Blake's hair was dark, almost black, his eyes green. *He looks like a Blackstone.* Matt pushed the errant thought from his mind before it could take a stronger hold.

"It'll just be a phase he's going through," he managed to say.

"I think it's more than that. He needs some stability in his life. With Marise gone and you overseas so often, he's almost afraid to trust an adult. Next to Mum, who doesn't cover all his day-to-day care, I'm his only constant." She sighed. "Look, I know it's been hard on you, losing Marise and all the hideous media intrusion, but you have to think of Blake. He's your son. You have to be there for him."

Matt took a step back. She may have grown up here but she'd been gone for ten years. She had no idea how hard things had been and had no right to comment on them. And now she was his employee. A fact it would do to remind her of.

"Matt, I'm sorry, but you're going to have to do something. I can't stay here forever. You know when I took this job on it was supposed to be temporary—only through December until Marise returned from Australia. My agency in London is pressuring me to take up a new permanent assignment. With Blake being so attached to me the way he is right now, it will destroy him when I have to go."

Go? She couldn't leave. Not now. Not when he was juggling so many metaphorical balls right now. Aside from being on the verge of taking control of Blackstone Diamonds, he had the signature range launch coming up, and then there was the matter of tracking down the last of the missing Blackstone Rose diamonds. His plans weighed on his unstinting concentration. Concentration he couldn't afford to have broken by any further disruption to Blake's routine. As much as it tormented him to have her there—a constant reminder of the one time he'd overstepped the mark between chivalry and temptation—she had to stay.

Rachel watched as Matt absorbed her news. Short of battering him over the head with an encyclopaedia on paediatric psychiatry, she had no idea of how to get through to him. Blake needed his daddy now more than ever before, yet Matt remained so distant. It was crucifying to watch them and be helpless to do anything about it. When Blake had called her Mummy as she'd picked him up from his exclusive private preschool earlier that afternoon, she knew it was past time to swallow her fears and stand up to Matt Hammond. He'd been through the wringer these past few months with Marise's death and the subsequent media circus that still refused to end, but the man had to take responsibility for his little boy. Only he could provide the stability Blake so desperately craved.

"You can't go. I need you." His voice was hard, flat, as if he was holding on to his temper by a thread.

"We both know that's not true." She managed to keep her voice level, belying the tightly coiled tension in her body, even as his words scored a line across her heart. He couldn't even bear to be in the same room with her for five minutes longer than absolutely necessary. Matt Hammond and his unstinting sense of honour would go to hell and back before he needed her in the way she'd always dreamed of. She'd waited what felt like a lifetime to hear those words from him, but now that he'd actually given them voice they sounded painfully hollow. "If anything, having me here for Blake has made you distance yourself from him even more."

His eyebrows drew together ever so slightly at her words. She'd managed to score a definite hit. Ever since the night of her graduation dance he'd been totally and utterly aloof with her, hiding behind some cloak of misplaced honour. As if he'd taken advantage of her that night, instead of the other way around. In her youthful foolishness she'd thought their lovemaking would have brought them closer, not driven them eternally apart. That distance between them had made their current situation increasingly difficult, at a time when his son needed all the stability he could get.

"I have a business to run. I can't be home all day every day. Correct me if I'm wrong but you are a nanny, aren't you? That is why I hired you when Marise went to Australia." His grey eyes resembled cold, dark slate, the only visible indicator that she was getting under his skin.

"As a last resort only. Be honest with yourself, even if you can't be honest with me. If I hadn't been the only person you'd been able to get hold of at Christmas, you would never have hired me. I told you at the time it was a stopgap only. I have my own commitments in the UK that I need to meet."

Rachel shoved her hands in her jeans pockets to hide the trembling that would give away how upset she was. For Blake's sake, she couldn't afford to give an inch on this issue.

"Commitments? A boyfriend who's getting tired of waiting for you to come back perhaps?"

"Not that it's your business, but no."

"I'll double what I'm paying you to make up for the inconvenience. I need you to put your plans on hold, at least until your mother returns."

"Matt, you can't throw money at this problem and hope it will go away!" Rachel wanted to stamp her feet in frustration. "He needs *you*."

"I know exactly what my son needs and I'll make sure he gets it. Do I have your agreement to stay on?"

He had her in a corner. She wouldn't leave in the lurch the beautiful child sleeping upstairs. Despite how she'd grown to love him in his own right, he was Matt Hammond's son, and for that reason alone she'd walk over broken glass to protect him.

"Yes. I'll stay. But I'm giving you fair notice. When Mum gets back from Wanganui I'll be returning to the UK."

He gave a sharp nod in acknowledgement. "If there's nothing else to discuss, I'll see you in the morning."

Rachel nodded and turned to leave, determined to put some distance between them before her anger and frustration found a new vent. His hand on her shoulder halted her in her tracks, the heat and strength of his fingers imprinting her skin beneath the thickness of her fleecy sweatshirt. Instantly her body leaped to life, her senses attuned to his touch, her heart craving more.

"Rachel?"

"What?"

"Thank you."

Her eyes were drawn to his sensuously full lower lip as he said the words. A faint shadow of dark-blond bristles marked his jawline, throwing his skin into relief and accentuating how pale and drawn his features were. It occurred to Rachel with renewed understanding how hard he must be fighting to keep his life together—both on a family level and on a business one. She knew only too well what he'd been struggling with.

Lost for words, she could only nod, and pulled from his grasp and his overwhelming presence before she did anything stupid. Like try to offer him comfort. To offer him herself.

Two

The next morning dawned with one of those impossibly clear blue sky days that you only get in winter. A vapour trail from a passing aircraft streaked a straight line of white across the azure background as Rachel loaded her car with a small suitcase packed with her limited winter wardrobe. Most of the summer clothing she'd brought with her to New Zealand she'd left behind in the wardrobe. After all, she'd only come to New Zealand at Christmas to spend a few weeks with her mother. She hadn't expected to stay on beyond the warm, sticky Auckland summer, nor had she expected to end up working for Matt Hammond.

When Matt had initially approached her and asked if she could help with Blake when Marise had gone to Melbourne to attend her dying mother, Rachel hadn't spared a thought. Her answer was an instant and irrevocable yes born of sympathy. As much as she'd never warmed to Marise, she couldn't refuse to help under such sad circumstances. But when Marise had continued to stay away after her mother's death, and her name had subsequently been linked in the press with Howard Blackstone's, Rachel's sympathy had been firmly quashed.

She couldn't understand why the woman chose to stay away from her husband and little boy at Christmas. Even if she had been having an affair with Howard Blackstone, as the media seemed intent on proving, how could she have rejected her son like that? Especially when he was old enough to understand the holiday and all it entailed.

Marise had never been right for Matt. From what Rachel had seen on her infrequent and brief visits home, she was nothing but a controlling and calculating woman who cared for little but lifestyle and money. Lots of it. There'd always been something inherently unsettled in Marise's nature, as if she wanted more, felt as if she was due more somehow. For the life of her, Rachel couldn't understand why Marise couldn't have tried to be happy with Matt. The Hammond wealth wasn't, quite possibly, on a par with the Blackstones', but it wasn't far off it.

And then, of course, there was Matt himself. Rachel felt the familiar tug of longing from deep within. Marise had been a fool, and she certainly hadn't deserved a man like Matt.

Rachel slammed shut the hatch of her mother's car

with a satisfying bang and climbed into the driver's seat. As she drove from the apartment complex in Takapuna towards the historic township of Devonport, she mulled over her discussion with Matt last night.

It hadn't exactly gone as planned. For a start, she hadn't expected to fall asleep while waiting for him, but then he'd been a lot later than she'd anticipated and her day with Blake had been trying on many levels. The boy had been overexcited at the prospect of his daddy coming home from yet another trip. When his bedtime had passed and there'd still been no sign of Matt, he'd thrown a tantrum of epic proportions, with behaviour quite unlike his usual bright and biddable nature. The gradual change in Blake over the past couple of months had begun to give Rachel cause for genuine concern, and she knew she was right to have brought her fears to Matt's attention. How he handled it was another matter.

The trip to Devonport was always a pleasure. Rachel had loved growing up in this bustling and interesting suburb. Her dad was a naval officer at the nearby base, and with his long periods away, her mum's job with the Hammonds had meant she'd spent a lot of time in their spacious and elegant family home nestled on the side of North Head, facing across the harbour towards Auckland city itself.

As she let herself into the house her ears were assaulted by Blake's excited squeal as he tore through the downstairs wearing nothing but a towel. He launched himself straight at Rachel, forcing her to drop her handbag and suitcase at her feet to catch him midair.

"Hey, you! Stop! Come back here."

Matt followed down the hallway, his longer legs eating up the distance before he came to an abrupt halt within a metre of her. Rachel clutched her giggling charge a little tighter, anything to hide the sudden flare of desire that swept through her body at Matt's appearance.

His dark-blond hair was in disarray, as if he'd just towelled himself dry, but that wasn't all that was in disarray. The towel he'd knotted at his waist had started to slip, exposing the hard, lean lines of his hip and the tapering 'V' of his groin. With a monumental effort Rachel dragged her eyes up towards his face, skimming ever so swiftly over his tanned, ridged abdomen and muscled chest.

Her heart skittered against her ribs. This man was nothing like the coldly formal businessman who'd arrived home so late last night. No, the guy standing before her was as different as a diamond from an emerald, and she wanted him just as much.

"Come here, you," Matt mock-growled, reaching for his son. "You have to shower before preschool. We made a deal, remember?"

Blake shrieked again and turned his face into the curve of Rachel's neck, his little body shivering with delight at the game.

"I'll get him ready if you like," she offered, doing her best to maintain eye contact with the man she'd willingly given her innocence to eleven years ago. The man who stood at dire risk of losing the only covering on his delectable body.

"I'll do it."

There was an edge to his voice that gave her no

recourse. Instead she stood there as his strong arms reached out and he plucked his giggling, wriggling son from her arms.

"You might like to—" Rachel started. Too late, the towel at Matt's hips slid away. She caught a glimpse of untanned flesh, a thatch of dark hair, before she tilted her gaze towards the ceiling. "Grab your towel," she finished lamely, her cheeks flaming hot.

Blake was in total paroxysms.

"You little stinker, look what you've done." Matt was clearly trying to hold back his own laughter.

In her peripheral vision Rachel saw him bend at the knee and scoop up the towel, before spinning around to go back the way he and Blake had come. It said a lot for his self-possession that he slung the towel across his shoulder, letting it drape down his back to almost cover his taut backside, instead of putting Blake down and re-affixing it to his waist.

The view of the ceiling was no contest against the long, strong muscles of his legs and his now semibare back as he marched down the hall. Rachel drank her fill of the vision, letting her eyes caress the length of his frame. A tug of longing struck deep inside. The whole exchange had taken little more than two minutes but it had left her shaking. Her fingers itched to trace those strong, lean muscles and intriguing indentations that made his masculine frame so incredibly beautiful.

She shook her head slightly to clear the mental image of doing just that. People like Matt Hammond didn't dally with the staff—he'd made that patently clear eleven years ago. Once had been a mistake. A mistake he had no intention of repeating.

She was his son's nanny. No more, no less.

As much as it hurt her to admit it, that would never change. And aside from what her length of stay was doing to Blake, it was also slowly killing her inside. You couldn't love a man for most of your life and not be affected when he refused to acknowledge you existed as a desirable woman.

Rachel collected her belongings and trudged upstairs, choosing the guest room closest to Blake's. She dropped her bags on the bed, deciding to unpack later, and went back down to the kitchen to put on a carafe of coffee, then started to make French toast, Blake's favourite. As she went through the motions, she realised she'd better start making some notes for her replacement as to Blake's likes and dislikes. For the most part he was easy to please and ate his vegetables with little coercion, but he had his favourite meals. With the first slices of bread sizzling in the pan she got Blake's backpack ready for preschool.

The phone rang just as she was putting the second batch into the pan.

"Hammond residence," she answered.

"This is Quinn Everard." The slightly accented male voice had a smooth, soft tone. "Could I speak to Matt Hammond?"

"I'm sorry, Mr Hammond can't come to the phone at present. Can I get him to call you back?"

Everard rattled off an Australian-based phone number before thanking her and hanging up with "Please get him to call me as soon as possible."

By the time she'd sprinkled cinnamon sugar over the French toast and put two servings onto plates in the oven, Matt and Blake had come through.

"Something smells great," Matt said.

"Yay, French toast!" Blake clambered onto the booster seat on his kitchen chair and waited expectantly for his plate.

Rachel slid the plate onto the place mat in front of him. "Be careful. It's hot," she admonished as the little boy snatched up the first slice in his little fingers. She took the second plate from the oven and laid it at the second place setting at the table.

"Here, this is for you," she said to Matt. "Take a seat and I'll get your coffee."

"You don't need to wait on me, Rachel. Blake's your charge. Not me."

"It's no bother. I was making breakfast for him anyway."

He accepted the cup of strong coffee complete with a splash of cream before replying. "And what about you? Where's your breakfast?"

"Oh, I'll get something later. After Blake's gone to preschool."

"Look, you've made far more than I can manage. What do you say, Blake? Should Rachel have breakfast with us?"

"Yeah, yeah, yeah!" Blake shouted excitedly. "Here!" He shoved a slice of bitten toast towards her, almost knocking over his glass of milk at the same time.

"Hold on, tiger. You finish what you have on your plate and I'll give her some of mine."

"Okay, you give Mummy some."

The air in the room thickened. Rachel shot Matt a worried look. How was he going to handle this? She saw him take a deep breath, the fine white cotton of his business shirt expanding slightly across the breadth of his chest.

Matt's cool grey eyes met her gaze steadily before he broke contact and looked directly at his son.

"Blake, you know Rachel is your nanny, not your mummy."

"But I want her to be my mummy." A tiny frown appeared between the little boy's dark brows and he set his lips in a mutinous line.

"Sweetheart, you already have a mummy." Rachel hunkered down beside Blake's chair. "We talk to her at bedtime, remember? And tell her about each day."

"But she's not here and I want a mummy that's here! I want you." Tears pooled in the lower lids of Blake's sharp green eyes, before one big, fat drop spilled over the edge and tracked down his chubby cheek.

"Son, you can't just have a mummy like that."

"Why not?" the tearful child demanded.

Rachel's heart ached at the expression on Matt's face. There was no easy answer. His next words twisted her heart even more.

"Because a mummy and a daddy have to love each other first."

"Don't you love Rachel, Daddy?"

Rachel caught her breath. She wished she could

disappear from the room. She didn't want to hear Matt's denial.

"We're friends, Blake. We've known each other a long time."

Rachel could tell Matt was hedging, trying to find the most diplomatic, yet firm, way out of the situation.

"But why don't you love her? I love her."

As if it could be as simple as that. It was time to step in. She didn't know if she was capable of standing up to hearing Matt's answer.

"C'mon, buddy, have you had enough to eat? Let's go and get your teeth brushed. We'll talk about this later, okay? I'll race you upstairs."

She helped Blake down from his booster seat, wiped off his sticky hands and face with a damp cloth and gave him a little tickle to distract him. Suddenly she remembered the call.

"Someone called for you, Matt, said his name was Quinn Everard. I've left the number on the pad by the phone. He wanted you to call him back straight away."

She heard the rapid scrape of Matt's wooden chair on the tiles behind her.

"Did he say what it was about?"

"No, just that he wanted you to call back as soon as you could."

"Okay, thanks."

It must have been important, Rachel realised, when she came back downstairs with Blake. There was an edge of excitement about Matt that hadn't been there before.

"After you've dropped Blake off at preschool, can

you pack a few things for me? I know it's not in your job description, but with your mother away—"

"You're going away again?" Her voice rose incredulously. "But you've just arrived home."

Hadn't he listened to a word she'd said last night? Had this morning's incident with Blake not shown him how important it was that he be there more for his son?

"This trip is unavoidable."

"So send someone else, someone from the office. Surely you don't need to go yourself."

"This is something I've been waiting for, for a long time. Everard believes he's tracked the owner of the fifth diamond."

Rachel's blood thrilled in her veins. The last of the infamous Blackstone Rose diamonds? She'd been here looking after Blake when Matt had received the news he'd inherited four incomparable pink diamonds in Marise's estate—diamonds that had been proven to be from the Blackstone Rose necklace, which had mysteriously gone missing thirty years ago. The necklace Matt's father, Oliver, had been accused of stealing. She knew how important it was to Matt to bring the stones back together and to show the world that his father was innocent of the slur on his name.

A sudden solution presented itself.

"Good, we'll come with you, then. Where are we going?"

Matt gave her a piercing look. "I beg your pardon?"

"I said, where are we going?"

"I'm going to Tahiti, but you're not coming with me."

Rachel braced her feet firmly and took a deep breath.

"Oh, yes we are. Blake needs to spend time with you. Your business will take, what? A few hours? It's a perfect opportunity for both of you, and it's away from here, from the memories. You're planning to be there what—two, three nights?"

"And then I'll be back."

"And you'll be gone again. Didn't this morning show you anything? Honestly, Matt, I just don't understand you. Don't you *want* to strengthen your bond with your own son?"

He took a step back, as if she'd given him a physical shove. His face paled slightly and the line of his jaw firmed. She knew, from past experience, he was weighing his words very carefully. Eventually he spoke.

"Rachel, this is a business trip. Not a holiday. You're not coming with me. Simple."

"Then you'll have to take Blake on your own, because I won't be here."

"What are you talking about?"

"I mean it, Matt. You have to put Blake first for once. If you don't take *us,* you'll be taking him by yourself because I'll be walking out that door and I will not come back. I'm not bound to you in any way, I'm not on contract and I'm tired of my life being on hold while you sort out yours. So what's it to be?"

As much as it would kill her to do so, Rachel had every intention of following through on her threat. Obviously something in the tone of her voice made him realise it, too. Finally he let go of an exasperated sigh.

"Fine. Have it your way. I'll have my secretary make

the arrangements and let you know when we're leaving."

"Good." Rachel scooped Blake up in her arms and danced him around the room. "Hey, Blake, we're going on a trip with Daddy, isn't that neat?"

The little boy laughed in her arms and started enumerating the toys he wanted to take with him. Over Blake's dark head her gaze met Matt's. She knew he was angry. Very angry. A tremor of an aftershock ran through her body. She'd never stood up to anyone like that before, least of all Matt Hammond. There was one thing he hated above everything else and that was to be manipulated, and she'd thoroughly manipulated him just now.

But it was worth it. Somehow she had to break through the invisible barrier he'd erected between himself and his son, and then maybe, just maybe, he could make room in his heart for another.

For someone like her. Someone who would stand by him, love him, no matter what.

Three

Rachel had worked for some very wealthy clients over the years but the speed with which the trip to Tahiti was organised gave her a new appreciation of the power of Hammond money. By the time Matt had arrived home that afternoon, a private charter jet had been organised for departure at nine the next morning.

Rather than be snarled up in rush-hour traffic, they covered the distance to Auckland Airport by helicopter, touching down outside the Skycare terminal, where the charter company's staff greeted them and introduced them to the customs and immigration officials assigned to process their flight.

Blake was beside himself with excitement and it took every ounce of Rachel's skill and patience to keep him occupied. Eventually, though, he settled into his plush leather seat on the Gulfstream jet and watched goggle-eyed through the window as the plane was pushed back in readiness for departure. Once they were at altitude, Rachel watched in some relief as, with the somnolent hum of the jet's engines, his eyelids started to drift closed. He'd been so excited the night before he'd hardly slept, ensuring, in his regular visits to Rachel's bedroom to see if it was time to get up yet, that she had little sleep also.

"You look tired," Matt commented as he unclipped his seat belt and stood. "Why don't you see if you can get some sleep, too?"

Just what every woman wanted to hear. Mind you, she did feel as though she was a bit of a wreck.

"I think I will. Blake's bound to be full of energy when we get there. I'll need a head start on him," she replied, her eyes skimming over him.

He'd surprised her this morning by coming through from his master suite dressed in his usual business wear. Not that there was anything wrong with the cut of his suit or the set of his tie, it was just that she'd expected him to dress down for the journey. Tahiti was, after all, a tropical holiday mecca. She hoped he'd loosen up once they were there. It would be no fun for Blake if Matt ended up involved in business matters for the duration of their stay.

"That'll be a good idea. By the way, Tahiti is twenty-two hours behind New Zealand time. We'll arrive about four-thirty in the afternoon, yesterday."

Rachel adjusted her watch to the new time zone.

"Right, I've got it. So are you planning to meet with the diamond's current owner straight away?"

"Yes. Everard teed up the meeting yesterday. I'll see you and Blake settled at the hotel then I'll call my contact. I expect to head straight out. I probably won't be back before Blake's dinner time."

"Will you be there to put him to bed?"

"To make certain, he can stay up a little later tonight. Given the time difference and the sleep he's having now, he'll probably be wired."

"I'm sure he will be," she said with a slight smile on her face. "But he'll be thrilled if you're there for him at bedtime." Rachel leaned over and smoothed a dark lock of hair from Blake's face, unaware of Matt's intense expression as he watched her do so.

"I have work to do. If you or Blake need anything, just signal the attendant."

The Gulfstream was spacious and comfortable and offered a full office set-up, which was one of the reasons Matt preferred this aircraft. He opened his briefcase and sorted through his papers, but his mind wouldn't focus on the work he needed to get through. Instead, his line of vision kept travelling down the cabin.

Rachel had reclined her seat, her eyes closed. One hand was tucked up against the chair back, her cheek resting on it. In his mind's eye he saw her reach out and touch Blake as he slept. It was foolish to envy his son that unconscious gesture but envy him he did. He shook his head ever so slightly. He'd been mad to let them come along with him. He would have been back at home by tomorrow night if everything went according to plan. But still, the prospect of a little rest and relaxation in the sunshine with Blake held no small amount of allure. As much as he hated to admit it, Rachel was right. He spent too little time with his son.

Matt forced his attention to the jewellery designs he'd spread out in front of him. He'd had personal input into each and every piece of the Matt Hammond Heirloom Range. A swell of pride grew from deep within him. The launch would see him realise a dream he'd held since he'd entered House of Hammond under his father's wing while in his late teens. Although House of Hammond specialised in antique and estate jewellery, he'd always dreamt of developing a range of his own— a blend of the past and the present with reproduction antique jewellery. His own personal and irrevocable stamp on the world.

It was no small personal pleasure to know that time had come. As had the time for a lot of things.

Growing up, Matt had always been aware of the undercurrent of jealousy that had tainted his father's life when faced with Howard Blackstone's success. The rift between the families had widened irrevocably when Howard had accused Oliver of stealing the Blackstone Rose necklace at the thirtieth birthday celebration of his wife, Oliver's sister, Ursula. Worse, Blackstone had even gone so far as to suggest that Oliver and his wife, Katherine, had had something to do with the kidnapping of James Blackstone, Howard and Ursula's first-born son.

As soon as Matt had been old enough to understand, he'd sworn he'd help his father clear his name and take

Blackstone down in the bargain. Well, he might have lost his chance to take down Howard Blackstone, but he would succeed at the next best thing. Taking control of Blackstone Diamonds.

Share by painstaking share he'd acquired power within the company. Now, with only a minor additional share holding, voting power would be his. For a moment Matt allowed the anticipation of success to wash over him, imagined the surprise and pleasure on his father's face when informed of the news. It had been hard graft, and risky, getting here. But it had been worth every cent.

And now he was only hours away from another success. The acquisition of the last of the missing Blackstone Rose diamonds.

The balance of the flight passed swiftly and it was only as they began their descent into Papeete that Rachel and Blake stirred. The flurry of disembarking, going through customs and transferring to a ferry flight to Moorea was accomplished in minimum time, one of the pleasures of charter jet travel. Matt wondered what was going through Rachel's mind as their limousine drove them to the resort where they were staying. Her sparkling hazel eyes were glued to their surroundings, drinking in the startlingly colourful array of flora around them. Blake chattered a mile a minute, gasping at the colour of the ocean, and he squirmed with excitement when Rachel promised him a swim once they were settled.

Would she wear a bikini? he wondered. A spasm tightened muscles deep in the pit of his stomach. It didn't matter whether she did. The creamy flesh she chose to expose was totally off-limits. He should be grateful that he wouldn't be there to witness their aquatic foray.

The resort they were booked into was beautifully set on a private lagoon on the northern shore. Matt had specified a garden bungalow, knowing his son's curiosity would literally lead him into deep water if they'd utilised the over-water bungalows available.

"This looks marvellous," Rachel commented as they entered the comfortably appointed bungalow. "Which bedroom shall we have, Blake?"

"Blake will bunk in with me," Matt said before his son could reply. "That is the point of this, isn't it?"

"Yes, of course. Lucky you, honey." She ruffled Blake's hair. "You get to sleep with Daddy."

Rachel's hand stilled before flying to her mouth to cover her lips. Her stricken eyes caught his. Matt watched as a flush of peach bloomed over Rachel's cheeks.

"I didn't mean—"

"Of course you didn't," he replied smoothly, but his voice contradicted the instant reaction of his body. The sudden hungry need that uncoiled inside.

"Could you get his swimsuit out? I'll take him to the lagoon while you're at your meeting."

"Sure, see you in five."

Rachel was standing out on the terrace when he finally brought Blake to her. The low afternoon sun promised a spectacular sunset, but its gilded kiss through the gauzy long shirt she wore over her bikini sent a fierce shaft of heat through Matt's body as he drank in the silhouette of her lushly feminine curves. Suddenly his business suit and tie were uncomfortably tight, less of the armour he'd subconsciously chosen for today and more an instrument of torture.

She turned to face them. "I was just admiring the sunset. It's early here, isn't it?"

"Between five and six, from what I understand. You guys had better make the most of the light that's left and I'll see you when I get back."

Rachel reached for Blake's hand. "See you later then. Say bye to Daddy, Blake."

Matt watched them stroll along the garden path towards the lagoon, feeling a twinge of envy at their carefree chatter. How long had it been since he'd allowed himself to simply feel pleasure? Damn, he couldn't even remember. But pleasure would be high on his agenda very, very soon. And it would start with the acquisition of the elusive pear-shaped diamond he needed to complete the Blackstone Rose set.

He went inside the bungalow and lifted the phone, quickly dialling in the local calling number Quinn Everard had given him.

"Mr Sullivan, please," he asked as the phone was answered at the other end. "This is Matt Hammond."

"One moment, sir."

After a short time another male voice came on the line.

"Mr Hammond, welcome to Tahiti. I trust your journey was a pleasant one."

"Thank you, yes. I'm calling to confirm our meeting tonight."

"Certainly, that is still in place. I understand that you have travelled here with your son and a companion. Please, bring them with you."

"My son's nanny." Matt corrected the other man's assumption. "It isn't necessary that they come with me. This is a business matter."

"Ah, but, Mr Hammond, we're inclined to be a little more informal in our business matters than perhaps you're used to. I will send a car for you at seven o'clock. And please, dress comfortably. I don't believe in standing on ceremony."

Because he would not jeopardise the successful outcome of the meeting, Matt had no other recourse but to accept. He threw off his jacket and ripped his tie undone, throwing them both on the bed Blake had chosen for him. Making tonight a social occasion didn't sit comfortably, but he would do what he had to do to achieve his goal. Acquiring the diamond was the only thing he needed to worry about.

He changed into chinos and a short-sleeved shirt and went in search of Blake and Rachel to tell them of the change in plans. He found them both splashing and laughing in the shallows of the lagoon. From the lengthening shadows cast by a stand of palms, he watched Rachel unabashedly frolic in the water. Her muslin blouse clung to her, moulding to her breasts and the curve of her hip, as Blake splashed water in her direction. Her hair was loose, and hanging in wet ringlets down her back. Blake squealed as she chased after him in the water, her longer legs making short work of the distance between them. As she bent to scoop the little boy up in her arms Matt caught a tantalising glimpse of bikini-clad backside.

Blood pooled low in his groin, a simmering heat that had nothing to do with the balmy evening air. He pushed his hands into his pockets and clenched them into fists. He shouldn't allow himself to be affected by her this way. The waters of his life were muddied enough without complicating things further by this uncontrolled reaction to a girl he should never have touched in the first place.

Girl? No. She was all woman now. The enticing teenager had matured into a beautiful woman. One who deserved to be made love to with painstaking intensity and focus. Not taken on the back seat of a car—her ball dress pushed up around her hips, her expensively coifed hair in total disarray—by a young man who should have known better. A man who should have refused what she'd so innocently, willingly, offered.

Any man who was not Matt Hammond.

He stalked out from the shadows. Rachel noticed his approach immediately.

"Hello. I thought you had a meeting."

"There's been a change in plan. We've all been invited up to Sullivan's house for dinner tonight. You and Blake will need to be ready by seven."

"No problem." She cast a glance at Blake, who was investigating something in the sand on the shoreline. "Is everything all right?"

No, it certainly wasn't. Not with her standing there as she was, her tempting body all but broadcasting in neon signs how available she was to him. As his eyes skimmed her form he noted how her stance stiffened, her nipples peaking into sharp points through the dual layers of muslin and Lycra.

"Matt?" she prompted softly, a note of entreaty in her voice.

"Fine. Everything's fine. I'll see you back at the bungalow."

He strode away with long, loping steps and castigated himself for every kind of fool for agreeing to bring her here with Blake. He should never have believed she would abandon Blake. Instead, he'd been so single-minded about acquiring the fifth Blackstone Rose diamond that he'd been prepared to agree to anything to make her stay on and had landed himself in an untenable situation at the same time.

When their limousine pulled up outside the traditionally designed home up in the hills, a casually attired tall, slender man moved out over the deep front porch. If this was Sullivan, Matt was surprised. This man couldn't have been more than a baby when the necklace was stolen; he looked to be no more than a few years younger than Matt's thirty-three. His stomach sank. Was this all going to turn into a wild-goose chase after all?

"Welcome to my home, Mr Hammond. I'm Temana Sullivan."

Matt took the other man's hand in a warm, strong grasp. "Pleased to meet you." Rachel and Blake climbed out behind him. "And this is my son, Blake, and his nanny, Rachel Kincaid."

"Ah," said Sullivan with a warm smile. "Welcome to Tahiti, Miss Kincaid. I trust you are having a lovely time so far?"

He offered his hand and when Rachel took it, lifted her hand to his lips, grazing her knuckles with an old-fashioned gallantry that sent a surge of protective instinct through Matt's veins.

"Miss Kincaid, your skin has the beautiful lustre of the famed Japanese white pearls. You will need to be careful in our climate. It would be a tragedy for you to bear any damage."

"Thank you, I'll be fine. We brought plenty of sun-block," she responded with diplomatic pragmatism.

To Matt's delight Rachel extracted her hand from Sullivan's grasp with a smile that didn't quite meet her hazel eyes, but he didn't like the way the other man's gaze lingered on her, or the charming smile he bestowed in her direction.

Their host gestured to the front entrance of the house.

"Come inside and we'll have a drink on the balcony before our meal."

They followed Sullivan inside. Matt was intrigued by his appearance. Of mixed heritage, his host had the darker colouring of the Tahitian people but his features were dominated by startling blue eyes and a shock of chestnut hair streaked with blond. Matt sensed an undercurrent of amusement from the other man—the sense that Sullivan knew his appearance had put him off stride.

"Please, take a seat." Sullivan gestured to a collection of deep-cushioned hardwood-framed chairs positioned in a semicircle on the wide deck facing the ocean. A working pearl farm could be seen not too far away.

Matt lowered his frame into the chair and forced himself to keep a lid on his eagerness to cut straight to business. Clearly Sullivan wasn't in a mood to be hurried, and while it was frustrating being obliged to wait, Matt knew how to play the game.

Conversation remained general not only through pre-dinner drinks but the meal, served al fresco on the patio beside the subtly lit infinity pool, where Sullivan appeared to command most of Rachel's attention, explaining the pearl farming process in answer to her questions.

"So you're saying the colour of the host shell influences the colour and lustre of the pearl?" Rachel asked before taking a sip of her wine.

"Yes, and in the case of the black pearl there is only one variety of oyster in which it is grown, the *Pinctada margaritifera*. The pearls can vary in colour from pearly white to nearly black and many colours in between. Despite its name, they are never truly a complete black."

"The whole process sounds fascinating," Rachel enthused.

"Perhaps, if Matt is in agreement, you can all visit the farm the day after tomorrow? We have our expert over from Japan who will be grafting our next crop."

Sullivan flashed Rachel a smile that left Matt in no doubt that it wouldn't bother him in the slightest if Rachel had to make the visit on her own. It was definitely time to intercede.

"That would be fascinating. I'd like to talk to you

about a new range of jewellery that I'm working on and for which I'm looking specifically for baroque pearls. It would lend some real interest to the collection if we used a variety of black pearls rather than the traditional whites."

"If you gentlemen would like to continue your discussion I'd like to take Blake out to see the garden, if that's okay with you, Mr Sullivan?"

"Call me Temana, please, and certainly. Make yourself at home. When you come back inside, Philippe will show you to my study."

The men rose as Rachel stood and took Blake from the table. Matt waited in silence for his host to open the proceedings. It was a tool he'd found especially useful in business where people were altogether too eager to open their mouths. He wasn't disappointed.

"I imagine you would like to get to the point of tonight's visit. I have to say, I admire your patience and restraint. Another man might have tried to steer conversation but you've been satisfied to wait." Sullivan put his drink down on the table and leaned back in his chair.

"I'm not other men." Matt's answer was short, but within it lay a veiled warning. Don't underestimate me.

The other man smiled and nodded, acknowledging the unspoken message, then continued.

"I have something you want, something you're prepared to pay a considerable sum for. Am I right?"

Matt inclined his head.

"Something that by rights I shouldn't have."

"Correct again."

"And you are the legal owner of this item?"

"I have documentation to show so, yes."

"That won't be necessary. Quinn does his homework. His word is enough for me. Look, to be honest, I'm not entirely certain how my father came into possession of the stone. All I know is that it formed a part of a large collection of loose cut stones he'd amassed in his lifetime. As I said to Quinn, I will sell you the stone on one condition."

"That your family name remains out of any possible publicity about its recovery. Quinn told me. No problem."

Sullivan looked him square in the eye. Matt met his stare unwaveringly. Whatever the other man saw in his face must have satisfied him because he nodded.

"Quinn said you were a man of your word. I believe him. He doesn't do business with cheats or liars."

"You say you're not entirely certain about how your father came by the diamond. Does that mean you have some idea?" Matt probed.

"My father was Australian. He settled here in the late seventies, married a local girl and they established the pearl farm. He started collecting precious gems in the mid- to late eighties and I believe it was a short time after that, that he acquired the diamond, although I can't be certain of the date.

"He was meticulous about his records, which was why, when he passed away, I was surprised to find little documentation to authenticate the diamond. There was, however, a file with copies of his correspondence with someone in Melbourne at around that time. He only referred to his contact by their initials. B.D."

Barbara Davenport. Marise's mother. So they'd been right after all. She *had* been the missing link. Matt couldn't wait to tell Jarrod, his brother, the news. It explained why the original four diamonds had come to be in Marise's possession at the time of her death. Obviously Barbara had only ever sold the one stone. Had she kept the others as a nest egg, he wondered, or had the sale of the first stone been so difficult she'd elected to hold on to the others? Whatever her reasons, they'd never know the full truth behind them.

"May I see the stone?" He kept his voice low and steady, yet inside his chest his heart hammered in excitement.

"Certainly, come with me."

The room they entered was a type of study-cum-workroom lined with glass display cases of pearls in varying colour, shape and texture. Matt watched his host open a wall safe and remove a single black velvet case.

His chest tightened as Sullivan put the case down on a matching velvet cloth on the work desk and turned it to face Matt.

"Here, tell me if it's what you're looking for."

He flipped up the lid on the case. Matt's breath momentarily shuddered to a halt in his lungs at the sight of the pear-shaped pink diamond as it sparkled against its white satin bed. He reached blindly into his pocket, extracted his loupe and fitted it to his eye. He reached out with tingling fingers to lift the stone from its resting place, drinking in the flash of pink fire that blazed from the stone's core.

Mentally he ran through the checklist as he held the stone closer for inspection. Fancy Intense Pink, pear cut, virtually internally flawless, weight approximately ten carats. The match in colour and clarity to the other four seven-carat stones he'd inherited on Marise's death was undeniable, even without more specialised investigation. Deep in his gut he knew this was the one.

Carefully he placed the stone back on its cushion.

"It's what I'm looking for."

"I'm glad. For whatever reason my father acquired the stone, it doesn't do us any good to be associated with stolen property."

Sullivan closed the lid on the velvet case, and Matt felt a pang of loss as he put the stone back into the wall safe and swung the dial to reset the lock.

"Now we know I have what you want, let's get down to business."

Four

Matt stretched out on the sun lounger and soaked up the glorious heated rays of the sun. He couldn't remember the last time he'd relaxed like this. The sensation had become alien to him, yet at the same time remained as familiar as a long-lost habit.

His mind skimmed over the success of yesterday's meeting. Not only had he and Sullivan come to an arrangement about the diamond, which he would collect as soon as the confirmation of funds transfer came through, but they'd discussed a mutually lucrative arrangement regarding the black baroque pearls which would take the Matt Hammond Heirloom Range to even greater heights.

Now there was only one fly in the ointment. Rachel.

His hearing became attuned to the gentle sound of her breathing, his senses on full alert and prickling with awareness at her close proximity on the lounger next to him. Blake had begged at breakfast to participate in the junior guests' treasure hunt and sand castle competition on the beach. After checking into the details, Matt had left Blake in the care of the children's group supervisors. Right now he knew he'd made a terrible mistake. Without the buffer of his son there was nothing to dilute Rachel's presence. Or his reaction to it.

She was wearing a turquoise bikini, the one she'd barely managed to hide yesterday. On its own it was quite innocent, cut neither too low nor too high. On any other woman Matt knew it wouldn't have bothered him in the least, nor attracted his attention. Yet he could barely keep his gaze to himself. Damn. He shifted again on the lounger as his body stirred and he became increasingly uncomfortable.

She was torment in a compact package. In his peripheral vision he could see the light sprinkling of freckles on her shoulders, their pattern trailing down her chest and into the valley between the gentle swell of her breasts. An image of him slowly, painstakingly, tracing his tongue, from one pigmented patch to the next, burned onto his retinas sending a fireball of need deep down to his groin. Damn, this had to stop.

"I'm going for a swim," he announced suddenly, and pushed up off the lounger before Rachel could respond.

He dove from the edge of the pool, determined that distance from temptation would be his rescue, but the water's temperature did little to soothe the ache of desire that simmered through his veins. The silky glide of the swimming pool water across his almost-naked body only heightened the growing want inside him. With the volume of holiday makers in the pool, swimming one punishing lap after the other was impossible. Surcease, it seemed, was equally so.

Distraction, that's what he needed. He slowed his pace and changed to a slow breast stroke, using the opportunity to scan the occupants at the pool's sunken bar. Yes, a perfect opportunity presented itself with a slender blonde seated in the water. One way or another he'd scour Rachel from his thoughts.

An hour of distinctly unscintillating conversation later he returned to the bungalow. Rachel had long since left the poolside and there was still another hour to go before he needed to collect Blake from down at the beach. He'd taken a stroll past the activities on his way back and the sight of his little boy industriously and happily engaged had been a welcome one.

As he stepped inside the main lounge of the bungalow he heard a small cry of pain from Rachel's room. Concern overrode any desire to preserve her privacy and he covered the distance to her door quickly.

"What is it? Are you all right?" he asked as he opened the door.

Rachel spun around at the intrusion. Dressed in her bra and panties, she wore no less than she had poolside, yet here, in the intimacy of her bedroom she felt infinitely more vulnerable. Quickly she reached for her sundress, holding it to her like some outraged maiden determined to preserve her dignity. Her body, though, instantly reacted in contradiction to her action. Her nipples tightened in response to his presence, and her breasts grew full and heavy, aching for his touch.

"It's nothing," she answered a little unsteadily. "I just caught a bit too much sun today, that's all. I was trying to put some aloe gel on but I can't reach all of my back."

"Give it to me." Matt came closer and took the tube from her suddenly nerveless fingers. "I thought you used sunblock."

"I did, but it's been a while since I've just lain about like that doing nothing. Really, it's all right. I'll stay covered up from now on. You don't have to— Oh!"

The sensation of his fingers, slicked with gel, across the back of her shoulders and down her spine sent a shiver through her body that had nothing to do with the temperature of the gel and everything to do with his divinely gentle touch. The soft pressure of his strong fingers sent electric tingles up and down her back with each sweep of his hand.

As he stroked across the small of her back, her womb contracted tightly and she fought to hold back a moan. This felt so good. *He* felt so good. Her intensely heat-sensitive skin felt the warmth that emanated from him as he stood at her back.

"I'm going to undo your bra strap," he said in a voice that sounded surprisingly unaffected. "There's no point in missing anywhere. You don't want to peel."

"Of…of course," Rachel stammered, clutching at the cups of her bra as the shoulder straps threatened to slide down her arms.

"You have a line from the strap of your bikini."

"I suppose I'm burnt on either side?" She fought to keep the tone of her voice level, but inside she was a tangled mess.

"Pink, but not too bad."

Her breath caught in her throat as he traced one finger along the upper and lower line of her strap mark, inadvertently touching the side of her breast as he did so. Suddenly his hand dropped away.

"I'm sorry, Rachel, I didn't mean—"

She whirled around. "No, it's okay. Thank you, the sunburn feels much better now."

He was so close she could feel his breath on her skin, see the tiny silver striations in the irises of his cool grey eyes. It would be so easy to let her dress slide away, to lift her arms to his shoulders, slide her hands around his neck and lift herself up to kiss him.

She watched as his pupils dilated, heard his breathing become uneven.

"Matt?"

The soft slither of cotton, swiftly followed by the scratchier lace of her bra, across the front of her body was the last conscious sensation she was aware of before she followed through on her instincts. Beneath her hands the strong muscles of his shoulders flexed as she skimmed her fingers across their breadth, linking them behind his neck. She went up on tiptoe, offering her mouth to him, offering herself, maintaining eye contact as if she could will him to surrender to his feelings.

She drew her body in alignment with his, a groan of

pure pleasure rippling from her throat as her aching breasts pressed against the hard muscles of his chest, as the soft curve of her belly pressed against his. There was no mistaking the hard ridge of arousal in his swim trunks, nor the scorching heat that shimmered in waves off his skin.

With an answering growl he bent his head, pressing his lips to hers in a hard possession that took her breath away and replaced it with a clawing need that had remained unanswered for eleven long years. She pressed closer into him, shuddering in delight as his arm swept around her waist, drawing her hard against the lean strength of his body.

She drove her hands up into his hair, clutching him more tightly to her as her hips ground against his erection. She wanted him more than she'd ever wanted anything in her life. Her body remembered his touch, his inexplicable scent, and it excited her even more to feel him and know that she wrought this reaction from him.

His tongue slid past her lips to meet and duel with hers. Even the taste of him was addictive. She suckled his tongue, drawing him deeper into her mouth the way she craved to draw him deep within her body. A throb of pure lust pulsed within her, sending sensation spiralling through her body, weakening her knees. She buckled, falling back onto the bed, drawing Matt with her, over her.

She reached for him again, her hands running across his chest, tracing the outline of his nipples, a small smile playing across her lips as she felt them retract and tighten at her touch. She caught his top lip between hers and softly, gently, traced the tip of her tongue along the moist heat of his skin. When he groaned again, she repeated the action, this time taking in his bottom lip, relishing the tremor that ran through his body at her touch.

Her hands glided down his torso. Lord, he was magnificent. His strength and muscle were overlaid by the goose bumps that rose on his flesh as she outlined his ribs, then dipped one hand lower to his belly. She travelled lower still to the 'V' of his groin that had so enticed her only two days ago.

She slid past the still-damp constriction of the waist band of his swim trunks to find the hard silken length of him. At the light brush of her fingertips she felt his arousal buck against her palm, and she closed her fist around his shaft, sheathing him with a gentle stroke.

His body stiffened at her touch, as if he was about to pull away, but she strengthened the stroke of her hand, drawing to the tip before sliding like a hot cuff to his base again.

Rachel caught his lower lip between her teeth and sucked against it in a rhythmic motion that mirrored the movement of her hands, increasing in pressure and speed until she lost all track of intent and could focus only on the sensations that wound tighter and tighter still deep within her core.

His body began to tremble at her assault and he pressed against her hand, his hips straining as if to amplify her actions. She felt him grow even harder, his tip swelling, then suddenly he thrust hard against her hand, a raw groan ripping from his throat.

"No!"

Matt broke free and staggered to his feet. His body screamed in denial, begging the release her touch promised. This was wrong. It was all wrong. She was Rachel, his son's nanny, his housekeeper's daughter! He'd taken advantage of her trust once before, when she'd been just shy of eighteen and he twenty-three—a young *man* who should have known better. He would not do it again.

"What is it? What's wrong?" Rachel's voice intruded on the fog that encapsulated his mind.

"You can ask that?" he growled.

He flung an angry scowl at her and forced himself to ignore the flush of desire across her sun-tinted skin and the pointed tips of her nipples, which begged for his touch. He clenched his hands into fists to halt his instinct to reach out and gather her silky curves against his now bereft body.

"Matt, please. Don't fight this thing between us. At least let us have this."

His eyes locked on her lips. Lips that were swollen with their kisses, lips that begged to be kissed again.

"No. This was a mistake. I should never have touched you."

He spun and turned away. He needed distance— right now.

"But I touched you. I wanted to do it, Matt. You wanted it too. How can you say it's a mistake? We're consenting adults. There's no reason why we can't—"

"No reason? For me there's every reason. Aside from the fact that as your employer I'm accountable for you, I have no desire to be caught up in another scandal—

let alone another relationship. Can you imagine what the press would do if they found out we'd been intimate after your high school dance and that you were now working for me? Under my roof every night? You'd be roasted in the media. Give me some credit for taking responsibility for what's mine to protect."

"I'm not asking for your protection, dammit! Matt, I lo—"

"Don't. Don't say it."

Rachel went up onto her knees, totally unashamed of her near nakedness. "So you're running away again?"

"I don't run, Rachel. I create distance when it's necessary."

"Matt, get real. When it comes to running away you're an emotional marathon champion. It's okay to face the truth. We've always been like this together. What happened eleven years ago was going to happen sooner or later. And it will always be there between us. It's not a crime to give in to that attraction."

"It is for me."

As her bedroom door slammed shut behind him, Rachel sank back on her heels. Her mind reeled with his rejection, yet her body still screamed for his touch. Slowly she got up from the bed gathered her sundress and bra from the floor and redressed. Somehow, someday, she'd get through to him. He'd responded like a flare to her touch. As much as he tried to deny it, his attraction for her equalled hers for him. That much between them, at least, had never changed.

When she came through to the lounge Matt was dressed in shorts and a polo shirt and stood at the door, looking out across the gardens. As she approached him he turned to face her, his face an inscrutable mask. Even though he was dressed casually there was something about the set of his shoulders and the expression in his grey eyes that told her his defences were up in full force. She supposed she should take some consolation in that he thought he needed to armour himself against her.

"I've contacted our pilot. We leave in the morning."

"So soon?" Shock poured through her with the efficiency of iced water. "But what about the diamond?"

"If my transactions with Sullivan aren't complete by morning I'll arrange for the stone to be safe-handed directly to Danielle Hammond in Australia."

"And the trip to the pearl farm? We're expected there tomorrow."

"So eager to see Temana Sullivan again, Rachel? Don't tell me you're planning on using him as a backstop because I said no."

Rachel saw red. How dare he tar her with the same brush as his ex-wife? But she drew short of bringing Marise's name into the mix. "Don't judge me by other people's standards. I was thinking nothing of the sort. You're overreacting."

"Overreacting? I don't think so. As you'll remember, this was supposed to be a business trip, not pleasure. If you want to see Sullivan again you can do it on your own time."

"For the last time, I'm not interested in him." *It's only ever been you,* she wanted to scream but knew it would be useless. "What about Blake? He's having such a wonderful time. This was a perfect opportunity for the two of you to spend more time together."

"Blake's young. He'll cope."

And you say you're not running away? The words remained locked in her throat. As much as he denied it, Matt was running away again—from her. And worse, with her actions she'd destroyed the precious little time he'd been enjoying with Blake. Sadly, there was nothing she could do now but accede to his instructions.

"I'll start packing his things. What time do we have to be ready?"

"By ten, and don't worry about his things. I'll take care of them."

If he'd slapped her with a chilled wet flannel, his rejection couldn't have been more complete. Cold fingers of failure, tinged with regret, tightened like a fist around her heart. He was so closed up emotionally, driven by those damned diamonds and what Howard Blackstone had done to him and his family, that there was room for nothing and no one else in his heart. The knowledge that she'd been instrumental in effectively sealing up that window to his heart was a heavy mantle to bear.

Five

As their jet lifted off from Papeete's airport at midday the next day, Matt let his head fall back against his chair in relief. By later this evening they'd be back home in Devonport, and life as he had come to know it would resume. The past twenty-four hours had been absolute torment. He was used to denial; he'd lived with it for longer than he cared to remember. But the systematic breakdown of his marriage with Marise prior to her jaunt to Australia was not on a par with the craving for Rachel that shredded his very soul.

He could barely look at her without reliving the feel of her touch on his body. He hardened in response to the memory. Yesterday had been categorical proof he should have trusted his instincts and stayed well away. Even after all this time, she remained his one great weakness, and weakness couldn't be tolerated. Under any circumstance.

It would have been all too easy to lose himself in the comfort of her body. To forget the infidelity of his wife, the failure of his marriage, as well as his own failures as a husband and father, and to take whatever respite he could. But he refused to allow himself the pleasure, however fleeting it would have been. Rachel deserved more than that. Despite whatever confused link she imagined between them, she did not deserve someone like him.

He focussed instead on the rectangular shape of the box in his breast pocket, the box in which the final Blackstone Rose diamond lay. Sullivan had called him and suggested they meet for dinner again last night, as the monetary side of their transaction had been approved. For as long as Matt could remember, his father had been passionate about the recovery of the Blackstone Rose stones. Now Matt had achieved what his father had never been able to do. All his life he'd strived to prove himself worthy of Oliver Hammond, worked hard to be the son the man deserved. In this, at least, he hadn't failed.

The Auckland evening was bleak with darkness and frigid driving rain when they landed at Auckland International Airport. As they climbed into their limousine for the journey home, Matt flipped open his cell phone to call his parents.

"It's Matt. Are you two busy tonight?"

"No, we're not. Aren't you home early? I thought you were going to be gone a few more days."

Matt ignored his mother's reference to the early demise of the first break he'd had in years. "Do you mind if we swing around? I have something special to show Dad."

"Of course you can. You know you're always welcome. Are you bringing Blake and Rachel, too? Did you eat on the plane? Why don't you all stay for a light supper?"

Matt let his mother's voice wash over him in a flood of motherly concern. If he had his way he'd be leaving Rachel at her apartment, but he knew if he did, it would elicit unwanted explanation. Explanation he had no intention of making.

"That would be great, Mum. We'll see you in about forty-five minutes to an hour, depending on traffic."

He slid his cell phone back into his pocket, anticipation thrumming through his veins at the prospect of seeing his father's reaction to the diamond. Ever since the night thirty years ago when Howard Blackstone had accused his father of stealing the Blackstone Rose necklace, it had been Oliver's self-appointed mission to find it. The accusation had rankled between the brother-in-law business rivals for many years, and every so often was raked over by the press, eager to flesh out an old story for its scandal value. Now Matt had categorical proof that his father had been innocent.

"We're going to your parents'?" Rachel's voice interrupted his thoughts.

He looked across the dim interior of the car. She'd barely addressed him since he'd told her they were leaving Tahiti and frankly, that was the way he preferred it.

"Yes."

"Are you sure you want me there?"

"My mother included you in her invitation."

"Oh, okay, then."

She settled back in her seat for the rest of the journey, although Matt could sense she wanted to say more.

When they pulled up outside the single-storey unit in the luxury assisted-living complex where his parents resided, the tension inside him ratcheted up a few more notches. Since his father's stroke five years ago, little had given him pleasure. Always a hands-on man, he hated the disability that now left him paralysed down one side and unable to speak. Oliver Hammond had given so much to both his adopted sons; Matt was both humbled and deeply satisfied to be able to return a small measure of that love now.

After giving his mother a quick hug at the front door, Matt went straight to his father, who sat in the elegant sitting room in his wheelchair. He squatted down in front of Oliver Hammond.

"Dad? I have something to show you."

He reached into his pocket and drew out the velvet case, holding it on the flat of his palm.

"You know how four of the Blackstone Rose diamonds were found among Marise's things when she died?" Matt prompted.

His father nodded his head slowly, never once taking his gaze from the black velvet case.

"I have the last stone."

He put the case in his father's lap and opened it, watching his father's expression closely. He was unprepared for the raw sound that erupted from his father's throat, the sheen of tears that reflected in the older man's eyes, for the grief he read there. He'd expected jubilation, excitement, perhaps smugness, but not overwhelming sorrow.

"Dad, are you all right? This is good news. It means we have proof Blackstone lied all those years. You've been vindicated, totally and utterly. When I make a press statement to say we have located all of the major stones from the Blackstone Rose, the whole world will know the truth."

His father shook his head from side to side.

"What, Dad? You don't want me to make a statement? I don't understand." Matt rose to his feet, his eyes locked on his father's face. His mother's hand on his shoulder made him turn.

"Son, he is happy you brought this to show him, but it brings back old memories. Hurtful ones. Despite the fact he was the one who cut off contact with Sonya and Ursula he never stopped missing his sisters. You have no idea how he grieved when Ursula drowned. He blamed Howard for the rift that grew between the families, but he blamed himself, too. Wished he'd done more. We all wished we'd done more. It's enough for us now to know the diamonds have been recovered. Let's not turn this into another tabloid frenzy, Matt. Your father's health, and mine, couldn't stand it."

"Are you absolutely certain about that, Mum?" Matt couldn't believe he was being actively discouraged from publicly exonerating his father from a crime that many had said he was justified to commit.

"Yes, I'm certain."

"Tell me what exactly happened that night the necklace went missing." Matt looked up at his mother. "I know what the papers have said over the years, but you've never really talked about it."

Katherine sighed and looked to her husband. Oliver nodded slowly once, and reached his one good hand out to finger the stone, tears still rolling one by one down his cheeks.

"I persuaded your father we should attend Ursula's thirtieth birthday party. Oliver wasn't keen on going. There'd always been a note of competitive tension between him and Howard, which only got worse after Jeb died, but I felt it was important for Ursula that we be there. She'd been so fragile since James had been kidnapped and with Ryan being born only a year after…" Katherine's voice choked up a little. "We didn't call it postnatal depression back then. Maybe if people had been more open about things she'd still be alive today.

"Anyway, Ursula was so happy we made it over and, oh, she looked amazing that night. With the Blackstone Rose around her neck she was the epitome of Howard's success. I wondered how comfortable she was with the necklace. She kept fingering it during the course of the evening. It was quite a heavy, ostentatious thing. It must have been quite a burden around her slender neck. She kept, you know, lifting it away from her skin, playing with the clasp—adjusting it, as if it was coming undone all the time.

"As the night drew on she started to drink heavily. I was surprised to see her like that. She'd always been the perfect hostess—seeing to everyone's needs, making sure everything was just so—but that night she left everything to Sonya. When the dancing started she was near the pool, and Oliver noticed she was a bit unsteady on her feet. He went to guide her away from the edge but before he could get to her she fell in. Everyone was so shocked. No one moved at first—not even Howard. Oliver raced forward to help her from the water. He was furious with Howard for letting her get drunk in the first place and accused him of being incapable of looking after anything properly. As you can imagine, Howard was none too impressed."

Katherine reached over and took Oliver's paralysed hand in hers, stroking the mottled skin gently, her eyes distant as she recalled the events of the evening.

"Sonya and I helped Ursula upstairs, but she twisted away and shouted that she wanted to go back to the party, that Howard expected it of her. Obviously she was in no condition to do so and I have to admit we did kind of manhandle her a bit up the stairs and to her room. I imagine that must have been when the necklace fell off because later the pool was drained and checked thoroughly, as were the grounds where Ursula had been during the evening, and of course there was no sign of it.

"Once she was in her room she started to cry. It was heartbreaking. She just couldn't stop. It was as if all the stress and misery of the past two years had come to a head. She was inconsolable. Sonya and I undressed her and dried her and put her to bed. Howard came up to check on her, asking where we'd put the necklace.

Neither of us could remember when we'd last seen it on her. Of course, Howard left us straight away saying he had to find it. He wasn't terribly sympathetic to Ursula, not that it surprised me, but I had expected better of him. Eventually she fell asleep and Sonya told me she'd stay with her. I went back downstairs. That was when I heard the shouting."

"The shouting?" Matt prompted.

"It was awful. Howard and Oliver were toe to toe. I really thought they were going to come to blows. Howard had his fist knotted up in Oliver's shirt front and was accusing him of stealing the necklace. Of course your father denied it but Howard was vicious in his attack, even going so far as to accuse your father of somehow being behind James's kidnapping! I couldn't believe my ears, no one could, but Howard was like a man possessed."

"What did Dad do?" The words his father had spoken had become legend in the tabloids, but the actual facts had been muddied by various tellings over the years.

"You know your father." Katherine smiled. "Never one to back down from a challenge or to accept unjust behaviour. I can hear his words as clearly in my head now as he said them that night. He plucked Howard's hand off his shirt front and told him he'd take diamonds from him in an instant, but never a child. It was the last time Oliver spoke to Howard, ever. Of course what he'd said just made everyone think he had somehow stolen the necklace but now you've proved he didn't, and with the truth out about James, as well, hopefully we can put all this behind us."

"Put it behind us? You have to be kidding! The Blackstones will pay for what they put you through."

Rachel got up from the table where she'd been supervising Blake as he coloured in a book.

"Matt, stop it, you're upsetting your mother. Can't you see this has been difficult enough for her?"

She perched on the arm of Katherine's chair and put her arm around the older woman's shaking shoulders. Katherine gave her a watery smile of gratitude and swallowed hard before facing her youngest son.

"We've already suffered enough for the past thirty years. Your dad asked Sonya to come back home with us but she insisted Ursula needed her. She couldn't abandon her sister, not after everything she'd been through. Oliver told Sonya that when Ursula was better he wanted both of them to leave Howard, to come home. But they stayed." Katherine squeezed Oliver's hand gently, a sad smile pulling at her lips. "He felt as if they chose Howard's care and protection over his. It created a division between all of us that's never healed."

"Which is exactly why this isn't the end of things." Matt paced the width of the room, coming to a halt in front of his father. "I'm bringing them down, Dad. All of them. By the end of the month I'll hold enough shares to have controlling interest in Blackstone Diamonds. It'll be ours, just as it always should have been."

Rachel froze. A cold chill crept over her skin. Matt sounded so bitter, so driven. He'd always been focussed, even as a teenager, but this was different. This bordered on obsession. Suddenly her share broker's recent repeated e-mails made sense. For a couple of months he'd been asking her if she wanted to sell the stock she held in Blackstone Diamonds—stock which formed a large part of her investment portfolio. Obviously Matt had been working for some time to buy out other shareholders in his single-minded objective.

As much as she loved him, she had no desire to see him succeed in this venture. It was born of hatred and could only continue to fester, even if he achieved his goal. It wasn't healthy, for him or for anyone around him.

A worried frown creased Katherine's brow.

"Matt, are you sure you're doing the right thing? What about Kim? Have you discussed any of this with her?"

Matt's face hardened at his mother's words.

"I know what I'm doing is right. And as for Kimberley, she made her choice when she left us at the beginning of the year."

"That's not entirely fair, son. Her father had just died. She had to go home." Katherine's hand fluttered up around her throat.

"Home? It's where the heart is, isn't that what you always taught us? Well, her heart obviously lies in Sydney with Blackstone Diamonds because that's where she stayed." He bent down to wrap an arm around his mother's shoulders. "Mum, we've let them take enough. It's time to bring it to a halt."

Rachel's heart squeezed in sympathy as she watched the battle of emotion play across Katherine's features.

"But when will it end, Matt? When will it end?" his mother asked, the tremor in her voice betraying her anguish.

"When everything that bastard took from us is restored to Hammond hands, and not before."

"And Blake? Where does he stand in all this?" Katherine persisted.

Matt visibly stiffened. "What do you mean?"

"What the papers are saying about Howard and Marise. About Blake."

"He's my son. That's all that matters."

"Are you certain? Can you live with not knowing for sure?"

Rachel felt as though she was caught on the periphery of a Greek tragedy as she watched the scene before her unfold. Her heart ached and her eyes burned with unshed tears as she saw the fleeting shaft of pain in Matt's eyes. He held himself so rigid, as if to give voice to that pain would see him crumble.

He looked straight at the little boy at the dining table, happily absorbed in his activity and oblivious to the undercurrents swirling around them. As they watched, Blake pushed back his hair from his face, exposing the widow's peak at his forehead. The genetic hairline trait that was identical to Howard Blackstone's.

Matt's response was emphatic and final. "He's *mine*."

When they'd arrived home at the Hammond residence, Matt had told Rachel her services weren't required over the weekend. The first Monday in June being New Zealand's observance of the Queen's Birthday meant it would be a long weekend, and he told her he had no plans to go into the office and was more than capable of managing Blake on his own for the next three days. He suggested she needed the break, given all the extra days she'd worked for him lately, but Rachel was certain that Matt wanted the break from her more.

Disheartened by the realisation, she'd packed up some of her things into a weekend bag and gone back to her serviced apartment, telling herself the time off would be welcome no matter how it pulled at her heart to be away from him.

On the Saturday morning Rachel got in touch with her mother, who mentioned her sister was in better spirits but struggling with everyday things like bathing, so she'd be staying on at least until the end of the month. Taking advantage of the unexpected leisure time, she spoiled herself with long walks, soaking up the blustery wind conditions on Takapuna Beach and relishing the sight of the churning water with its garnish of white caps, catching up on her reading and watching a little television.

She was thoroughly sick of her own company by Monday night and had flicked over the television channels to watch the latest edition of a worldwide syndicated current affairs programme. She was about to flick back to the crime drama she'd been watching when a photo of a little boy made her sit up.

What the heck was a photo of Blake doing on the television?

There was one thing Matt had been vigilant about in the entire media circus that had erupted with Marise's death, and that was that Blake should never be subjected to public scrutiny. It had made the transition from car to building at his preschool an ongoing challenge. While Blake had been happy to play a game of hide and seek for a week or so earlier in the year, it had soon grown lame. It had been a complete relief to both Rachel and her charge when the interest in the circumstances around Marise's death had dwindled to the occasional tabloid speculation.

Matt would be furious that she'd somehow failed to protect Blake from being photographed. A lump formed in her throat at the thought that she'd somehow failed both of them.

She turned up the sound on the remote. All the fine hairs on the back of her neck stood at full attention as the announcer's voice introduced the next segment.

"And coming up next in tonight's show we have the amazing story of James Blackstone, better known as Jake Vance—the little boy who came back from the dead."

James Blackstone? The returned Blackstone son? But how, when the photo was so like Blake? The similarities were too obvious to be overlooked. Oh no, please no, she thought as she dropped to her knees and scrabbled around in the TV cabinet for a blank DVD to put in the recorder. It could only mean one thing, and that would destroy Matt completely.

With a shaking hand she set the recorder, then sat back to watch the segment. Twenty minutes later her head was reeling.

With her mother working for the Hammonds, as she had for so many years, Rachel had grown up knowing a little of the mystery surrounding the disappearance of

Howard and Ursula Blackstone's first-born son, even though it had happened long before she was born. When the furore had erupted last month over his return to the family fold she had paid scant attention. It was all too little too late for the mother who'd committed suicide and for the father who'd died before the truth was known.

But the story she'd just seen cast an entirely different shadow on the whole drama. One that would impact the man and the child she loved beyond all else.

On Tuesday morning the DVD burned a hole in her bag as she let herself in Matt's house. He and Blake were in the kitchen finishing breakfast, and Blake jumped down from his chair to run and give her a massive hug as she came into the room.

"Hello, handsome. Did you have a good weekend?"

"I missed you. Why didn't you come see me?" he demanded, giving her another chubby-armed squeeze for good measure.

"You were busy with your daddy. It was special time, just for the two of you. Did you have fun? Tell me what you got up to."

She let the chatter of Blake's weekend run over her like a balm. They'd been busy by the sounds of things.

Matt got up from the breakfast table and put his things in the dishwasher.

"I'm glad you're early. I need to get away early today, too."

So he was going to be all business, was he? It hurt that he could shut himself down like that. Had he even spared her a thought over the weekend? He'd certainly been on her mind.

"Before you go, I was hoping you'd have a few minutes. I have something you need to see." She took the DVD case out of her bag and showed it to him.

"It'll have to wait until tonight," he answered coldly.

Rachel put her hand on Matt's arm to stop him walking past her. Through the fine cotton of his shirt sleeve she felt the muscles of his forearm bunch into a knot, as if he couldn't bear her touch.

"Matt, people will be talking about this. I saw a television van at the front gate when I arrived today. Please, you need to see the DVD."

"What is it?" he demanded, shaking her hand off his arm and taking the disc.

"There was a feature on Jake Vance last night."

Matt snorted. "Jake Vance? James Blackstone, you mean." He shoved the disc back in her bag. "Thanks, but no thanks. I have no interest in hearing about the 'second coming' again."

"It's more than that, Matt. Look!"

Rachel grabbed the case from her bag and popped out the disc, inserting it into the DVD player attached to the small TV set fitted into the custom-built kitchen joinery.

The programme started and the screen filled with the photo that had arrested her in her tracks last night. The photo of the young boy who looked just like Blake at the same age.

"Hey, that's me." Blake's voice came from the doorway as he came back into the kitchen.

"No, honey, that's your cousin. His name is Jake."

"Jake. Blake. Jake. Blake." He started to run around the room, chanting as he went.

Matt picked him up in his arms and whispered something Rachel couldn't hear, but whatever it was, Blake fell silent and when Matt put him down again he raced away. She heard his feet hammering up the stairs.

Matt watched the DVD in absolute silence, reaching over to switch off the set when the segment reached its end.

"What are you going to do, Matt?"

"Nothing."

Rachel was incredulous. "Nothing? How can you say that?"

"It doesn't prove anything. They look alike. It happens."

"Look alike? They could've been twins. That likeness didn't happen by accident."

"So you're telling me that the media is right? That Marise was not only being unfaithful to me when she died but she was already pregnant to Howard Blackstone when she married me? You think this proves Blake isn't my son? You're overstepping the mark, Rachel. Back off."

"Surely you can see you have to find out now. The press is going to be all over you again, and all over Blake. Please, for both your sakes, find out for certain."

"Perhaps you didn't understand me last Thursday night, Rachel. Blake is *my son*. No paternity test will change that."

She wouldn't give up. She couldn't. Both of them needed the truth more than anything if Matt was to be able to continue to forge a strong bond with his boy. And, if the evidence that presented itself was true, Blake had a whole other family he deserved to be a part of. She had to push one more time.

"It might not change the legalities, Matt, but have you asked yourself why you've spent so much time away from home, away from Blake? Could it be that deep down you're afraid the rumours are true?"

Six

Anger flooded him like a tidal wave. How dare she insinuate he was deliberately staying away. Him? As an adopted child, he knew better than anyone that it made no difference who donated to your gene pool. Your father was exactly that. Yours. And you were his. As Blake was his.

But before he could unleash his fury and tell Rachel in no uncertain terms where she could stick her accusations, a pinprick of doubt stabbed at his mind. Had he subconsciously done exactly as Rachel had suggested? Was his need to be Blake's biological father stronger than he even dared admit to himself? Not for the first time he rued the estrangement between himself and his cousin Kim. This was just the type of thing they'd have been able to discuss at length in the old days, weighing the pros and cons of each scenario. True, there'd been a little distance between them when he'd married Marise—Kim had expressed surprise at the whirlwind courtship—but their working relationship had always been incredibly strong. It had been bolstered by a kinship they'd built together because they'd wanted to, not because they were related.

He reminded himself of her betrayal. Even she'd reverted to kind when the chips were down.

Was that what he was afraid of? That Blake would *want* to be a Blackstone when he grew up? No. The thought was impossible to contemplate.

"I'm late for work." He snatched up his briefcase and headed for the garage before Rachel could say another word.

Leaving later put him in the thick of rush-hour traffic, and as bad luck would have it, there was an accident on the harbour bridge. He cursed his decision to drive into work today. The ferry would've been swifter and simpler all round, but he'd planned to stay late to catch up on work he'd missed during the foray to Tahiti.

His gut clenched into a tight ball of frustration as the memory of Rachel's silky-soft skin beneath his hands flooded his senses. Tahiti—he'd been crazy to take her, but she was like a dog with a bone over the issue of Blake, and he didn't have the time or the energy to fight her. He should have. He should have put his foot down, made it clear in no uncertain terms he was the boss, she the employee. Except he'd crossed that line. Crossed it well and truly.

Goodness only knew he'd been on the verge of total loss of control at her touch. It had taken an immense strength of will to pull away and not to finish what they'd started.

And now it wasn't enough that she'd seeded herself under his skin, ensuring his nights were plagued with wanting to sink himself into her soft, warm curves again and again until he purged himself of the last hellish few months. No, now she'd insinuated her thoughts into his mind, questioning the thing that defined *him* most.

Fatherhood.

By the time he swung into the basement car parking of his building he was in a filthy mood—a state of mind not helped in the least by the brash visual reminder of the Blackstone's storefront dominating the adjacent corner to House of Hammond. Blackstone had been on his way to Auckland for the official opening when the plane carrying him and Marise had gone down. If the man had wanted to create a more dominant reminder of his unfortunate influence on the Hammonds' lives he couldn't have chosen a more obvious statement to do it with.

Well, Matt would see to it once and for all that there were no more questions. If settling Blake's paternity was what it took to rid himself of at least one persistently niggling problem then that's exactly what he'd do.

It was surprisingly easy to research paternity testing in New Zealand, and Matt was relieved to discover that, confidentiality guaranteed, he could acquire a home testing kit. After all, the last thing he wanted to do was take Blake with him to a diagnostic lab with reporters trailing behind them.

With the home testing kit he could courier the samples to the lab and for an additional fee have conclusive results within three to five days. He clicked on the order form on his computer screen requesting the kit. One way or another, he'd soon know the truth about Blake.

But one question still plucked incessantly at his mind. Even if Blake was conclusively proven to be his son, had Marise, in a final fit of defiance, been having an affair with Howard Blackstone when she died?

The next few days passed in a blur of activity at House of Hammond. The shipment of baroque black pearls had arrived, together with the first of the Pacific pearls Matt had incorporated to be set into existing designs. His hands itched to get back into his workroom so he could work up some samples, but all the while, in the back of his mind, he was waiting for that one phone call that could set his mind at rest.

On the Rachel front they seemed to be observing a truce, both of them focussing on Blake's privacy. Rachel and Blake had been virtually house bound. The pre-school had warned them of a media presence every day since the documentary piece on Jake Vance had aired, and they'd all agreed it would be best if Rachel kept Blake home and out of the glare of publicity that the documentary had rekindled.

With Mrs Kincaid not returning home before the end of the month, Rachel had taken on most of her mother's duties along with the care of Blake. Much as Matt tried to ignore it, there was a certain comfort in coming home to the two of them each day—a sense of home that had been missing from the house for far too long.

Now, almost a week after sending away the test kit, Matt was impatient for the result. One way or another.

He'd decided to finish work early today and surprise Blake, who was due home from a rare play date in the next hour. If the rain that had been forecast held off, maybe he could forestall Rachel cooking dinner and suggest she go back to her apartment for the night, leaving him to take Blake to nearby Cheltenham Beach for fish and chips. Rachel was still on him about spending more time with Blake and she was right. He'd been so fixated with vengeance against the Blackstones he'd pushed aside his obligations to his son.

He'd just pulled the Mercedes into the garage at home when the breast pocket of his jacket vibrated. The caller display said "unknown number." Matt's heart leaped in his chest.

"Matt Hammond," he answered.

"Mr Hammond, it's Liz Walters from the testing lab. Could you give me your security password please?"

Matt gave her the password he'd meticulously written onto the sample submission form.

Two minutes later he snapped his phone shut, adrenaline coursing through his body together with a sense of relief so immense it brought tears to his eyes. Finally he had the proof. The confirmation that what his heart had always told him was true. He had someone of his own. Flesh of his flesh.

Blake was his son. Categorically and irrevocably his.

"Matt? Is everything all right?" Rachel stood in the doorway to the garage. "I heard your car come in but you're taking forever. Is everything okay?"

"Yes. Everything is more than okay." A wide grin split his face as he stepped towards her, grabbing her from the top of the three stairs that led down into the garage and swinging her around and around.

Her laughter bubbled in the air around them.

"Put me down," she choked. "You're making me dizzy!"

"He's mine, Rachel. He's mine. I got confirmation just now."

He slowly stopped spinning, although his head and his heart felt as though he was still on a fast-moving carousel. Every nerve in his body went on full alert as her soft curves brushed against his chest, his abdomen, as he lowered her to the ground.

"Confirmation? You mean you had the test done?"

"Yes, to both."

Rachel lifted a hand to cup his cheek, her eyes shining with unshed tears. "Oh, Matt, I know how much this means to you. This is wonderful news."

Her fingers, so small and warm, branded against his skin. Her hazel eyes sheened over, the gold glints inside her irises glowing with pleasure. Slowly he saw the light in her eyes change and deepen into something else. Something that made him lower his head, take her lips and obliterate the last remnants of doubt that had lingered in his mind.

The taste of her was intoxicating, heady. He pulled her more tightly to him, feeling her frame melt against the hard planes of his body and intensifying the swiftly building tension in his groin to new heights. Her arms slid under his suit jacket, her hands gripping at his back, clutching at his shirt as if she'd fall if she let go.

He angled his head so he could take her mouth more deeply and plunder the hot recess with his tongue. Each taste was more enthralling than the last. The texture of her lips, her tongue, gave rise to an insatiable desire that started where their skin touched and burned through him like molten metal.

He pushed one hand up under her sweatshirt and pulled her T-shirt from the waistband of her jeans, desperate to touch her skin, to feel her warmth against his skin. The clasp on her bra was an easy victim to his able fingers, and her full breasts fell free of the binding Lycra and lace. He cupped one breast with his hand; she fit perfectly, as if she'd been made for him and him alone.

His thumb abraded her nipple, feeling it tighten into a hardened peak of want. Matt shoved her clothing up, baring her breast to the cool air. Goose bumps peppered her skin but she made no protest. He bent his head to her breast, taking the questing nipple between his lips, biting gently. Her guttural moan of response sent a spear of sensation straight to his groin. He wanted her, right here, right now.

With his other hand he cupped her buttocks, pressing her mound against his increasingly hard erection. She flexed against him in a natural rhythm as old as time. He pressed her back against the side front wheel guard of the Cayenne. When he reached for her belt buckle her hands flew to help him. As soon as her zipper was undone his hand pushed aside the denim and delved into her panties, into the hot secret part of her.

She was slick with need. Need for him. He felt all-conquering. Supremely male. He pushed her jeans down farther, allowing him better access to her soft, moist folds. Her breath rushed past his throat on a heated sigh as he probed her entrance, delving first one, then two fingers inside her. Her inner muscles clenched against him, drawing him deeper.

"I want you inside me. All of you." Her voice was strained, as if the very effort of speech was too much. "Matt, please?"

He wanted it, too. Wanted it so much his head was ringing with it. Ringing? No, that was the chime on the front gate intercom. The sound was a sharp thrust of reality, forcing Matt into painful awareness of his sur-roundings—of the woman in his arms, of what he was doing to her, with her. Again.

If he'd stepped off an ice floe in the Antarctic and into the ocean his senses couldn't have been jolted harder.

He pulled his hand slowly from the liquid heat of her body, feeling her shudder as he did so, and helped her rearrange her clothing.

"That'll be Blake coming home." Her voice sounded thick, as if the words were sticky toffee coating her tongue.

"I'll see to him." Matt stepped back, away from her, away from the siren-like enticement of her body. "I'm sorry, Rachel. It seems I'm destined to keep making the same mistake with you. We will discuss this later."

She was refastening her belt, with some trouble as her hands shook violently. She looked up. Her lips were swollen with their kisses, her eyes still awash with the heated pulse of desire that had almost seen him take her up against the side of his dead wife's car. If anything, that was even more sobering than the chime at the gate. This was the second time in as many weeks he'd almost lost control. It wouldn't—couldn't—happen again.

Rachel stood completely still as Matt strode away to the intercom at the connecting door to the house, and after a few short words hit the button to admit the car waiting outside. She knew she should move, say something, do anything, but her limbs remained frozen at her sides, her body still racked with the aftermath of emptiness after being stoked to such heights.

She forced her legs to move, deliberately stepping one foot in front of the other as she made her way back into the house, focussing on each inhale and exhale in an attempt to force her heartbeat back into some semblance of normality. She fled upstairs to her room.

Sorry.

Mistake.

The words hurt more than his withdrawal from her two weeks ago in Tahiti. He could have said anything but that. Anything else might have given her hope that she stood a chance with him, that her love for him could finally make a difference to his life. Instead, he was sorry. Incapable of seeing that the attraction between them went beyond the incendiary physical need they incited in one another.

Rachel refastened her bra beneath her clothing, then

splashed cool water on her face. Outside she heard Blake's ride pull up at the front portico and Blake's shout of glee when his father opened the door to let him inside. She knew she should go downstairs and start dinner. But right now all she wanted to do was curl into a ball in the darkest corner of a closet and hide.

For the briefest moment, when Matt had told her he'd received the result of the paternity test, he'd been the old Matt. The Matt she'd known as a teenager. The one who laughed and loved life and took every challenge head-on and with a smile on his face. Not the coldly driven and single-minded stranger he'd become in the past six months.

She reached for a towel and buried her face in its thick softness, then straightened and pulled her shoulders straight, regarding her reflection in the mirror.

Nothing visible remained of their uninhibited connection in the garage. But inside, the wounds still cut deep. She'd lived with this for the past eleven years, she reminded herself. It was nothing new. She'd survive. She always had. Except this time the hurt went deeper than before. The love she'd borne for him as an idol-struck teenager was nothing compared to what she felt for him now.

Back then she'd been driven by little else than hormones and the firm belief that if they made love everything would be all right, that he'd acknowledge his feelings for her and she'd be his girl. But she'd been wrong. So very wrong. If anything it had made things worse. And these past two encounters had only served to drive him farther away from her.

Rachel neatly folded her towel back on the rail and left her bathroom, determined to paint an expression on her face that left him in no doubt that she was unmoved by their passion. That she could withdraw from him as effectively as he had from her.

She'd do it, even if it killed her inside.

Seven

Downstairs she followed the sounds of Matt and Blake talking, finding them both in the family room, their heads bent together over a large floor puzzle. Matt looked up as she came into the room. He'd changed into jeans and a cable-knit sweater and looked far too sexy for her shattered senses.

"I was thinking I'd take Blake to the beach for fish and chips for dinner. You can take a break and head off home now if you'd like. Have a night to yourself."

At first she was at a loss for words. She hadn't expected outright rejection of her presence, not by any means. She was on the verge of acceding to his suggestion when Blake leaned forward and whispered in Matt's ear.

"No, son. Rachel needs time alone, too." Matt's voice was firm.

Blake rocked back on his heels, a recalcitrant pout marring his features.

"I want her. I want Rachel!"

"It's okay, Blake." Rachel interrupted before a full-scale tantrum could develop. "You and Dad go and have some fun feeding the seagulls. But you'll have to hurry. There are rain squalls forecast early this evening."

Matt looked outside, a frown pulling at his face. "Looks like they're here already."

Another idea occurred to Rachel. "Have you given your parents the news yet?"

"No, I was going to call them this evening. Why?"

"Well, I can put dinner together for five as easily as three. Why don't you invite them over, make it a celebration." Be damned if she'd show him how much his rejection had stung. "Honestly, it's no problem. Blake can come and help me get things ready while you go and pick your mum and dad up. You know how your mother hates driving in this weather."

For a moment it looked as if Matt would refuse and insist she leave, as he'd suggested, but Rachel held her ground under his steely gaze.

"Fine. I'll call them now."

Rachel let go of the breath she'd held hostage in her lungs as he stalked out the room and across the hall into his study. She reached out a hand to Blake.

"C'mon, honey. Let's go and get some dinner ready for Nanna and Poppa."

* * *

Matt's parents had been ecstatic about the news. Although there'd been an awkward moment when Katherine discovered Rachel had set four dinner places in the formal dining room.

"Rachel, aren't you eating with us?" Katherine asked.

"No, thank you, Mrs Hammond. I'll have mine in the kitchen," Rachel said as she put the steaming platter of chicken and zucchini pasta on the table.

"Don't be silly, you're one of us. Isn't she, Matt?"

Matt looked up from where he was settling Blake at the table. "Mum, if Rachel's more comfortable eating in the kitchen, that's her choice."

Rachel looked at him in shock. Could he have been more blunt?

"That's just ridiculous," Katherine protested, moving over to the sideboard to collect an extra place mat and table setting. "You've gone to all this trouble to prepare a lovely meal. The least you can do is enjoy it with us."

She shot her son a look that spoke volumes and patted Rachel on the hand. "There you are, dear, now we can all celebrate as a family."

Despite the rocky start, the meal turned out to be a relaxed affair. They'd lingered at the table for a while after they'd eaten. Then Katherine suggested she bathe Blake and get him ready for bed. Rachel went through to the kitchen to make coffee and tidy up the last of the dishes. She was surprised when she saw that Katherine had followed her.

"Rachel? Can I have a word with you?" she asked.

"Of course," Rachel replied as she rinsed off a plate then stacked it in the dishwasher.

"I just wanted to say thank you."

Confusion furrowed Rachel's brow. "Thank you? Whatever for?"

"For talking Matt into getting that wretched paternity test done." Katherine put up a hand to stop Rachel's protest. "Now, now. I know exactly how intractable Matt can be, so I'm sure you had something to do with persuading him to go ahead and get the proof he…" Katherine's voice wobbled precariously close to a sob but she pulled herself together on a sharply indrawn breath and continued. "The proof he needed to move on."

"Move on?"

"To put this whole sordid business between Marise and Howard behind him. It's eating him up. I'm just grateful you helped make him see sense. You can tell it's made a difference for him already."

Rachel nodded. She had seen a difference in Matt tonight when he dealt with Blake. As much as he'd tried to deny it, the fear that Blake wasn't his biological child had influenced his behaviour towards the boy. With Blake's paternity no longer under question Rachel knew their relationship would now grow stronger.

Katherine put an over-tired and overexcited Blake to bed at nine-thirty before coming back downstairs. It was getting on for ten by the time Katherine and Oliver left, insisting they take a taxi rather than have Matt drive them home. Rachel was unloading the dishwasher before heading off to bed herself when Matt came into the kitchen.

"Did you need me for something?" she asked, then instantly wished the words unsaid.

They'd already established he needed her for nothing more than the succour of his son. But a part of her still wanted to believe in miracles—to believe that he could embrace the feelings he had for her and admit them to himself as well as to her.

"I wanted to thank you for tonight. Having Mum and Dad over was a great idea. They really enjoyed it and, as you saw, they're over the moon that the whole paternity question is resolved."

"Are you going to issue a press statement? At least to stop the media hounding you both."

"I'll speak with our PR people tomorrow and discuss the best way to handle it."

"Good idea." Rachel finished wiping down the bench top then wiped her hands dry on a towel. "Matt?"

"Yeah?"

"What made you change your mind about the test?" She hoped like crazy that he'd done it for Blake's sake. To remove all and any doubt about the boy's parentage as he was growing up and to prevent the question being raised in the media again and again.

"Several things." Matt pulled out a chair at the kitchen table and sat down, gesturing for Rachel to do the same. "It was partly to halt the speculation, but essentially I wanted to ensure that no-one else could stake a claim on him. There's no way I'll ever let anyone take him from me. I meant what I said before I got the results. Blake's mine. This means it stays that way."

"But why would anyone—?"

"Marise was divorcing me. She was suing for full custody of Blake."

Rachel sat back in her chair as if she'd been slapped. "She what? When? How did you find out?"

Matt swallowed and she watched the muscles in his throat work before he spoke again. His eyes were a flat grey, as cold and lacklustre as unpolished silver.

"I was served with papers on my way out of the mortuary where her body was held. Ironic, isn't it?" His mouth twisted in a mockery of a smile. "In death she prevented the one thing she seemed hell-bent on. Taking me for everything I hold dear."

Rachel yearned to comfort him. But she daren't reach out, not again. Instead she held in the cry of denial that Marise could've been so foolish as to throw away her marriage, let alone to believe that someone like Matt would let go of his son without a monumental battle. If there was one thing in this world he was passionate about it was family. Even his business came second to that. Or at least it had until recently.

Now it made even more sense. His bitter plan to take over Blackstone Diamonds, his refusal to accept overtures from the Blackstone family. No wonder. He had all the proof he'd needed that Marise had been having an affair with Howard Blackstone and Rachel could only imagine the depth and breadth of his anger when he'd been served the papers at such a horrific time.

"Which leads me to my next decision." He paused and levelled his gaze directly at her.

A sense of foreboding prickled down her spine.

Whatever he had to say next she was certain she wouldn't like it. Rachel lifted her chin and met his stare face on.

"And that is?"

"About what happened earlier on, and in Tahiti. It has to stop. In fact it's going to stop. There's no way I want the entanglement of another relationship, or even marriage. The situation with Marise has taught me to hold on to what I love and hold it fast. Nothing and no-one will ever jeopardise Blake's wellbeing again. Ever. And, as it seems I can't keep my hands off you, and I clearly can't offer you what you seek with me, as soon as your mother returns from Wanganui I'll start looking for your replacement and let you get back to your life as you asked."

"What do you mean, 'what *I* seek with you'?" Rachel pulled together every ounce of courage she could muster. She couldn't let him see how drastically his words had affected her if she was going to be successful in carrying off the biggest lie of her life. "We can be adult about this, surely. I certainly don't expect a relationship from you. We go back far too long for me to think that. Don't worry. I know exactly where I stand."

She pushed up from her chair and painted a smile on her face that made her cheeks ache.

"Rachel, be honest. I've abused my position as your employer, abused your trust. I don't want my actions to be misconstrued by you into thinking I want a relationship with you."

Rachel managed to force a gentle laugh from her constricted throat. "Oh, don't worry about me misconstruing your actions. You've made your position quite clear. Let's just say it was an aberration. And as for abusing my trust, it was nothing of the sort. We both have needs that temporarily overtook our reason. Let's face it, it's been a while for you, right? Me, too. Can we please just leave it at that?"

Matt watched Rachel's stiff back retreat as she walked from the room and turned for the stairs. Yeah, it had been a while. A long while. Things between him and Marise had been strained for months before she'd gone back to Australia. Marital relations were nonexistent for the better part of the year—hell, if he was honest with himself he had to admit that Marise had actively avoided sex after Blake's birth, arguing that no form of contraception was a hundred percent safe and that she didn't want another child so soon.

Despite Rachel's departing statement, there was more to it, he was certain. Just as he was certain that his behaviour with her was no aberration. He was in the company of beautiful women on a regular basis. He'd never once had the urge to take one against the side of the nearest vehicle the way he'd nearly done with Rachel.

And that urge still simmered below the surface. It was only a matter of time before they'd be hot and naked, relieving this awful pressure that had been building inside since she'd taken over as Blake's nanny—and that would be disaster, because he was certain once would never be enough.

As soon as her mother was back he'd release her, whether this thing with Blackstone Diamonds was in the bag yet or not. She could go back to her life in the UK. That way the temptation would be gone. He'd meant every word he'd said when he'd told her he wasn't in the market for a new relationship or marriage ever again. He'd allowed his instincts to overrule good sense only twice in his life, once with Rachel after her high school ball, the other time in the intoxicating whirlwind of courtship with Marise. Both times had proven to be damnably wrong. He wasn't fool enough to go three for three.

Matt straightened up from the workbench and examined, from every angle, the pearl and diamond ring his team had been working on. The platinum setting brought out the best in the colour of the large semi-hemispherical pearl.

Technically named a blue pearl, it drew from the myriad colours found in the species of abalone found in New Zealand waters, called Paua, and usually reflected pinks through to purples and blue through to green. This particular pearl, nine millimetres in diameter, was predominantly green, with a hint of blue here and there. He'd drawn from a 1930s jewellery catalogue when perfecting and personalising this design, and surrounded the pearl with twelve old-mine-cut diamonds. While the old-mine cut didn't offer the flash and fire of the more modern brilliant cut it was more in keeping with the sedate beauty of the pearl.

He nodded his satisfaction. This was perfect, exactly as he'd imagined it. It would be the crown in his collection of brooches, rings, pendants and earrings all modelled on designs from the 1930s. The drawings for his next range release, inspired by the earlier Victorian trends in jewellery, and which would incorporate the delicate white and pale-pink pearls he'd sourced from Japan earlier in the year, were in his office awaiting his final inspection before coming into the workroom.

He held the ring up to the light one more time, savouring the chameleon-like beauty of the pearl, the blues and greens showing a faint shimmer of gold here and there. What you initially saw was not necessarily what you got with these stunning pearls. Each one was a precious gift of colour. This one in particular was exquisite.

It reminded him of Rachel.

Hell, where had that come from?

He placed the ring in its display case and snapped it closed and wished he could turn off the thought as easily as he'd shut the lid on the box.

Rachel. She invaded his thoughts on a regular basis. Not just his thoughts, he admitted to himself. There was an ache deep inside that she'd awakened—an ache he'd suppressed since the estrangement with Marise and which he'd kept firmly tamped down in the months since her death.

Damn. It was wrong, unforgivably wrong, but he wanted Rachel with a longing he dared not give in to. No, he had to remind himself it was an abuse of trust, an abuse of her position in his home. He was a father first, head of House of Hammond second, and on the verge of having the controlling say in the company of the man who'd brought his family nothing but pain and regret. That was enough. It had to be.

Matt returned the ring to the vault, slipping it into the drawer housing each of the pieces of the collection.

He paused in his actions to savour the sense of anticipation that came with imagining the Blackstone family's collective reaction when he achieved his goal. He'd given his vow over Howard Blackstone's grave that Blackstone would regret having messed with the Hammonds. Matt's next move against them would show them all he was a force to be reckoned with. Howard Blackstone would spin in his grave if he knew that a Hammond would be pulling his company's strings very shortly.

Back in his office Matt attended to his paperwork, most urgent of which was a press release waiting for his approval. He skimmed over the details. In it his PR team issued the DNA results and thereby quelled any further speculation about Blake's paternity. They also stated that the family had no further comment and wished to continue with their lives uninterrupted. Matt scrawled his initials on the sheet in approval. He was about to fire the sheet into his out-box when he suddenly hesitated. The timing of the release could be important. To ensure it had maximum exposure, he decided to wait a few days.

He pushed his chair back from his desk and leaned back, staring at the photo on his desk. He'd become so accustomed to its presence he barely even looked at it these days. Taken early on in his marriage to Marise, it was one of those fun candid shots that take a slice out of time and preserve it forever.

They'd known she was pregnant when the picture was taken, and he'd been ecstatic about the news.

Marise had been more reserved. It had happened far sooner than she'd expected; in fact, she'd already been expecting when they'd exchanged vows in a rapidly cobbled-together wedding earlier that year. Looking back, they'd rushed everything, so they hadn't taken a moment to see the cracks that formed early on in their relationship.

Matt picked up the photo and held it in his hand, one finger tracing the outline of Marise's face. With her lush red hair pushed back off her face by the breeze, she was a picture of feminine beauty, but that old familiar pull that he'd felt when he'd first met her was gone. She'd been like a sought-after precious and rare gem and he'd had to have her. He'd believed that all he needed to complete his life was a wife and a family. Kim had urged him to be cautious when she'd heard of the romance, calling him from Auckland when news of his liaison hit the tabloids. But he'd been drunk on the power of passion and excitement, and it had clouded his judgement just as effectively as alcohol would.

He thought back to the first time he'd seen her. She was tall and slender, a lot like her sister, Briana, in build. But where Briana was blonde, Marise had red hair. A red so rich and intense it had perfectly offset her fair skin and green eyes. Everything about her had been full of energy and activity, yet underlined with an air of fragility that had appealed to his masculine instincts on every level. And then there was her charm, which had melted even the stoniest hearts.

She'd loved her job at Blackstone Diamonds' marketing division and had been intensely proud to be associated with them. He'd taken her away from all that. From everything that had given her life and vigour. He'd believed his love for her would be enough to compensate for it all. But he'd been horribly wrong.

His finger stilled as the last image he remembered of Marise poured back into his mind—of her body, cold and lifeless in the steel drawer of the mortuary. The glorious red hair lank and matted against the side of her head.

Matt slid the photo into his briefcase. He'd give it to Blake to keep in his room. Rachel had said that every night they "told" Marise what Blake had been up to that day. Perhaps the photo would help delineate the line between Rachel and his mother in the little boy's mind. Make it easier for him when Rachel left for good.

As he went to shut the case, his eyes lingered on the photo one more time. Something niggled beneath the surface of his mind. Something he just couldn't put his finger on. It wasn't until he was in the Mercedes and heading over the Auckland Harbour Bridge that the niggle developed into a full-blown realisation.

Marise had usually worn her hair in layered feathers brushed forward to frame her face, but in the photo he'd had in his office her forehead and hairline had been exposed by the wind. Although her widow's peak wasn't as prominent as Blake's it was, nevertheless, there. The documentary piece the other night had laboured the point, ad infinitum, that such a hairline was hereditary, but to Matt's knowledge, neither of Marise's parents had such a hairline, nor did Briana.

He slammed his hand on the steering wheel in disbelief that he hadn't realised the importance earlier. He had to be sure before he could make any kind of statement, but if he was right then everyone had been barking up the wrong tree all along.

Howard Blackstone had indeed fathered a child out of wedlock. But instead of it being Blake, could it have been Marise?

Eight

Matt splashed a generous measure of whiskey into the cut-crystal tumbler on his desk, then lifted the single malt to his lips.

He was right. He knew he was. Now all he had to do was prove it. His desk was scattered with photos and news clips. Pictures of Marise, of Howard, of Blake— and of Barbara and Ray Davenport, and of Briana.

It was all there in front of him. Proof.

He picked up the picture of Barbara and Ray and studied it carefully. They looked happy enough together but if his theory was correct it hadn't always been so. Barbara Davenport had been Howard's secretary thirty years ago. It was looking more and more likely that she'd been a lot more than that.

So how, then, had she managed to get hold of the Blackstone Rose necklace? Had she been at Ursula's thirtieth birthday party that night? He knew his parents had been there, but after the distress it had caused Katherine to relive the evening the other night, he knew he couldn't ask her. Maybe Briana would know. Granted, she hadn't yet been born when the necklace was stolen, but things had a way of being discussed in families that over time left dormant knowledge sitting in a child's mind.

He looked at his watch and judged the two-hour time difference between Melbourne and Auckland. It wasn't too late to call. He lifted the phone from its cradle. It'd been too long since he'd talked with his brother, Jarrod, anyway. This way he could kill two birds with one stone.

An hour later Matt reset the telephone handpiece in its stand. With what Briana had been able to tell him, he was convinced that Barbara had been pregnant by Howard. What had driven her to steal the necklace he could only speculate, but he would lay money on the fact that Howard had rejected his secretary once she'd told him she was expecting his child.

Marise's birth date was circled on the sheet of paper in front of him, together with the date of Ursula's party and the time he now knew Barbara had left her position as Howard's secretary. Given the timeline of when Temana Sullivan's father had acquired the pear-shaped stone, now safely in Danielle Hammond's creative hands, coinciding with the date the Davenport girls were enrolled for a private-school education, it all made sense.

Had Marise had some idea of the ramifications of the possession of the four round pink diamonds that she'd secreted in Briana's safe? Had she suspected, or even known, that Howard Blackstone was her real father?

All this time Matt had been plagued with the belief that he had failed Marise in some fundamental way, that the collapse of their marriage had been his fault entirely and that he'd been too focussed on business to hold on to his wife in the months before she'd left. But now he realized many of the failures in her life had occurred long before he'd come onto the scene. She'd been raised living a lie. Possibly even spurned by her real father before her birth.

Still, Marise must have convinced Howard of the truth. The vast private jewellery collection she'd been bequeathed was worth millions. A man like Blackstone didn't just give something like that away to someone as ephemeral as a mistress.

Had it been Blackstone's idea that she divorce Matt and go for full custody of Blake? Anger coiled tight and low in his belly. He'd lay odds on that being true.

He owed it to Marise to prove it. Theirs might not have been the happiest marriage on the planet but failure came on both sides of the marital bed. If he could do anything for her now, it would be to prove that Howard Blackstone was her father.

But a photo alone wasn't proof. Somehow he had to convince the Blackstone children to release their father's DNA information so it could be proven without a shadow of a doubt that Marise had been his child. With the current climate between them, and with what they had coming to them when he achieved the majority share holding he was after, he doubted they'd be forthcoming. But in all his years of business he'd learned one thing was paramount—if you waited, nothing came to you. If you wanted something, you had to reach out and take it with both hands.

"Matt? What are you doing still up?"

He wheeled around at the sound of Rachel's voice at the door. She was wrapped up in a voluminous dressing gown, her hair tousled and a pressure mark on her cheek from her pillow case. His fingers itched to reach out and touch the pink line on her face. Instead he gripped the tumbler in his hand that much tighter.

"Just expanding a theory."

Rachel moved around the desk, and he watched as her eyes scanned the pictures and papers he had spread there.

"A theory? I thought you'd sorted out the whole thing about Blake to your satisfaction. You can't go much further than the DNA result you got. What are you trying to prove now?"

Rachel reached for the picture he'd brought home from the office and he watched as her expression changed slightly, a quizzical frown appearing between her brows. Had she noticed what he had?

"I haven't seen this picture before," she said.

"I brought it home from work today. I thought Blake might like it in his room."

"That's a great idea."

The frown on her face deepened.

"I never saw her with her hair like this before. Is that a widow's peak at her hairline?"

"Yes, it is. I don't know why I didn't consider it before." Matt took the picture from Rachel and laid it back down on the table, next to the one of Howard Blackstone that he'd printed off from an archived newspaper article on the internet.

"My goodness! Am I seeing what I think I'm seeing?" Her voice was laced with incredulity.

"Tell me what you see."

If Rachel had made the same connection he had, then it lent weight to his theory.

"The hairline." She pointed with her finger to first Howard's photo, then Marise's. "The shape of their foreheads, their eyes. Granted her nose and chin are different, but anyone could be forgiven for thinking they're related."

"I think they're related, all right. I believe that Blackstone was her father."

"Her father! But how?" Rachel snapped up the pictures again and studied them more closely.

"Marise's mother, Barbara, worked as Blackstone's secretary back in the late seventies. She resigned in seventy-eight. Marise was born a few months later."

"Why would no one have noticed the resemblance before? Why now?"

Matt took a sip of his whiskey, then put the glass down; he didn't really feel like drinking anymore. Instead, his senses were being drummed into awareness by Rachel's closeness, by the warmth that radiated from her body so close to his, by the subtle scent she wore and which wove around him like a silken trap. He stepped away from the desk and sat down in his chair on the opposite side.

"No one had ever looked for it before. Barbara and Ray moved to Melbourne when she left Blackstone Diamonds. They'd been married a few years. It was only natural to assume that Marise was Ray's daughter."

"So what are you going to do now?"

"I'm going to prove that Marise wasn't having an affair with Howard Blackstone."

"Is that the only reason? To prove that she wasn't being unfaithful to you?"

"Isn't that enough? Don't you think it's better for Blake to know that his mother wasn't an unprincipled money-grabbing tramp like the media have referred to her since before the crash? One day it'll all come out again. You know it will. For all her faults, he needs to know she wasn't that kind of person."

Rachel rubbed her hand across her eyes. "Of course, that makes sense. I'm sorry. I'm tired. I should have thought of that."

"You should go back to bed. What are you doing up, anyway?" He flicked a glance at his watch. It was one o'clock in the morning. They should all be in bed.

His body tautened at the thought. In bed. Together. He resolutely shoved the thought back down into the dark place it belonged.

"I wanted to get some eucalyptus for Blake's humidifier. He sounded a bit chesty at bedtime and his coughing woke me a while ago. He settled straight down again, but I thought it would be a good idea to get the humidifier going just to make sure it doesn't get any worse."

"You head back to bed. I'll take care of it."

"It's no problem."

"You're dead on your feet. Don't worry. I'll see to him."

"Okay then." She turned to leave the room, but hesitated at the doorway. "Matt, how are you going to prove that Howard Blackstone was Marise's father? Kimberley Perrini and Ryan Blackstone aren't going to be too happy about a new skeleton in their father's closet, especially not so soon after their brother has resurfaced."

"It's not their happiness I'm concerned about. Don't worry, I'll deal with it."

Matt flexed his hands and counted the minutes to the time when Kimberley Perrini would be at her desk at Blackstone's head office and he could call and tell her what he wanted of her.

Six months ago it would have been simple. He'd have known that no matter what, he could have counted on his cousin's support. But things had changed. Drastically. So drastically they were barely even on speaking terms anymore. Her doing, his choice. By returning to Blackstone's the way she did with no notice, no warning, she'd effectively cut herself off from him and House of Hammond. It was little wonder he'd rejected her overtures after Marise had died—who wouldn't when it was Kim's own father Marise had been with. But in the light of what he now believed, he had to hope that Kim would see things his way.

He switched on his laptop and attached to an e-mail two pictures that showed the similarities between

Marise and Howard. The more often he looked at them the more he was convinced he was right.

But would Kim feel the same way? Would she want to find out that a woman she'd only tolerated for Matt's sake was in fact her half sister? He didn't doubt that Ryan would do his best to forestall any attempt to create a familial link between his father and Marise. The guy's tenacity knew no bounds, and protecting the Blackstone empire was inherent in him. If he sensed any additional threat, he'd close everything down as fast as he could.

Matt picked up his phone, punching the numbers and waiting for the burr of the call connecting through to Sydney. He momentarily rued that he'd deleted her mobile number off his phone but reminded himself they'd gone past that type of closeness. As he identified himself to the telephonist and asked to speak to Kim he wondered how long it would be before anyone else knew who was calling and to whom. No doubt Ryan or Ric Perrini's minions would spread the news with the speed of an Aussie bushfire.

"Matt, this is a surprise. How are you? And Blake, how's he keeping?"

Kim's voice sounded achingly familiar in his ear. He'd always admired Kim's directness and honesty and he missed working with her more than he'd ever admit to anyone. But underlying the warmth and familiarity in her tone, her voice held an element of caution.

"We're fine. Look, this isn't a social call."

She sighed. "No, I didn't expect it was, although I'd hoped that by now we could start to mend some fences between us. Don't you think it's time?"

He could hear the hope in her voice, the gentle plea to let go of his anger. The last words he'd exchanged with her had been bitter, laced with shock and grief, and above all, anger at what her father had wrought upon his family.

"Time? You tell me. I need to ask you something, but before I can explain why, give me your e-mail address. I need to send you a couple of attachments." As Kim gave him the details, he typed them in then hit the send button. "Let me know when you've got them."

He heard the hitch in her breathing as she opened the file.

"What do you want, Matt?"

"Have you looked at the pictures?"

"Of course I've looked at them. What are you getting at? Is this some kind of cruel taunt?"

Matt expelled a sharp breath. "Look at them again. Very carefully."

"I don't know what you expect me to see here. It would help if you told me what I'm supposed to be looking for."

He could hear the frustration in Kim's voice and felt a momentary pang for forcing her to look at the photos of her father and the woman she'd known so well. The woman who the world at large thought had been having an affair with Howard Blackstone.

"Kim, just concentrate. Try to get past the fact you knew them both and try to look at the pictures with a fresh eye. Tell me what you see," he coaxed.

"Okay, but I still don't see… Oh."

Matt gripped his phone tight as he waited for Kim to speak again. When she did, she obviously chose her words very carefully.

"The widow's peak. I never noticed Marise had one before."

"We never really notice what we're not looking for."

"Am I meant to assume you think there was a relationship between Howard and Marise that wasn't sexual?"

"Yes. I do."

"But that's ridiculous."

"Is it? Was Howard so devoted to your mother that it's outside of the realm of possibility he had an affair? We already know he wasn't a saint and your mother was withdrawn and depressed after James was taken. Howard was a virile man. As much as he supposedly loved your mother he could have had an affair, and he could have had other children. After all, no-one had trouble believing he was having an affair with my wife." Matt pressed home his point with the subtlety of a hammer on an anvil, strike after strike.

"Matt, look. I know you must still be hurting, but seriously, what are you hoping to achieve with this? It'll just start up the media merry-go-round again. Do you really want that? And how do you hope to prove your theory?"

"A DNA comparison will satisfy any question over their relationship. I want it clear that my wife wasn't having an affair with your father."

"So this is all down to your pride and this stupid feud? I don't think so, Matt."

"My pride has nothing to do with it. Would you rather continue to believe your father was having an affair with someone young enough to be his daughter when he died? Think of it from a public relations angle,

Kim. Think of the damage that has been done to Black-stone's since he died."

"Damage you've been capitalising on!" Kim inter-jected.

Matt rubbed his fingers across his forehead. Damn. Arguing with her wouldn't get the answer he wanted.

"Barbara Davenport was your father's secretary. She left his employ around the same time the Blackstone Rose went missing. We both know what a bastard How-ard could be. If he cut Barbara off when she fell preg-nant, what better revenge could she have had on him than stealing from him the one thing he prized above all else? The one thing he believed symbolised his success. Marise had four of the stones when she died. It makes sense that her mother gave them to her."

"And the fifth stone? Tracing that would be the only way to prove whether your outrageous theory holds water."

"I have the fifth stone."

"You...you what?"

Matt swiftly explained his recent trip to Tahiti and meeting Temana Sullivan.

"Trust me on this, Kim. Barbara Davenport stole the original necklace and broke it down. I don't know whether the heat around selling the largest diamond put her off selling the others or whether on its own it got her enough money to live the lifestyle we both know that her husband couldn't have provided on his income, but whichever way you look at it, she's the common denominator."

"Okay, for argument's sake, let's say she is, and that you're right. What do you want from me?"

"I need authorisation from all of you to allow me access to Howard's DNA results. I need to know, Kim, for Blake's sake. I don't want him to grow up with a mass of lies and speculation about his mother hanging over his head. You know what that's like. You don't want to put him through that, do you?"

He waited for what felt like an aeon before she replied.

"Okay, I'll do what I can to ensure Ryan and Jake give their consent."

"Thank you, Kim."

"Don't thank me yet. You might have my agreement, but Ryan and Jake are going to be a lot harder to convince. We have a meeting scheduled shortly. I'll try to call you back later today."

Nine

Matt spent the better part of the day working desperately to distract himself from the agony of waiting for Kim's call. In the end it was after five before his secretary buzzed through to say she was on the line.

"What did they say?" Matt asked as he picked up the phone.

"It wasn't easy, but I have their agreement." She sounded weary even though it was still only midafternoon in Sydney.

"Excellent. I'll get things rolling from this end." He wanted to punch the air.

"Hold up a minute. They have made some stipulations and, to be honest, we're in unanimous agreement on this."

A frisson of disquiet skittered down his spine. "Go on."

"Obviously you want some kind of public statement about the outcome of the DNA comparison if it proves your theory is correct—and I'd like to say that both Ryan and Jake are very doubtful of this."

"I had considered that a press release would be the best way of nipping this whole thing in the bud." He didn't want to tell her about his own recent fears about Blake and that he was sitting on the release of a statement that proved his fatherhood of his son. He was glad now he'd waited. Imagine the impact if both statements were released at the same time.

"We've done a little research and understand that if you can provide something of Marise's—a toothbrush, a hairbrush, even some hair that might still be on an item of clothing—the lab in Canberra that identified Howard's remains is prepared to rush through the comparison. However, the results will be returned to us. We are prepared to inform you of the outcome, of course, but even in the event you're proven correct you will have no physical proof, there will be no statement issued and no acknowledgement of the relationship, unless you agree to one thing."

"What?" Matt bit the word out through a clenched jaw. He could see where this was going and he didn't like it one little bit.

"You are to withdraw from the takeover bid, stop your buyout."

A wave of fury swelled through him. His first instinct was to growl "Never!" and slam down the phone, but he reined in his fury just that little bit and harnessed the control he needed.

"You can't be serious."

"That's our offer, take it or leave it."

"And if I leave it?"

"How can you even ask that? Maybe you should be asking yourself the real reason why you want to know about Marise and Howard. From here it sounds more like you're doing it for yourself than for Blake. When you can answer yourself honestly, call me back and let me know what you want to do." Then she hung up.

Matt was furious. With himself and with Kim. But he had to admit it, they held all the cards and they knew exactly how to deal them. Without the Blackstone children's permission he'd never get access to their father's DNA records. At a stretch he might be able to get some comparative kinship test done if he could find anything of Kim's still lying around, but he'd been ruthless in purging her workspace—and the Hammond-owned town house that had been provided as part of her employment package—when she'd told him she was staying in Australia. He'd overseen the movers as they boxed up every last item and had it shipped to her without so much as a personal note.

Given how thorough he'd been to strip every last thing of Kim's from wherever she'd left her personal stamp, Matt wasn't prepared to think about why he still hadn't let go of his dead wife's possessions.

He'd allowed himself to be manipulated into a tight corner, and there was only one way out. To agree. But agreement went against everything he'd been working so hard for. Was it enough simply to know for himself what the results were? Would that be enough for Blake in years to come?

Ever since his grandfather, Jebediah Hammond, had signed over his mining leases to Howard Blackstone, it had been his father, Oliver's, greatest goal to regain control of the diamonds that Blackstone had built his empire on. That goal had become Matt's and with the rift between the families wider than ever, he had been even more determined to see his father's dream realised.

But if Marise was truly Howard's daughter, wasn't his agenda thereby altered? Weren't the anger and the bitterness that had festered deep inside him falsely bred? His entire perception had to shift.

Matt wasn't a man accustomed to making mistakes. Every last detail had to be perfect before he would commit. Not for him the highs and lows of speculation and risk. No. He had to be certain that if he called a halt to his buy up of Blackstone Diamonds shares that it was for all the right reasons.

If he agreed to the Blackstone children's condition he was faced with the prospect of fielding his father's disappointment. While he'd been able to privately vindicate his father of the theft of the Blackstone Rose, and while the re-emergence of James Blackstone, as Jake Vance, had cleared his parents in his abduction, there still remained his father's one bug bear.

The mines.

Legend had grown around his father's final words to Howard Blackstone on the fateful night the necklace had been stolen. *"Diamonds that belong to the*

Hammonds I would take from you in a heartbeat, you bastard, but never a child."

There was no argument. A child's needs came before everything. Even a father's. And Blake deserved to grow up without the cloud of scandal over his mother's death hovering over his head. Damn. For his own peace of mind he needed to know the answer. The rest, well, he'd have to think about that.

He picked up the phone. They thought they had him, but he'd find some way out of this. A way to break beyond their conditions. Right now it was more important to get things under way. When Kim picked up at the other end he cut straight to the point.

"I'll send you what you need to get this started," he enunciated carefully, determined not to show so much as a crack in his control.

"So you've agreed? You're withdrawing from the takeover? Matt, I'm so relieved, I knew you'd—"

"No." He said the word quietly.

"No? What do you mean, no?" Kim's confusion was clear in her voice.

"Just get the tests done."

"But—"

"The tests, Kim. That's all for now." He put down the receiver. Without his agreement would they change their minds about getting the comparison done? It was a risk he was willing to take. Their consent to go ahead with the testing had been a telling moment. By now he'd lay odds they wanted answers almost as much as he did.

* * *

When he got home he was surprised to find the house in darkness. Rachel's car wasn't where it was usually parked and there was no sign of either her or Blake. It was late. A sense of alarm washed through his body. Where were they? Had something happened to them?

From the kitchen he started to dial the numbers to Rachel's mobile phone when he heard her key in the front door. He sped through to the entrance hall. She was alone. He caught her by the arm as she swung the door shut and reset the dead lock.

"Where have you been? Where's Blake?"

Rachel shook herself free. "Blake's with your mum and dad. Mrs Hammond called me to see if she could have him overnight. I didn't think you'd have a problem with that. Do you?"

He was overreacting. The by-product of too much frustration, and not all of it centred on his conversation with Kimberley Perrini.

"Of course not. Just keep me in the loop next time."

He stepped back and Rachel brushed past him, sending his body into instant full alert. He ground his teeth together silently. Yes, the frustration he suffered had a lot more to do with his son's off-limits nanny than with anything else. The faint imprint of her warmth where her hip had grazed his was like a burning brand. He wanted that brand over his entire body, skin to skin.

An aberration, she'd called their last encounter. But this sensation that held his body captive was no aberration. It was desire and need and longing all bundled into one aching mass centred deep within his body. It would be so easy to give in. To take Rachel in his arms, to taste her sweet essence and plunder her softness in the pursuit of release. If for one minute he thought that would soothe the disquieting ache within, if to take her and have done with her would bring it all to an end, he'd have followed her through to the kitchen where he could hear her preparing dinner. He'd take her by the hand and lead her to his master suite where he'd peel the winter layers of her clothing from her body, one piece at a time, until he exposed her pearly white skin. Then he'd explore every inch of her in as leisurely a fashion as he was capable of.

His hands shook. Okay, so leisurely probably wasn't in the cards. Nor was the realisation of the fantasy that plagued him night and day. Matt dragged his fractured thoughts together and locked them away in a cold, dark corner of his mind.

In the kitchen Rachel started to put together a quick meal for herself and Matt. Her mother always had a selection of pre-made dinners in the deep freeze in the utility room off the kitchen. Rachel had selected a home-made lasagne and popped it into the convection oven to warm through.

Her arm still tingled from Matt's touch when he'd grabbed her at the front door. Not in a hurtful way, but with a definite show of strength and dominance that from any other man would have made her feel vulnerable, even frightened. But she knew him so much better than that.

She hadn't planned on getting home this late; in fact she hadn't planned on leaving Blake with his grandparents. But both Katherine and Blake had been so excited at the prospect, that she hadn't seen the harm in it. At least not until she'd walked through the front door and come face-to-face with Matt.

There was a different air about him tonight. Something she couldn't quite put her finger on. Had he followed through on his plans to confirm this new link between Marise and Howard? Matt wasn't the kind of man to let something like that lie. Had he been in touch with Kimberley Perrini? Was that the reason he seemed so…on edge? She was dying to ask but knew she'd be overstepping the boundaries of their employer/employee relationship if she did so—the boundaries he was so determined to keep firmly in place.

She snatched her handbag up from the kitchen table where she'd left it and picked up her jacket. With dinner under way she'd put her things away in her room.

Upstairs, she was surprised to hear noise coming from one of the other bedrooms. She quickly put her things away, then went to investigate. To her surprise Matt was in the room, the wardrobe was pulled open and he'd taken several garments from inside and was inspecting them before laying them on the bed.

"Matt? Can I help you? What are you doing?"

"Looking for hair, Marise's hair. I need it to send to Australia."

"So you talked to Kim, then."

"Yes."

"And it went well?" she prompted.

"They've agreed to the DNA testing."

Rachel chewed her lip and watched as he moved

from the wardrobe to the dresser on the opposite side of the room. Suddenly it occurred to her that the room was full of Marise's things. Why was that, when the master suite was downstairs? Just how long had they been estranged? Her mother had hinted at trouble between the two of them, a distance and coldness that she couldn't understand in a couple that were still essentially newly wed. Away in London at the time, Rachel hadn't paid much attention to it. Matt's marital problems were the last thing she'd wanted to dwell on. Ever since her mother had told her of his sudden nuptials, Rachel had fought to lock her feelings for him out of her heart and mind.

She turned his response over in her mind. There was something he wasn't saying, she was certain.

"Just like that? They agreed? You must be quite relieved."

"It wasn't that simple." Matt stopped what he was doing and sat on the edge of the bed. "They had some conditions of their own."

"Conditions?"

"Yeah, can't say I'm surprised. They want me to withdraw from the takeover. They won't release proof of the results of the test unless I do."

"And will you?" Rachel walked over to the drawers and began refolding all the things Matt had pulled out.

"I haven't decided yet. First I have to find something of hers that can be used for the test. Without that it's all relative, anyway."

"So what sort of thing are you looking for?"

"Something on which she'd have left a trace of her

DNA. Kim said a toothbrush or hairbrush would do, but all of those things have been cleared away. There's not so much as a lipstick-stained tissue left in a handbag or a loose hair on a garment. Nothing."

Rachel closed the drawers on the dresser and systematically started to put away the gowns and suits Matt had thrown onto the bed. Everything was of the finest quality, everything typical of Marise in cut, style and colour. But not so much as a trace of fragrance lingered on her things. It was as if these were the clothes of a stranger. Someone who'd gone without leaving an imprint of their passage.

A thought suddenly struck her.

"What about her car? Did she keep a hairbrush or lipstick in the glove compartment? She always was meticulous about her appearance. She's bound to have something still in there."

"Good idea. I'll check. Leave those." He gestured at the things she hadn't yet put away. "It's time they all went."

"Would you like me to see to it?" Rachel offered.

He hesitated a moment at the open wardrobe. One hand reached out to touch the shimmering gold-coloured satin of an evening gown Rachel recognised from a society shot that had been plastered across the papers worldwide shortly after Matt and Marise had married. He fingered the fabric for a moment, then dropped it again as if its touch was like acid against his skin.

"Yes. Get rid of it all. I don't care where to. Just get it out of here."

He left the room on quick strides, and she heard him

head down the stairs. She looked around the room and wondered anew at the estrangement between him and his dead wife. When her mother had told her of their marriage, Rachel had tried to convince herself that she was happy for him that he'd found love even if it wasn't with her.

Up until that call she'd still harboured hope that one day she'd be able to win his heart. For as long as she could remember she'd loved him. First with the hero-worship adoration of a child, but then, as she'd hit her teenage years, the five-year age difference between them hadn't seemed so monumental anymore, and a new attraction had burned within her. One that had seen her take the lead the night he'd stepped in to escort her to her school ball.

She still remembered vividly how he'd looked that night. His blond hair was combed straight back off his strong forehead, making him look older, more distant than she was used to. When he'd come to her mother's apartment to pick her up she'd been breathless with excitement. Finally, she'd thought, he'd see her as he was meant to see her. Finally he would realise that she loved him and that he loved her, too.

Rachel's mouth twisted at the memory. He'd seen her, all right. He'd even allowed her to woo him, seduce him, with her newfound maturity and confidence. When he'd taken her in his arms and they'd made love in his car, she'd embraced the crossover between child and woman, welcomed the brief discomfort she'd experienced, revelled in the heights of pleasure he'd brought her. Finally she was his.

Except once the heat of their passion for each other

had ebbed, as surely as the outgoing tide on the beach where he'd parked, he'd become a stranger. He'd straightened his clothes and then hers, plucking her arms from around his neck when she'd reached for him again.

The expression on his face had said it all. He'd apologised for taking advantage of her, had said it would never happen again. Each word had been a death blow to her hopes.

When he'd agreed to accompany her to her ball she'd believed that finally he had begun to see her as the woman she'd become, but instead he'd seen her as a charity case. Someone who'd been let down by her own partner and whom he'd agreed to take so she wouldn't lose face among her peer group. He'd looked out for her like a brother. Except her feelings for him had never been sisterly. Not then and certainly not now.

Rachel sighed as she turned off the bedroom light and left the room, closing the door with a firm click behind her as she went. The last thing she needed tonight was the ghost of Marise's presence plaguing her sleep. She'd inventory the contents of the room and deal with them tomorrow while Blake was at preschool. Maybe they'd all rest a bit easier when that was finally done.

Matt met her at the bottom of the stairs, a sealed plastic bag in his hand.

"You were right. She did keep a hairbrush in the car. I'll get this away to Sydney in the morning. Thanks for the suggestion."

Rachel smiled and nodded. "Sure, no worries. Dinner should be just about ready. Where would you like to eat tonight?"

"Since Blake's not home I'll take advantage of the quiet and do some work in the library. Can you bring a tray to me there?"

Rachel nodded. So he was shutting himself away again. Suddenly she couldn't wait for her mother's return from down country and the chance to leave here again. But this time she wouldn't be in a hurry to return. There were some things a woman just couldn't keep putting herself in line for and flat-out rejection was one of them.

Ten

Matt's head spun with unanswered questions as he hung up his telephone. Kim's words still echoed in his ears. The results of the DNA testing were irrefutable.

Howard Blackstone was Marise's father.

Somehow the knowing didn't do much to ease the anger he still felt towards both his wife and his family nemesis. If Marise had believed Howard was her father before the plane crash, why had she not simply picked up a phone and told Matt? Because she'd been planning to divorce him, that's why, he reminded himself grimly. And with the full and financial support of Blackstone to do so. It was just the kind of leverage Howard would have relished.

But now he had another problem to consider. In light

of the results, Kim and her brothers had offered to see
to it that Marise's remains be removed from their resting
place at Waverley Cemetery and have her reburied in the
Blackstone family plot at Rookwood.

His first instinct was to leave her where she was, but
he knew deep inside that, with her love of pomp and circumstance, Marise would have preferred to be buried a
Blackstone. His hand fisted around the pen he'd been
taking notes with, snapping the tube into splinters.

A Blackstone. How bitterly ironic that he'd married one.

He dropped the fragments of his pen into the wastepaper basket and brushed off his hands. If only it was
as easy to brush off the knowledge that his wife had
taken that final irrevocable step to dissolve their marriage and take Blake from him.

It was time to break the news to Briana. How did one
tell someone that their mother had been unfaithful to
their father? That the sister they'd grown up with, loved
and fought with in the way that sisters did, was only a
half sister after all. He took in a deep, steadying breath.
It had to be done. He picked up the phone and called
Briana and Jarrod's number, expelling that breath in a
rush when Briana answered on the fourth ring.

"Briana, it's Matt. I have some news about Marise
that you really need to hear."

"News?" Briana sounded wary. She wasn't the only
one reluctant to uncover Marise's skeletons, not after
the way her discovery of the four Blackstone diamonds
that Marise had secreted in her safe had almost ripped
apart her relationship with Jarrod.

"Yeah, you might want to sit down. You know how I had tests done to prove Blake is my son? Well it led me to wondering about a possible link between Howard and Marise. It wasn't until I did a little more research that it became apparent that there were several links between your mother, Howard and Marise." He paused while the news sunk in. "Briana, Howard was Marise's father."

Her sharply indrawn breath resonated in his ear.

"You mean Mum had an affair with Howard Blackstone? Oh my God! No! I don't believe it. She couldn't have done something like that. She loved Dad."

"I'm sorry, Briana. I know the news is difficult to stomach." He concisely explained about the DNA matching that had been done with the hair from Marise's brush and the data used to identify Howard. "The test results are indisputable. It's possible that Blackstone turned on the charm and coerced your mother—goodness knows he knew how to do that to his advantage. And Ursula wasn't well then. Whatever their reasons, I think he rejected Barbara when she told him the news. We know she left her position suddenly. The more you look at it, the more it makes sense."

"That's true, but an affair? How on earth could they have kept that a secret, and for so long? And what makes you think he rejected her? It could have been the other way around."

"Because I believe Barbara stole the Blackstone Rose. Maybe she approached Howard for financial help with the baby, maybe she even threatened to blackmail him. Whatever, we'll never know for sure. But if I'm right, and all the evidence points that way, she must have broken down the necklace and, when the heat died down over its disappearance, sold the central diamond."

"Evidence? Have you recovered the last diamond?"

He quickly explained about the trip to Tahiti and buying the stone back from Temana Sullivan.

"Maybe selling just the one stone gave her enough that she never needed to sell the others. Or maybe she found the whole process too risky, the danger of being exposed too high, that she didn't attempt it again."

"This is all too much to take in at once. Matt, are you absolutely certain?" She sounded shaken.

"As certain as I can be. The Blackstones hold the proof that Howard and Marise are father and daughter, and they're not prepared to release that into the public domain. As to Barbara and the necklace, we know she was at Ursula's birthday party that night, and from Marise's date of birth we also know that Barbara was pregnant at the time. You know how she loved and protected you girls. She'd have fought Howard for what she believed was her daughter's right. And to avoid raising any questions, or create any disparity between you two, she'd have made sure that whatever Marise got you also received."

"Do you think Dad knew?" Briana whispered.

"I doubt it. He might have had his suspicions, but really, without the kind of proof we have today, he wouldn't have known for sure." Matt wondered briefly whether Ray Davenport might not have had some inkling about the affair, and whether that inkling had been a contributing factor to his embezzlement of Howard Blackstone's private account. But he pushed the idea from his mind. If Ray had been driven by revenge, he would never have been so adamant about returning the funds. "How's he doing?"

"He's accepted the conviction but he's not looking forward to the court sentencing date in October. All things considered, he's holding up okay."

"That's good." He hesitated a moment. "Do you want me to break the news to him about Marise and Howard?"

"No, I'll do it. It'll be a hell of a blow to him. I think it'd be better coming from me."

"There's one other thing." Matt clenched his jaw, fearful of Briana's reaction to the next bit of news. In one breath he told her about moving Marise's remains to the Blackstone plot.

Briana was silent for several moments, then she finally spoke. "It's going to raise all sorts of questions, stir up the waters all over again. As much as Marise would probably have preferred it that way, do we really want to get back on that media merry-go-round?"

"You're right. Marise would have preferred it. As I said before, there'll be no public announcement about Howard being her father." Matt hesitated a moment, anger rising to bubble just below the surface at the reminder of the Blackstones' attempt at manipulating his takeover attempt.

"I think we should accept the offer." Briana interrupted his thoughts, her voice suddenly firmer, more confident. "But, Matt, there's something else I'd like to do. As much as I disagreed with you over it, I know you had your reasons for Marise's private burial. This time I want all of us to have an opportunity to say goodbye to her properly, to remember how she was before she died. If you have no objections, I'd like to organise a memorial service to coincide with her reburial."

Matt considered her request. He'd been so full of anger back in January that he'd wanted her funeral over and done with. He was no less angry now, although it was better controlled, better directed.

A startling new thought surfaced in his mind. In itself, the memorial service would negate Kim, Ryan and Jake's withholding of the DNA results unless he withdrew from the takeover.

A grim, satisfied smile pulled at Matt's lips. He had them over a barrel. They couldn't deny or control Briana's right to say farewell to her sister with a proper funeral. He could both make it up to Briana and ensure he continued to have control over Kim and her brothers. Public announcement or not, the media would draw its own conclusions about Howard and Marise.

"Yeah, okay. Do what you need to do and let me know. Blake and I will be there."

"Thank you, Matt. You won't regret it. It'll give us all closure."

Briana's conciliatory tone washed over him in a wave of compassion. But she was wrong. Closure was still some distance away and would remain so while Howard Blackstone's influence still hung over Matt like the Damocles sword.

Matt had made an interesting discovery in the past few days. The solicitor's letter accompanying Marise's demand for the divorce and full custody of Blake had come from none other than the same firm retained almost solely by the Blackstones—giving weight to Matt's belief that Howard had been behind Marise's request to dissolve their marriage all along.

Matt would have his final revenge, one way or another.

Rachel held on tight to Blake's hand as they left the Sydney memorial service, but his lower lip started to quiver as the barrage of photographers rent the air around them with flashing bulbs of light. She scooped him up into her arms, turning his face into her shoulder. Inside she was seething that Matt could subject his son to this after all the months they'd struggled to keep Blake secure from the public eye.

She made a dash for the black stretch limousine, Matt at her side, one arm protectively around his son. Inside the warm confines of the limousine she baled Matt up with a furious glare.

"What the hell were you thinking?"

"Rachel, you overestimate my ability to control the media if you think I could prevent them finding out about Marise's memorial service." Matt sat back in his seat opposite her, his grey eyes like flint as he fielded her anger.

"You know you could have done something. Why put Blake through all this? And having your PR people make that paternity statement just yesterday was underhanded even for you."

Blake had turned in his seat next to his father and was up on his knees staring out the back window at the procession of similar black luxury vehicles behind them for the long, slow journey to the Rookwood Cemetery.

"I never did a thing to draw the media's attention to today." His mouth settled in a grim line. His expression should have served as a warning, but Rachel would not let go.

"No, you didn't. But you didn't take any steps to keep the memorial confidential, did you?"

"It would have come out anyway. No matter what Briana and I did to keep a lid on it."

"But they have every detail! From a copy of the exhumation order right down to a copy of the service. It was supposed to be a memorial for Marise. Not a three-ring circus!"

She slumped back in her seat and stared out the side window. She couldn't bear to look him in the eye anymore for fear of what she'd see there. She didn't want to find proof that Matt had orchestrated the whole thing. He hated the media but in the past six months she'd seen he wasn't above using them for his own means, and she had the deep suspicion that there was a great deal more to this whole debacle today than met the eye.

Blake had lost interest in watching the cars outside and had crawled into his father's lap. When Rachel looked at the two of them, her heart ached for the father and son. She'd worked so hard to bring them together again, and now that they were, she felt totally left out. A stranger. But that was no more than she should be, she reminded herself. There was no room for her in Matt's life—at his side, in his bed or anywhere else. No, she'd set out to make him a bigger part of Blake's life and she'd succeeded. Her time with them both was drawing to a close. After the roller coaster of emotions she'd been through so far this month she told herself it was no more than what she'd wanted all along.

As their car swept along Centenary Drive and turned onto Weeroona Road, another phalanx of reporters and photographers could be seen, grouped at the Strathfield Gates at the entrance to the cemetery grounds. Uniformed security guards at the gate endeavoured to keep the driveway clear, but little could stop the surge of activity as the funeral procession made its way through the gates. Overhead, news helicopters circled the necropolis.

Rachel gave Matt another pointed look as their car made its ponderous way through the throng and into the cemetery grounds before winding along the road that followed the serpentine canal.

"Don't worry, they're not allowed near us at the burial site." Matt's voice was clipped, and small lines of strain bracketed his lips.

Rachel felt a pang of remorse. As much as he and Marise had been estranged at the time of her death, he was faced with having to say goodbye to her all over again.

At the Blackstone family plot in the heart of one of the older sections of the cemetery, their limo slid to a halt behind the hearse that had preceded them from the memorial service in the city. A cool wind whipped around Rachel's legs as she stepped from the vehicle when the driver opened the door.

"Do you want me to take Blake?" she asked, turning to Matt as he and Blake exited the vehicle dressed in their identical charcoal-grey suits.

"No, I'll look after him. Thanks."

Briana, Jarrod and Ray Davenport, Briana's father, alighted from the car behind and walked up to them. Ray had been given dispensation by the court to leave his home state and attend Marise's service and burial. He looked tired and frail. The past six months hadn't been easy on anyone.

Briana looked upwards at the circling helicopters. "Marise would have loved this," she said, a break in her voice belying the emotion behind her statement.

Rachel watched as Jarrod put an arm around her and drew her comfortingly against his body. Such a simple gesture, but one that visibly bolstered Briana's confidence again. A shaft of envy speared through Rachel's heart as she stood slightly back and to the side of the gathering group of mourners.

Almost everyone seemed to be a part of a couple. A pale and drawn, although still classically beautiful, Kimberley on the arm of her husband, Ric. Ryan and his glowingly pregnant wife, Jessica. Jake Vance with his new fiancée, Holly McLeod. Even Sonya Hammond, Matt and Jarrod's aunt, was there with Garth Buick, Howard Blackstone's oldest friend. Despite the growing crowd, Rachel had never felt more alone in her entire life.

The funeral director gestured to the six men, Ray, Ric, Ryan, Jake, Jarrod and Garth, to step up to the hearse. Rachel swallowed the lump in her throat as the men slowly bore the coffin along the path to Marise's newly prepared final resting place.

Once again she was amazed at the power of money. How many families could have pulled this off in such a short time—being granted an exhumation, cutting through the red tape and bureaucracy and arranging a reburial in the Blackstone family plot.

While there'd been no official statement from the family, the press had buzzed for days with the news. It hadn't taken long before they'd made the connection, and the headlines had shrieked with banners such as Blackstone Love Child and Another Prodigal Blackstone. Matt had read each paper without expression, but Rachel had overhead Ryan's growled greeting to Matt as he'd arrived at the memorial service.

"Cunning, Hammond, very cunning. I should have given you more credit for finding a way past our embargo on releasing the truth. But you haven't won, not by a long shot."

Matt's response had been lost in Blake's excitement as he'd spied Kimberley and had broken free of Rachel's handclasp, shouting, "Aunty Kim, Aunty Kim!" Despite Kim's obvious joy in seeing her Godson again it was clear in her expression and that of her brothers that they were none of them impressed with the publicity that had mushroomed beyond their control.

The burial was a quiet and sombre affair. The celebrant expressed a few words before inviting the family to say their final farewells. Briana wept quietly as she stepped forward to lay a single white rose on her sister's casket. Matt held a surprisingly quiet and compliant Blake in his arms as the coffin was lowered into the ground, his face a mask of reserve.

The journey back to the Carlisle Grand hotel where Matt had arranged a small reception in his suite seemed endless. Blake peppered him with questions about his mummy, Matt answering in a low, steady voice until eventually Blake fell silent again.

Matt watched as Rachel circulated around the room, ensuring everyone had a drink and something to eat. Her warmth had lightened the atmosphere considerably compared to the tension associated with the memorial earlier. He fought to hold himself back. It would be so easy to go to Rachel's side, to accept her comfort, to gain some surcease from the deepening sense of failure that hung about his shoulders like a lead cloak.

Kim, seated on the couch with Blake, laughed and hugged his little boy with delight as they played finger games together. Blake's quietness had disappeared the moment they'd arrived back at the hotel, and he exuded energy and mischief as he bounced on the furniture. Kim exchanged a look, over Blake's head, with her husband that spoke volumes towards the closeness they'd rebuilt together.

Bitterness flooded his mouth. He and Marise had never shared such a link. Once the heated flare of their initial infatuation with each other had died down, her obsession with wanting more out of life than she had, had effectively destroyed any chance of a happier marriage together, or of providing Blake with two parents who loved him. His own failure to be the husband she needed, to be able to meet her constant demands, to shore up her frailties, struck a raw nerve. Failure, at anything, didn't fall under his umbrella. There was no way he'd risk that again. Ever. He had Blake. He had

House of Hammond and soon he'd have Blackstone Diamonds. That would be enough. It had to be.

"Matt, is everything all right?" Sonya Hammond touched him lightly on the arm. "It's been a tough day. Perhaps you'd like us all to leave."

"No, I'm fine. Don't worry."

"Well, if you're certain." Sonya sounded unsure.

"I am, absolutely." Matt hastened to reassure his aunt.

"Rachel's doing a wonderful job as hostess. You're lucky to have her." Sonya smiled. "You know, I was so incredibly happy and relieved when we heard that you'd solved the mystery around the necklace. I was wondering… Danielle mentioned that you've commissioned her to make a new necklace. Will it…will it be the same as before?"

"No, I've asked Danielle to come up with a new design. It won't resemble the old necklace in any way." He clenched his jaw. Aside from the stones there would be nothing in common with the previous necklace although he'd yet to come up with a name for the new one. It was his plan to tour the necklace together with the balance of Howard's gem and jewellery collection he'd inherited through Marise.

"You know Ursula came to hate that necklace with a passion. That night of her thirtieth birthday she'd begged Howard not to have to wear it, but he'd insisted. He loved her, in his own way, but he loved being able to show the world how successful he was, too. I often wondered whether things would've been different if my father had never assigned those exploration leases over to Howard." She sighed, a heartfelt sigh that came from deep inside. "Ah well, we can't change the past, can we?" She reached up and gave him a gentle kiss on the cheek before moving back to Garth Buick's side where he stood on the other side of the room talking with Ryan and Jessica.

Words stuck in Matt's throat. Change the past? What he wouldn't give to be able to do that. His eyes fixed on Rachel again, following the curves of her body in the long-sleeved Sherwood-green dress she wore, slipping down over her sheer black stocking-clad legs and down to her dainty feet encased in high-heeled black shoes. A far cry from the frills she'd worn to her high school dance but no less enticing. His body leaped to life; his blood thrummed in his veins and pooled in his groin.

No matter what he did, no matter what he'd been through, he still wanted her with a physical yearning that refused to be denied. What the hell was wrong with him? He'd just buried his wife for the second time, yet still he lusted for Rachel? He lifted his glass to his lips, letting the alcohol burn past his throat in one hefty swig, then turned away totally disgusted with himself. He stalked over to the wet bar where a waiter stood ready to refill the tumbler of whiskey he'd just drained.

"Matt, wait up a minute, would you?"

It was Kim, with Blake firmly and very happily holding on to her hand.

"What is it?" He wasn't in the mood to be convivial.

"Ric and I would like to take Blake for tonight." She put up one hand as he started to say no. "Now wait a minute. You look shattered. Come on, things might not be the best between us but I still know you, Matt. Today's been hell for you. Be honest with yourself. It's just one night. Besides, I've missed the little guy so much. I'll deliver him back in the morning, safe and sound. I promise."

"Rachel is more than capable of taking care of him if I should fall apart," Matt responded, his voice laced with sarcasm. But his words failed to strike at their intended target.

"Don't be silly. She's dropping in her shoes. Have you even looked at her today? Cut her some slack, Matt. Rachel's as strung out as you are."

Looked at her? He'd hardly been able to keep his eyes off his son's nanny. They darted once again to where Rachel stood to one side of the gathering, weariness visibly pulling at every delectable line of her body. Reluctantly he admitted Kim was right. Rachel looked about as shattered as he felt.

"Okay, but just tonight," he growled.

"Don't worry, I won't steal him from you," Kim promised with a sad smile. "I'll get Rachel to help me get some things together for him, then we'll be off."

By the time Ric and Kim had left with Blake, the rest of the group had begun to drift away. The brief formal handshakes he'd received from Ryan and Jake were due more to habitual manners than a genuine gesture of friendship. As he left with Holly, Jake hesitated in the entrance way to the suite.

"You know the ball's in your court. How about we meet tomorrow morning, say nine? See if we can't find a way through all of this." Jake's eyes narrowed as he waited for Matt's response.

"Fine. We'll meet. But be forewarned, I don't plan to make any changes. As you said, the ball's in my court. I prefer to keep it that way."

Eleven

Rachel went around the room checking that the hotel staff had completed their duties properly. There wasn't so much as an empty dirty glass to be seen anywhere, nor a discarded toothpick left on a table. There was nothing else she could do now but go to bed, but despite her tiredness, sleep was the last thing on her mind.

She hadn't been oblivious to Matt's distance this evening, how he'd held himself apart from everyone. She'd ached to go to him—to offer a touch, some gesture of comfort—but he'd made it quite clear that wasn't her place.

After the last of the guests had gone, he'd excused himself and gone to his bedroom. Now there wasn't even so much as a glimmer of light from under the door. She hesitated at his door on the way down the hall to her own, pressing her hand briefly on the wooden surface as if she could feel him through its solid shield.

She'd overheard his exchange with Jake Vance, and it made her chest hurt to realise that even after all the Blackstone family had done to set Marise to rest today, he was still as determined as ever to pursue his share acquisition. Her hand dropped from the door. Nothing would deter him from his path, that much was clear. There was nothing she could do to sway him back to the compassionate man she knew lingered beneath the bitterness left behind from the longstanding feud and his unhappy marriage.

She went to her own room and peeled off her dress, throwing it carelessly across a chair before padding on stocking feet to her bathroom. She took off her makeup and brushed her teeth then unpinned her hair and let it tumble down around her shoulders in a cascade of curls. She gave a half laugh at her reflection as she stood there dressed only in her black bra and panties with matching suspender belt, her sheer black stockings showing a creamy ribbon of flesh at the top of her thighs. Anyone would think she'd dressed for a lover when she'd prepared for the funeral.

And she had.

As hopeless as her love was for Matt, as angry as she was at his continual denial of their attraction, she knew she had to give their future one last chance. Before she could change her mind she dragged on a robe, exited her room and made straight for his.

Matt's room was dark; not even the spill of light

from her open door reached his. Her feet sank silently into the carpet as she crossed the room towards the bed. As her eyes adjusted to the darkness she dimly made out his naked upper torso as he sprawled across the sheets. A prickle of awareness danced across her skin as she reached out to touch him, his warmth filling the air between her hand and his shoulder like a tangible thing.

She lowered herself to the bed as her hand skimmed across his shoulder and down his bare chest.

"What the hell are you doing?" His voice was cold and angry. His hand whipped up to grab her by the wrist.

"I'm giving in, Matt. Giving in to what we both know we want."

"I don't want this," he growled and threw her hand off him and rolled away, getting up off the bed. "Get out of my room. Now."

"No." Rachel got to her feet and felt her way around the bed in the dark.

Waves of heat poured off his body as she felt, rather than saw, him in front of her. She lifted her hand again, taking his and laying it against her breast where the crossover of her robe had fallen apart.

"You want this, you want me, as much as I want you, too. Please, Matt, we need this. We *need* each other. Tonight, just for tonight." She was beyond shame anymore. If she had to beg, she would.

She waited for what felt like forever as her whispered words hung on the air. The warmth of his hand on her flesh seared her like a brand. Slowly she felt his fingers move, spreading softly over her breast and over the fabric of her demi-cup bra.

"There can't be anything between us beyond this, Rachel. I'm not in the market for a wife or a long-term lover. You're the kind of woman who wants it all, who deserves it all. I have nothing left to give."

"I know. I understand."

She reached up in the darkness and cupped her hand around the back of his head, drawing him down to her willing mouth. She felt the tiniest resistance in the corded muscles of his neck and then he succumbed and bent his head. A hot rush of blood coursed through her body as his lips met hers, as he allowed her to take the lead and probe his mouth with her tongue. A tremor ran through his body as she plunged her tongue into the hot, dark recess of his mouth and then withdrew, only to do it again.

"I want you to do this to me," she whispered against his mouth, "again and again. I want you to forget today, forget the past. Focus only on us, on now."

She slid her hand down over his shoulders, across his chest and lower, following the fine seam of muscle down his abdomen and lower still. He wore only satin boxers, and the elasticised band proved no restriction to her questing fingers. He was already aroused, his erection tenting the silken fabric. She used both hands to ease away his boxers, letting them slither down his long, powerful legs.

Gently, she pushed him back down on the bed and straddled him as she joined him there, running her fingers gently up and down his torso, lingering in the curve of his groin before tracing their way back up over his rib cage and up to the hard, pointed disks of his nipples.

His hands whipped up, lightning fast, and captured her wrists. His grasp, though not as tight as before, was no less masterful.

"Not slow, not this time," he growled as he flipped her over on the mattress, covering her body with his and burying his face at the curve of her neck where he nipped and suckled, sending a wild pulse of hunger throbbing through her body. "Not after what you've put me through these past few weeks."

He reached between them, tugging apart the robe and reaching for her panties. She was already wet with need and cried out in shock and desire as he pulled her panties away with a twist and tear of fabric. Rachel's heartbeat quickened as his hand reached between her legs to cup her. She heard his grunt of satisfaction as he felt her moisture, and she pressed against his palm, the pressure sending a tingle of electricity through her body.

"Do you have protection?" Matt rasped.

"I'm on the Pill. We're safe. I promise. No mistakes." Rachel hastened to reassure him, squirming against his hand again.

"You're wearing garters." His voice thickened as he skimmed his hands across her hips and down her upper thighs.

"Yes," she whispered in reply, reaching for him with her hands, guiding his straining erection to the heated core of her.

"I want to see you."

Rachel bit back a moan of protest at his hesitation

but took heart in the fact that in the glow of the soft light provided by the bedside lamp there could be no question of who he made love to. There would be no ghosts in this bed with them tonight.

"Beautiful." Matt's voice was strained and his hands shook as he reached for her again.

He wrapped her stocking-clad legs about his hips and positioned himself at her entrance, nudging her sensitive, slick flesh.

"Now, Matt. Please, now," she implored him.

Matt buried himself inside her with a groan, unable to resist any longer. There were no more excuses, no more regrets. Only sensation, feeling, need. Excruciating need that accelerated as she opened her body to him, welcomed him into her fiery inner heat. He strained to hold himself back, to prolong the acute pleasure of skin-to-skin contact, but instinct took over at its basest level and he surged against her, faster and deeper with each stroke. Beneath him he felt her body begin to tremble, felt her inner muscles tighten and spasm around him, drawing his climax from him in a rush of pleasure so intense and yet so harsh at the same time that he collapsed into her welcoming arms as the shudders of release racked through his body with the force of an earthquake.

Dimly he became aware of her fingers stroking gentle, lazy circles across the backs of his shoulders, down his back and to his buttocks before trailing their path back up to his shoulders again. He shifted against her and felt the answering clench of her body.

"Don't leave me yet," she said softly against his ear. "Please, not yet."

"I'm not leaving you, just making you more comfortable."

He shifted them both on the sheets, rolling slightly to one side and hitching her outer leg over his thigh, remaining joined as intimately as a man and woman can be joined.

"Are you okay?" he asked, almost afraid to look into her hazel eyes in case he saw recrimination there. He'd never taken a woman so frenetically before in his life, but suddenly all the holding back had crashed through like a floodgate being opened. And he still wanted her; although this time he would take his time.

Rachel smiled. It started with her eyes, then slowly her lips curved in a sensuous curve of satisfaction.

"Yeah, you?"

In answer Matt flexed his hips against her. An unfamiliar teasing smile pulled at his lips as he watched Rachel's eyes flare open in surprise, her pupils enlarging in response.

"So soon?" she asked. Her voice caught on a hitch in her breath and warm colour flooded her cheeks.

In answer he lowered his head and captured her lips, drinking of her generosity as he plundered the soft recesses of her mouth. He lifted himself from her body for only long enough to help her out of her robe, then he lay down on the bed, pulling her over him, tracing his hands over the soft mounds of her breasts as they remained restrained by the soft black lace of her bra. He could see the darkened points of her nipples semi-exposed at the tops of the delicate fabric.

Under his gaze Rachel reached behind her and unclasped her bra, letting the restraints fall from her and expose the lush globes of her breasts to his stare. She wriggled her arms free of the straps. As she met his gaze with heavy-lidded eyes, she ran her hands up over her rib cage and up farther to cup her breasts, rolling her nipples between thumb and forefinger, as if offering them in supplication for his pleasure. Matt's hands coasted to her waist, holding her as he lifted himself up to take first one, then the other proffered nipple, in his mouth, giving each hardened bud a tiny bite after suckling it.

Rachel was a vocal lover and her moans and cries of pleasure drove his desire for her to new heights. How far they had come from that long-ago night when he'd taken her in the back seat of his car with no more finesse than a randy buck. Five years her senior, he should have known better, should never have given in to the torment and temptation she'd so blatantly offered him during the last dance. But take her he had, and then shattered her like a fragile creature when he'd spurned her afterwards.

This time there'd be no misunderstandings. This time was only for the here and now, as she'd said, and he'd make damn sure it would supplant her earlier memories. They were both adults now, he rationalized. Adults with a magnetism between them that needed to be addressed and resolved—and resolved it would be by morning. But in the meantime, they had the night.

Rachel sensed the change in him as he played with her breasts, laving attention on each one alternately and driving her to the brink of desperation. It was as if he'd reached a point of acceptance, where he no longer had to fight whatever it was that pulled them together yet kept them apart.

She tunnelled her fingers through his hair, holding his head to her, pressing her flesh deeper into his mouth, relishing the tiny jolts of electrified pleasure that spiralled through her body as he bit gently on her sensitised skin. When he dropped back against the pillows, she arched her back and rocked her hips slowly, undulating them with a promise of greater pleasure still to come to him.

She reached down and took him in her hand. His skin was velvet heat as she slid her hand along his length to the tip, trailing over his sensitive head with a featherlight touch—allowing him close to her entrance, yet still denying entry—before sliding her hand back down again. His grey eyes grew dark, almost black, as she repeated the movement. She expected at any moment that he'd take control, but he seemed content to allow her to take her time, to relish the sensations she felt quiver through him as she maintained her slow, steady pace.

Suddenly she could take it no longer, the pleasure of prolonging the inevitable surpassed by her need to feel him inside her, to feel his possession of her body, the connection she'd never stopped craving from him since the first time they'd made love. She lifted her hips and positioned him at her entrance, a tiny groan of hunger escaping her throat as she felt him nudge her with a tiny flex.

With a slowness that almost was her complete undoing she lowered herself onto his rigid length, relishing the stretch and pull of her muscles as she took him deeper and deeper still, until she felt him press against the entrance to her womb. A shudder ran through her and she waited for it to dissipate before clenching tightly with her inner muscles, drawing him up and inwards before slowly letting him go again. She rocked her hips ever so gently, and squeezed again, repeating the action over and over until she saw a hot flush of colour spread across Matt's chest and felt his fingers clench at her waist.

She'd bear his marks with pride tomorrow. It would be all she'd have left. She knew without doubt this was their swan song. He wasn't a man who let go easily of what he wanted, and he'd made it clear that he only wanted her for tonight. If she had it in her, she'd make sure he was left with the memory of powerful lovemaking that he'd never forget, never find anything to compare it to.

Her own climax was building as she felt Matt swell inside her. She tilted her hips forward, so she could press harder onto his pubic bone and find the relief she knew lay in store for the tightly bound bundle of nerve endings at her core. And then she felt him shatter beneath her, his hips heaving upwards in an uncontrolled surge, driving her to orgasm in a splintering mass of colour, light and sensation. Deep inside she felt the heat and force of his climax as he pumped inside her, over and over until he was completely spent.

She fell down against his chest, hearing his heart hammer against hers in the same crazy tattoo. Never before had she attained such heights of pleasure with any man. She fought to hold back the burning tears that prickled behind her eyelids as she tried to accept that she had to walk away after tomorrow. Say goodbye to the man she loved beyond reason, to the hope that they could have made a new future, a new family together.

She swallowed against the sob building in her throat and buried her face instead in the strength of Matt's heaving chest. She'd get through this, somehow.

Twelve

Rachel slid slowly from the bed, determined not to disturb Matt. After their second time together they'd taken a long, lingering shower, making love in the steamy confines of the shower stall before tumbling back into the bed to sleep. How much later, Rachel wasn't sure, but he'd reached for her twice more in the night, each time subtly more intense than the last, until he'd fallen into a deep sleep.

She'd lain there for the past hour, watching him, unwilling to bring this episode to a close. Eventually reason had won out over emotion. She picked up her discarded underwear from the floor and scooped up her robe before quietly letting herself out of his room, softly closing the door and going to her own room.

There were matters she needed to attend to today. Matters that couldn't wait a moment longer. She took a brief shower before dressing quickly in her usual trousers and long-sleeved T. Their private flight home was scheduled for later in the afternoon but if she could manage it she'd be on the first available commercial flight out of Sydney. She knew she had a responsibility to Matt for Blake's care but she had no doubt that Kimberley Perrini would step into the breach and help for the short time before Matt's expected return to New Zealand.

While Rachel accepted she couldn't change Matt back to the kind of man he'd been before, maybe she could help him achieve his goal. It tore her heart apart to know that she could help him in this regard, but that by doing so would drive him away from her forever. She couldn't, wouldn't, love the man he'd become if he accepted what she was about to offer him before she left and returned to New Zealand.

She reached deep into the inside flap of her suitcase lid and drew out the envelope her share broker had forwarded her before their departure for Sydney the day before yesterday. With shaking fingers she drew out the single sheet of paper and skimmed its contents.

The share transfer form was simple enough. It was hard to believe that with nothing but her signature, and Matt's, he'd finally have what he wanted most—control of Blackstone Diamonds.

Briefly she wondered whether he'd have looked upon their relationship any differently if he'd known she held his trump card all along. She grabbed up the hotel pen from the table in her room and quickly signed the

Transferor section of the form before she could change her mind. This was what he really wanted above all else. Not her. Not ever.

A quick phone call to the airlines confirmed she could be on a flight as early as lunchtime, a good three hours prior to the private flight. As quickly as she could she jammed her things into her suitcase. She hesitated a moment as she grabbed up the underwear and stockings she'd worn yesterday, then stuffed them into the rubbish bin in her room. She could never wear that set again anyway. It was time to let everything from the past go.

A betraying click of her door heralded Matt's entrance.

"What the hell do you think you're doing?" he demanded.

Despite their torrid night he looked none the worse for wear. In fact, if the truth be told, he looked even better than before. The careworn lines about his eyes had gone; the deepening grooves that had furrowed his brow were softer now.

"I'm packing. I've arranged to go home on an earlier flight. I'm sorry that this leaves you in the lurch with Blake but I'm sure Kim will help you. It's only for a few hours. I can't stay any longer." The words gushed from her lips like river water rushing over stones.

"Is this some bid to make me beg you to stay? Because it won't work. I made it clear to you last night was one night only."

Rachel zipped up her case and lifted it off her bed and to the floor before facing him.

"Matt, I'm perfectly aware of the conditions of

our…our…" She searched for the right word but for the life of her couldn't think of anything. She waved her hand in the air between them. "Whatever. You made that patently clear to me, and if you think I regret for even one minute what we shared last night you're completely wrong. I loved every second of what we did together.

"That's the difference between us, Matt. I couldn't have made love with you last night that way if I didn't already love you so much it's killing me inside to be with you. I've always wanted you. I know you said it was just a teenage crush that first time, that girls often say they love their first. But with me it was always more than that. I've loved you for as long as I can remember and that will never stop, never go away. Why do you think I stayed away from New Zealand for so long? Why do you think I always timed my visits to Mum when you'd barely be around?"

"And you expect me to feel the same way? To declare my undying love for you because we had a night of great sex?" His voice was as hard as hailstones flung against glass.

"No, not at all. I know you're completely incapable of loving another woman again. There's only one thing that matters to you more than Blake, and even then I question which has priority in your mind anymore." She snatched up the envelope she'd folded the share transfer form into and shoved it at him. "Here. I don't want these anymore. Do what you want with them. I just hope you can live with yourself afterwards."

Rachel grabbed the handle of her suitcase and wheeled it to the door. She turned back to Matt. "You're not the man I fell in love with anymore. There's a monster inside you now. One hell-bent on destroying your own family—and whatever you think, Matt, the Blackstones *are* your family, too."

Matt watched in rigid, angry silence as she left the room, and listened as she opened the front door. The sounds of Blake and Kim at the door galvanised him into action. He shoved the envelope in his pocket and went through to the main living room.

Rachel was in the doorway, reaching down to give Blake a big hug. She lifted him into her arms and smothered him with teasing kisses, then put him back down again.

"So you're heading back to Auckland now?" he heard Kim ask.

"Yes, I have a chance to make a connecting flight to London via Los Angeles tomorrow night and there's a bit I need to clear up before then. I'd better get going. The concierge has arranged a taxi for me."

Matt's blood ran cold in his veins. She'd planned that far ahead? She was returning to the UK? Even from where Matt stood he could see the glimmer of tears in her eyes as she said goodbye to Blake and Kim. It struck at something deep inside him. She really was going through with it. It wasn't some grandstanding trick to get him to say he loved her. She was leaving. For good this time.

He swallowed against the bitter taste in his mouth. He could stop her, prevent her from leaving. All it would take was three little words. Words he'd promised himself he'd never share with another woman again. Before he had a chance to second-guess himself the door was closed.

Kim covered the short distance to where he stood.

"What have you done this time, Matt? Can't you see she loves you?" Kim asked, a worried frown creasing her forehead.

Matt snapped his gaze from the closed door and met Kim's concerned look. "How did last night go with Blake? Everything okay?"

"I take it you don't want to talk about it?"

Matt remained silent.

Kim's short laugh lacked any humour. "Fine. Yes, everything went fine last night. Blake's an angel, aren't you, honey?" She reached down to ruffle the child's dark hair and watched as Blake reached up for his father.

"Up, Daddy, up!" he demanded.

"Hey there, tiger. Did you have fun with Aunty Kim last night?"

Matt let his son's prattle wash over him as Blake enumerated his activities since he'd left the hotel suite the day before. It felt good to have his son back with him again. Right. Although it would be years before Blake made his own way in the world, Matt suddenly wanted to slow down time so he could linger over every moment with his boy. It hit him anew how aloof he'd been with Blake since Marise's death, how much he'd risked by removing himself both emotionally and physically from Blake. Sure, he'd convinced himself that he'd seen to Blake's immediate needs and requirements. What parent didn't? And in choosing Rachel to care for him over the past six months he'd ensured Blake would continue to receive the love and attention he'd deserved.

But nothing beat a parent's love for a child. Nothing else was quite the same. Rachel had at least made him see the light in that regard. She'd pushed him and pushed him until the scales had fallen from his eyes. Made him find out the truth. His pride would never have let him do so if she hadn't been so determined.

Blake started to squirm in Matt's arms, ready now to be put down. As he scampered down to his room Kim spoke again.

"You know, Matt, you never used to be this closed, this angry. I was hoping now that the business with Marise and Howard has been resolved and you have all the Blackstone Rose diamonds back together again, we could begin to take down the wall that stands between us. I miss you, Matt. I miss our friendship. Are you ready to forgive me yet for leaving you like I did in January?"

Matt thought about how holding Blake in his arms had felt. How the bond between parent and child had formed and strengthened over the years. How he'd almost destroyed it before Rachel's intervention. Suddenly he understood fully the inexorable pull that had taken Kim from his side and back into the folds of her family when Howard's plane had been reported missing.

Her estrangement from her father had been hard on her. Howard had been a difficult man to love but there was no questioning his power over his family, or his intense pride in his children.

His voice sounded raspy when he finally spoke. "It's got nothing to do with forgiveness, Kim. I behaved like a total bastard. You did the only thing you could. Family comes first. Always."

Rachel's parting words to him suddenly echoed in the back of his mind. Through Blake the Blackstones were his family, too, which put him in an untenable position if he was going to go through with his takeover. Was he prepared to risk it all for revenge?

"Thank you. You have no idea how much that means to me." Kim leaned forward and brushed his cheek with her lips. "Jake mentioned you guys have a meeting this morning. With Rachel gone, did you want me to keep an eye on Blake for you until you're all done?"

Matt took a glance at his watch. "Yes, if you don't mind. I'd better get on if I'm going to be on time."

As he went to go back to his room and grab his jacket he felt in his pocket the envelope that Rachel had given him. He pulled it out and slid open the flap. His heart shuddered in his chest as he unfolded the sheet of paper and skimmed its contents.

It was here; he had it all in his hands. Finally he had the leverage to fulfil his plans to avenge his father. His hand shook slightly as his gaze fixed on Rachel's neat signature on the Transferor line. He sank slowly onto the bed as the immensity of what she'd done bloomed in his mind.

His recent words to Kim—family comes first—tormented him. His promise to his father—the man who'd adopted him, brought him up, taught him everything he'd ever hoped to learn about the jewellery industry and more—could now be realised. Surely his vow to this man came first beyond all other commitments.

But what of Blake? What of his right to be a part of his extended family in every sense of the word? Matt would be carving an uncrossable line in the sand if he continued with his plans.

He wondered what had been going through Rachel's mind when she'd signed the transfer form, whether she'd believed in her heart that he would utilise it. He'd treated her badly this morning, spurned her love, when deep down inside he craved it beyond all else. More than revenge, more than the satisfaction of gaining control of all that Blackstone Diamonds symbolised to the Hammond family.

He wanted to be the man she'd fallen in love with again. He wanted her love and he wanted her to accept his love in return.

"Matt? Here, you can take my car if you want." Kim stood in the doorway, proffering the keys to the silver Porsche Carerra Ric had given her for her birthday. "I know she's probably not on a par with your McLaren but treat her gently, won't you?"

"Yeah, sure, thanks." Matt stood up and took the keys, letting the paper fall to the floor at his feet. "I promise I'll take good care of it."

"Here, you dropped this." Kim bent down to pick the form up, her face paling dramatically as she saw what the paper was. She pressed a hand to her stomach.

"It's not what you think," Matt hastened to assure her.

"Well, it looks like a sizable share transfer. What the heck else am I supposed to think? You say family comes first and that you've forgiven me but you're still going ahead with it, aren't you? How could you, Matt? After everything you just said?"

Matt took the sheet from her, tore it in two, then slowly crumpled the transfer form in his hand, fisting it into a ball of wadded paper before dropping it on the bed.

"No. I'm not going ahead with it. Not now. Enough's enough. I meant what I said, Kim. Family does come first. Both our families. I can see that now. And, since it's up to me, I'm going to work with Jake to find a solution to all this. It's not going to be easy but we'll get there. We have to."

He grabbed his jacket from its hanger. Jake Vance was expecting him, but he wouldn't be expecting what Matt proposed discussing. Not in a million years.

Thirteen

Rachel hung up the phone and gave her mother a wan smile. It had been a delightful surprise to find her mother back home when she'd arrived from her flight at midday. They'd spent the afternoon catching up and had shared a quiet dinner together here in the kitchen. It would be their last meal together for some time, Rachel realised with a pang. As soon as it was time for her agency to open in London she'd make her call.

"Looks like they'll be happy to have me back at the agency, Mum. They have a long-term contract waiting for me. I probably won't be able to come home again for some time."

"Are you sure you're doing the right thing, love?" her mother asked as she wiped her hands on a towel before coming over and giving her daughter a much-needed hug.

"It's the only thing I can do. I can't stay here any longer. Not feeling the way I do."

Her mother nodded sadly. "It's a crying shame. The silly man doesn't know when he's on to a good thing. Speaking of which, that sounds like them home now."

Rachel flung her mother a stricken look. "I don't want to talk to him, Mum. Can you make my apologies? I'll head back to my apartment and finish packing."

She was off and out the back door just as she heard the front door swing open and her mother's voice filter down the hall in a greeting to Matt and Blake as they came inside.

Back at her apartment the air was chilled. There was little she needed to pack. All of her clothing she'd already separated out into seasons and had packed only what she'd need when she arrived back in London's latest heat wave. Her mother would mail on to her the rest of her things over the next few weeks.

She flipped on the television set so she wouldn't feel quite so alone, although the sound would do little to ease the pain in her heart. It was the late-night news announcer's next words that made her stop halfway through making a cup of coffee and turn the sound up.

"And in breaking news, from Sydney, rumours abound of an upcoming merger between Australia's largest diamond retailer, Blackstone Diamonds and New Zealand's House of Hammond. Sources at Blackstone have reported of a meeting between the CEOs of both companies earlier today."

A merger? Rachel sat down before her shaking legs gave out on her altogether. How could the news have it so wrong? They should be reporting of the takeover, not a merger.

Her doorbell sounded, driving her back to her feet. She opened the door, still in shock at what she'd heard, but the sense of surprise swirling through her was nothing compared with the disbelief that slammed into her when she saw Matt standing on her doorstep.

"Can I come in?" Without waiting for her answer, he nudged her out of the way and closed the door behind him.

"What are you doing here, Matt? What's going on?"

He flicked a glance at the news bulletin on the TV set. "I see you've seen the news. I'd hoped I could beat them to it. But first things first," he rumbled, reaching for her.

Rachel's heart skittered in her chest as his strong arms pulled her to him. Her hands fluttered to his chest, and a question hovered on her lips but was instantly forgotten in the heat of his kiss. Matt's lips were firm and insistent as he teased and coaxed hers open, his warm hands sliding around her back and drawing her even closer to him. Tears sprang to her eyes. How dare he do this to her again. One night, he'd said, one night only, and now here he was tearing her heart apart all over again.

But try as she might, she couldn't push him away, couldn't stem the flood of desire that poured through her body and galvanised her hands into action. They stroked him through the sweater he wore, burrowed underneath it to touch the searing heat of his skin. He shuddered at her touch, then mirrored her actions, sliding his hands under her knit top, skimming her waist, her rib cage, higher.

"Where's the bedroom in this place?" he demanded, suddenly sweeping her off her feet.

He didn't wait for her answer, instead making his way down the small passageway. Every cell in Rachel's body wanted to accept his lovemaking, but every part of her brain shrieked "No!" She couldn't make love with him and survive to walk away again. It had taken every last ounce of her strength to leave him in Sydney this morning.

Matt laid her down on her bedcovers and went to lie next to her. As he reached for her, Rachel spun away and rose on shaking legs.

"No."

"Come on, Rachel. You know you want this. We both do."

"Of course I want you, Matt." She backed up until she hit the wall behind her. She put out one hand in protest as he swung his legs over the edge of the bed to sit up. "That's just the problem. I've always wanted you—and it's never been enough for you. Never been right. We had last night, and it was beautiful. But that's where it ends with us. I can't love you like that again and then leave. I'm not like that."

"Then stay."

He rose off the bed and crossed the short distance between them, planting one hand on either side of the wall behind her, effectively trapping her where she stood. The scent of his cologne wove around her, and she inhaled deeply, committing the delicious fragrance to memory. Something to take out and treasure at a later date, when she could remember this time with him without it scoring lines across her heart.

She shook her head. "I can't."

"Stay. Please," he growled, and lifted one hand from the wall to cup her chin and force her to look up into his clear grey gaze.

"Don't you understand anything I've said to you? I can't stay with you, Matt. You don't need me anymore. Blake is happy now since you've started to spend more time with him again. The night he spent with Kim in Sydney is proof positive of that. No. I've done all I can."

"And me, Rachel? How about me?"

"You know you don't need me. You've said as much all along. I'm not such a sucker for punishment that I'm prepared to be available for you whenever you want me and be shoved aside when you've had enough."

"And if I said I needed you?"

When she went to shake her head, he held her face between both his palms.

"I mean it, Rachel. I need you. I'm begging you to stay. I love you. Curse me for all kinds of fool for denying it for so long if you like, but don't deny me this. I can't imagine a future without you beside me, sharing my life, my heart, my bed." He bent his head and kissed her softly, sweetly, on lips parted with shock at his words.

"No, I can't," she whispered against his lips. "Not when you're so hell-bent on destruction. Not when you harbour so much anger. It'd destroy us both in the end."

"It's all right now. I changed my mind."

Rachel pushed him away from her. "What? Just like that? After all this time?"

"I finally listened to you. You were right. The Blackstones are my family as much as they are Blake's. It was time for the hatred and feuding to end. Conquering Blackstone Diamonds meant nothing to me anymore once I realised how truthful your words were. When I looked at myself I didn't like the man I'd become any more than you did. I don't want to be that person anymore. I want to be the man you fell in love with. I want you to let me love you the way you deserve to be loved, by a man who deserves to love you."

Rachel sank down onto the bed. Words failed her. Matt sat beside her, taking her hand and lifting it to his lips before pressing it over his heart.

"I've fought my feelings for you for far too long. That night when we first made love, I knew I should have held back. Hell, you were only seventeen. But I wanted you so very much. I thought one taste would be enough, but afterwards, when you thought we could continue with a relationship, all I could think of was how I'd shamed you and my family. I'd betrayed a trust that both our families had in me when I escorted you to the dance that night. I'd betrayed your innocence."

Beneath her fingers Rachel felt the steady beat of Matt's heart.

"Matt, I wanted you to take me. I wanted to be your girlfriend and more."

"But I couldn't give that to you. Not then. Not when

you still had your whole life ahead of you. You hadn't been to university, travelled, done any of the things you'd always talked about. If you'd stayed you would have come to resent me in the end. And I would've resented you, too. I had big dreams for my future, and they didn't involve a steady girlfriend at the time. I know it sounds selfish but you have to understand where I'm coming from. Mum and Dad never hid the truth about my birth parents from me. My birth mother was only seventeen when she had me, my birth father a few years older. I couldn't bear it if we'd allowed history to repeat itself."

"But, Matt, even if we'd had a baby we'd have had the support of our parents," Rachel protested.

"You don't understand. I couldn't do that to Katherine and Oliver. Not after all they'd been through. Not after all the support and love they'd given me all my life. I just didn't have room in my life to be the person you needed then. We were on different paths. Mine was to support my father in his endeavour to keep House of Hammond strong and growing and to take back what he'd always felt had been taken from him by Howard Blackstone. You deserved better than that."

"And what happened to that path, Matt? What are you doing with Blackstone now?"

Matt smiled, a genuine smile that lifted the intensity from his eyes and lightened his face. "We're doing what we should have done years ago. We're merging the companies together. It won't happen overnight, obviously. It'll take years of planning and hard work, but it'll be good work and it'll mean that the old hatred can die a natural death, leaving the way clear for Blake and the rest of his generation to keep the peace between us."

"Are you sure that's what you really want?" Rachel couldn't believe her ears—couldn't believe that after decades of anger and accusations between the families it was all coming to an end. A happy end.

"I'm certain. It's time to look forward, to put the past in the past where it belongs. People make mistakes, horrible mistakes, and I'm not immune from that. But you've shown me that nothing built in anger can survive. It takes genuine love and commitment to make things last. The kind of love and commitment you've offered me and that I was too stupid to accept." He cupped the back of her head, tilting her head so she faced him eye to eye. "I want to accept that now, Rachel. I want to accept everything you've so generously and selflessly given me. And I want to give it back to you in return.

"I let the failure of my marriage smother my true feelings towards you. I let it make me believe that I couldn't succeed in the kind of relationship you deserve. But I was wrong. My marriage failed for myriad reasons but I know I will never fail you, if you'll only give me a chance to show you how much I love you. I need you to keep me human, to remind me daily of what's important in my life. You, Blake, my family—*all* my family.

"Will you marry me, Rachel Kincaid? Do me the utmost honour of being my wife?"

Tears streaked down Rachel's cheeks. She could barely draw breath, her heart had swollen so huge in her chest as she finally heard the words she'd always waited to hear.

"I love you with everything there is inside me, Matt. Of course I'll marry you. You're all I've ever wanted or ever will want."

She reached up to kiss him, to show him in every possible way how much his words meant to her and how heartfelt were her own.

When Matt broke the kiss, he put his hands on her shoulders, pushing her back gently. "Will you wear this?"

He reached inside his jeans pocket and drew out a platinum-set pearl and diamond ring. The pearl and pink diamond were of equal size, set side by side with a semicircle of four smaller pink diamonds on each side to ring the two together. Rachel gasped as she held out her hand for him to put it on her ring finger.

"It's a *toi et moi* ring. You—" he pointed to the iridescent pink pearl "—and me." He lightly touched the pink diamond. "Your gentleness and beauty to balance and soften the hardness of my heart. If you don't like it I'll make you something else."

"No, it's perfect. I love it, Matt. I love you."

Their clothes disappeared as they sought each other to affirm their love. When finally, on a joyful sigh, their bodies cleaved together again, it was with a sense of rightness and purpose that overrode past sorrows and disappointments, replacing them with a hope for the future that was as strong and bright as the many facets of a brilliant-cut diamond reflecting the light of a new dawn.

Epilogue

"You look beautiful, Rachel." Kim's smile belied the tears in her voice.

"Absolutely stunning," agreed Danielle, who together with Kim had helped Rachel prepare for the wedding.

Rachel stood in front of the cheval mirror, her eyes sparkling in disbelief at the reflection that faced her. She *felt* beautiful in the strapless sweetheart-neckline gown that hugged her torso before cascading to the floor in a cloud of tulle and organza. She hadn't wanted traditional white, instead opting for a fabric that shimmered with the faintest shade of pink through the layers, much like the pearl in the ring Matt had put on her finger only two weeks ago.

Two weeks. She had to pinch herself to even believe

it was true. She felt like Cinderella about to go to the ball to meet her fairy-tale prince—except today was real. So very real.

She smiled at Kim's reflection as Kim adjusted the short veil pinned to her hair with clasps decorated with pink diamonds—Kim and Ric's wedding gift to her.

Kim gave her a quick hug. "I'm glad he finally saw sense and didn't let you go."

"I know. I'm so lucky," Rachel replied, her throat constricting on the words as she remembered how close she was to leaving Matt for good.

"*You're* lucky? More like the other way around." Kim laughed softly. "But either way, I couldn't be happier. He's the old Matt again. It's great to have him back."

A knock at the door made the women turn. Butterflies did double loops in Rachel's stomach. Was it already time?

Matt stepped into the room, tall and debonair in a charcoal-grey morning suit.

"Matt! You can't come in now. It's bad luck to see the bride!" Kim exclaimed and tried her best to push him out the door again.

"We've finished our run of bad luck. Trust me. Besides, I wanted to be the one to ask Rachel to wear this." He revealed a large white velvet case. He cupped the base with one hand and opened it towards Rachel with the other. Kim and Rachel gasped in unison as he revealed an exquisitely crafted necklace on a cushion of white velvet.

"Oh my, that's the most stunning piece I've ever seen

in my life. I recognise your work," Kim said as she turned to Danielle with a bittersweet smile. "You've outdone yourself with this. And I recognize the stones. My mum would've approved if she could see it today."

Rachel knew for certain then that the five pink diamonds had once been part of the legendary Blackstone Rose.

Danielle looped one arm around Kim's waist and gave her a quick hug as Kim dabbed at the moisture that had suddenly sprung to her eyes.

Rachel cast a worried look in Kim's direction. "Kim, I don't want to wear it if it'll upset you or your family."

"No, it's time the old ghosts were all laid to rest," Kim hastened to reassure her. "And this is the perfect way to do it. Put it on her, Matt."

He looked to Rachel for confirmation. "If you're sure?"

Rachel nodded, her heart swelling with pride that this man was about to become her husband.

As Matt lifted the necklace from its case he said, "I've renamed it the Bridal Rose. I'd like to think all future Hammond and Blackstone brides will be able to wear it as a symbol of the new unity between our families." Then, lifting Rachel's veil slightly to o side, he looped it around her neck. "We can't forget e past or remake it. We can't bring back the loved es we've lost. But we can make sure our families he a strong and happy future together."

The stones settled against Rachel's skin with flash of rose-tinted fire, and the three women gazed uon her reflection in brief silence. While the chainlooked fragile, on closer inspection Rachel could see ne links were doubled, each one woven into the other, giving a softly rounded foxtail effect that belied the delicate appearance of the necklace. But the chain was nothing compared to the five priceless pink diamonds graduated to drop in a 'V' featuring, at the apex, the teardrop-shaped stone Matt had recovered in Tahiti.

"It's perfect," Rachel whispered. "Matt, thank you."

His eyes met hers in the mirror. "Yes, perfect. I love you, Rachel. Don't keep me waiting, okay?" He lifted her hand to press a kiss quickly to her knuckles, then left the room.

"Did he say all Hammond and Blackstone brides?" Kim said with a twinkle in her eye.

"Yes, he did," said Danielle. "I know it was his original intention to tour the necklace with the rest of Howard's collection but I have to say I like this idea better. It ties it all off so perfectly, letting go of the old and moving on with the new. The feud affected us all. So glad it's in the past."

"I agree. And I look forward to the day when my daughter can wear the necklace, too," Kim said quietly.

"Kim!" Rachel exclaimed on an excited gasp. "Your daughter? You mean—"

"Wow! That was quick." Danielle laughed.

"Yes, and very unexpected." Kim laughed as Rachel and Danielle crowded around her. "Ric and I are having a daughter, our own little miracle. We've hardly got used to the reality yet ourselves, but we're incredibly happy.

"I can't believe it. You barely even show!" Rachel put

her hand to Kim's softly rounded belly. That explained the wonderful glow of happiness she'd noticed in Matt's cousin. "I'm so happy for you both. That's just the best news. Oh, heck, I'm going to have to redo my makeup if we keep this up!"

Kim's news was truly wonderful. Evidence that miracles did happen—like the miracle of Matt's love for her. She reached for a tissue to dab at her eyes.

"Oh, no you don't! We haven't got time. You heard the man." Danielle chuckled and handed Rachel the posy of pink rosebuds she'd chosen as her bridal bouquet. "Let's not keep him waiting."

The three women made their way downstairs, pausing at the entrance to the ballroom where the rest of the family was assembled awaiting Rachel's arrival. Rachel's father, on shore leave, stepped forward, looking strong and handsome in his naval dress uniform. Kim gave Rachel's veil and dress a final primp and gave a tiny nod when she was finally satisfied everything was just right.

"Remember, give us a couple of minutes, and don't run down the aisle. He's waited this long, he can wait a few seconds longer."

As Rachel stood in the passageway, her hand on her father's forearm, she suddenly felt an overwhelming sense of calm descend over her. All the nerves, all the butterflies she'd been beset with since she'd woken this morning, disappeared. Only a few metres away, the man she loved with every beat of her heart waited to pledge his love to her. The moment couldn't have felt more right.

"Ready, honey?" her father asked, his weathered face wreathed in a happy smile.

"Absolutely," she replied, reaching up to give her father a quick kiss on the cheek.

"I now present to you, Mr and Mrs Matt Hammond!" The celebrant's voice rang out across the ballroom.

"*My* mummy!" Blake shouted as he squirmed to get down from Katherine's lap and raced towards the couple standing at the altar.

Matt scooped him up in his arms, holding him out so he could give Rachel a kiss. "Yes, son. Your mummy, just like you said." His eyes met Rachel's and he knew his life couldn't be more complete than it was at this very moment.

He looked around the room at the small but close-knit gathering of family members who'd made it at such short notice to their wedding. His mother and father were seated with Sonya, and for the first time in Matt's memory a sense of peace and calm was evident on his father's features. Garth Buick stood a little to one side, but there was no denying the adoration on the man's face as he watched Sonya renew her family ties with her estranged brother.

"Congratulations, Matt." Jarrod and Briana stepped forward from the group of witnesses to their exchange of vows. Jarrod bent to give Rachel a quick kiss on the cheek. "Welcome to the family, Rachel." He winked at his brother. "Can't stop her tagging along now."

Matt looped his other arm around Rachel's waist. "And I wouldn't want to," he said emphatically.

Jake and Holly joined them, also expressing their

good wishes, shortly followed by Kim and Ric and Danielle and Quinn.

It was during the speeches that Jake's cell phone began buzzing rather obviously in his breast pocket. Holly gave him a strong nudge and an admonition to turn it off, but, unperturbed, Jake flipped the phone open, his voice a low rumble until he snapped it shut again.

In the next break in proceedings he stood and clasped his champagne glass in one hand. "I'd like to announce a double celebration. Would everyone charge their glasses, please."

Catering staff hastened around the tables ensuring that everyone had their glasses topped up. Satisfied everyone was ready, Jake cleared his throat, raising his glass in the air.

"I'd like to announce the safe arrival of Ryan and Jessica's twins, a boy and a girl. Mother and babies are doing well. Father is a complete wreck!"

Laughter resounded in the room as everyone toasted the new babies.

As the afternoon progressed into evening and the ballroom was cleared for dancing, Matt took Rachel into his arms in step to the waltz being played by the string quartet in the corner of the room.

"Happy, Mrs Hammond?" He bent down and nuzzled behind her ear.

"Ecstatic, Mr Hammond, and you?"

He felt her pulse step up a beat under the pressure of his lips, and acknowledged the answering surge in his blood. "I can't wait until they're all gone and I can have you to myself again. The past two weeks have been torture."

A happy laugh bubbled from Rachel's throat, and he swung her around in time to the music. "Hey, it was your idea to wait," she reminded him. "Just think how good it's going to be. Tonight and every night for the rest of our lives."

The rest of their lives. The overwhelming sense of happiness that emanated from deep inside him settled like a mantle across his shoulders. As they spun around the room once more he realised anew how close he'd come to losing it all—and how lucky he was to have the woman in his arms.

* * * * *

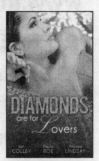

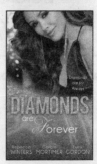